YESTERDAY'S ECHO

Also by Matt Coyle

Yesterday's Echo

A Novel

Matt Coyle

OCEANVIEW PUBLISHING
SARASOTA, FLORIDA

ISBN: 978-1-60809-173-7

Published in the United States of America by Oceanview Publishing, Sarasota, Florida

www.oceanviewpub.com

10 9 8 7 6 5 4 3 2 1

PRINTED IN THE UNITED STATES OF AMERICA

To my wife, Deborah, who has supported me unconditionally; to my late mother, Carol Coyle, who believed in me more than I did myself; and to my late friend, Tom Burke, who inspired me in life and continues to do so from the hereafter.

ACKNOWLEDGMENTS

This book could not have come to fruition without the help and guidance of many people who deserve special thanks:

My wonderful agent, Kimberley Cameron, for believing in me.

The great folks at Oceanview Publishing, Pat and Bob Gussin, Frank Troncale, David Ivester, and Susan Hayes for getting behind a rookie author.

My father, Charles Coyle, who undertook the heroic task of reading the very first draft of this book.

Nancy Denton who line edited a much later version, making it suitable to send out.

My writers' group, led by sharp-penciled and sharp-witted Carolyn Wheat, and composed of an assemblage of great writers over the years: Cathy Worthington, Judy Hamilton, Lisa Davis, Murray Hagen, and Cindy Tocci.

Friends who have helped me in ways that will remain secret: Joanne Murphy and Holly West.

Alan Russell and Ken Kulken for their generosity of experience.

Gar Anthony Haywood for his keen eye in early chapters.

Law enforcement experts: retired Chula Vista Homicide Detective Thomas Basinski, Sergeant Ken Whitley of the Garden Grove Police Department, and my brother-in-law, retired Los Angeles Police Department Detective III Gene Wolfchief.

Medical and forensics expert, D. P. Lyle, M.D.

Veterinarian John Morizi.

Any errors in law enforcement, medical, forensics, or veterinary issues are solely the responsibility of the author.

My wife, Deborah, for putting up with me and helping fine-tune many a phrase.

Finally, Raymond Chandler. I'd have never made it here if I hadn't read him first.

ACKNOWLEDGMENTS

YESTERDAY'S ECHO

Muldoon's

CHAPTER ONE

The first time I saw her, she made me remember and she made me forget.

She sat at the bar in my restaurant sipping wine and turning heads. Her roots stretched back to somewhere in the Pacific Islands. Along the way, a dash of Anglo joined the lineage. Her skin had taken the sun and turned it into dark caramel. Black hair flowed down over toned shoulders, matched by a cocktail dress worn the way many women tried, but few could. Black slingback heels showed off her legs.

I watched her from the entrance to the bar. She caught me looking and I held her eyes, dark slices of Asian mystery that dared me to turn away. I'd turned away from a lot of stares over the last eight years. Some had accusations in them, others just questions coupled with faint recognition. All haunted me like echoes from my past. Her eyes were harder to read. There seemed to be hunger hiding underneath cool detachment. Or maybe it was just bored certainty. A veil she pulled down to separate herself from men's leering eyes.

Before I could decide if I wanted to risk getting behind that veil, a flash of blonde caught my eye. Angela Albright, wife of the mayor of San Diego, steadied herself with a hand against the wall adjacent to the bar's entrance.

"He's late." Her words were slushy with alcohol and she seemed to be talking to herself, no one in particular, and everyone all at once. Her attire matched her condition: distressed blue jeans, baggy coat, and a homeless-woman-sized shoulder bag.

"The mayor?" I took her arm and guided her to a table and

barstool against the wall. She smelled like a margarita left out all day in the sun. I'd seen her cheerfully tilted before, but never stumbling drunk.

"No. Not him, Rick." She pinched her eyes closed and waved a hand in front of her face. "He's up in L.A., begging fat cats for money and votes."

Her husband was running for governor of California. His wife, seen frat-boy drunk out in public, wasn't the kind of publicity his campaign needed a month before the election. I liked the mayor okay, but I didn't care whether or not he won. Politics was best viewed from a distance. But the mayor and his wife were loyal customers and good for business.

"Let me get you some coffee and you can tell me who you're looking for." I caught Pat the bartender's eye, held out my hand like I was holding a mug, and mouthed, "Coffee."

Angela shook her head like a little girl told to eat her vegetables. In her early thirties, she still carried the youthful looks of a slightly sophisticated surfer girl. But the life of a politician's wife had started to pull at the corners of her blue eyes.

Pat arrived with the coffee, glanced at Angela, and raised an eyebrow at me as he left.

"I don't want coffee!" Angela pushed the cup away and some liquid sloshed onto the table. "Where is he?"

"Who?"

"The devil."

We got all types at the restaurant, but I'd yet to see Satan. Maybe Angela was even drunker than she looked. She was usually the pretty wallflower who faded into the background. Tonight I smelled a scene about to explode. I owed it to my customers to keep things Southern California laid-back. I owed it to my regulars to keep them from making asses of themselves in my restaurant.

"I don't think he's coming in tonight."

"No." Her eyes went wide. "He'll be here."

I stole a glance at the woman in the black dress with the mysterious eyes at the far end of the bar. Apparently, she'd been stealing one of me. She looked down at her wine glass when my eyes met hers.

"Angela, if the devil comes in, I'll tell him you were looking for him. In the meantime, I'm calling you a cab."

"No!" She sprang off the barstool and bumped into the next table, knocking over a half-full Corona. I grabbed the bottle before it toppled all the way over, but a stream of beer splashed across the table and cascaded onto the board shorts of a sun-aged surfer.

"Dude!" He shot up and looked down at his damp crotch.

I felt heads swivel and eyes lock onto me. Angela swerved around the surfer and out of the bar.

"Next two are on the house," I said and followed Angela down the hall toward the dining room. She bumped into the hostess, managed to stay upright long enough to make the turn toward the front door, then crashed onto one of the leather sofas in the entranceway, her purse spilling its contents.

Makeup, lipstick, keys, tampons, a wallet, a cell phone, and an overstuffed manila envelope lay strewn across the floor. Kris, my ace hostess, bent down and started shoveling the items back into the purse. Angela bounded off the sofa and grabbed the envelope before Kris could get to it.

"Thanks." She took the purse from Kris and shoved the envelope inside.

I nodded Kris back to the hostess stand and knelt down next to Angela. Tears slid down her cheeks and her watery eyes were the color of a shallow bay.

"I can't go back there." Her voice, a wet whisper. She fell back onto the sofa, mashing the purse to her belly like a fullback protecting a football.

"We'll just stay out here." I sat down and gently laid an arm around her shoulder. "I'm buying the guy a couple rounds. He'll be fine."

"No. You don't—" She jerked out a breath and tucked her head into her shoulder. The tears became a steady flow.

I slipped my cell phone out of my pocket and called a cab. After a couple minutes, Angela finally let me lead her out of the restaurant, through the terra-cotta courtyard, and up the stairs to Prospect Street. The October night had a hint of winter in it and the stars hung low in the sky. A taxi waited at the curb.

"Time to go home, Angela." I opened the cab's door.

"He doesn't know who I am." Angela looked at me through tear-drained eyes.

"He'll get you home." I steered her into the cab, gave the driver two twenties, told him her address, and then shut the door. I watched Angela lean over the front seat and say something to the driver as he drove away. Maybe she redirected him. Maybe she asked for a barf bag. It didn't matter.

I liked Angela, but she was someone else's problem now. People were free to screw up their lives as they pleased. Just not in my restaurant.

I surveyed Prospect Street, La Jolla's restaurant row. The sidewalks were almost empty.

Most of the tourists had gone home and paradise was again left to the locals. Old-money natives felt safe enough to venture down from fortresses high on hillsides above the ocean. Type As were back from their Hawaiian vacations, packing in overtime until they could jet off to Aspen in the winter. And pub crawlers could again publicly slip into private stupors in peace.

Kris waited for me back at the hostess stand. "The women's bathroom is backed up again and a lady needs to use it."

One crisis averted, another one to solve.

Muldoon's Steak House was an old-school restaurant with a casual atmosphere. Redwood slats and polished copper on the walls, big gas grill out in the open flanked by a salad bar, hardwood tables, captain's chairs, waitstaff in Dockers and golf shirts. We kept our prices reasonable and our labor costs down. Sometimes that meant me waiting tables or helping out behind the bar or the grill. Whatever it took to keep the doors open and the creditors from walking through them.

Tonight it meant playing plumber.

The ladies' john was just outside the kitchen door, opposite the grill. A woman in a green baby doll dress stood outside it. Blonde, but not by birth. The gold around her neck and the diamond on her finger glowed like hard-won trophies. She looked to be holding off middle age with the help of a personal trainer and a plastic surgeon.

"Sorry about the inconvenience, ma'am." I pointed to the busboy station ten feet away. "You can use the men's restroom around that corner. I'll have someone watch the door for you."

"Thank you for coming to my rescue." She gave me a perfect smile.

The busboy stood loading place settings into water glasses at the bus station.

"Justin, make sure the men's restroom is empty and then guard the door while our guest uses the facilities."

Justin, a gangly high school kid, looked at the woman, blushed, and went around the abutment that separated the bus station from the men's room.

The woman didn't move. "You look familiar to me."

It could have been a line. It could have been a ghost from my past. Either one led me down a path I didn't want to go. "I'm here almost every night."

"I've never been here before." She peered up at me. It felt like she was staring into my past. "I think it was on TV. Have you ever been on TV?"

A familiar knot tightened my stomach.

"It must have been someone who looked like me." I pointed toward the bathroom. "The restroom is right around that wall."

The woman kept staring and smiling. Then the smile fell and her hand went to her throat.

She recognized me now.

The knot in my stomach grew tighter.

She took a step backward, then spun and hurried to the men's bathroom.

I slipped into the kitchen and pushed aside memories of Santa Barbara.

And Colleen.

They were always there, just out of reach, waiting for a trigger to shoot them back across my consciousness. But, after eight years, I learned how to lock them back up in the box of my old life. Work helped. Duties, responsibilities, tasks that required a narrowed focus. Tonight it was a clogged drain.

I wheeled the plumber's snake out to the drain cleanout just outside the ladies' restroom. The snake was electric and as temperamental as a North Korean dictator. I got it running, bent down, and fed the metal auger into the cleanout pipe. Fifteen feet in, the snake hit resistance then gave way. I reversed the drive, and the device pulled out the obstruction. A bloated, used tampon flopped out of the pipe and splatted on the floor like a dead mackerel.

I looked up from the engorged cotton blob and saw tanned, athletic legs. They belonged to the woman in the black cocktail dress from the bar.

"There's always a woman somewhere clogging up the works, isn't there?" Her voice buzzed my spine like a wet finger in a light socket. It was gravelly and deep. Just like Colleen's had been. Long ago. It lingered in my ears, warm and rumbly.

The shock subsided, and I straightened up.

"And usually a man left bent over, cleaning up the mess," I said.

She gave me a polite laugh.

The busboy was out on the floor, so it was up to me to play bathroom sentinel. I asked the woman to wait, then rolled the snake back into the kitchen, washed my hands, and delegated mop and tampon duty to the dishwasher.

I reemerged and led the woman to the men's bathroom. In heels, she was almost as tall as me. Maybe five eleven. She moved with an easy, unpracticed sensuality. A whiff of cinnamon rode off her bare shoulders.

After I'd made sure the men's room was empty, I held the door open.

"I'm Rick." I put out my right hand. "I'll be your doorman tonight."

"I'm Melody." She gave my hand a gentle squeeze. Her skin was warm. "This is exciting. The men's bathroom!"

"Try not to clog up the works."

"Don't worry." She stopped in the doorway and flashed me a near perfect smile, flawed by one crooked incisor. "I clean up my own messes."

She didn't take long.

"It wasn't as exciting as I hoped, but thanks for guarding the door."

"This is La Jolla. Excitement here is a rainy day." I turned to lead Melody away from the bathroom, but she stood still.

"Then shuffling a very drunk next First Lady of California out of the restaurant must rate high on the excitement meter." She smiled and her mahogany eyes brightened, almost as if the veil had been lifted.

I didn't say anything.

"Why was she so upset?" Her voice was low. Conspiratorial. She moved in close and rested warm fingers on my forearm.

Melody was good. She had me going, but I knew I was being played. The smile, the touch, the whisper. She had an agenda that had more to do with Angela Albright than my magnetism. Maybe she was a reporter looking for a headline or from the rival campaign looking for dirt. It didn't matter.

"I'd better get back to work." I extended my hand. "Nice meeting you, Melody."

Her eyes tried to dig beneath mine for an instant. Then she took my hand in a slow shake and gave me another perfect, imperfect smile.

"You're an old-fashioned gentleman." Melody let go of my hand. "It's been a pleasure, Rick."

She walked through the dining room toward the bar. I watched the smooth swirl of her hips. She shot a glance over her shoulder and caught me looking. Again.

The next half hour I made a few rounds of the kitchen and the dining room. The night inched along. It was a little before nine and not busy enough to keep the hostess on beyond the top of the hour. I checked the bar before I sent Kris home.

We had live jazz Wednesday through Sunday starting at nine, and the band had yet to take the small stage to the left of the bar. They were chatting up customers, probably in hopes of scoring a round of free drinks. Leron, the front man, held court before two women half his age. I caught his eye and tapped my watch. He nodded, bowed to the ladies, and started rounding up his mates.

I glanced toward the corner where I'd first seen Melody. She was still there, but no longer alone. A man with slicked-back red hair and a soul patch under his lower lip hovered over her. A dark blue neck tattoo peeked above his collar. He seemed miscast in a gray sport coat and black slacks. Prison orange was more his color. His lips were moving near Melody's ear. She didn't look happy. He looked like he made a lot of people feel that way. And enjoyed it. Why was a scumbag like that talking to Melody? Maybe she needed an out.

I fought the pull to intervene. It was none of my business. If it didn't affect the restaurant, it didn't affect me. I didn't know Melody. She was a look, a cinnamon scent, a tug at my gut. My days of interceding in strangers' affairs were long past. You needed a badge for that. Or empathy. I didn't have either.

Not anymore.

Muldoon's

CHAPTER TWO

I let the waitstaff go home at nine thirty. We stopped serving food at eleven, but the dining room was empty and the bar half full. I'd handle any late diners myself. Anything to keep the labor costs down during slow months.

At nine forty-five, a man in a navy pinstripe suit entered the restaurant. The suit had to be Italian and fit him like a two-thousand-dollar suit should. He had a couple inches on six feet and was lean. His gray widow's peak knifed back from an angular face that dead-ended in a square chin. He peered down at me through gray eyes that took in light and reflected none back.

I said hello. He didn't say anything. He looked past me like I wasn't there and sauntered toward the bar. I didn't mind being ignored. Especially by the wealthy elite. If they'd ignored me back in Santa Barbara, things would've been different. Well, most things.

After The Suit passed by, I noticed Red Soul Patch returning from the bathroom. His eyes locked onto the back of the man and he stopped. He waited until The Suit disappeared into the bar, then buzzed by me out the front door. A shade paler than when I'd seen him earlier.

You see all kinds of wealth in La Jolla. Old money, nouveau riche, oil sheiks, professional athletes, trust fund slackers. But none who could send a scumbag with prison tats running in the opposite direction just by being seen.

I trailed The Suit into the bar.

The band had just come off a break and opened with a cover of "Eleanor Rigby."

Leron's tenor sax took the place of the lyrics. He was on tonight and he made that sax sing.

I scanned the bar and found The Suit. With Melody. He had his hand on her shoulder, leading her toward the exit. She looked as happy as she'd been when Red Soul Patch whispered in her ear.

None of my business. Except that they stopped right in front of me.

"Is it too late for dinner?" Melody asked. Her voice was higher than before. Slightly brittle. The man loomed over her, his dead eyes held me at a distance, an imitation smile lifted the corners of his mouth.

I grabbed a couple menus and a wine list from the hostess stand and led them to a candlelit booth. I ran the night's specials and asked if they wanted drinks. Melody ordered a glass of Mer Soleil chardonnay and then Italian Suit finally spoke.

"I'll have Macallan, single malt. That is, if your bartender can find it behind the flavored vodkas." His voice was a deep ooze. A note of superiority rode underneath a baritone that filled the booth like hot tar spilled over cement.

"Twelve- or eighteen-year-old?" The GenY'ers covered the bar costs, but you didn't stay open in La Jolla as a restaurant without catering to old money.

"Well then, you didn't really have to ask. Did you?" He showed me teeth. It was either a smile or a show of dominance. "Neat, of course."

"Of course."

I liked him better when he ignored me.

When I returned to the dining room with the drinks, the man's voice spilled out of the booth, "—a dangerous game." An edge broke through his syrupy cadence.

He held Melody's right hand across the table. The muscles in her arm at full cord. Her left hand hidden in her lap. A flame from the candle danced in a mild draft. Anger flickered in her eyes and the candlelight disappeared into his.

Whatever was going on was none of my business. Domestic

dispute, argument among friends, or enemies. It didn't matter. I had a restaurant to run and, at the end of the night, a quiet life to retreat back into.

I set the drinks down and looked at Melody. The anger in her eyes melted down into a plea. I hesitated. I lived by a code that kept me out of the spotlight and out of trouble. It had worked for eight years. Before I could decide whether to break it for a woman I didn't know, The Suit interrupted.

"That will be all for now, waiter." The certainty of his command of the situation hung off each word.

I checked the table. His hand still clutched Melody's.

"Everything all right?" I looked at her.

She stayed silent, but the plea remained in her eyes. The man grinned up at me. This wasn't his boardroom, it was my restaurant. I glanced back down at his hand then into his eyes. It was like staring down a well.

"Everything all right." I left the question mark off the end.

He looked at Melody and then back at me. He kept showing me teeth, then finally let go of Melody's hand. She pulled it back and dropped it into her lap. I noticed her table setting was short a steak knife.

I turned to leave when the molasses baritone stopped me. "Is the proprietor in tonight?"

"If you need to talk to an owner, I'll do." If he wanted to complain about my service, he'd have to do it to me. This was my boardroom.

"You mean we've had the pleasure of Mr. Muldoon's company and weren't aware of it?" He smiled at Melody. She didn't smile back.

"I'm his partner," I said.

"Why, that's odd." With the dead eyes and the white teeth, he looked like a Great White zeroing in on a sea lion. "My realtor saw this property on the market a month ago and the only owner listed was Thomas Muldoon."

His statement landed in my gut like a sucker punch. I had to fight just to breathe and stay upright. My partner and best friend trying to sell the restaurant out from under me? Couldn't be. This guy was just flexing his muscles to remind me he was still in charge.

"We have a private arrangement." Like any good fighter, I tried to convince my opponent that his punch hadn't hurt me.

"Business seems to be a bit down." He surveyed the empty dining room. "Now might be a good time to explore new career opportunities."

He was right. We'd lost money in September and were running darker red in October. All of which was none of his damn business.

"I'm happy here." I matched his lifeless look with one of my own. "Thanks."

"Well, apparently your partner isn't." He pulled a business card from a silver case and lifted it toward me. "Have him call me."

The name "Peter Stone" was embossed on the card with a phone number. Nothing else. I snatched it and retreated to the kitchen.

I delegated all further interaction with booth one to Justin and went back into the tiny office at the end of the storage hallway behind the kitchen. I sat in the captain's chair in front of the chipped oak desk. Corkboards tacked with pictures chronicling the life of Muldoon's hung on the walls.

I zeroed in on my favorite picture. In it, Thomas "Turk" Muldoon and I were going nose to nose over some long-forgotten dispute in a pickup softball game. We were always opposing captains and played every game like it was the World Series. After a few beers and a rehashing of the highs and lows of the game, we'd get back to being best friends.

If the restaurant really was for sale, there wasn't enough beer in the world for Turk and me to be best friends again. I looked at the black rotary phone below the picture and remembered Turk couldn't be reached. Tough to get cell service while hanging off the face of Half Dome in Yosemite. After he mounted that summit, we'd have to convene one of our own.

Justin popped his head through the doorway. "Booth one decided not to eat. They just want the check."

I left Justin in the kitchen with the dishwasher to get a head start on the nightly floor scrub and went into the dining room. I'd just printed out Peter Stone's check at the wait station when a crash of broken glass snapped my head up. Melody stumbled out of booth one onto the floor. She sprang up, feral eyes wide. Stone lunged at her and grabbed her wrist as she started to run for the exit.

I was on Stone in three strides. I grabbed his wrist and twisted. Melody broke free and ran toward the front door. I let go, but my force had already sent Stone backward and his leg caught a chair and he hit the floor hard on his back. I glanced over my shoulder at Melody and she did the same. Our eyes locked for an instant. I saw primal fear in them. Nothing else. She spun her head back around and sprinted down the hall and out the front door.

I turned back to Stone. He was already to his feet and moving forward. I stepped in front of him. He tried to move around me, but I shadowed him like an offensive lineman fending off a pass rusher.

"Are you adding holding me against my will to assault?" A smile cracked his face.

What was I doing? Playing hero to a woman I'd never see again? Getting back at my past through an asshole in my present? The right thing? None of the motivations justified my getting involved. Not even the last. I'd moved on instinct and adrenaline. Reason hadn't entered into it.

"I wanted to make sure you weren't running out on the bill."

Stone pulled out his wallet and I noticed that his left hand was bleeding. Melody must have put that missing steak knife to good use. He handed me a one hundred dollar bill and stepped around me. I let him go. Melody'd had enough time to get lost and I had a quiet life to try and find again.

The deep-water voice turned me around.

"Good luck on the job hunt, Rick." He gave me the dead eyes. He knew my name without me giving it to him. What else did he know? "If you need a character reference, feel free to have your next potential employer give me a call."

Stone flowed out of the dining room like a lazy stream. No hurry, now back in command of his world. He pulled a cell phone from his breast pocket as he turned down the entry and out of the restaurant.

When I locked up the restaurant at twelve thirty a.m., a shadow moved across the etched glass window as I double-checked the front door. I spun around and found Melody. A dark leather coat now covered the upper half of the killer dress and her hair was pulled up under a black San Francisco Giants ball cap. Black tennis shoes had replaced her heels.

"Melody." In the light of a patio lamp I noticed that her left eye was swollen and bloodshot. Stone must have found her in spite of my schoolboy heroics. "Are you okay?"

"Yes, yes I'm fine." The words came out fast and ran together. Her good eye, a black drop in a white circle of fear, scanned the night. "But I need your help. I think someone's following me."

"Stone? Did he hit you?"

"No. I don't know."

I'd already broken my rule of not getting involved once tonight and now that had mutated into a black eye and a midnight cry for help. What would my next involvement lead to?

I offered my cell phone to Melody. "Call nine-one-one. I'll wait with you until the police arrive."

"I don't want the police. I just need to go someplace safe." Her eyes tugged at me like a scared child. "Just for a little while."

Even rookie beat cops know the danger of getting involved in a domestic dispute. But that's why they were cops, and I wasn't anymore. They got paid to run into danger; I got paid to lock and unlock a restaurant.

"There's nothing I can do that the police can't do better." I slid my hands around her leather-clad biceps. There were taut, ready for fight or flight. "The safest place for you is the police station.

It's only a couple blocks away. I can walk or drive you over there."

"I'll be fine on my own." Her eyes shimmered as they filled with liquid. She backed away from me into the night. "Goodbye, Rick."

The husky gravel in her voice cracked into raspy sand. The way Colleen's used to when our fights ended in tears. Just like the last night I'd ever see her.

"Come on." I extended my hand.

"Where are we going?" She stayed in the darkness.

"Someplace safe."

She took my hand and we climbed the steps that lead up from the courtyard to Prospect Street. When we hit the top step, I saw headlights creeping down the street toward us. I spun and hugged Melody.

"Play along while this car passes," I said.

She tightened, but hid her face between my neck and shoulder and wrapped her arms around my waist. I caught the scent of cinnamon and a trace of lavender as I pressed my cheek against her head. Her breath was warm on my neck.

I gently turned us so I could spy the street. The headlights belonged to an SUV. Big, black, tinted windows. A Ford Expedition. It passed in a steady crawl. No front plate. Parked cars blocked the view of the back. I watched it until it disappeared around a bend.

"Okay." I loosened my grip around her waist, but didn't let go.

Melody stayed still for a second, then slowly turned her head, sliding her cheek along mine until she was facing me. The only thing between us was the bill of her Giants cap pressed against my brow. Her lips, full, cushiony, inviting. Her eyes, obsidian ciphers. We hung there, suspended, our breath comingling.

Melody moved first. A half step backward. "I guess we'd better go."

I grabbed her hand like it'd been my idea to break the trance and led her onto the street.

We hustled down Prospect toward Cave Street and the bank

parking lot that held my car. A thick breeze off the ocean chilled the night. I scanned both sides of the street as we passed palm trees, restaurants, jewelers, and art galleries, but didn't see anyone who wanted to steal my restaurant or punch Melody. Just another autumn night in the Jewel by the Sea.

When we hit the parking lot, a rat the size of an heiress's purse dog shot out from a hedge and scampered up a palm tree. Melody whiplashed but didn't scream.

Safely nestled in the palm fronds on top of the tree, the rat could look out over paradise and plan its next intrusion into it.

CHAPTER THREE

The drive home I made every night in my Mustang GT suddenly seemed unfamiliar. The night was cast-iron black and every pair of headlights assaulted my eyes. Melody didn't ask where we were going. She sat hunched down with the brim of her hat pulled low over her eyes. Her right hand clutched the door handle. She was scared, hiding from the night, but ready to escape into it.

We drove in silence along Torrey Pines Road, the main artery out of downtown La Jolla. I lived in North Clairemont, a few miles east of La Jolla off Highway 52. There the ocean was only a memory, occasionally recalled through one of the cooling breezes it sent inland. The coastal hills rolled flat as they made their way east and then climbed one final time up to a mesa where houses, duplexes, and apartments sat cramped together.

A pair of headlights followed me off the freeway. I made a couple of turns, but the headlights were still there. They were wide set and high off the ground like they belonged to an SUV. Just like the one I saw crawling down Prospect Street.

"Was the person following you in a black Ford Expedition?" I asked.

"I don't know." Her voice unsteady. "It was a big, dark SUV."

The Expedition seemed to rule out Stone. A Cadillac Escalade seemed more his style. Whoever it was, they were still behind me.

When my next turn came up, I kept my foot on the gas until the last second then slammed on the brakes and made a hard right. Melody rolled toward me until her hand on the door handle stopped her. Her eyes were wide as she looked at me and then over the seat at the night behind. I stood on the gas and glanced over my shoulder. Our pursuer slid around the corner and accelerated toward us.

My heart jackhammered in my chest, and I gunned the car down the dimly lit street. The charging headlights flashed to brights. I downshifted hard and cranked a left turn on the next street, cut my headlights, and dropped down another gear. The transmission groaned and the car bucked, but I made a quick right without flashing my brake lights. I gunned it a hundred yards, then slammed to a stop in front of an RV parked under a towering eucalyptus tree.

Melody had already slid down in her seat and I followed her lead, but kept my eyes on the driver's-side mirror. A cone of light appeared in the intersection behind us and then a dark mega-SUV sped by. I'd lost them. For now. But they knew my car and, if they were friends of Stone, they knew my name, too.

"Melody, who's after you?" My voice matched my elevated heartbeat.

"I don't know!"

I didn't believe her. But right now it didn't matter. The truth could come later. Safely home came first.

I eased back onto the road leaving my lights off. We were only a few blocks away from my house and I figured I could Braille my way there. Neither of us spoke again, perhaps afraid that if we broke the silence we'd give ourselves away and the SUV would return.

A block from home, another set of headlights approached from the opposite side of the street. Too low to the ground to belong to an SUV. Still, Melody sank down in her seat. When it got closer, I could make out a light bar on top of the vehicle. A cop car or private security. This was North Clairemont, not La Jolla. Closest people here got to gated communities were tailgate parties at the stadium before Charger games.

I switched on my headlights. Too late. A blast of white light exploded inside my car. I braked to a stop and threw an arm in front of my face to block the invasion of light. It stayed pinned on me, but also caught Melody below the bill of her cap. I expected a command to turn off the ignition and step out of the car. Nothing.

I rolled down the window and squinted behind my arm.

"Is there a reason you were driving your vehicle with the lights off?" A gruff voice hidden behind the floodlight.

In my experience as a cop, there were only two reasons people drove at night with their lights off. They were drunk or they were casing a house. I could now add evading mysterious SUVs to the list, but I didn't think that would sound plausible. But telling the cop the truth could be a way to turn Melody's problems over to him. Then I could deal with my own. I glanced at Melody. Eyes hidden under the bill of her cap, lips pinched tight, and a hand squeezed around the door handle.

Scared, but brave.

"My girlfriend and I were arguing so I pulled over and turned off the lights. I was just a bit late turning them back on. Sorry." Maybe I thought I could handle someone else's problems better than my own. Maybe I thought I'd get lucky if I played hero for Melody. Maybe I wasn't thinking at all.

The floodlight shifted to Melody's face, the mouse under her eye highlighted in white relief. Melody put her hand on the bill of her cap, shielding her face.

"Is everything okay, ma'am?"

Great. Now I was in the middle of my own domestic dispute. I shot a glance toward the voice, but the floodlight blasted my face again before I could see who was behind it. I did get a look at the car, though. Black-and-white cruiser. Real police.

"I'm fine, officer." Melody's voice was calm, friendly. She was good. A chameleon. "Just tired and anxious to get home."

This cop was operating off the manual for a late-night vehicle stop. He should have been out of his car with my license in his hand or had me against my car assuming the position if he wanted to be a hard guy. I'd given him enough ammo; driving with lights off, woman with a freshly swollen eye.

No complaints. I'd never been a manual guy myself.

"Try to obey the law from now on."

The black-and-white drove off, but kept the floodlight plastered on me until it finally went black half a block down the street. Must have gotten lucky and caught the cop at the end of his shift. He'd probably had a long day and just wanted to get home safely. Just like me.

"Thank you." Melody touched my hand on the steering wheel.

"For what?"

"For still being that old-fashioned gentleman who guarded the bathroom door tonight."

If old-fashioned meant stupid, then call me a gentleman.

I pulled down my street and parked around the corner from my house and left the carport empty. If the Expedition stumbled onto my block, I didn't want to make it easy for them to find my house.

Melody clung to my hand as we hustled the couple hundred yards to my house. Inside, I tossed my keys onto an end table and led Melody through the dark living room over to the front window. I peeked out at the street through Venetian blinds.

"Is anyone out there?" Her hand squeezed mine, nervous breath on my neck.

"No. Must have lost them." I dropped Melody's hand, found the switch on the wall, and turned on the ceiling light.

The room illuminated and Melody came into clear view for the first time since she surprised me outside Muldoon's. A purple welt on her left cheekbone pinched in on a bloodshot eye. The rest of her looked just fine. Beautiful. Magnetic. Her leather jacket was cut short and tight to her black dress. Tanned, athletic legs gleamed below the hem. Only the Giants cap and the tennis shoes didn't belong. And yet, they did.

"You were pretty impressive in that car." The worry now out of her voice, replaced by a confident growl that again reminded me of Colleen. "I'm guessing you've done that before."

"I've done a lot of stupid things." I went into the kitchen.

"I hope helping me isn't one more of them." Melody stood in the doorway, hip against the frame like she owned it.

"Me, too." I smiled like it wasn't a big deal. "You want some ice for that eye?"

"No, thank you. but I wouldn't mind some in a glass."

"What would you like to go with it?"

"Anything that will make me cough if I take a big enough sip."

I grabbed two rocks glasses from the cabinet above the sink, then pulled down a bottle of Herradura Tequila off the top of the refrigerator and some orange juice and ice from inside it. Just enough ice for a chill, three fingers of tequila and a splash of OJ for color.

I handed Melody her drink, walked over to the back door, and opened it. Midnight, my black Labrador retriever, bounded in. He reared up, slapped his front paws on my chest, and licked my chin. He walked over to Melody, and she scratched his square head and cooed dog talk to him.

"Looks like Midnight has a new friend."

"He's adorable."

Melody liked my dog and seemed to like me. But her world was dangerous. Nowadays, my idea of danger was a green guarded by water with a long iron in my hand.

"Time to tell me what's going on."

I took Melody's hand and led her back into the living room to a beige chenille sofa fronted by a maple coffee table. I set my drink down on a coaster and pulled the sleeve of her jacket off her free hand. She slid her back to me and I caught another whiff of her perfume as I took the coat off her bare shoulders. She took off her baseball cap, shook down her hair, and sat down on the sofa. I hung her coat in the hall closet and tossed the Giants cap onto the pile of hats on the upper shelf.

I sat next to Melody and she pushed off her tennis shoes and tucked bare feet underneath her. She took a sip of her drink and eyed me above the rim of the glass. Comfy. Cozy. Inviting. Tempting me to forget about the night's events and roll with the moment.

The moment didn't pass, but I tried to ignore it. For now.

"Who hit you?" I took a long, double swallow of my drink. The sweet tang bit my throat and warmed my face.

"I was in a hurry when I left my motel room and bumped into the door."

I'd heard similar lines dozens of times from spouses on domestic dispute calls when I was a cop.

"Melody." My voice caught an edge. "I knocked down some rich fuck, played hide-and-seek with an SUV, and lied to a cop for you tonight. I deserve the truth."

"You're right." She touched my hand. "I'm sorry I dragged you into the middle of this."

"Into the middle of what?"

"I'm a reporter for Channel Five News, the CBS affiliate in San Francisco."

Another buzz along my spine.

A reporter. CBS. The network that had blown my face up nationwide in prime time eight years ago on *48 Hours*. The guilt about what I'd done that long-ago night in Santa Barbara reawakened in my gut. It was always there, just beneath the surface, waiting to breach. Surely, Melody knew my story. Why would she choose me for help?

"I'm down here on a story about Mayor Albright's run for governor." She left it there like that was enough.

"Who hit you?" I shoved down my past and concentrated on Melody's present. "Stone?"

"No." She went for her drink again, but I stopped her with my hand on her arm.

"I'm tired of the cat and mouse, Melody. Who hit you?"

"One of my sources for the story."

"Who is he? Why did he hit you?"

"I can't reveal his name." A silken strand of hair fell across her eye. She let it hang, obstructing the view. "He got angry when I wouldn't pay him for information."

"Was he the one chasing us?"

"I don't know." She hit her drink, harder this time. "He got mad, and I left the motel and then the SUV started following me. I tried to lose it, but I couldn't. I finally parked in front of the La Valencia Hotel and went in pretending that I was going to get a room. I ran out the back. That's when I thought of you."

"Why?"

"Your restaurant was just down the block." Her eyes went soft and her mouth turned sad. I thought she was going to cry. But she didn't. "You took on Peter for me. I've never seen anyone do that before."

That made me stupid, not heroic.

"Where does Stone fit in?" I asked.

"He's someone I used to know when I was young and not very smart."

"So, he's an ex-boyfriend." A spring-autumn relationship. I'll bet Stone made for a cold, dark autumn. "How does he play into the story?"

"He doesn't. I thought it would be nice to visit him while I was down here." Her eyes found the floor. "It wasn't."

Stone didn't seem to be the kind of man you'd want to visit at any time. Especially as an ex. I figured she had another reason, but I let it go for now.

"Why no police?" I asked.

Melody took another long tug of her drink and set the glass down empty. She was pulling strength from a tequila bottle. In order to deal with the truth? Or deliver a lie?

"I'm sorry, Rick. This isn't fair to you." She swung her legs out from under her and her feet found her shoes on the floor. She put them on and stood up. "I shouldn't have gotten you involved. I'm going to call a cab and go back to the bungalow."

Melody was still evading my questions. She had something to hide. But, she wasn't the only one. Even with all *48 Hours* thought they knew about me, I had something to hide, too. Some things needed to stay hidden in the dark corner of one's soul. Melody and I didn't know each other well enough to venture there. I didn't know anyone that well.

I stood up. "That SUV might be there waiting for you."

"I know." Her voice creaked high and her shoulders slumped. "But I have to go."

"Stay."

"No, I can't." Her eyes went liquid.

She wouldn't go to the police and shouldn't go back to her hotel. She only had me.

"You don't have to tell me anything. I won't ask any more questions." I swallowed her in my arms and pulled her to my chest. "Just stay."

There was no redemption from the sins of Santa Barbara, but Melody needed me. Maybe life could finally start over.

Melody's face grew wet against my neck. Tears in silence. I held her and stroked her hair until she stopped crying. She looked up at me. One eye swollen, both bloodshot, nose red. Yet still beautiful. Her lips met mine half way. Soft, delicate. Then eager. Fingers fumbled at clothes, mouths explored freshly exposed skin. My bedroom was a five-second walk down the hall.

The couch was more immediate.

Muldoon's

CHAPTER FOUR

We went at each other hard and hungry like our first time might be our last. Lips, teeth, fingernails. Her body was firm and soft and wrapped around me like a velvet vine. She filled my wants before my body could scream them out. Rough, smooth. Prolonged, quick. When I caught Melody's eyes, they were dark mirrors hiding their content even as her body convulsed. My eyes were more revealing. The mask the public, my friends, even my last lover saw, came off. I was vulnerable, exposed. At ease.

When we were done, we were both spent. I'd had more than a few one-night stands over the years. Celebrity junkies who got off by having sex with anyone who'd been on TV. Adrenaline junkies who got off by having sex with someone dangerous. And lushes who thought I was cute and just wanted to get off. This was different. The sex was ravenous, yet intuitive, with a resonance underneath the physical attraction. Maybe it was the events of the night and the flush of raw sex, but I felt more alive than I'd felt in years. Eight years.

I was splayed on my back, the sofa under me, Melody over me. Her naked body a warm blanket. We lay mute, content to loll in the syrupy afterglow of sex.

Melody ran a finger along my ribs and finally broke the silence. "I don't think you did it."

"Did what?"

"Killed your wife."

My body clenched. The sight of Colleen's pale body laid out on the cold steel of the coroner's drawer assaulted me. The red indentation encircling her neck. Her eyes were closed, but her white-purple face still accusing me. The image was burned into my mind. An indelible stain that had marked me for who I was. The disgust and the shame slowly bled out and the image faded away.

Melody's finger continued its track along my ribs. I relaxed and exhaled from down deep within me. Melody knew the story everyone else knew and she had deemed me innocent. She saw the man I used to be. But like everyone else, she didn't know the whole story. Only God and I knew the truth about my innocence or guilt. He'd make his judgment when the time came. I'd already made mine.

"When did you decide I was innocent?"

"Well, I remember thinking at the time that you might be." She tilted her head up at me. "But tonight, after I spoke with you the first time, I was sure."

"That's all it took?"

"I read men very quickly. Women are a bit trickier."

"Yes. They are."

I hoped we were done with the subject and could move on to the weather, the Chargers, the Pythagorean theorem. Anything but Santa Barbara.

"That must have been a horrible thing to go through," she said. No such luck.

Melody laid her head back down on my chest and continued to unbury my past. "Your wife is murdered and you're arrested by your own police department. Then *48 Hours* does a hit piece on you even after you've been exonerated. I can't imagine what that must have been like."

"I wasn't exonerated." I didn't deserve anyone's sorrow or want anyone's pity.

"But, the charges were dropped."

"Not the same." SBPD made that very clear at the time in their statement to the press. Eight years later, I was still a "person of interest."

"One thing always bothered me about that *48 Hours*."

"Only one?"

"Well, that's just it." She rose up on an elbow wedged between me and the rise of the couch. "You were innocent. Why didn't you talk to them and give your side of the story? You came off looking guilty."

"I would have come off looking guilty either way. That's how they spin it. I wasn't going to be interviewed just to make for good television." That was mostly true. But I also didn't trust myself enough to sit in front of a camera and not look guilty.

"I think maybe you should have." Melody peered at me and the mirror that separated us during sex disappeared and warmth radiated from her dark, almond eyes. "If people had gotten to know you, they wouldn't have believed you killed Colleen."

The mention of Colleen's name opened up the ache in my chest. It always did. Even when I said it silently in my head. But Melody mentioning it also set off alarm bells. She seemed to know a lot about my past. Her tears and fears earlier had been real, and I hoped our roll on the couch had had the same meaning for her as it had for me. But she was a reporter. Five hours ago she'd pumped me for information on the mayor's drunken wife. Had I become the next possible story?

"How did you remember Colleen's name?"

"I Googled you on my iPhone after we met tonight. I wanted to see if the police ever arrested anyone else. I hoped that you had at least gotten closure." She kissed me on the chest. "I'm sorry you haven't."

I wanted to believe her.

I didn't say anything and we lay quietly for a while. No more questions. No more memories. Finally, Melody inched up my chest and kissed me on the lips. Natural, easy, like we'd known each other longer than just one night and one eight-year-old TV show. In that moment, I wished we had.

I checked the clock on the DVR: 2:03 a.m. I had to open Muldoon's in five and a half hours.

"Let's go to bed."

I took her hand and led her to my bedroom and into my bed. We spooned in an intimacy beyond our time together. In the movies, we would have made love again. In real life, I was asleep in five minutes.

A rustling woke me up. I saw Melody's shadow pass in front of the bed and then heard the bathroom door close. I checked the time on my clock radio: 4:07 a.m. I closed my eyes and didn't open them again until the alarm woke me at 7:00 a.m. Midnight sat beside my bed wagging his tail, smiling at me through his eyes the way Labs do. Time to start the day.

I slowly eased out of bed so as not to wake Melody. I looked over and saw that I needn't have worried.

She was gone.

I checked the bathroom and the kitchen to be sure, but the house felt empty and I sensed she wasn't there. The absence of her coat from the hall closet confirmed it.

I felt empty, too. And, I felt foolish for allowing myself to feel anything. It was a one-night stand that was never meant to make it to night two. That's how it worked. Take the flowery talk and the soft caresses and stick them in a forgotten file. It was sex. It was over. Melody just figured it out before I did. I couldn't blame her for that.

Knowing all that still didn't fill the vacuum in my gut.

Midnight snorted and ran his head under my hand to remind me of my priorities. I opened the broom closet in the kitchen and filled his bowl with dog food from a forty-pound bag. I allowed myself a glance at the refrigerator to see if there was a note under a magnet. Nothing.

Get over it.

I let Midnight outside, then went into my bedroom and threw on shorts, T-shirt, and tennis shoes.

On the way out the door, I opened the hall closet to grab my black Callaway hat. My hand came down with Melody's Giants cap instead. So, she had left something behind. Surely, a lapse of memory and not an excuse to come back. I held the hat up to my face and caught a whiff of Melody's shampoo. It brought me back to last night on the couch and in bed.

Move on.

I tossed the Giants cap back onto the stack and grabbed a dark-blue Chargers hat. It smelled like me and fit my head the way it was supposed to.

Back to normal.

Muldoon's

CHAPTER FIVE

I unlocked the front door to Muldoon's and Peter Stone's image took supremacy in my mind. His barb about seeing the restaurant listed for sale sat undigested in my stomach. I wondered if my mornings unlocking Muldoon's might soon come to an end. I'd given the restaurant my heart and soul. It was home. No one was just going to take it away from me.

The phone rang as soon as I hit the kitchen. I grabbed the wall extension hanging on the pillar next to the meat-cutting table.

"Rick Cahill?" It was a man's voice that I didn't recognize.

"Yes. How can I help you?" He didn't reply, and then a couple of seconds later I heard the dial tone. Not a great start to the day. Hopefully, not a continuation of last night. I let it go and focused on the restaurant and my real life.

I grabbed eight rectangular pans from the rack opposite the dishwasher and walked out to the cook's station in the grill area. I pulled the pans that held steaks from their slotted drawers in the under-counter refrigerator and rotated the meat into the new containers. After I'd done the same with the fish, I dumped the empty pans back in the kitchen on the dishwasher counter and washed my hands.

Nothing had started to turn yet, but we needed a busy night. I decided not to call in a fish order. Better to sell out of what we had than to dazzle customers with a variety of fish that would go bad before it sold. The restaurant business was different from most. You couldn't have a year-end sale or even a week-end one. When the product got old it went into the garbage and your tiny profit went in with it. Still, it beat wearing a badge for a police department that wanted to put you behind bars as much as you did the gangbangers on the street.

I grabbed the clipboard with the meat order sheet off the hook next to the phone and went into the walk-in refrigerator. I usually checked the inventory at night before I shut Muldoon's down, but last night Melody and Stone had knocked me out of my routine. We were pretty well stocked, and it would be another light order. I grabbed a shrink-wrapped strip loin from its box to get started on my meat cutting for the morning. When I came back out of the walk-in there were two large men staring at me from across the butcher-block meat cutting table.

"Are you Cahill?"

The speaker was at least six four and must have come through the door sideways or he would have gotten stuck. His head was square like his body, evenly leveled by a crew cut. He had a few years on me and they looked like they'd been spent pumping iron. Gray sweats, stretched well beyond XXXL, clung to his body.

His partner was as tall but not as wide. He had unkempt blond hair and a faint goatee anchored his angular face. Metal rings pierced both eyebrows and stair-stepped up his ears. He wore a lazy Generation Y grin and lounged against the cutting table. A black leather coat and baggy jeans filled out the attitude.

Those two weren't there to make dinner reservations.

"I'm Rick Cahill." I dropped the meat on the table. "What can I do for you?"

"Where's the girl?" The bigger one was in charge. His voice had an edge to it and a faint Brooklyn accent.

Looked like my friends from last night's car chase had finally caught up to me. I liked it better when I couldn't see them. And, when they couldn't see me.

"What girl?"

"Don't be a hero, pal." He tugged on his sweat top with his ham-hock right hand. "Melody, the drop-dead Filipina. We just wanna talk to her. Where is she?"

Some of the edge had rubbed off his voice. It was almost weary, like he'd done this so many times before that he was tired of the routine. His partner didn't look tired. He'd snapped out of his slumping attitude and was poised like a puma ready to pounce.

My morning crew wasn't due for another twenty minutes. It was just me and them.

"That sounds like a woman who had dinner here last night. But I don't know where she is." True, but now I had competition if I wanted to find her. Double-barreled competition. I sank my weight into the balls of my feet. "Why don't you leave me your names and phone numbers, and if this Melody comes back in, I'll have her call you."

"Still playing the hero." The big fella took a step toward me, and I spring-loaded my body.

The kid beat him to me. I let him get close, then grabbed the lapels of his coat and spun him into his partner. The big one took the impact like a concrete pillar. The kid bounced off him and slammed against the stainless steel wine refrigerator. His boss loomed in front of me filling up my vision, a crooked smile below hard pebble eyes.

Adrenaline pulsed in the place of blood. I eyed the knife block on the meat-cutting table two steps away.

"Hey!" A voice boomed from the other side of the kitchen.

Everyone turned to see Thomas "Turk" Muldoon standing in the doorway. My partner, my best friend, and the toughest man I knew. He'd put on a couple pounds around the middle since his linebacking days at UCLA, but most of him was still hard and agile. He held a meat mallet in his right hand. Used to tenderize meat. Sometimes the two-legged kind.

The concrete pillar worked his eyes over Turk. "You interrupted our little talk."

"By all means, let's talk." The whites grew around Turk's pale-blue eyes. I'd seen that look before. So had a drunk who once insulted Turk's sister. Right before unconsciousness.

The head tough moved his eyes from Turk over to me and finally rested them on his partner. "Let's go."

The younger one held his ground for a second and then walked toward the kitchen door, eyeballing Turk with each step. The leader followed him, but stopped at the exit and turned to face us.

"You two be careful, now." He grabbed a water glass off the shelf opposite the dishwasher and held it with his palm over the top. He squeezed and it exploded into shards and crashed down onto the cement floor. "Life can be dangerous. Even in La Jolla."

He gave us one more tough-guy look and then went through the door.

Turk followed him through the restaurant like a controlled avalanche flowing down a mountain.

I rode his wake.

It wasn't the first time Turk had covered my ass. Back in the early days after Santa Barbara, there were always a few latent frat boys brave on booze who wanted to test the "murderer." I tried to hide in public under a low profile. The first year back, I even grew a beard. But when challenged, my anger was quick and punitive. I rarely needed Turk's support, but he was always there. No matter what.

After the tough guys left, I closed the front door behind them. The backsplash of adrenaline twitched in my hands.

"What the hell was that all about?" Turk sat down on the couch in the hall and ran his hand through a tangle of red Chia Pet hair that hadn't felt a comb since the '80s.

"They were looking for a woman who had dinner here last night." I sat down next to him and let go a sigh.

"They had a funny way of looking."

I replayed the night for him, leaving out the sex and Stone wanting to buy Muldoon's. The former was between Melody and me. The latter would come out soon enough.

"So, those two assholes were Stone's boys?" His eyebrows rose.

"So, you know Stone." I stood on my anger and waited for Turk to come clean.

"Not personally, but I know of him. Everybody does."

"I don't."

"Don't you ever read the newspaper?" He looked at me like I was the dumb kid in school.

"Not in the last eight years."

"Oh. Yeah." He squeezed my shoulder with his massive hand. "Sorry."

My anger throttled down. Turk was the man who'd given me a life after my old one had died. No one would hire me after SBPD pushed me off the force. Not in Santa Barbara, not down here. Then Turk called and offered me a job as kitchen manager at Muldoon's. He took some heat for it in the local paper and sales dipped for a time, but he never blinked. I handled the back of the house while he handled the front. After about a year, I was general manager of the whole restaurant and he was a semi-absentee owner off rock climbing in Joshua Tree, Yosemite, or Grand Teton.

I'd first worked at Muldoon's as a fourteen-year-old kid prepping veggies for Turk's father. The money I made on weekends made a difference to my family after my dad had lost his job with the La Jolla Police Department. Turk was an all-city high school linebacker with scholarship offers from all over. But he took the time to show me the restaurant ropes and became a big brother to me. And my best friend.

"So, tell me about this Stone guy." Maybe Stone had been lying to me about buying Muldoon's just to get under my skin.

"Breakfast first."

Turk walked down the entry hall and made a left at the hostess stand into the lounge. He stood behind the bar under a set of Irish bagpipes mounted on the back wall. The uilleann pipes bore the Muldoon family crest. They were Turk's prized possession. A family heirloom his father brought over from the old country. Every St. Patricks' Day, Turk would pull them down and play "Danny Boy" just like his father had before him. A collector once offered him $10,000 for them, but he turned him down. One night in a quiet moment over too much Jameson, Turk confessed that he hoped to someday hand the pipes down to a son.

After he finally settled on one woman and quit playing on the sides of mountains thousands of feet in the air.

I sat on a stool and watched Turk concoct his version of breakfast. He pulled a banana, an orange, a lime, two eggs, and some cranberry juice from the under-counter refrigerator. After he peeled the orange and banana and tossed them into a blender, the raw eggs and cranberry juice followed. He topped everything with a few squeezes of lime, ran the blender on high for a few seconds, then poured in a pint of our house dark amber from the beer tap.

"You want some?" He set an empty glass down in front of me.

I just stared at him. He shrugged his shoulders and took a swig directly from the pitcher. Dirty foam hung from his three-day growth of mustache.

"Which route did you climb on Half Dome?"

"Regular Northwest."

"That's the one we did that time, right?" My only trip to Yosemite, rock-climbing Mecca, way back in college. I remembered Turk ascending nature's monument, heaven just out of reach and a view of the granite valley below. His movements were sure and fluid like an orangutan swinging through the trees. I fought my way up behind his lead, muscling against the rock instead of working with it. But somehow I made it to the top.

"You should come next time." Turk took another gulp of his breakfast, then came around the bar and sat down next to me.

"I don't think my knee or your restaurant would allow it." I rubbed my left knee that had been shredded in a college football game. "So tell me about Stone."

"He was part owner of a casino in Vegas before he moved out here. Back when the mob still had a piece of the action. I think it was the Starlighter, before they blew it up and built whatever the hell they put in its place."

"What brought him to San Diego?"

"Evidently he was forced out of the casino." Turk took another slug of breakfast and made a sour face. "He got into real estate out here. Owns a few hotels. Now he's a big time philanthropist. He's clean and shiny like Vegas never happened. He just donated a pile of cash to put a new wing on the La Jolla library."

"Does he own any restaurants?"

"I don't know. Why?"

"He told me he was interested in Muldoon's and that you should give him a call." The anger welled up in me like steam in an overheated radiator. I tried to keep the cap on. "Said his realtor told him it was listed for sale."

Turk shook his head and glanced down at the bar. When he looked back at me his eyes were squinted and his mouth closed tight.

"Yes, the restaurant is listed." His voice had a little snap in it. "You could have just asked me and I would have told you."

"Or you could have volunteered it." I bit the words off harder than I expected to.

"I'd never sell without telling you. I'm just testing the water to see where the market is. If I do sell, you'll get back what you've invested."

"I don't want my investment back." Stone's entitled arrogance, Melody's abandonment, and now Turk's betrayal boiled up in me and the cap blew off. I shot up from the barstool. "I want the restaurant. That was our deal!"

"Our deal? You gotta be kidding." Turk planted catcher's-mitt hands on the bar and leaned toward me. "You're giving me seven fifty a month. That's barely enough to get you a minority share. The rate you're going, we'll both be dead before you own this place."

"We had a deal."

"It was contingent upon you getting a loan." His voice was low, like a father explaining life to his son. "It's been two years."

"Any other buyers?" I lowered my voice and tried not to sound like a petulant son.

"None right now, but you need to come up with some real

money soon. I can't wait forever." His eyes showed friendship with a hint of pity. "Have you talked to any new lenders lately?"

I'd talked to plenty of lenders, but there wasn't a bank who'd give me a loan with only a 2006 Mustang GT as collateral. All I had was seven years of sweat equity in the one place I felt at home. Until now.

I left the bar without answering.

Muldoon's

CHAPTER SIX

Eleven forty-five a.m. I left Muldoon's and headed south on Prospect Street instead of north toward my car. Turk and Stone were still rattling around in my head, but I had a more immediate concern. Melody.

The muscle I'd met that morning didn't seem like the kind to give up the chase. I was afraid of what they might do to Melody if they found her. I had to get to her first. It was time to convince her to put the police between her and Stone and his hard boys. A call to her cell phone would have been the easy way. If I'd had enough sense between sex and snuggle time to get her number.

One thing I did mange to absorb was that Melody'd mentioned she was staying at a motel that she later called a bungalow. I knew of only one place that fit that description. Shell Beach Motel. It was just a few blocks away, down by the ocean.

The sun was hiding behind a gauze of morning fog when I hit the narrow alley that sluiced down a hill toward the sea. The motel was a series of small bungalows opposite the beach and sat on Coast Boulevard, a winding strip of seaside paradise. The bungalows were weather-beaten and could only generously be called quaint, but they did have an ocean view. Today the low gray sky smothered the ocean, leaving a gunmetal gray reflection on the water. Even paradise had its off days.

I angled over to a brick three-story building on the south side of the alley that housed the front desk. Maybe someone in there could help me track down Melody.

I was about to enter when a cop car blurred by on the street and then hot-rubbered to a stop on the north side of the alley. I walked down to the corner and looked. Three other squad cars and two slick tops were parked haphazardly in the street blocking any would-be traffic. A uniformed patrolman stretched yellow crime-scene tape around two bungalows and part of the parking lot. A plainclothes detective squatted in front of a Hispanic woman seated in the one of the unmarked brown Crown Victoria cop cars. The woman was crying and wore blue latex gloves against her white smocks. A maid who'd seen something horrible.

Melody?

Had I been too late? Had the two thugs found her while I was arguing with Turk? An image of Melody lounging naked on my couch flashed in my mind. Then she morphed into Colleen laid out on the coroner's table. My face burned hot and sweat beaded my hairline. Had I failed again? I had to find out what happened. And who it happened to.

A crowd had gathered outside the tape, pushed back onto the sidewalk by a couple of uniforms. Wet-suited surfers, sweat-suited geriatrics, and a small group of German tourists craned their heads to get a better view. I slipped into the middle of them. There wasn't much to see. The door was opened on a bungalow fronting the street and a woman in a white lab coat brushed black fingerprint powder on the doorknob.

Members of the crowd murmured to each other, and I heard the word "dead" a couple times. The number of cop cars suggested as much. But nobody knew for sure. I heard another vehicle pull up and glanced over and saw a coroner's van. My stomach knotted tighter. All doubt now erased, I was just left with the "who."

On the far left-hand side of the parking lot, a woman talked to a detective up against the crime-scene tape. She had her back to me, but something about her was familiar. Designer jeans, powder-blue sweater, natural brown curls. The detective was short, but made up for it with attitude and attire. Herringbone jacket, tan slacks, slicked-back hair, and an '80's porn mustache. He said something and the reporter laughed and flicked her hair away from her eyes. I guessed it wasn't the first time they'd been together at a murder scene.

The woman turned, stuffed a notepad in her leather shoulder bag, and hurried across the parking lot.

"Heather?" I said.

She looked over at me and flashed a high-wattage smile under big brown eyes. Heather Ortiz, *San Diego U-T* food reporter. She'd done a story a few years back on family owned restaurants versus the big chains. Turk had talked on the record for the story. Afterward, Heather and I'd had a couple of drinks in the bar that had ended with breakfast in her bed. Seemed she'd moved up the food chain to the cop beat.

"Rick? I never took you for a Lookie-Loo."

"What happened in there?"

"You're white as a sheet." She put a hand to my forehead. "Are you okay?"

"Fine. What happened?"

Heather examined me with reporter's eyes looking for a scoop. She must have read my desperation, and realized I had more than the normal prurient interest in whatever had happened inside the bungalow. She looked over my shoulder at the crowd and then took me by the hand and led me over to a red Mazda Miata convertible parked on the street.

"What's going on, Rick? Do you know someone who was staying in that room?"

"I know someone staying here, but I don't know what room she's in."

"Your friend is probably all right." She rubbed my hand. "It's a he, not a she, they're about to zip up in a black bag."

I let out a sigh, louder and longer than I could control.

"She must be someone special."

"A friend."

I wasn't sure yet whether or not Melody was special. I wasn't sure of anything about her. Except that sometime between stepping out of the shadows last night and disappearing from my bed this morning, Melody'd become my responsibility. I hadn't realized it until the two toughs tried to beat her whereabouts out of me. There was no reason to it, although I'm sure some shrink would tell me I was trying to make up for past sins. Responsibility didn't need reason. It only needed commitment. Now I just had to find Melody.

"Well, I trust her stay was more pleasant than the DB's."

"DB?" I smiled. "You've really taken to the cop beat, haven't you? You just need a fedora with a press badge under the hat band."

"I left it at home. Right next to my Turner Classic movie collection." She sighed and her eyes went skyward. "I wish it were that exciting. This is my first dead body in weeks."

"Yeah, it must be tough with the San Diego murder rate dropping. I'll bet the DB is happy he could spice things up for you."

"Smart ass. It's not all that spicy." She dropped her voice and I had to lean in to hear her over the waves whooshing on the beach, the mutterings of the crowd, and the squawks from the police radios. "The inside scoop is that it looks like a drug overdose, not a homicide. You can read all about it in the *U-T* tomorrow morning."

"A lot of cops and crime-scene tape for an overdose."

"The overkill is a CYA move by La Jolla PD." She pulled me away from her car into the alley that split the motel units. "There's a push by the La Jolla town council to disband the police force and contract with San Diego County Sheriff's department to handle law enforcement. Del Mar does it and saves a bundle in tax dollars. The council is looking for any excuse to take their agenda to the voters. If this turns into a homicide, it will be all over the news and the whole department's existence is going to be on the line. They'll do whatever it takes to close the case."

Heather and I exchanged business cards and then hugs and said our goodbyes. I went back to the front desk and found out that Melody had checked out earlier that morning.

•   •   •

The sun had started to burn through the haze when I made the climb up to my car. Strict parking enforcement pushed us day workers up the hill from Restaurant Row into residential neighborhoods to park our cars. The homes along the way were mostly small and at least fifty years old. Some had sprouted new additions or second stories. None had views of the ocean, and all were worth more than I'd make in twenty-five years. I was from this town, but not of it. And yet, this is where I'd returned for a second chance at life. If Turk sold Muldoon's, I didn't know where I'd go for a last chance.

Feet shuffling on the sidewalk behind me pulled me out of my head. My car was twenty feet away. Too late. A fist smashed into my right kidney before I could turn around. Pain shot through my back. A python, or maybe an arm, squeezed around my neck. I grabbed at it with my hands and felt taut flesh. A lot of it. I pulled at the arm and fought for air and saw Gen Y tough guy smiling in front of me. Then I heard the big one in my ear.

"Muldoon's not around to help you this time, Cahill."

They must have staked out my car after Turk kicked them out of the restaurant.

I tightened my stomach, but didn't get my hands down in time to block the kid's punch. It went through clenched muscle and into my solar plexus, and all the air left my body. I tried to bring oxygen back into my lungs, but another punch landed on my right rib cage. Pain exploded up my side. The only thing that kept me from hitting the ground was the arm clamped around my neck. But it sealed off the chance any air would return to my body. I gasped. My face flashed hot and tight. I pulled at the arm, and it eased its pressure. Not from my effort, but because the man-mountain wanted an answer.

"Where's the girl?"

It was probably time to tell him the truth. Maybe that would be worth a couple of gulps of air. I mulled this for a millisecond when I saw the front door of a house across the street open a crack, and a withered woman's face popped out.

"What girl?" My voice rode out on a gasp.

"Motherfucker!" Spittle flew out of the Gen Y kid's mouth and hit my chin.

He drew back his right hand, but his punch never landed. I kicked him in the crotch like I was punting a football. It would have been a fifty yarder. He yelped and fell to the ground in slow motion, curling into a fetal position.

The boss tightened his grip on my throat. I stomped my right heel down on his instep but only made him squeeze harder. I tugged at his arm. It was like trying to pull a branch off an oak tree. My face burned, and my head pounded. Then he relaxed his choke hold and moved his arm two inches down. My mouth opened wide and vacuumed in as much air as it could, then I heard a shout from across the street.

"The police are on their way!" The voice was a high-pitched whine. It was the most beautiful voice I'd ever heard.

The huge arm now clamped both sides of my neck. A police choke hold, back when they were still allowed. I could breathe, but felt dizzy. I grabbed his arm with all I had left but couldn't budge the tightening vise. My legs wobbled and everything turned red.

Then I heard it again.

"I called the police! They're coming!"

"Talk to the cops and you're dead." The Brooklyn-accented voice hissed in my ear.

Then he let go of my neck.

My knees hit the sidewalk first, and then my hands and face. I heard the neutered one struggle up off the ground, then running footsteps, car doors slamming, and finally a vehicle peeling out and zooming away. I didn't see any of it because my eyes were closed. When I opened them I saw the sidewalk, up close.

"Are you all right?" It was the voice from heaven again.

I rolled over on my back and groaned. My whole body felt like an open wound. After someone had rubbed salt in it and squeezed on some lemon juice for flavor.

"Yes. I'm fine."

"The police should be here any minute!"

I rolled back over onto all fours and stood up in stages. My car sat twenty feet away. The police would have to question my savior across the street alone. Brooklyn's threat hung in my ears under the pounding in my head.

When I finally made it to my car, the seat belt felt like an iron maiden when I cinched it around my torso.

I got home safely, locked the front door behind me, then glaciered through the kitchen to the back door and let Midnight in. He bounded in and jumped up to greet me before I could stop him. I stepped aside and tried to avoid his clawed embrace. My right foot caught the leg of the kitchen table and my back hit the ground at the same time Midnight's front paws landed on my rib cage. Pain shot through my front and my back and met in my middle. Laughter came instead of tears.

Midnight raked his tongue along my asphalt-scraped cheek.

Love hurts.

Muldoon's

CHAPTER SEVEN

Three hours later, after ice on my kidney and ribs and Motrin down my throat, my house phone rang. I struggled off the couch and answered it, hoping it was Melody.

"Rick, it's Dan Coyote."

Not even close.

Dan was a detective for the La Jolla Police Department. He was the only cop I knew who liked me, and that was probably because he didn't know me very well. We'd met playing golf at Torrey Pines a couple years ago. We hit it off and now hit the links together every month or so. He'd joined the LJPD from the Phoenix PD when La Jolla was short on manpower. It was a few years after I'd returned from Santa Barbara. If he knew or cared about my past, he never mentioned it.

"Hi, Dan. If you have a tee time, I'll probably be out of action for a couple days." I didn't think I could put a tee in the ground, much less make a golf swing.

"Actually, I'm calling about an incident that occurred today that may involve you." His voice was more detective than golf buddy.

The ancient Good Samaritan who saved my life must have given the police my license plate number. I didn't know whether the goon's threat had been idle or serious and I didn't want to find out. Beyond that, I'd had enough police involvement for a lifetime.

"If you're talking about a couple of guys roughing me up, it's not a big deal. I'm fine. I don't want to press charges."

"I'd still appreciate it if you'd come down to the station and tell me about it." His voice, now full detective, brought back bad memories from Santa Barbara.

"I have to be at work soon. It's really not worth your time."

There was a pause and then a deep exhale. "Look, Rick, the woman who filed the report is the owner of *The La Jolla Lantern*. She's making this a big deal. I'd really appreciate it if you'd come down."

The *Lantern* was the tiny local paper. Apparently its bite was bigger than its circulation. I didn't want the one cop I had as a friend to join my long list of enemies in blue.

The La Jolla Police Station was on Wall Street, just a few blocks from Muldoon's. The cops called it the "Brick House" because it was constructed of white brick. It had been a library in its early days before the police took it over. I guess the "Library" wasn't as intimidating as the "Brick House."

I hadn't been there since my dad got kicked off the force twenty-five years ago.

The two-story station house had polished wood floors and ex-posed wood-beam ceilings. I could see how it would have made a charming library, but my body tensed and my breaths quickened when I walked through the front door. It was a police station. A place where I used to belong, but never would again. A place where you were forced to face the truth, even when you lied.

The desk sergeant, a blue sack of wrinkles with a gruff tone, phoned upstairs to Detective Coyote in Robbery/Homicide. This was La Jolla. They might as well have called it Robbery/Died of Natural Causes. The town averaged maybe a murder a year. Still, the murders were usually high profile and became grist for books and TV crime shows. Jilted ex-wife murders her rich husband and his new trophy wife, white-bread wannabe gangbangers beat to death a surfer buddy, rich kid murders his whole family. The mur-ders probably got big publicity because of their rarity and locale.

Just like Santa Barbara.

Dan came downstairs to usher me up to the second floor and

Robbery/Homicide. His greeting was professional and lacked the warmth of a first-tee handshake. He had less hair and more stomach than when we'd first met, but still had an athlete's grace. His Native American ancestry showed in prominent cheekbones and dark hair. Tan slacks, a brown blazer, and a conservative tie made up his uniform. There were no jeans and T-shirt detectives on the La Jolla police force. Those were for TV cops and Levi's commercials.

Robbery/Homicide was housed in a square room that stank of day-old coffee. There were four low cut gray cubicles in the middle of the room adorned with computers and family photos. A large window faced the street and let in palm tree-filtered sunlight. An American flag hung on the wall opposite the window next to a map of La Jolla with red-and-black pushpins stuck in it.

In the far-left corner of the room there was a large glass-enclosed office with "Police Chief Raymond Parks" stenciled on the front panel. I guess in a small PD like this, the chief had to slum it with the gold shields. Open blinds cut shadows across Parks's face as he sat at his desk in his dress blues. He turned up dark eyes and gave me a flat-faced stare for an uncomfortable three count. My reputation preceded me. I wanted to get the hell out of there and back onto the streets where the tough guys didn't have badges.

The only other person in the room was the detective I'd seen talking to Heather Ortiz at the Shell Beach Motel earlier in the day. A nameplate on the outside of his cube opposite Dan's read "Detective Moretti." Hair slicked back hard, olive skin deeply tanned like a guy who spent his days at the beach or his nights under a sun lamp. He was hunched over a trash can clipping his fingernails. I guess the DB turned out to be an overdose. One less murder to solve for the busy boys at Robbery/Homicide.

Dan pulled a chair from the empty cube next to his and offered it to me. My ribs and kidneys hurt as I lowered myself down into the chair. He opened with some preliminaries, name and address to get everything on the record if needed. Then he asked me to describe my day leading up to and through the assault.

I gave him the rough and tumble at Muldoon's and then the ambush. The rest was between Melody and me. Nothing about taking her home last night, nothing about looking for her at the motel. I didn't even give him her name or what she looked like. Until I knew different, Melody didn't want the cops involved and I certainly didn't want to be involved with the cops.

"And you don't know the woman that these men were looking for?" He looked at me like "no" would be the wrong answer. I gave him a version of it, anyway.

"Like I said, they were looking for a woman they claimed had dinner in Muldoon's last night. I don't necessarily see or remember every guest who comes into the restaurant."

I'd probably never see Melody again. If I did, I didn't want it to be because I'd betrayed her trust.

Dan stood up and looked down at me like I'd betrayed his. Sometimes in life you have to make hard choices.

"All right, Rick," Dan said.

He walked over to a file cabinet against the wall and grabbed two large three-ring binders, then came back and dropped them on the desk. They made a loud "clunk" that brought Moretti's head over the cubicle wall. He gave me cop eyes and then disappeared below the partition.

"Look through those mug books and let us know if you find the men who assaulted you." He gave me the same look Moretti had. "I'm going to go grab our sketch artist in case the suspects aren't in the books."

I flipped through the mugs and didn't see anyone I recognized. I sat quietly and waited for Dan's return. The quiet didn't last long.

"Those two hard boys seemed pretty certain you knew the woman they were after. Why do you think that is, Cahill?" Detective Moretti's coal eyes bore into me over the top of the cubicle.

He must have been listening while he worked on his manicure.

"I don't know." I held his glare. "Maybe they didn't like getting kicked out of the restaurant and decided to take it out on me."

"Just an innocent victim." He hit each syllable hard like the drop of a guillotine blade. "Is that it, Cahill?"

I'd never met this guy before and wished I hadn't then. His contempt for me was boldly up front, even for a cop. I hadn't faced such hatred since my last encounter with Colleen's father.

"I didn't even want to press charges." My voice had some hiss to it. "I came down here as a favor to Dan, so—"

"You're a real sport, Cahill." He smacked gum, loud and hard with an open mouth. "Doing the police a favor by reporting a crime that you seemed content to cover up. You could have saved us all a lot of time and trouble if you would have waited around for the uniforms. That's what people with nothing to hide do."

"Yeah, I can see you're very busy. Not even enough time for a decent manicure."

Moretti sprang up from his chair to his full height, which would have been right at the police department minimum, if they still had one. He walked over and let his short-man frame tower over me as I stayed seated. I glanced at the chief's office behind Moretti to the left. Parks's eyes were on me and not his belligerent detective.

"How the hell were you ever a cop, Cahill?"

Finally, a good question. I hadn't planned on being one. I was going to be a football coach. Start in high school and then move my way up the ladder. My father had been a cop for LJPD. At least until he "retired" early without a pension. There'd been an investigation, but no charges filed. I remembered playing kickball in grade school the first time I heard the word "bagman." Neither the kid who'd repeated his father's words nor I knew what it meant. Until later.

My dad died when I was a sophomore in college. The man I'd loved as a child, feared as a kid, and hated as a teenager. His ex-partner was the only cop who attended the memorial service. That was the day I decided to become a police officer. I never let myself believe that I was doing it to erase the tarnish my father had brought to the family name. It was only after I'd turned tarnish to rot that I realized what I'd been trying to do.

I didn't think Moretti was interested in the details, so I kept my history to myself.

"You had to go all the way to Santa Barbara to find a place where no one could smell the stink of your old man on you." He smacked his gum louder. "But you fouled the world and that poor girl with your own stink. Didn't you?"

If he didn't have a badge and it had been five years ago in a bar, I would have stopped his mouth with my fist. That may have been what he was hoping I'd do now. Give him a reason to put me in a cage where I belonged. Where my family blood had fated me. I tamped down the anger and shoved it into a compartment in a dark hole in my mind.

"You practicing interrogation methods for when you catch the guys who jumped me?" I smiled up at him like a good citizen. "After you've buffed your nails, of course."

He raised his foot up and rested it on the arm of Dan's chair and leaned in on me. Up close, I could see the tip of a jagged cleft lip scar under his black mustache. I caught a whiff of his cologne. It was subtle, like ox musk mixed with gasoline.

"Something's not right about your little story, Cahill." He smiled but drilled small, mean eyes into me. "Just like the story you told Santa Barbara PD a few years back. The rotten apple doesn't fall far from the rotten tree."

I stood up. Moretti dropped his foot back to the ground and straightened up. It didn't matter how straight he made his spine, he'd never catch up to me. This time I crowded him and looked down at his forehead. "Tell Dan I'm sorry I couldn't wait around for the sketch artist." I crouched down a few inches so we were eye to eye. "Okay, Detective?"

Moretti grabbed me by my shirt and sent his cologne in first before his face. "Sit down!"

He tried to push me down into the chair, but I stayed upright. My ribs and kidneys screamed pain, but I swallowed it. I caught the chief's office out of the corner of my eye. Parks still had his eyes only on me.

"Sylvia's ready to sketch for Mr. Cahill." Dan's voice broke the tension, but I kept my eyes on Moretti.

"Cahill and I were just discussing his father." Moretti relaxed his shoulders and looked over at Dan. "Bags Cahill left quite a reputation behind. Just like his son, Rick, here." He turned back to me. "I told your friend Dan all about your, ah, interesting past this afternoon."

He gave me a snake grin, patted me on the shoulder, and then left the room.

I turned and saw in Dan's eyes that I'd need a new golf partner. Now every cop I knew was on the other side of the thin blue line.

I sat down and worked with the sketch artist. Not because it was the right thing to do. I'd already done enough wrong to negate the right. I did it to show Moretti and the rest of them that, although I was my father's son, they'd never know me. They could label me a bent cop, a guy who got away with murder, but they'd never know who I really was.

No one ever would.

Dan had left me alone with the sketch artist. After about a half hour she had two good renderings of my attackers. I didn't think anyone wanted to pat me on the back or shake my hand about being a good citizen, so I thanked the artist and got up to leave.

Moretti sauntered into the room just as I stood up from Dan's desk to leave. He ignored me and took the sketches from the artist and headed over to the copy machine next to the coffeemaker. I'd started to turn to leave when I noticed Moretti stop and stare at one of the sketches. He gave a quick glance in my direction and then went into the chief's office, closed the door, and shut the blinds.

I didn't wait around to find out who he'd recognized or why the chief had to see the sketch in a sealed room. It could have been a suspect in a high-profile case they wanted to keep the lid on. It could have been an ex-cop they knew. It probably had nothing to do with me. But when that door shut and those blinds snapped shut, the memory of Santa Barbara Police Department and another sealed room rushed back at me. My body flashed hot and my breath caught in my throat. I bolted out of the squad room, down the stairs, and out of the station house.

CHAPTER EIGHT

I shut down Muldoon's early and was home by eleven thirty. Three or four beers and then bed was the plan. I'd had enough excitement for one day. And one night. I had a Ballast Point Ale in my hand even before I opened the back door to let Midnight in. I put a hand out before he could jump up and knock me over again. I was almost knocked over anyway.

Melody rushed in behind Midnight and planted her lips on mine before I could wipe the surprise off them.

This time we made it to the bedroom. Despite the fast start, we took our time, explored and savored. The passion of last night was muted, but the feeling was more intense. Like it was more than sex. That it had meaning. Unlike last night, her eyes allowed me in. When I looked into them, I saw desire, yet vulnerability. A vulnerability that I shared and hadn't felt since the early days with Colleen. It scared me, but in that moment I loved her for it.

I rolled onto my back when we were done, and Melody nuzzled against my shoulder.

"What happened to your face?" She traced a finger along my scab in the dark.

The hair lifted off the back of my neck. Those were the first words Melody had spoken to me tonight. Her voice floating in the dark sounded so much like Colleen's that I could have been back in Santa Barbara lying in bed with her eight years ago. Or standing over her grave, her voice accusing, coming up through the earth. Guilt flooded in through the cracks of my memories.

"Hey, come back to me, Rick." Melody gently squeezed my chin. "Where did you go?"

A place that's always there, no matter how far I run from it.

"I'm right here." I took her hand off my chin and held it in my own. "I'm not the one who disappears in the middle of the night."

"Ouch. I guess I deserved that." She rolled onto her back but kept hold of my hand. "And you deserve an explanation."

"If you hadn't come back, that would have been explanation enough. But you did."

"I wasn't going to." She blew out a deep breath. "I'm sorry I didn't say goodbye last night or leave you a note. I thought it would be best for both of us if I just disappeared. I wanted you to forget about me."

"Why?"

"Because my life is—complicated—right now."

"You mean there's a man in it."

"No. My career. Things." She squeezed my hand. "It just seemed that a relationship didn't make sense right now."

"Then why did you come back?"

"Because all the reasons why I shouldn't have weren't enough to stop me." She rolled over on top of me and kissed me. "And I wanted to see if you felt the same way."

"Am I going to wake up tomorrow to an empty bed?"

"No, but you might wake up to breakfast in bed. I make a mean stack of pancakes." She rolled off me and rested her head in her hand. "Now, what happened to your face?"

I told her about my adventures with the hard boys and the cops. I left out my trip to Shell Beach Motel. My pride didn't want her to think that I'd crawled after her when she left me behind.

"Rick, I'm so sorry about all this." She ran fingers along my scalp and kissed my forehead. "You tried to protect me and look what happened. Why didn't you just tell them what they wanted to know?"

"I didn't know where you were, so I couldn't have told them if I wanted to."

"But you could have least told them the truth. That you knew me. Maybe they wouldn't have hurt you."

"What happens between you and me is no one's business but our own." I rolled up on an arm so that we were face-to-face. "But if there is going to be an 'our,' I need to know why these men are after you."

She didn't say anything and I waited. Her face was outlined in the dark, but her features hid in shadows. Finally her voice came out of the night. "They must be working for Peter."

"Stone?" I asked.

"Yes."

"So, he's more than some jilted lover. What's going on?"

She turned away from me and rolled onto her other side. "I don't know."

"Melody. These guys are dangerous. If you won't tell me what this is about, then go to the police." I laid my hand softly on her hip. "Or I will."

She was silent again. Then her voice, barely above a whisper, drifted over her shoulder. "I think my source is blackmailing Peter."

"I thought he was giving you information about Mayor Albright. What's that have to do with Stone?"

"He knows a lot of things about a lot of people. I don't know what he has on Peter, but I don't want to be the person who brings the police into it." She sat up and faced me. Her eyes still pools of shadow. "Peter is a very vindictive man and knows a lot of ways to hurt people. Please stay away from him, Rick. I don't want him to hurt you, too."

I didn't want him to either. Stone had already pushed some pain my way through the restaurant before he even knew me. Now I was probably on his to-do list.

"Who was the other guy?" I asked.

"What other guy?"

"Red soul patch with a prison tat on his neck. I saw you talking to him in the bar last night."

"Oh." She turned slightly, her profile shadowed by the night. "He was just some guy hitting on me."

At that moment Midnight banged his head against the door

from outside the bedroom. He had no qualms about being a third wheel. I got up and let him in and he went over to Melody's side of the bed and sat in front of her.

"Midnight has a crush," I said.

"We bonded while I waited for you to come home."

"Do you always make your entrances through the back door or were you hiding because you'd been followed again?"

"I don't think I was followed." She scratched Midnight behind the ear. "Midnight started barking when I knocked on the front door, so I went in the backyard to quiet him."

"It looks like it worked."

"I've tamed my share of wild beasts."

The next morning was déjà vu of the one before. Midnight wagging his tail in front of me, empty sheets next to me. Well, most mornings started that way, but not with the essence of Melody lingering in my empty bed.

Game over. I wouldn't try to track her down this time. Fool me once, fool me twice. There were only two strikes in this game. I got up to let Midnight outside.

The smell hit me as soon as I left the bedroom.

Pancakes. A whole new ballgame.

Melody stood next to the stove barefoot in my T-shirt, hair in a ponytail. Breakfast never looked so good. I wrapped my arms around her tight belly and kissed her neck. She purred. I could get used to that.

"Smells fantastic," I said.

"I told you I have skills."

"Yes, even in the kitchen."

I grabbed Midnight's bowl and filled it with dog food from the bag in the broom closet. After he'd chomped down his breakfast, I let him out and then went and got dressed. It was Turk's turn to open Muldoon's, so I had the day to myself. And Melody.

Breakfast was waiting for me when I returned to the kitchen.

Steaming pancakes, melting butter, and Vermont maple syrup from my pantry. I sat down and noticed there was only one plate.

"You're not eating?" I asked.

"I'm going to get dressed first."

"Not on my account."

"Then on mine." She smiled. "Your skillet only has room for three pancakes at a time, anyway. I'll get the next batch."

She lingered at the table waiting for me to take a bite. I did and fell in love.

"You weren't lying about your skills. These are fantastic!" I rubbed my thumb and fingers together. "There's a layered richness to them."

"I used brown sugar instead of white." She bounced slightly on her toes. "Glad you like them. I'll be right back."

I finished my pancakes and dropped three dollops of batter down onto the cast-iron skillet Melody had pulled down from my pot rack. I had them flipped and on a plate for Melody by the time she returned. She wore the same jeans and green blouse that she'd had on only briefly last night. A touch of makeup around her left eye covered the residue of the fist to the face her source had given her two nights ago.

She complimented me on the flapjacks, making it seem like I'd been the genius behind the batter. After we'd each polished off six, we pushed aside empty plates and lolled, full bellied, at the kitchen table.

"Rick." Melody's eyes dropped to the bleached-oak kitchen table before they met mine. "I'm flying back to San Francisco today."

"Okay." Well, we'd always have pancakes.

"I'm filling in on the anchor desk." She almost sounded apologetic. "It's a great career opportunity."

"That's great." I tried to sound sincere. I don't think I pulled it off.

I was happy for her, but sad for myself. Melody had a career and deserved success. But, I had finally met someone who made me remember what life could be like before Santa Barbara.

"This isn't the end, Rick." She reached for my hand across the table. "It's the beginning."

Midnight's growl from the backyard sounded right before a loud knock on the front door. I thought about letting him in to play bodyguard. But I headed out of the kitchen alone. I didn't think the tough guys after Melody would make another play in the middle of suburbia while the sun was up.

I opened the door and realized that I'd been thinking about the wrong tough guys.

Muldoon's

CHAPTER NINE

Dan Coyote and Tony Moretti stood together crowding my porch with their police presence. If given a choice between them and the two hard guys, I might have gone the other way. They flashed their badges like we were all strangers. I wished we were.

"Mr. Cahill, we have a few questions we'd like to ask you involving a police investigation." Moretti's voice had none of yesterday's contempt in it. I liked the new version better, but braced for an angle.

"Did you get a hit on one of the sketches of the guys who jumped me?" I couldn't think of any other reason, in my new life, that I'd have cops on my porch to start the day.

Moretti's eyes squeezed down and his lips went tight. Dan examined my welcome mat. I'd struck a nerve without even intending to. The sketch that had stopped Moretti in his tracks and sent him into his chief's office was the nerve. How it was connected to LJPD, I didn't know and the cops didn't want me to. That was fine by me. Anything that kept the police out of my life was my first choice.

But here they were, hiding their truth and wanting to know mine.

"We're here on another matter, Mr. Cahill." Moretti hid his obfuscation under his new tone. I changed my mind. I liked his old voice full of hate better. At least I knew where I stood.

"And what would that matter be?"

"Rick," Dan finally found his voice and then my eyes, "why don't you invite us inside and we'll explain."

I liked cops in my house even less than on my porch. But I didn't want to give Moretti a reason to dislike me more than he already did. I waved them inside. Dan grabbed the morning news-paper off my porch and handed it to me as he passed through the door. I dropped it on the end table. Melody was still in the kitchen, quiet beneath Midnight's huffing outside the back door.

Moretti surveyed the living room. His pursed lips showed he was unimpressed with the maple bookshelf, mismatched furniture, department store entertainment center, and dog-worn carpet. He wasn't in La Jolla anymore. Had to slum it in North Clairemont with the common folk. I maintained the manners of my class by not offering the cops a seat or anything to drink.

We stood, an abbreviated football huddle, in the middle of my living room. I figured Moretti would want to play quarterback. The short ones always do. I shut up and waited.

"Do you know a Melody Malana?" Moretti finally asked.

I thought they'd come by to bullshit their way through a few questions to find out what I knew about the man in the sketch they were protecting. Not questions about Melody. And how had they linked Melody to me? The man in the sketch? Or, had the police themselves been following me? I flashed back to the cop who'd stopped Melody and me Sunday night and had hidden behind his floodlight.

"Who?" I asked.

"Don't try to play smart, Cahill." He stepped in under my chin and drowned me in his cologne. "You don't have enough practice."

Now we were back on familiar ground.

"Rick." Dan's voice was calm against Moretti's sudden agita-tion. "It's important that we talk to Miss Malana. Please tell us where she is."

"What's so important?" I wasn't just going to roll over.

Maybe Moretti was right about my level of smarts.

"You going to lie to us again? You're just itching to wear the bracelets. Aren't you, Cahill?" He stepped in so close that his nose almost bumped my chin. "We'll start with obstructing a police in-vestigation and see what else sticks."

"Aren't you a bit out of your jurisdiction to be slappin' on handcuffs, Detective?" I looked down my nose at him. "This is San Diego PD's beat."

"Try me."

The sound of a cabinet door closing came from the kitchen before I could say something else smart. All eyes shot to the doorway into the kitchen. Melody walked into the living room. She wore the same leather shoulder bag she'd had on last night when she surprised me with a kiss at the back door. The kiss suddenly felt like a fond memory from a long time ago.

"What can I do for you gentlemen?" She smiled, her voice calm. She made it seem like starting the day with cops in your living room was as normal as sunshine in San Diego.

Moretti eyeballed her up and down before he spoke. "Miss Malana?"

"Yes."

"I'm Detective Moretti." He showed her his badge and nodded toward Dan. "This is Detective Coyote. We need to ask you a few questions."

"Okay." Melody joined our huddle.

"Do you know a Mr. Adam Windsor?" Moretti asked.

"Yes." Melody said, the smile now tight on her face.

"I'm sorry to have to tell you that he was found dead yesterday morning."

Melody sat down on the sofa and stared at Moretti, but I don't think she saw him. Some of the tan had washed out of her face, but her eyes revealed nothing.

"Are you okay?" I sat down next to her.

"I'm fine."

"Who's Adam Windsor?"

"Mr. Cahill," Moretti interrupted, "we'll ask the questions, if you don't mind."

"My ex-husband." Melody said, her voice flat like her emotions.

Ex-husband?

"What happened to him?" Melody asked, still under control. "How did he die?"

"Undetermined at this time." Moretti's eyes bored in on her, a cardsharp looking for a tell. "His body was found at the Shell Beach Motel."

Melody gave away nothing. I tried to do the same.

Adam Windsor. Heather Ortiz's DB. Melody's ex-husband. Found dead at her motel. You didn't have to be a cop to raise an eyebrow at Melody. She hadn't necessarily lied to me, but she hadn't been free with the truth. Maybe her ex staying at her motel would have come out eventually. I'd done my own share of withholding. But now there was a dead body, and I was still dealing with one of those from my own past. I wasn't sure I knew Melody well enough to handle hers, too.

Moretti said Windsor's death was undetermined. But, Heather Ortiz had already labeled it an overdose yesterday after talking to Moretti. Maybe he was waiting for the coroner's official determination before he told the whole truth. When would Melody do the same?

"Miss Malana." Dan stood over the sofa. "It would really be helpful if you'd come down to the station with us."

"Am I under arrest?" Melody's eyes widened.

Dan shot a look at Moretti and so did I.

"No." Moretti gave her a compassionate cop smile. "We just need to ask you a few more questions in a more appropriate environment."

"I'll make coffee if you like." I stood up. Moretti could smile all he wanted; nothing good ever came out of a station house talk. "But Melody stays here."

Instinct. Stupidity. Masochism. Any or all could apply, but heavy emphasis on stupidity.

"I warned you, Cahill." Moretti resumed his position as a wart on my chin. No compassionate cop smile for me. "Miss Malana may or may not be joining us, but you are."

Moretti reached behind his back on his belt and I heard the clink of handcuffs.

"Detective Moretti?" Melody stood up. Her voice was high

and caught in her throat. "Please let Mr. Cahill stay here. I'll go with you to the police station."

Moretti snapped one cuff around my left wrist and shot hard, black eyes up at me. "You remember this feeling, don't ya, Cahill? Cold steel pinching your wrists?"

I figured he was bluffing, but I'd been wrong before. Even though I talked around the truth about knowing Melody yesterday, Moretti didn't have anything arrest worthy on me. But if his partner backed him up it didn't matter. He had a badge, he made the rules.

"Please." Melody's voice quivered. "Detective."

Dan didn't say anything else, but trained basset hound eyes on his partner. Maybe he was the kind of cop I had tried to be. And failed.

Moretti shot a key into the cuff and had it off my wrist in an instant. He gave me a contented smirk that said he'd had his fun at my expense. I couldn't argue with the smirk, but I wouldn't have minded putting my fist through it.

"Miss Malana," Moretti stepped around me toward the front door, "if you'll come with us, we'll make sure you get a ride to wherever you like after we done."

Melody let out a quick breath and gave her head a minute nod. Composed, she rested a hand on my shoulder and kissed me on the cheek. "I'll be fine," she whispered. Then she followed Moretti to the front door.

I didn't think so. "Let me call you a lawyer first."

Dan looked at me like I worked for the ACLU.

Moretti opened the door and said. "This shouldn't take very long."

Melody turned back and gave me a weak, crooked incisor smile. It sucked a breath out of me. "It's okay, Rick, I'll call you when I'm done."

Dan followed her outside and closed the door, sealing me inside my empty house.

Muldoon's

CHAPTER TEN

I washed the breakfast dishes and cleaned up the kitchen, hoping that if I kept my hands occupied my mind would follow. It didn't. Melody kept creeping in. A woman I hadn't known three days ago now seeped into my thoughts, flooding me with feelings I hadn't had for almost a decade. Feelings I never thought I'd have again. Love? I couldn't tag that label on it yet. But something strong, visceral. A need to protect. And I couldn't protect Melody when she was down at the La Jolla Police Department's Brick House.

Of course, she was only there for routine questioning. Cops always called it routine when they took you down to the station. Just a few routine questions. Next thing you know, you're in a holding cell waiting for the chance to call a lawyer.

Until the coroner's report came back with a cause of death that wasn't homicide, Melody's freedom was in the hands of a small-town cop with a big-city ego. And there was nothing I could do about it.

When I was done in the kitchen, I headed for the front door. I didn't have to be at Muldoon's until five p.m. Normally I'd play golf or get a workout in. I was too beat up to do either and probably wouldn't have been able to concentrate, anyway. I needed to take a drive to either clear my thoughts or focus them.

I grabbed my keys and wallet off the end table by the front door and noticed the *U-T* newspaper that Detective Coyote had brought in with him earlier. Ever since Santa Barbara, I'd made a practice of skipping the front page and the local section and going right to the sports page. Everything else ended up in a pile and then in the recycle bin.

Today, I scanned the front page and inside looking for Heather Ortiz's article on Adam Windsor's death at the Shell Beach Motel. I wondered if she had more information than Moretti had let out when he took Melody away. I found the article on the front page of the local section.

The headline alone told me more than Moretti had: Son of Windsor Bank Founder Found Dead. And the accompanying picture of Adam Windsor told me more than Melody had been willing to. He looked younger in the picture and didn't have a neck tattoo, but Adam Windsor was the red-haired man I'd seen talking to Melody in the bar at Muldoon's Sunday night. Not just "some guy" hitting on her. Her ex-husband. The man who ended up dead.

This wasn't a matter of Melody not telling the whole truth, of holding something back. This was a lie. I'm sure there were plenty of legitimate reasons to lie about talking to your ex-husband. Especially, as Heather Ortiz's article stated, after he just got out of prison. Embarrassment over bad choices, didn't want to burden the new boyfriend with old baggage, wanting a fair chance at a fresh start. All that kind of bullshit. But the fact remained, Melody had lied to me. After I'd taken a beating for her, shielded her from the police, and shared my bed with her, I still hadn't earned the right to the truth.

What else had she lied about? Could I believe her stunned surprise at hearing about the death of her ex-husband? Or had that been a lie, too?

I tried to set aside my anger and went back to the newspaper article. It said that Windsor had just been released three weeks ago after serving an eight-year term in Nevada's High Desert State Prison for drug distribution. He hadn't been a guest at the Shell Beach Motel, and his body had been found in an unoccupied room. The article closed by stating that the cause of death was believed to be from a drug overdose.

It wouldn't be the first time an ex-con died of a drug overdose, but according to Detective Moretti, Heather appeared to be jumping the gun. He had said the cause of death was still undetermined.

I didn't know Heather that well, but she didn't seem like the kind of reporter who would let the need for a scoop get in the way of verifying facts. Maybe information about the cause of death had changed since the newspaper's deadline yesterday.

Windsor not being a guest at the motel bothered me. He got into a room somehow. Melody had told me the first night we were together that her source had hit her and she fled the motel. Had Windsor been her source? And had he been staying with her?

Ugly scenarios started speeding out in front of me. I needed some answers to reel them back in. Melody wasn't around to give them to me. I'd have to find them on my own.

I looked up the number for the Shell Beach Motel on my iPhone and dialed it.

"It's a great day at the Shell Beach Motel," a chipper, young female voice said. "How may I help you?"

"I'm going to be in town for a few days and have heard great things about your motel." Except for the dead bodies. "A friend of mine was just there and she loved her room."

"That's great to hear. All of our cottages have ocean views and offer cozy amenities."

"I was hoping to stay in the same bungalow she did, but I forgot to ask her what number it was. Her name is Melody Malana and she checked out yesterday."

Suicide or homicide, the room that Windsor checked out in wouldn't have been released back to the motel yet. Even if it had, management would give it an intense cleaning before they allowed anyone to stay in it again.

I heard fingers clicking a keyboard for a few seconds. "I'm afraid that bungalow is unavailable. I can reserve another one for you that is equally as nice. In fact, it has a little better view."

"Wow, rented already. I thought October was the slow season in La Jolla." I let out a little grunt like I was disappointed. "Do you know how long the new occupant is going to stay? Maybe I could stay in another room and then move over when the person leaves."

"Well, there's . . . it's not really . . . ah."

"Oh, my word!" I tried to sound giddy and shocked at the same time. "It's not the room where the dead body was found. Is it?"

"Ah, well . . . we're not supposed to really . . ."

Bingo.

"Oh, there goes my other line," I said. "Let me call you right back."

So, Windsor's body had been found in the room Melody had checked out of earlier that morning. The morning I woke up and she was gone. She must have taken a cab from my house to the La Valencia Hotel where she'd left her rental car the night before and then gone back to the motel to get her belongings before checking out. Unless she'd thrown everything into the rental when she left the motel the night before. Hard to imagine she'd had time to pack a suitcase when she was fleeing an ex-con who just punched her in the face. One thing was certain. Melody didn't have a suitcase with her when she showed up on Muldoon's doorstep asking for my help.

Unless Windsor broke in after Melody checked out, he must have been in her room when she returned to get her stuff. Was he lying on the floor with a needle jammed in his arm or a crack pipe lodged between death-clenched teeth or was he still alive?

Some answers required Melody. Maybe she was giving them to the police right now. I'd have to wait for mine, but not locked up in my own house looking for distractions.

I went outside, got into my car, pointed it toward La Jolla. I'd gotten Melody's cell phone number over breakfast and now dialed it. Her voice mail came on immediately. I hung up. She'd been with the police for an hour and a half. Plenty of time if everything was just routine. Not nearly enough if it wasn't.

The sun had sweated off any remnants of fog and left the sky a crisp blue. I broke off Highway 52 up the ramp into La Jolla, breaching the first rolling hill that protected its east end. The ocean came into view out beyond a canopy of evergreen trees that hid homes with million-dollar views.

I hit the bottom of the hill and merged onto Torrey Pines Road, winding up the next rise into La Jolla proper. Multimillion dollar homes clung to a hillside on the left, on the right a view of the coastline below arced its way from La Jolla Shores north to Black's Beach. I turned right on Prospect Street, still not sure where I was going, but felt the pull of Melody at the La Jolla police station. A chill crept up my spine at the thought of going back inside the Brick House. I'd seen enough of that place and the people inside it.

Restaurants, art galleries, and curio shops drifted by until I approached Muldoon's. I thought about stopping in, but kept going. Turk's putting the restaurant up for sale still stung. Muldoon's no longer felt like a second home to me.

Traffic was slow, and I got caught behind a Mercedes that was older than I was. A mop of blue-gray hair was just visible above the back of the driver's seat, level with the steering wheel. Whether it was granny tanks or rentals driven by swivel-headed tourists, traffic was slow in La Jolla year-round.

The Mercedes had a red, white, and blue Albright for Governor bumper sticker. It reminded me that the mayor was having a rally at the La Jolla Recreation Center at eleven a.m. I'd seen a headline about it in the paper this morning while I searched for the story about Adam Windsor. One local son made good and striving for more. Another, a ne'er-do-well done with striving, good or bad, forever.

Melody had told me, way back when I could trust her, that she'd come down to San Diego to cover Mayor Albright's run for governor. If that were true, she'd probably try to make his rally before she had to fly back up to San Francisco. That's if she got out of the Brick House in time. And providing everything she'd told me since we met hadn't been a lie.

Muldoon's

CHAPTER ELEVEN

The La Jolla Recreation Center was on the southern end of Prospect Street, a few blocks down from Muldoon's. I'd played football there as a kid and still played in an occasional pickup basketball game there when my knee allowed. The Rec was old when I was young. Hell, it was old before my father was born and was now considered a historic site. That meant nobody wanted to spend the money to modernize it.

Three to four hundred people sat on the recreation center's truncated flag-football field in metal folding chairs and listened to Mayor Albright speak as he stood at a podium on top of a small wooden stage. Albright was in his early fifties and kept in shape, though his white hair and sun-worn face made him look older. Physically, he wasn't a big man, but he had a powerful presence motored by nonstop energy that filled up any room he entered. Today it spread out over the football field.

Behind him on stage were his wife, Angela, looking more sane and sober than the last time I saw her, their six-year-old daughter, Cassandra, and Chief Parks. I guessed Parks was there to lend law-and-order support. Albright won loud cheers from his audience as he talked about education reform, lower energy costs, lower taxes, and holding Washington, D.C., accountable for safeguarding the border. He then segued into the safety of the people of California.

"We can't expect the federal government to do all our policing." Albright gripped the podium and looked out over the crowd. "They've got their hands full and we need some hands-on leadership right here in California!"

He waited for the cheers and the crowd obliged.

"That's why when I become the governor I'm going to create the Department of California Security that will work in conjunction with the federal government." He paused and smiled. "I know you're probably thinking, 'not another bureaucracy.' But bureaucracies are created by bureaucrats, not men of action. And I can promise you that the man who'll run the department is a top-notch investigator, an inspired leader, and a proven law enforcement officer. He's made La Jolla the safest town in the state. Please show your support for the man who will travel with me to Sacramento to ensure California's safety, La Jolla's own, Police Chief Raymond Parks!"

Albright turned and motioned behind him. Chief Parks, attired in his dress blues, rose from his chair and waved. He smiled, but on his black-mustached, coal-eyed face it looked more like a wolf snarl. He sat down before his charm vacuum sucked up some of Albright's charisma.

The Mayor finished his speech and invited everyone to a reception inside the Rec Center's meeting room. I scanned the crowd looking for Melody. I didn't see her but did find a familiar face. Or more precisely, a familiar head. A square one atop a square body. My old kidney-punching pal from yesterday. He looked like a block of granite in a Men's Warehouse suit. He stood next to the door of the building that housed the room where the mayor's reception was to he held.

A horde of people in front of me broke for the reception and obstructed my view of the man with the python arms. I jostled through the mass of three-piece suits, sundresses, and Hawaiian shirts, catching glimpses of him every few steps. When I finally edged into the clear, his billboard-size back was disappearing into the reception up ahead. I followed him inside the old, mission-style building.

The rectangular room had a creaky wood floor and was packed shoulder to shoulder with Albright supporters. Red, white, and blue bunting hung from the walls, and two refreshment tables held punch and red, white, and blue cookies. The mayor and his entourage stood at the far end of the room shaking hands with supporters at the front of a roped-off reception line. The big guy filled a doorway that led outside. He ushered people through it after they had their fifteen seconds with the mayor, his family, and Parks. My attacker was working security for the mayor, ten feet away from the police chief.

The only way to get to him was to join the slow-motion conga line of true believers. Not that I knew what I'd do when we were face-to-face. I decided I'd let the chief decide. Give him the chance to arrest a dangerous criminal or, if I was right, continue to cover up for one. I got in line.

Every few seconds I shuffled a couple feet forward, wedged between an aging surfer in shorts and flip-flops and a 1970's beauty queen showing silicone cleavage and a surgically reborn face.

After a couple minutes, I finally stood in front of the guests of honor, only twenty feet from the goon who'd tried to squeeze Melody's whereabouts out of me. First up was Mayor Albright.

"We've missed you in Muldoon's, Your Honor." My attempt at small talk.

"Well, yes, the campaign you know—" Albright gave me a strained smile like I had European youth hostel BO and he just found out he had the bunk under me. "Thank you for your support."

He turned to the beauty queen, and I was already forgotten. The mayor had always been friendly in Muldoon's, but that was out of the way of reporters. Best not to be seen too chummy with a suspected murderer in public. I wondered if he knew the pedigree of his security bulldog.

I peeked over at man mountain as I shuffled in front of Angela Albright. His eyes glanced off mine just before I turned them on Angela. I couldn't tell if he recognized me.

Angela grabbed my hand with both of hers. She wore a turquoise blouse that made her blue eyes pop. No residue of Sunday night's drunkenness shone in them.

She leaned into me and spoke in a low voice under the din of the crowd, "Rick, thanks so much for looking after me the other night." She looked over and made sure her husband was busy with the beauty queen. "The campaign has been so hectic. I'm afraid that when I let down my hair, I went a little bit too far. I'll send a check over to you at the restaurant to reimburse you for the cab fare."

"No need. Consider it my contribution to the campaign." I started to release her hand, but she held on and pulled me closer and whispered in my ear, "No one's asked you about me being in the bar that night, have they?"

"No." Melody had, but nothing seemed to have come of it. I didn't see the need to add to a nice lady's worries.

I moved off Angela over to little Cassandra Albright, a mini version of her mom. She smiled up at me and put out a tiny hand. "Thank you for your support."

I shook her hand, patted her on the head, and shot a glance at my extra-large nemesis. But he was gone. Replaced by another mountain of testosterone in a suit. I doubted that it was because it was the mauler's turn for a break. He'd seen me. He was in the wind. But Chief Parks was still there, the last of a line of glad-handers.

He didn't look glad to see me. I'd become as popular with La Jolla's Police Department as I was with Santa Barbara's.

Parks was as stiff and starched as his uniform and looked as approachable as a porcupine at full quill. Up close, his cheeks were smooth and shiny like someone had taken a belt sander to them and finished with a buffing brush. His dark eyes burned into me. No attempt to hide their malice under a politician's smile. His out-stretched hand, a bayonet waiting to impale me. I grabbed it any-way. A cloud of Moretti's cologne wafted over me, but I had it backward. The mustache, the cologne; Parks was Moretti's icon, not the other way around.

"Hi, Chief." I smiled. "I got a tip that will help your arrest stats. One of the men who attacked me was working security here and just disappeared out the door behind you."

"I'll report it to the detectives in charge." His voice was flat, uninterested, yet somehow familiar to me.

The cover-up was on. The investigation into my assault was dead. My attacker had juice with LJPD and, maybe, the mayor. He was probably an ex-cop who'd gone private and still had pals on the force. I was an ex-cop with sore ribs and enemies on every force.

Justice ignored for some greater good that I wasn't a part of.

Parks dropped my hand like it was a sack of dirt, and the new security goon ushered me through the door to the outside.

Sunlight splashed through trees, birds chirped, and a sweet whiff of the ocean wafted in the air. Paradise with a dirty back room.

Muldoon's

CHAPTER TWELVE

I went home and let Midnight inside from the backyard. I gave him a Milk-Bone, then went and sat down on the sofa. Midnight chomped down his treat and then came over and sat in front of me. He looked up at me with big brown eyes. No judgment, no disappointment, no manipulation. Just acceptance and love. I went back into the kitchen and got him another Milk-Bone.

My cell phone burred in my pocket. I pulled it out and checked the screen. Melody. A warm tingle spread across my chest. Even with the lies and the doubt, my body chose to believe. I sided with my brain, but still answered the phone.

"Rick, my plane's about to board, but I wanted to call you before I left." Her voice was animated like she was happy to talk to me. But I'd been wrong before.

"What happened with the police?" I asked.

"They just asked me some questions about Adam. When I'd seen him last. Did I know if he'd been taking drugs. Things like that."

If Melody felt any sorrow over the death of her ex-husband, I didn't hear it in her voice. She could have been discussing the weather. Maybe being married to a drug addict had used up all her pity.

"So they must have asked you how he ended up dead in your room."

"Who told you that?" Now I had her attention.

"I figured it out." Irritation shaded my voice. "I figured out a lot of things today."

"What do you mean?" Defensive, maybe hurt.

"Why did you lie to me about not knowing the red-haired man

you talked to in the bar Sunday night?" I paused, then hit home. "You know, your dead ex-husband."

"I didn't want you to think—I hoped he'd just go away. I'm sorry, Rick." A PA system in the background murmured something about a flight boarding underneath Melody's halting voice. "I have to go now. My flight's leaving. I'll call as soon as I can. We can talk things over then. But it's going to be hectic for the next couple days. I'm anchoring the eleven o'clock news tonight and both the five and eleven tomorrow. I'll call, Thursday at the latest. I promise."

If she was waiting for an "I'll be waiting by the phone" or an "I'll miss you," she'd miss her flight. I didn't say anything.

"Rick. Thank you so much for all you've done for me." She sounded sincere, but her words spelled out brush-off. I expected her to tell me she liked me as a friend or that we'd always have pancakes. "I don't know what I would have done without you." Another boarding murmur in the background. "I have to go. I'll call you soon."

"Goodbye, Melody." I hung up.

Midnight gave me more black lab love eyes. My buddy, at my side no matter what.

Or maybe he just wanted another Milk-Bone.

The next morning at Muldoon's I was trimming the fat off a top sirloin butt when Hector, our cleanup guy, came over to me at the cutting table.

"*Policia esta aqui.*" Hector thumbed toward the dining room.

Great. More police. I wiped my hands on my once-white apron and followed Hector into the dining room. My two favorite detectives were waiting for me by the empty salad bar. Muldoon's had become a popular hangout for people I didn't want to see. I sent Hector back into the bar to finish his cleaning duties.

"Cahill, you need to come with us to the station," Moretti said, his mouth a sneer under the porn mustache. He looked like he hoped that I'd reject his command.

Dan's face was stoic, no trace of friendship in it.

"Why? Did you pick up the two suspects who assaulted me?"

"It's regarding another matter." Moretti snapped some gum at me. "But rest assured, we have unlimited manpower available to solve your, ah, battery case."

"Yeah, I know. I spoke to the chief about it yesterday."

Neither of them gave away anything. The chief could have told them about my attacker being at the Albright rally or he could have kept it to himself. The outcome would have been the same either way. Nada.

"Let's go, Cahill," Moretti said. "We don't have all day."

"Unless you can be more specific, I don't see how I can help." I started for the kitchen. "I've got work to do. You know the way out."

"Rick," Dan called after me, "we need your help buttoning a few things up on Adam Windsor's death."

I stopped and faced Dan. "I don't know anything about that."

"We just need to verify a few things concerning Miss Malana." Dan tried a smile. It wore better than the one on Moretti's face. "This won't take long."

Just a few routine questions.

"Okay. Ask whatever you want. But I'm staying here."

Dan gave me more golf-buddy smile. "We need you at the station to take a look at a few things—"

"Cut the bullshit, Cahill!" Moretti took up his position under my chin. "Come with us now or we'll come back tonight and have a little chat right here in front of your customers."

They'd need an arrest warrant then just like they did now to compel me to go with them. But the thought of a scene in the dining room and losing the trust of our regular customers after working so many years to earn it weighed heavily.

"Let me finish up in the kitchen first."

The ride to the Brick House was only a few blocks. We took it in silence. I'd only been in the back of a police car twice before. Once as an egg-throwing teenager, another as a murder suspect. I hadn't enjoyed either ride and didn't this one, no matter how short. The view was better from behind the wheel, adrenal glands on overload, jacked on the power of the badge. Veteran cops called it the "John Wayne Syndrome" and knew it either wore off or wore you out. I'd still been in full "Duke" mode when I left the force.

Moretti parked behind the Brick House and he and Dan led me into the police station though a back door. We walked under a cloud of silence. My stomach knotted and sweat spotted my forehead. Front door, back door, it was still a police station. I turned my head and quickly wiped my brow, hoping the detectives didn't sense my unease. They gave away nothing, and we walked up cement stairs in a hollow stairwell that echoed our silence.

We hit the second floor and went down a tile hallway that led to the back entrance into Robbery/Homicide. Dan disappeared through the doorway, and Moretti took me down the hall and opened the next door on the right.

"Make yourself at home." He left and closed the door.

I walked into a small, square, white-walled room with a wooden table and three chairs tucked into the far corner. A fluorescent light buzzed overhead and a closed-circuit camera above the door peered downward. A light burned red on the camera. Action. Just like the interrogation room in Santa Barbara eight years ago. My pulse quickened and the past shallowed my breath.

I had to fight not to bolt out of the room. They couldn't hold me. This time. But if they wanted to sweat me, they'd find a way. I just wanted to get it over with. I needed to pace the room to settle my nerves, but knew they were watching in black and white nearby. If I paced, they won. I sat down in a chair in the corner with my back to the camera.

I waited. Five minutes? Ten minutes? It felt like thirty; it could have been three.

Finally, the door opened and Dan entered the room. Moretti followed holding a stack of manila folders.

"You're in my chair." Moretti dropped the folders with a loud thud on the table and grabbed the back of my chair.

I stood up and Moretti sat down. I knew the folders were probably full of anything but information about me. They were a prop to intimidate me. He didn't need it. The square room was intimidation enough.

"Have a seat, Rick." Dan pulled out the chair that faced the camera.

I obliged. He sat down next to his partner, opposite me.

"Thanks for coming in and helping us out." He smiled at me like we were still golf buddies planning our next round. The Good Cop. My eyes slid over to his partner. I didn't need any help figuring out which role Moretti would play.

Dan pulled a small tape recorder out of his side coat pocket and set it on the table. A backup to the camera over the door. He turned it on, stated the date and time and named the three of us in the room.

Moretti got up and pulled his chair over next to me, the rubber foot glides squealing on the tile floor. He placed his foot on the chair and leaned toward me resting his crossed arms on his knee. Cologne and a smirk pushed down on me.

"Where'd you get the heroin?"

My pulse double tapped and my breaths quickened. I could feel the sweat squeezing out of my forehead and under my arms. The game had changed. Moretti was fishing. I had nothing to hide. Still, the walls were inching toward me. I swallowed it all down.

Routine questions.

"What are you talking about?"

"The heroin that killed Windsor." He leaned into me. "You see, that's where you made a mistake. He got clean in the joint. You should have noticed that when you stuck the needle in his arm. No tracks."

My temples pounded, echoing inside my head. I flashed back to Santa Barbara and Detective Grimes, his face in mine, telling me that my neighbors had heard a violent fight between Colleen and me the night of her death. That Colleen had confessed to a friend she was considering divorce. My lack of an alibi. And, finally, that I'd failed the polygraph and then reading me my rights.

I blinked and settled my breathing.

"I didn't stick a needle in anyone's arm." I tried to sound calm. "The newspaper made it sound like he'd OD'd on his own."

"The newspaper got it wrong." Moretti stared down at me from his perch, a vulture eyeing a fresh kill.

Dan stood up and left the room.

I didn't like being left alone in the room with Moretti. The red light on the camera above the door confirmed it was still recording. At least there'd be a record of anything Moretti might try. Unless somebody erased it.

"Look, I've seen Melody. I'd probably do whatever she asked me to do, too." Moretti's smile turned friendly like we were old pals. "I'm sure she made it sound reasonable. The guy made her life a living hell. He'd probably end up dead with a needle in his arm, anyway. That sort of thing. But you got caught and this is your one chance to be smart. If you put Melody behind this, the DA will cut you a deal. But you gotta get there first. She gets the chance, she'll roll on you before her tight ass hits the seat. Then you'll be looking at a needle in your own arm, but it won't be heroin."

I knew the game. He was still fishing. If he'd had enough on Melody, they would have booked her. Maybe they thought Windsor had been murdered, but had nothing and were throwing a Hail Mary.

I wasn't the answer to anyone's prayers.

"This is bullshit." I stood up and strode for the door.

Moretti chuckled and kept his seat. That scared me more than if he'd tried to stop me.

I got to within a step of the door when it opened. Detective Coyote came in carrying a brown paper evidence bag.

"You might want to sit back down, Rick." He walked over to the table and set the bag down.

I followed him over, but remained standing. He pulled a black

Callaway Golf cap out of the evidence bag. It looked just like the one I couldn't find in my hall closet the morning Melody disappeared.

I sat down.

Muldoon's

CHAPTER THIRTEEN

"We found this hat in the Shell Beach Motel room where Adam Windsor died." Dan took the seat across from me. "Looks like the one you wore when we golfed together. See how it's frayed at the tip of the bill. Even has a Lake Tahoe Golf Course ball mark clipped on its side, just like yours. Too many smudges on the ball mark for a good print. But forensics found a few hairs inside the cap." He leaned toward me and his eyes searched mine. "Anything you want to tell me?"

Melody had obviously grabbed the wrong hat before she left my house that first night. Her hair would be in it as well as mine. All perfectly innocent. Except for the dead guy in her motel room.

Could she have set me up? Was mine the only hair in my cap? Had she taken it to plant in the room? None of this made sense. They couldn't prove something I hadn't done. I was innocent. But my body betrayed me. I wiped my forehead, my breathing audible. The sweat under my arms reeked fear.

I'd waited too long before I called a lawyer in Santa Barbara. It had cost me a week in lockup and almost a lot more. "It's probably time for a lawyer."

"Sure, if that's what you want, Rick." Dan had his friendly face back on. "You haven't even been arrested. We just need some help to get the facts straight."

I looked at Moretti peering down at me. "Your partner has already made up his mind on the facts."

"You lawyer up and I'll know I was right." Moretti gave me the smirk.

"We just have a few more questions, Rick," Dan said.

I didn't know any criminal lawyers and I'd seen all I needed to of public defenders in Santa Barbara. I wanted to believe Dan. But I'd wanted to believe Melody, too, and now I was in a liars' room with cops wanting the truth. A truth I didn't know. I just wanted to get it over with. All of it. Now.

I pointed at the Callaway hat on the table. "That looks like a hat I lost."

"How do you suppose the hat ended up in the motel room where Windsor was murdered?"

"Someone might have borrowed it without asking or mistook it for their own and it ended up in the motel room where he OD'd." I didn't think Melody had killed her ex-husband, but I wasn't going to take the fall for it if she did.

"Who could that be?" Moretti pretended like he didn't know.

"Possibly someone who stayed at my house a few nights ago."

"And this person's name?"

"Melody Malana." I forced her name out in a low hum and felt like a kid who ratted out his sister to his parents for smoking cigarettes in the bathroom. Only Melody wasn't my sister, the cops weren't my parents, and the stiff wasn't a cigarette.

"Which night did Miss Malana stay at your house?" Dan asked.

"Sunday."

"Sunday night, October seventeenth. Correct?"

Dan was calm, relaxed. An insurance agent asking a few necessary questions.

"Yes." I waited for Dan to tighten down the timeline.

"And what time did Miss Malana leave your house Monday morning?"

"I'm not sure."

"What do you mean you're not sure?" Moretti moved in behind my ear. "She drop a sleeping pill on you, too?"

Dan squinted at Moretti and the two of them eyed a silent conversation. Moretti had cracked out of turn. The sleeping pills were to remain a secret. I didn't know what it meant, but I locked it away, a bullet to be used later if I could figure out how.

Dan turned back to me. "Why is it that you don't know when Miss Malana left your home?"

"She left while I was still asleep." Could Melody have drugged me so that I'd sleep through the night and give her the alibi she needed? I didn't remember leaving her alone with my drink, but if I'd been drugged maybe I wouldn't. No. I'd woken up when she got up in the middle of the night to go to the bathroom. I wouldn't have if I'd been drugged. Would I?

"So you don't know where she was from approximately six a.m. 'til nine a.m. Monday morning, October eighteenth?"

Eight years ago, in another small, square room with detectives bearing down on me, I'd lied. This time I told the truth. "No."

"And where were you during that same period of time?"

"At home, then at work."

"Can anyone verify that?" Dan studied me. I felt Moretti at my back.

"My dog, the two guys who jumped me that you stopped looking for, and Turk Muldoon."

Dan ignored my dig. "How well did you know Adam Windsor?"

"I didn't know him at all."

"But he was in your restaurant the night before he died." Moretti was back in my ear.

"A lot of people come into my restaurant. Doesn't mean I know them all."

"When were you last at the Shell Beach Motel?" Dan asked.

He knew the answer, that's why he'd asked the question. Hoped to catch me in a lie. Someone at the motel had seen me with the Lookie-Loos. That meant the cops had been showing my picture around or someone at the motel had recognized me. Heather Ortiz? Maybe information was a two-way street.

"I was there around noon on Monday, watching the police with everyone else."

"Is that why you went there? Because a dead body had been discovered."

"No." The walls pinched in on me and the stink under my arms rivaled Moretti's cologne. "I didn't know about a dead body until I got there. I was looking for Melody, but she'd already checked out."

Moretti's voice came over my shoulder. "You sure you weren't there to retrieve the hat you'd left there earlier?"

"I think you got what you wanted, Detectives." I stood up. "I'm going back to work."

"One last question, Rick." Dan rose and stood between me and the door. Moretti circled around behind him. "Why did you lie to us the other day when we questioned you about your assault?"

"I don't know what you're talking about." Except I did.

"You lied about not knowing the woman that the men were looking for." Dan folded his arms across his chest, a sentinel on the Blue Line. "It was obviously Miss Malana, the woman who'd just spent the night at your house, and who you'd been looking for at the Shell Beach Motel three hours before we spoke to you. Why'd you lie, Rick?"

I'd lied because Melody hadn't wanted to get the police involved, back when she was innocent and fragile. Now I had a better idea why. But admitting it now would only make me look more guilty. And I wasn't the only one holding things back. How could the cops be so certain the thugs were looking for Melody unless they questioned them? And then let them go.

"It wasn't obvious to me, Detective. But I guess it was to the big guy who jumped me. The same guy who worked security for Mayor Albright yesterday. You know, Chief Parks's buddy."

I walked around the detectives to the door and held my breath when I turned the knob. Unlocked. I opened the door and walked down the hall, fighting the urge to run. Any second I expected to hear the clink of handcuffs and feel Moretti's breath on my neck. I hit the door to the stairwell and thundered down the steps and out the back door of the Brick House.

Still a perfect day in the Jewel by the Sea. The sun blinding down through a cloudless sky mocked me.

CHAPTER FOURTEEN

Muldoon's was only a few blocks from the Brick House. Even if it had been a thousand, I wouldn't have gone back inside and asked for a ride. Hopefully, I was done riding in cop cars, front seat or back, for the rest of my life.

I threw a hand up to block the taunting sun and wished I'd remembered to grab my sunglasses when the cops escorted me away. I fled the Brick House parking lot and headed for Muldoon's, passing by the front of the police station. Out of the corner of my eye, I saw brown curls and white teeth coming at me.

"Rick!" Heather Ortiz waved as she hurried toward me from the front walkway of the Brick House. She wore her reporter's uniform: sweater, jeans, heels, and leather shoulder bag. Just like the outfit she wore at the Shell Beach Motel. And like the one she'd worn when we'd slept together two years ago.

Behind Heather, a man with a camera clicked photos of me.

I moved my hand from the sun's assault to block the camera's and kept walking. The camera kept clicking.

I'd become news. Again. I could make Muldoon's in two minutes if I sprinted full-out the whole way. How much farther would I have to go to outrun the spotlight? I kept walking.

"Rick." Heather finally caught up to me. "Please, do you have a minute?"

"Lose the photographer."

She stopped and turned to the man, his face one big camera lens. "Sam, I'll meet you back at the car."

The photographer peeled off, and I continued walking with Heather nipping at my heels.

"Come on, Rick." She hustled up alongside of me and pulled a notepad and pen from her purse. "Why were the police questioning you?"

"No comment."

"Did it have to do with the Windsor murder?"

I stopped. "What murder? You called it a drug overdose in the newspaper yesterday."

"I got a scoop." She flashed me a big dimpled smile, like having inside info on dead bodies was sexy. "But keep that to yourself. We want to break it in tomorrow's edition of the *U-T*."

"No comment." I started walking again, faster this time.

Pepper and palm trees splattered shadows across the sidewalk, providing brief cover from the pressing sun. We passed the T intersection of Cave Street and Ivanhoe. Another couple blocks and I'd be back at Muldoon's. Sanctuary from the intruding glare of the sun and the media.

"Why not tell your side of the story so you can control the spin?" Heather's high heels clacked along the sidewalk beside me.

"There's no side."

"Come on, Rick." She put a hand on my arm. I kept moving forward. "Maybe if you would have talked to the press back in Santa Barbara the story wouldn't still be following you."

I stopped and turned toward Heather, biting down anger. "It's not a story, a ten-second sound bite, a prime-time TV show. My wife was murdered. And she was still dead when the media moved on to exploit someone else's grief and she's still dead now." I stepped out of the shadow of a palm tree, the sun knifing my eyes. "No fucking comment."

I started for Muldoon's again. First walking, then jogging, then running. The clacking of Heather's heels fading, then silent in the background. My bum knee ached and Heather would never catch me, but I kept running. Still, no matter how fast I ran, my past stalked me like a coyote on the scent.

I hit Muldoon's at full sprint.

CHAPTER FIFTEEN

I pulled into my driveway a little after one a.m. Inside the house, I went through the kitchen to the back door to let Midnight in. I could usually hear him snorting outside, eager to greet me. But when I opened the door there was only the silence of the night. I threw on the backyard light and saw Midnight lying on his side next to the front gate, a circle of vomit pooled near his head.

"Midnight!"

I bolted across the yard to him. He didn't move. His tongue hung out of the side of his mouth and his eyes were white slits underneath his eyelids. I pushed opened his lids, but his pupils hung unmoving at the top of his eye sockets. Tears welled in my eyes as I held my hand to his nose. It was dry and the temperature of the night. Then a weak brush of warm air grazed my fingers. He was alive!

I scooped up some of the vomit in my hand. It looked like raw ground meat and was still warm. I ran into the kitchen and put the vomit into a Ziploc bag, then shoved it into my pocket and ran back out to Midnight. I picked him up. Eighty pounds of deadweight. His head hung limp off to the side. I got him through the gate and into the backseat of my car and peeled out of the driveway. When I turned onto the main drag, I heard Midnight's body slide along the backseat and thump against the armrest. He was running out of time.

My vet in La Jolla only kept normal office hours, but I knew of a twenty-four-hour emergency clinic in Mission Valley. I'd been there before when a cat dashed out of the darkness in front my car one night on my drive home from work. Neither the cat nor I had been quick enough to save its life.

I slammed to a stop in the clinic's parking lot and pulled Midnight's limp body from the car, and the memory of that cat leapt into my mind. I prayed that I'd been quick enough this time.

As I ran to the entrance with Midnight in my arms, the sliding glass doors opened, and a woman in a green smock wheeled a gurney out to me.

"What happened?"

"I don't know!" I set Midnight down on the gurney and we pushed him inside the clinic. "I came home and found him in the backyard. He was unconscious and there was vomit on the grass. He's barely breathing."

She stopped in front of a counter in the center of the room and picked up a phone and pushed a button. "Dr. Ramsey, we have a code red." She hung up the phone and turned to me. "I'm going to take your dog—what's his name?"

"Midnight."

"I'm going to take Midnight into the emergency room and the doctor will be out to ask you a few questions." She wheeled Midnight toward swinging doors leading to a room off the left side of the clinic.

Before she got there, the doors swung open and a man who looked barely out of his teens came into the room. "Dr. Ramsey" was stitched above the left pocket of his white coat. He stopped the gurney and pushed the rubber end of the stethoscope against Midnight's chest for too long. The world grew silent and the night crept into the clinic.

Finally, he pulled the instrument from Midnight's chest. "I'll be in shortly."

The woman nodded her head and wheeled Midnight through the swinging doors.

"Is your dog on any medication?"

"No."

"Has he eaten anything unusual recently?"

I remembered the warm contents in my pocket. "I don't know, but there was vomit on the grass where I found him."

I pulled out the bag and handed it to Dr. Ramsey. He examined it for a second then put the bag in the front pocket of his lab coat.

"I'm going to pump Midnight's stomach and expel anything that hasn't been fully digested. I'll also give him an enema to flush out any lingering toxins." He put his hand on my shoulder in a strained attempt at bedside manner. "He'll get the best care possible."

I wanted to believe him, but he looked like a kid wearing a coat with his father's name on it. "Thanks."

He turned and hurried through the swinging doors into the emergency room.

I slumped down into a chair along the wall. Dread tightened my throat and my eyes threatened tears. I scanned the clinic's waiting room.

I was all alone.

I checked my watch again: 2:20 a.m. I'd been at the clinic an hour and the vet and his assistant were still with Midnight behind closed doors. My body felt like a clenched fist. I did another circuit of the clinic's waiting room and watched the plaques, certificates, and pictures on the pale-green wall pass, again. I'm sure they all had some significance, but they never made it past my eyes into my brain. There wasn't any room left in there behind the fear, the regret, the anger, and the memories.

I'd had a dog as a kid. A basset hound named Baxter. We were both pups and, in my father's eyes, had a lot to learn. He was strict with both of us, but back then only Baxter had the courage to rebel. One night when I was ten, our family went out for our awkward annual restaurant dinner. My father had always worn his LJPD dress blues to the dinner while he was still on the job. This was our first night out since Dad had been kicked off the force.

He'd spent a lot of time earlier that night staring at his only two suits laid out on his bed. Once he decided, the rest of us put on our Sunday best and we all went out and tried to enjoy dinner.

I'd forgotten to put Baxter in the backyard before we'd left. He'd rewarded me by chewing up the suit that my father had deemed second best and left lying on the bed. Dad took his belt to both of us that night. Things were never the same after that night, between Baxter and my father and my father and me.

I never had wanted another dog until Kim, my last girlfriend, blindfolded me and drove me out to the back country in Alpine on my thirtieth birthday. When the blindfold came off, I was in a small pen with seven black Lab puppies. They were shy at first until one came over and licked my hand and sat down next to me.

Midnight had been at my side ever since. Now he might never be again. Someone had tried to kill him. If I ever found out who, I'd give the cops a legitimate reason to arrest me.

My temples throbbed and my breathing grew audible and then the vet's assistant came through the door in the back.

"The doctor will be in to talk to you in a minute." Her brown eyes matched the stoic expression on her pale, oval face.

"Is Midnight going to be all right?"

"The doctor is the appropriate person to talk to. He'll be in shortly." She walked behind the counter in the middle of the room.

"Don't give me that bullshit! Is my dog alive?"

Her face turned pink and she looked down at the computer on her desk. "Yes, he's alive. I'm not . . . the doctor likes to be the one to talk about the condition of our patients. I'm sorry."

I noticed for the first time that the name Donna was stitched on her smock. "Thanks, Donna."

The doors swung open and Dr. Ramsey walked in.

"Is Midnight going to be all right?"

"I'm afraid it's too early to tell." Ramsey didn't look like a kid anymore. "We'll need to monitor him overnight."

"Can I see him?"

"He's resting comfortably. Why don't you come back in twelve

hours?" He went to the counter, and Donna handed him a clipboard. "Please fill this out."

I took the clipboard without looking at it. "Could you tell what
he ate that made him sick?"

"I'd have to run a toxicology screen to be absolutely certain,
but it appears that someone put sleeping pills in some raw ground
meat and fed them to your dog. You can have the police call me
when you file a report."

I'd had enough of the police for one day.

It was after three a.m. when I walked through my front door
for the second time that morning. I had to be back at Muldoon's
in less than four and a half hours. The adrenaline that had surged
through my body when I found Midnight and carried me through
my hours of dread at the clinic now left me empty and spent.

I zombied into my bedroom and pulled off my clothes, left
them where they fell, and went to the nightstand to reset the alarm
to give myself an extra fifteen minutes of sleep. But something was
wrong with the nightstand. Its feet were slightly forward from the
ruts in the carpet they'd made after years of resting in the same
place. It looked like someone had pulled the nightstand out and
hadn't pushed it back in exactly the same place. The hair on my
neck went up and the adrenaline awoke from its slumber and my
stomach ground on empty.

Someone had been inside my house. Someone had poisoned
Midnight so they could search my home.

Stone's tough guys?

I didn't think anyone was still in the house, but I searched it
anyway. Even under the bed. No bogeyman, but he'd left something behind. My nose told me there was something familiar, yet
out of place on the carpet next to my bed. The stink of human
sweat mixed with something else that I couldn't identify, but knew
I'd smelled somewhere before. Wherever it had come from, it was
now the stench of my life being violated.

I checked all the locks on the doors and the windows. None
showed any tampering. Whoever broke in must have had a set of

lock picks and knew how to use them. He'd gone through the back door so he could have time to work the lock without worrying about being seen. And he'd come prepared to deal with a dog. What else had he been prepared to deal with?

I'd gotten rid of all things police after I'd been bumped off the force. Including my gun. Tomorrow I'd go to a gun shop and fill that void. I just hoped Midnight and I could survive the ten-day waiting period. I fell asleep with the stink of something foreign in my nose and without my trusted companion at the foot of my bed.

Muldoon's

CHAPTER SIXTEEN

The alarm rang at seven fifteen a.m., and I reached over to turn it off. I didn't know what day it was, but the surroundings looked familiar. Home. I staggered out of bed to let Midnight outside. Then it hit me like a left hook to the kidneys. Midnight! I dashed into the living room, grabbed the phone, and called the clinic where I'd left him.

"Mission Center Animal General." A woman's voice.

"I'm checking on my dog, Midnight. I brought him in last night." I held my breath. My heart pounded inside my head.

"Could you give me your name, please?"

"Rick Cahill. My dog's name is Midnight. I brought him in last night. He was poisoned."

"Oh, I'm sorry. That's horrible." I heard the clatter of fingers on a keyboard and then silence. "This computer is so slow."

I tried to breathe.

"There. Oh, there's no status listed here. Let me go check with a doctor. I'm going to put you on hold, okay?"

"Okay."

I stood naked, clutching the phone to my ear, and listened to the clinic's on-hold message warn about the dangers of heart-worms. The seconds passed as lifetimes. I paced the living room and noticed a picture on top on my entertainment center. It was of Midnight as a pup. He was about ten weeks old and sat staring directly into the camera. His ears were perked up and his head was tilted as if he'd asked a question. I didn't have an answer.

"Mr. Cahill?" A different woman's voice spoke into the phone.

"Yes?" I stopped pacing.

"This is Dr. Helmer. Midnight is awake, but still groggy. He answers to his name, which is a positive development. I want to keep him here for a few more hours to make certain that he's retained all his motor functions."

I exhaled for what seemed like the first time that morning. Life was looking up. "When can I pick him up?"

"Why don't you wait until around noon? If there's any change, I'll call you."

I thanked her and hung up, but still held the phone in my hand. Someone had poisoned my dog and broken into my house. It would have been a good time to call the police. I thought of Dan and Moretti and the interrogation room.

I put the phone back onto the receiver.

My cell phone buzzed in my pocket on my drive to work. I switched the call to my Bluetooth.

"Rick." The man's voice was smooth and patronizing at the same time.

I'd heard the voice before in person. It wasn't any more appealing over the phone.

"How did you get my cell number?"

"Oh, Rick." A dry chuckle. "In my world, a man like you can always be found."

Peter Stone. The man probably responsible for poisoning Midnight. I squeezed down my anger. I had a feeling he fed off of other people's rage. Like a wildfire riding the Santa Ana winds.

"Didn't your goons find what they were looking for last night?"

"You must have me confused with someone else." He managed to sound sincere. "However, if you give me what Melody took from Adam Windsor, your life will improve."

"I don't know what you're talking about." And I didn't. Whatever game Melody was playing no longer included me.

"I actually admire you. At first I thought you were just a boorish waiter trying to impress a woman who was out of your league. But you took a beating for her. That took courage. And stupidity.

But those two always go together, don't they?" He paused, but I didn't answer. "Now it's time to be smart, and I think you're capable of that. Do me this favor and your life will improve."

"You're not listening, Stone."

"You poor boy, you're in love. She could always make them fall in love with her. That's her greatest asset and her biggest fault." The superiority left his voice and he sounded human. "Listen to me, Rick. Melody's a puppet master and you're jiggling on command. Give me what the police didn't find and move on with your life."

"Melody didn't give me anything." The anger wrestled free from my grasp. "So call off your pit bulls and stay the fuck out of my life!"

"You're making a mistake, Rick. We could have been friends."

The line went dead.

Turk walked into Muldoon's around nine as I was cleaning off silver skin from a tenderloin. It was his day off. He held a newspaper in one hand and a quart of orange juice in the other. Half-zipped sweatshirt, board shorts, tangled red hair. A thought popped into my head that he'd heard Midnight had been poisoned and was there to lead a posse to track down whoever did it. My protector, my partner, my best friend. Just like old times. Or even four days ago.

"You read the paper this morning?" He took a gulp of OJ and a drop of it rolled down his chin and nestled in stubble. He tossed the front page onto the table.

"No." I looked at the paper. A lot had changed in four days.

A picture of me with my hand blocking my face sat below a headline entitled: Restaurant Manager Questioned In Windsor Murder. The article's author: Heather Ortiz. She'd twisted my "no comments" from our little talk yesterday into the empty denials of a guilty man.

Now it was murder. Now I was a suspect. Now it was Santa Barbara all over again.

"You get a lawyer, yet?" Concern lifted Turk's eyebrows.

"I don't need a lawyer."

Maybe I did, but I couldn't afford one. The cops had me spooked, but I wouldn't go into hock just because they were looking at me. When they stopped looking and started touching, then I'd mortgage my future for my freedom.

"Read the article." Turk tapped the newspaper. "They're making you out to be a serial killer."

"I don't need to read the article. I know the story."

Juan, the veggie prep, chose then to emerge from the walk-in refrigerator with a bag of carrots stacked on top of a box of broccoli and a flat of cauliflower.

"Juan, why don't you go pour yourself a Coke in the bar?" Turk nodded toward the kitchen door.

The kid looked at me and then set the produce down on his workstation and left the kitchen.

"Listen." Turk's voice was low and calm. "You should at least talk to a lawyer. The article rehashes Colleen's—um, the whole Santa Barbara thing."

"I know. Once a killer, always a killer."

"Rick, this is serious." Turk grabbed my shoulder with his huge hand and bore his eyes into me. The worry in them scared me a little. "You can't just make wisecracks and hope this goes away. I can't—you don't want to go through Santa Barbara all over again."

Turk had visited me while I was in jail in Santa Barbara before SBPD dropped the charges. He was the only friend who ever did. He had tried to keep things light during the visit, but I could tell that seeing me locked up had been hard on him. It had been hard on me, too.

"I know. You're right. If the cops pull me in again, I'll lawyer up." In that instant the past few days didn't matter anymore. We were friends again. "Thanks."

"I have to go out of town for a couple days." He dropped his hand from my shoulder. "When I get back, why don't you get away from the restaurant while this thing blows over? You haven't had a vacation in a while. The time off will do you good."

Friends with a caveat.

I'd become a liability. This was La Jolla, where image mattered. Old money didn't want a murderer to be the face of a restaurant they frequented. Things had changed since Turk first hired me. Times were tough now. Every lost customer counted. The only man willing to give me a job seven years ago now couldn't afford to have me seen doing it.

"Okay." I kept my head down and sliced the tenderloin on the meat table into steaks.

The knife's blade left deep channels in the wood.

I arrived at the veterinary clinic at noon. A green-smocked young woman with an "Annie" name tag and a mop of blonde hair gave me a warm smile. "May I help you?"

"I'm here to pick up my dog, Midnight."

"Ah, he's a sweetie." Her smile grew bigger. "Let me check with the doctor and make sure he's ready to go out and conquer the world again."

She left the desk and disappeared into the back of the building. I went over to the waiting area and stood next to the chair that I'd spent a long two hours in last night. There was a coffee table full of magazines that I'd ignored while I'd worried about Midnight. Today, the front page of the *U-T* sat on top of a copy of *Dog World*. My partially obscured face stared up at me, the same Chargers hat on my head that I wore today. Might have to switch to a Padres cap tomorrow.

I scanned the article while I stood over the table. It was as bad as Turk had said. Heather rehashed Santa Barbara and Colleen with emphasis on the fact that I was still a suspect up there and down here. A daily double. Moretti called me a "person of interest," but left plenty of room to read between the lines. Muldoon's was mentioned as the last place Windsor was seen alive. Free publicity, but at what cost? No mention of Melody. I wasn't sure if I should feel better or worse.

I heard Annie return to the desk. I flipped a couple pages and buried my story inside the newspaper, then dropped it onto the table.

"He's ready to go—" She shuffled some papers and found the one she'd been looking for. "—Mr. Cahill?"

Her smile dissolved into recognition. I lucked into one of the few people left who still read newspapers. Annie handed me a bill and studied me like a juror in a courtroom. My life had suddenly regressed eight years. Recognition, suspicion, judgment. I avoided her eyes like a cuffed felon and handed her a credit card. Eight hundred and fourteen dollars. Money I might soon need for a lawyer, but it was a fair trade. I got back my best friend. One of the last I had.

Annie gave me one last look. I avoided it again, and she disappeared into the back. A minute later, she led Midnight into the lobby on a leash. His head was down and his gait was measured as if he were trying out new legs. He didn't see me at first, but then he must have caught my scent because his tail started wagging, his head came up, and he strained against the leash to reach me. I dropped to my knees and hugged him as he lathered my face with his tongue.

Outside, the sun had broken through the clouds. Midnight needed help up into the car, a climb he'd normally ascend in one fluid leap. I rolled the window down, but he wasn't yet ready to stick his head out and fight against the wind.

I knew how he felt.

CHAPTER SEVENTEEN

I was half a block from my home when I noticed a TV van parked in front of it. Channel Ten News. The TV people had caught up with Heather Ortiz. I was news. Again. Back under the microscope. The dread I'd felt at the vet's late last night crept back up my throat. Maybe Turk was right. Maybe I should get out of town for a while. Or forever. I passed by my house and kept driving.

I needed protection. And not just from the media.

San Diego Gun was located in a strip mall on Convoy Street in Kearney Mesa. It sat next to a liquor store and a couple laps around the pole from a strip club. Guns, girls, and booze, all within one hundred feet of each other. Not even Walmart could offer that. The gun shop was crowded for a weekday afternoon. I guessed during hard economic times people wanted to protect whatever they had left. For me, that was my life and my dog.

Home protection usually called for a shotgun, maybe a Remington Pump Action 870 or a Mossberg HS410. You take out the intruder and a piece of your wall all at the same time. I wanted something more delicate with a narrower focus. I scanned the glass cases displaying handguns. Semiautomatic pistols dominated the space: Berettas, Glocks, Sig Sauers, a couple of high-dollar Kimbers. Calibers from .22 to .45. I moved down to the last section of the display case that held the revolvers. Wheel guns. Colts, Smith & Wessons, Rugers. My father taught me to shoot as a kid with a wheel gun, his Smith & Wesson service revolver. Santa Barbara PD issued recruits Beretta 92S semiautos, but I always liked the feel of my father's revolver.

A clerk approached me from the other side of the case. Like all the employees, he was strapped; a Glock 9mm was holstered on the hip of his camo pants. Buzz cut, wifebeater stretched by a beer belly, tinted range glasses. He looked like he'd spent an earlier part of his life getting paid to carry a gun. In the service or on the force. Maybe both.

"Anything in there you want to get a feel of?" he asked.

I wanted to get the feel of a lot of them. But I was already out eight hundred bucks today. I needed something solid but not too expensive.

"How about the Ruger SP101?"

"Two-and-a-quarter or three-inch barrel?"

"The snub."

He opened the case from his side and pulled out the revolver, opened its empty cylinder, and handed it to me. "Great conceal weapon. It's a .357 Magnum, but you can shoot .38 Specials all day long on the range to mitigate the recoil. I use Winchester 110 grain jacketed hollow points packed in a full .357 Magnum load when I shoot mine. That'll give you plenty of stopping power when the shit hits the fan. It's got five shots. The three inch has six, but you really only need one."

The gun had some heft to it for a snub nose. I closed the cylinder, sighted it away from the clerk, and tried the trigger. The double action was smooth, crisp.

"Show you anything else?"

I dropped my hand to my side and felt the weight. Solid, reassuring, lethal. I set the gun down on the counter. "I'll take this."

I filled out the paperwork and handed Buzzcut a credit card: $450 plus the government's take. A lot of money, but less than I'd paid to save Midnight's life. Seemed like a reasonable amount to protect my own. Now I just had to wait ten days. I'd known Melody less than half that time and had already been ambushed, fingered for a murder by both the cops and the press, had my house broken into, and my dog poisoned.

Ten days?

Buzzcut came back with my receipt.

"We'll call you in ten days to come in and pick up your weapon, Mr. Cahill." He lowered his voice when he said my name, like he knew it wouldn't be good to advertise. For either of us. "Remember to bring in your receipt."

Whatever vocation Buzzcut had performed in the past wearing a gun, he wasn't doing it anymore. Neither was I. And if he knew not to shout out my name, he probably knew my past. Maybe he had a story, too. Maybe he could help a brother out.

I checked the salesman name on the receipt: John.

"John," I leaned in over the counter, my voice now low, "I know the ten days is moot, but do you know where I could find something to hold while I wait? Something without so much paperwork."

John straightened up and the former cop in him took over his posture. I thought for a second he was going to ask me to spread 'em.

"Sir, your credit card is good, and if you don't have any felony convictions, I'm sure the State of California will okay your purchase in ten days." He kept his voice low, but it now had command presence. "But if I heard you correctly, you're asking me to break the law. Seems like you're in enough trouble all by yourself. I'll forget what I heard since you once wore a badge. I can see why you don't wear one anymore."

I left the gun shop nearly five hundred dollars poorer, empty-handed, and with a worse reputation than when I'd entered. But when I got to the car, Midnight still wagged his tail.

The TV van was gone when I got home. For now. I parked in the driveway and took Midnight inside, gave him a Milk-Bone, then went back outside and started up my car again. I drove around the corner and found my favorite secluded parking spot. I didn't want anyone to know when I was home. Not the media, not Stone's thugs, not even my neighbors. My life was now empty driveways, averted eyes, and glances over the shoulder.

The message light on my answering machine pulsed staccato when I got back to the house. I let it blink. Reporters, friends, family. What would I say to them, "No, I didn't kill this one either"? The one friend who didn't ask questions and trusted me unconditionally was alive and safe again. I owed it to Midnight to keep him that way. Whoever had broken in might come back when I wasn't home. I wasn't going to leave Midnight there alone to protect it.

My cell phone buzzed in my pocket for the ninth or tenth time that day. A call from the animal clinic would have been the only one that demanded a pick up. Midnight was safe with me now. So I was free to ignore calls for the rest of the day or longer.

I checked caller ID and answered.

"Rick!" Kim, my most recent ex-girlfriend, but still close. "I've been calling all day. You had me worried. Are you all right?"

She obviously still subscribed to the *U-T*. "I'm fine. Sorry. It's been a busy day."

"I thought maybe—"

"That I'd been arrested?" Not yet.

"Rick, my God!" Her voice rising with fear. "What's going on?"

"The police just asked me some questions." I kept my voice calm to try to settle Kim's nerves. "This thing will all be sorted out. Don't worry."

"Can I do anything to help?"

It wasn't a throwaway line for Kim. She meant it. Her heart was pure, her intentions sincere, and her love unconditional. That had been the problem. She was too good a woman to tie herself to a man who could never return what she so easily gave. I figured that out early. Kim hadn't yet.

"Well, there is something." I wasn't sure how much to tell her. I didn't want to worry her more than the newspaper already had. "Midnight's not feeling well, and I'm going to be real busy for the next few days. Would you mind if he stayed with you for a bit?"

"What's wrong with him?" Her voice had the worry I'd tried to avoid.

"He got into something that made him sick, but the vet said he's going to be fine. I just want someone who'll give him the TLC I can't right now. I know that's you, Kimmy."

She was the girlfriend who'd given me Midnight on my birthday three years ago. I knew she missed being with him as much she missed being with me.

"Oh, poor boy. Of course I'll watch him. I have to work late tonight. You can drop him by on your way to work." She still knew my schedule. "The spare key is still under the flowerpot in the backyard. You remember, don't you?"

There was a longing in her voice that made me feel guilty on a day when half of San Diego already thought I was.

Muldoon's

CHAPTER EIGHTEEN

I got to Muldoon's at five thirty, early so as to avoid customers and most of my crew. My plan was to hide in the office most of the night unless it was busy. Kris was hostessing and she could handle most anything on her own on a slow night. She'd work late and I'd just be there to put the restaurant to bed. I'd worry about the employee costs later.

I'd parked down by the beach and taken the long cement staircase that led up to Prospect Street from Coast Boulevard. I entered Muldoon's through the back door of the liquor room that was behind the bar. If the media was camped out in front of the restaurant, they'd never know I was there.

The bar was empty except for Pat, who was wiping down shot glasses. He gave me a surprised look as I entered through the back door. "Shit! You scared the crap out of me."

"Don't believe everything you read in the newspapers."

"No. I didn't mean that, but since you mentioned it—"

"Not now, Pat." I shook my head and headed out the bar on my way to the office.

I didn't make it.

"Rick!" Kris stopped me at the hostess stand, and I waited for the question.

I got one, just not the one I'd expected.

"Where have you been? Mark's been trying to get ahold of you all day. He's got food poisoning and can't find anyone else to wait tables tonight. There's no one but you to work his shift."

So much for my plan. I wondered how our regulars would like their slaughtered cattle being served to them by a murderer.

I'd deal with the customers as needed. I'd deal with my crew right now.

"Kris, go grab everybody who's here and bring them into the bar."

She gave me a puzzled look.

"Now!"

She hustled into the dining room, and I went back into the bar.

"It seems like that reporter has an axe to grind." Pat put a shot glass back on the shelf above the cash register. His eyebrows lifted on his round face. "Isn't she the one who did a story on the restaurant a couple years back? The one who took you home?"

Never spend an all-nighter drinking tequila with a bartender.

"What's your point?" I asked.

"Maybe she's bitter. Mad that you never asked her out again."

"Doubt it. The cops have a high-priority case and they want the public to think they're doing something. It'll pass. In the meantime, we need to keep doing our jobs."

Kris walked into the bar trailed by Blake, the grill man; Juan, the prep cook; Brittney, the waitress; and the busboy, Justin. They stopped just inside the door and looked at me with worried eyes, except Blake, who looked pissed to have been pulled off the grill. My kind of employee.

"I'll say this once." My voice was firm, but not loud. I scanned the face of each employee before I continued. "There is some shit in the newspaper that makes me look bad. There will probably be more of the same on the TV news. I haven't done anything wrong, but they'll make it sound like I have. None of that matters. When we're in this restaurant, we do our jobs. Nothing else. I don't care what you do in your free time, but the bullshit on the news will not be discussed inside these walls. If customers ask you about it, you don't know anything, because you don't. If any reporters try to enter the restaurant, you ask them to leave. If they don't, you get me. If you want to talk to reporters on your own time, that's your right. If it affects your ability to perform your duties at Muldoon's, you'll lose your job."

I laid eyes on each individual employee one last time. "Does everyone understand?"

A chorus of "yeses."

"Okay. Thanks for your attention. Now back to work."

Everyone left except for Kris. She walked over to me, her blue eyes liquidy.

"I know you're a good man, boss." She hugged me tightly, her head against my chest, a quiet sniffle.

I hugged her, then gently pushed her off me. "Thanks, Kris. Now go back to work."

Dinner service started slowly. I let Brittney's section fill up before I started my shift. The pace picked up and things were running smoothly. I didn't sense any looks of recognition or accusing eyes. Either none of my customers read the newspaper or didn't care whether I killed people in my free time. They just wanted good food delivered promptly and me visible only when needed.

My kind of people.

At least until some of our regulars showed up.

The Faheys arrived a little after eight, an hour later than normal. They were our longest-running customers and the oldest of old money La Jolla. When I approached their table, Mrs. Fahey didn't attempt her usual flat smile. Instead, she wrinkled her face like she smelled something foul.

"Hello, Mr. and Mrs. Fahey." I set the unneeded menus down on the table. "Gibson, easy ice and Jack Daniel's, neat?"

"We almost didn't come tonight." She looked at her husband who sat hunched over, staring down at the table through his whiskey-bottle glasses. "But it wasn't fair to deprive Mr. Fahey of his weekly steak dinner."

"Well, I'm glad you decided to come." I forced a smile. "It's always nice to see you."

"Jules Windsor is a friend of Mr. Fahey's." An edge crept into her haughty voice.

"We knew Adam as a child."

Walter Fahey still wouldn't look at me. He angled his head toward his walker, which leaned against the wall next to his seat. I didn't know whether he couldn't stand to see my face or was embarrassed that his wife was making a stink.

"I never had the pleasure of meeting any of the Windsors." I hoped she'd take my statement as an alibi and we could move on with dinner.

Mrs. Fahey hawkeyed me for a bit before she spoke again. "Well, if you say so."

She didn't sound convinced. But, apparently, a succulent filet mignon was too good to pass up.

The frost stayed on Mrs. Fahey the rest of the night, but she never came out and accused me of murder. Mr. Fahey warmed up and by the end of dinner he didn't seem to care how many people I'd killed. He still let me guide him through the restaurant and out the door as he teetered on his walker.

After my conversation with Mrs. Fahey, my antennae went up. Every look from a customer now had a hint of accusation, repulsion, or fear. I could feel eyes lasered on me with every trip through the dining room. Innate sensitivity or paranoia, it didn't matter. I just wanted out.

I was finishing my shift when the Slaters waved me over to their table. They sat in Brittney's section at their favorite table with a view of the courtyard. I barely had the "hello" out of my mouth when Dean interrupted. "Did you kill the little prick?"

"Dean!" Ann's lined, but attractive, face burned crimson. "That's a horrible thing to say. Rick, just ignore him."

"You would have done the world a favor." Dean ran a hand through a gray goatee that anchored his fry-pan face. "The kid was a bad seed."

"You shouldn't speak ill of the dead." Ann shook her head at her husband. "Think of the family."

"The family's probably relieved. That kid was nothing but trouble." He swallowed some Johnny Walker Black and rolled his red-tinged eyes toward me. "I hired the little prick to work for me one summer as a favor to his old man. We were doing the library renovation and tools started disappearing off the work site. I confronted Adam about it, and he threatened to tell the newspaper that I was charging the city for phantom work. I called his bluff and fired him. A few months later, Jules kicked him out of the house for a while. Turns out he was selling drugs out of his bedroom. Yeah, he was a real saint."

I excused myself before Dean had a chance to high five me.

The dining room had slowed enough to let Brittany handle it alone. I peeked my head into the bar for a quick check before I'd finally get my chance to hide out in the office. It was two-thirds full and the band had the customers boogying in their chairs and working up a thirst.

I was about to head back to the office when Pat caught my eye. He nodded toward the far end of the polished oak bar. I looked over and saw Eddie Philby huddled over a draft beer. He seemed to be minding his own business.

That's what I was afraid of.

Everyone I'd ever known who'd worked a while in the restaurant biz had had a habit at some point. Booze, weed, or blow. You got off work late, tired but wired, and there was always a friendly bartender to pour you two for one, or a fellow server to share a joint with in the alley, or a boozy dealer at the end of the bar you'd meet in the bathroom and give your night's tips to for a gram of blow.

Eddie Philby was holding office hours at the end of the bar. My bar.

It's not that I was a prude. Or without sin. I'd ridden the white powder roller coaster for a few rounds after I moved back down from Santa Barbara. It was a quick up out of the hole I'd dug for myself. But it had emptied my pockets and my soul. I went from feeling sorry for myself to feeling nothing but the next rush. I finally quit cold turkey when its grip was the tightest and all I had left was the memory of who I once was.

Philby hadn't been around back when I was snorting my

dinner, but he'd helped put Pat on tilt for a couple of years. I almost had to fire Pat one night when his hands shook so badly booze sloshed out of the drinks he tried to serve.

What my crew did with their free time was their business. When they brought it to work, it was mine. I'd sent Pat home and spent the rest of the night behind the bar in the weeds. I finally decided I had to call Pat the next morning and fire him.

When he came back into the restaurant after closing that night, I figured he'd saved me a phone call. But before I could pink-slip him, he asked for my help. I saw fear in his hollow, brown eyes. And it wasn't the fear of losing a job. He was the best bartender on the block and could have had another gig by morning. It was the fear I'd seen years before when I looked in the mirror after yet another all-nighter. The fear that you'd lost control of your life and could never get it back.

I took Pat back to my place that night, and we talked 'til dawn. He kept his job and spent the next few nights on my couch.

He'd grown a tire around his middle since then, but his ticker now had a better chance to keep ticking living on beer and pizza than it did riding the white powder rails.

I'd warned Philby that if I ever caught him dealing in my restaurant, I'd call the cops. He'd heeded my threat, and I hadn't seen him for a while. Until tonight. He could have innocently been in to nurse a beer and enjoy the music like the rest of the crowd. And the thugs who jumped me this week could have just been giving me a physical exam.

I went to the cocktail waitress station at the end of the bar where Pat made five empty glasses turn into five drinks in twenty seconds. I leaned over the bar, and he met me in the middle.

"I'll be in the office. As soon as he gets up, call me on my cell."

Pat nodded and I retreated to the back of the restaurant without Philby having seen me.

I'd just finished squaring my bank and counting the tips I'd distribute to the crew when my phone vibrated in my pocket. I pulled it out and saw that the incoming number was the restaurant's.

"He's up." Pat's voice shouted over the band in the background. "Need a hand?"

"Nope. Thanks."

I waited twenty seconds and then headed through the kitchen into the dining room. The men's bathroom was just around the corner from the busboy station. I eased the door open a foot and slid through the opening avoiding the squeak the hinges made when the door was opened wide.

The two urinals were empty, but the handicap stall was full. Of four shoes.

"This is the shit, man." Philby's voice was a high-boil whisper.

"How 'bout a taste before I fork over the dough?" I didn't recognize the other voice, but I did the need.

A quick tapping sound slid out of the stall. Probably a credit card on top of the toilet's tank chopping up the rocky cocaine into a powder. Then a snort and a loud exhale through the mouth.

"You're right, dude." The buyer. "Good shit."

Another snort, this one longer. "I wouldn't do you wrong, bro." Philby's voice was stuck in his throat. "A 'G,' right?"

"Yeah."

I took two quick steps to the stall and pounded the door. "Out!"

"Shit!"

Some shuffling, then the stall door slowly opened. First out was a guy I'd seen in the bar a few times, but I didn't know his name. He was in his late twenties and wore a surfer uniform: baggy shorts, T-shirt, and flip-flops.

"We were just—"

"Leave."

He hustled past me and out the bathroom door.

Eddie Philby stepped out of the stall and gave me a faded smile. He didn't look like the stereotypical drug dealer. He was closer to forty than thirty and dressed like a department store mannequin, blue blazer and tan slacks. But the coat, like its owner, was starting to show its age. Philby was a trust-fund baby from an old-money La Jolla clan who was living off the fumes of his family's largesse. His aristocratic good looks were unraveling around the edges like his coat and his hollow core was visible in his eyes. A junkie who dealt to feed his habit.

"I told you to keep your business out of my restaurant." I blocked his path.

"An impulse buy that was initiated by the customer." He'd dropped the drug jive and reverted to his roots. "I just came into your lounge to enjoy the fine music."

"Well, savor the memory because it's the last time. Leave now and don't come back."

"Okay." He straightened his shirt collar. "But, it's a shame because I had a business proposition for you."

I waited.

"Your bar is fertile ground for my product, and I need market share." He rubbed his nose. "I'm willing to offer you a percentage off the top of all transactions. You won't have to get your hands dirty. You just look the other way and, while you're looking, keep an eye out for undercover cops."

The irritation of the previous week started to bubble under my skin, but I held it at a simmer.

"What makes you think I'd go into business with you?"

"Well, I read the newspaper. Adam Windsor was obviously back to his old ways and last seen alive in your restaurant. I knew Adam way back when. He was a cheat. I'm sure his death was a well-deserved accident over his bad business practices."

"So, that's how it was."

"Look, I know it's tough to get ahead. I'm lucky. I've been blessed by my parentage." He put his right hand on my shoulder. "There's nothing wrong with doing a deal that blurs the line every now and then. Certainly your father understood that."

The bubbles hit boil and I shot my right arm under his and yanked it hard up behind his back and drove him into the wall opposite the mirror. He got his other arm up in front of his face to cushion the blow and save his nose from breaking. Still, his face made a loud splat against the wall and the air blew out of his body.

"Spread 'em!" My cop ancestry jolted through me all the way out from my father's grave.

I kicked Philby's feet apart and pulled his arm higher behind his back. A hoarse shriek leapt from his throat, and I searched his coat pockets with my free hand. When I found what I was looking for, I released his arm, shot my hand up to his coat collar, and pulled down as if I just put my last quarter in a slot machine. Philby's ass hit the ground and he skidded across the bathroom floor.

"What the hell's wrong with you?" He wiped away a thin trickle of blood from his nose.

"I'm a killer, remember?"

"I don't want any trouble. I just want my product back." Philby was back on his feet but kept a nervous distance from me. "Please."

The baggy I'd ripped from his coat contained ten or twelve paper bindles, each about one by two inches. If they were all grams, I held over a thousand dollars street value of cocaine in my hand.

"I'll leave. I promise. Just please let me have my blow." Philby's voice had the whine of a kid begging a bully to give him back his milk money.

I guess that made me the bully.

I went into the stall where Philby'd done his business and left the door open so he could watch. Then I dropped the baggy into the toilet and flushed. "Still wanna be my partner?"

"Fuck!" Philby bolted toward me but stopped short of the stall. "Why did you do that?"

"Get out of my restaurant and don't come back."

Philby glared at me and seemed to be weighing his options. Finally, he turned and slinked toward the door. I went to the sink to wash his residue off my hands and heard the door squeak open but not shut.

"At least your old man was smart enough to know how to get ahead." Philby stood in the doorway. "And just dumb enough to get caught."

He let the door go and exited. Adrenaline jolted me forward and I was on him before the door swung shut. I grabbed him by the back of his collar and his pants and ran him through the dining room toward the front door. The band was on a break and some of the crowd had spilled out of the bar into the hallway. Philby squealed and waved his arms, but I kept moving forward. Surprised looks bounced off me as I sped him through the gauntlet of spectators. The door opened just as we got to it, and I slung Philby outside past a wide-eyed man who was probably looking forward to a mellow evening of jazz.

Philby tumbled along the terra-cotta tile and slammed into a planter's box that housed an elm tree. My hands buzzed from the adrenal blast and my eyes bulged. I waited for Philby to do something stupid, but he crawled to his feet and limped out of the courtyard.

When I went back inside, murmured conversation fell silent, and all eyes were on me. Kris stood at the hostess stand, her eyes wide, uncertain. She'd seen me throw people out of the bar before, but this was the first time I'd done it literally. And violently. And the first time I'd done it after being accused of murder. I walked over to her, and she inched backward, fear creeping into her questioning eyes. The look shouted at me in silence; maybe I wasn't such a good man after all.

I went back to the office without saying a word.

Ten minutes later, the office phone rang. I let Kris answer it in the dining room. The red light on line two blinked and the phone rang again. Kris had taken the call up front and forwarded it back to the office. Someone wanted to talk specifically to me. Someone who didn't have my cell number. A reporter? The police?

I'd done enough running for one day. I answered the phone.

"I knew sooner or later that evil inside you would crawl out again." The voice was a little raspier than the last time I'd heard it, but the venom was still strong. "It looks like you may pay for your sins, yet."

"Hello, John." Somehow the news about my supposed involvement in the Windsor death had made it all the way up the coast, past San Francisco, into Marin County.

"She would have turned thirty-two last month." His voice now wavered, caught in his throat. "But you took all her birthdays away, you son of a bitch!"

"I miss Colleen, too, John."

"Don't you dare say her name! You don't have the right to say her name!" His words came out in gushes of hatred and sadness. "You lost that right when you took her away from us. When you murdered my baby girl!"

He started sobbing. The same raw wails of pain I'd heard over the phone eight years ago when I'd told him Colleen had been murdered. His only child, whose love for me had caused a rift between the two of them that had never healed. He'd always thought I wasn't good enough for Colleen.

He'd been right.

I held the phone to my ear while he sobbed, just like I had eight years ago. Only this time I didn't cry, too.

"May you rot in hell!" The line finally went dead.

CHAPTER NINETEEN

I hung the phone up, feeling the same sadness, regret, and guilt I felt after every one of John Kerrigan's yearly calls. It always came around Colleen's birthday. In the past, the call had been an expletive-laden message on my home answering machine. I guessed with my recent notoriety, he wanted to deliver his hatred live. I couldn't blame him. If I was convinced someone had gotten away with murdering my daughter, I would have done the same. Or worse.

But John's hatred of me went deeper than that. He'd never liked me from the start. I was an ex-jock turned policeman, born from the loins of a disgraced cop. Too low rent for the daughter of a Marin County multimillionaire.

I met Colleen at a party early my sophomore year at UCLA. She was a freshman at UC, Santa Barbara, and was down visiting friends for the weekend. Her laugh and gravelly voice pulled me to her from across the room. Well, her blue eyes and the way she filled out her jeans and halter top might have had something to do with it, too. But there were plenty of beautiful women at the party, just like all the jock parties I went to. None of them had Colleen's wit, confidence, and charm. And she didn't throw herself at me once she learned I was a football player, like the other women at the party had.

She was a challenge. I was an athlete, I thrived on challenges. But the flutter in my belly told me it wasn't just a conquest I was after. For the first time in my young life of easy-women bachelorhood, I wanted more.

We talked for hours by ourselves on a couch in the corner of a dorm living room, unaware of the debauchery going on around us. Literature, philosophy, politics, anything but what a stud I was to be the starting free safety on the Bruins football team. She mentioned her boyfriend a couple times, but he was just an obstacle to overcome, like a blocker between me and the ball carrier.

Colleen went back up to Santa Barbara the next day. We traded e-mail addresses and kept up an intermittent correspondence, but I wouldn't see her again for almost a year. It took a career-ending knee injury, a school transfer, and nine months of trading barbs and finally punches with her high school sweetheart and his posse to finally win Colleen's heart.

It took five years to break it. And one night to get her killed.

Line two on the office phone rang again. John Kerrigan calling back to fire more shards of his broken heart at me? He'd earned the right. And I'd forfeited the right not to hear him out.

I picked up.

"Rick?"

It wasn't John, but the caller's voice sounded so much like his daughter's it would have sent a chill down his spine, just as it did mine.

Melody.

"I want to see you." The sexy gravel.

"It's a long drive from San Francisco."

"I'm in San Diego." The words came out fast and ran together.

I hadn't heard from Melody since she left two days ago. I'd written her off as a two-night stand. One that had caused me a lot of grief, and one that I should have been glad was over. But Melody was back in San Diego, the woman who'd lied to me at least once, whose association had gotten me a front-row seat under a police spotlight and a front page perp picture in the morning paper.

"Where?"

"At the airport. I'm getting a car." She paused and I thought she was done speaking. Then, "I was hoping I could come by your house later."

I wanted to see her, but under my conditions. My house, my bed, her advantage.

"Things have gotten a bit hot around here since you left. The press already staked out my house once today. Why don't I meet you at your hotel? Where are you staying?"

"I don't have one, yet." Disappointment. "I guess I was hoping we could pick up where we left off."

"Do you know where Mount Soledad is?"

"You mean where the cross is?"

"Yeah. Meet me there in a half hour."

Another pause. "Okay."

I grabbed my coat and headed back into the dining room. Kris saw me as I approached the hostess stand and suddenly didn't know what to do with her hands.

"Kris, I need you to stay till closing and help Pat shut everything down." My natural inclination was to put my hand on her shoulder, but I kept it at my side. "Can you do that for me?"

"Yes," she said, but without a "Boss" on the end of it. She couldn't make her eyes meet mine. Another supporter lost to the other side, just like so many back in Santa Barbara. I didn't have time to win her back tonight. I hoped she'd give me the chance to do so in the future.

I went into the bar, leaned toward Pat, and shouted over Leron's sax solo of The Crusaders' "Spiral." "I need you to shut the restaurant down tonight. Kris will help. I have my cell if something comes up."

"No problem."

I pulled away from the bar, but Pat wasn't done.

"Before you go." He took a business card from his pocket and handed it to me. "This guy wants to talk to you. I think he's still in the bar."

I looked down at the embossed card: "Ellison Krandel Fenton III, Attorney-at-Law."

A lawyer. Great. The vultures were already starting to circle.

Something about the name seemed familiar, but I guessed I'd probably seen it on the side of a bus or something. I scanned the bar
and caught a few startled glances from people who were probably
eyeballing me because of Eddie Philby's grand exit a half hour ago.
Or maybe because of the article in the paper. Or maybe both. Time
to go. I turned and headed for the liquor room door to make my
escape out the back of the bar.

"Rick!" A voice I didn't recognize competed with the band.

My hand was on the doorknob. A short reprieve from what
was sure to be my life back under the floodlights just a twist of the
wrist away. But I still owned a piece of Muldoon's, and while I was
there, I was its face. Guilty or innocent.

"Rick, wait!"

I turned and saw a man who looked vaguely familiar under the
dim bar lights. He wove his way toward me through tables of customers. I made him for my age, give or take. He wore a smile that
was too big for someone I didn't know late on a Sunday night. No
doubt the illustrious Ellison Krandel Fenton III. I felt sorry for his
firstborn son.

He finally made it over to me.

"Rick!" Slightly goofy smile, now even bigger, showing perfect
teeth. He put out a hand. "It's me, Ellison."

That much, I'd figured out. Why that should mean something
to me, I hadn't yet. I shook his hand.

"Sorry, I'm in kind of a hurry." I pulled my hand away just before he could start the fourth pump. "Why don't you call me here
tomorrow morning? We can talk about whatever it is you want to
talk about then."

"Oh. Okay." Hurt look of a grade school kid who'd just found
out he hadn't been invited to the slumber party.

I'd seen that look before. On that same face.

"Elk?"

"Well, I go by Ellison now." Goofy smile back in place. "But
you can still call me Elk. If you're in a hurry, I don't want to keep
you."

"I've got a minute." I figured I owed him after fracturing his collarbone in football practice back in high school sixteen or seventeen years ago. "Let's go somewhere we can hear each other."

I led him out of the bar and into the dining room, which was nearly empty. We took a seat next to a window in the back.

"It's been a long time, Rick. I've missed all my buddies back here in San Diego."

I didn't remember Elk having many buddies and I didn't think I was one of them. He'd been the odd kid, the tagalong, who was tolerated because he was sometimes good for a laugh. Usually at his own expense. Back when I was young, stupid, and pissing testosterone. I thought of how I'd shown Eddie Philby the front door tonight and marveled at how much I'd grown since my high school days.

"Yeah. I haven't seen you since you moved to Colorado junior year. Life been good?"

"Mostly." The smile dropped for an instant, then realigned. "Got two beautiful girls who live with their mother in Los Angeles. That's why I moved back to Southern California, to be near them."

My life was in the headlines, I didn't feel the need to share. "So, you living in San Diego or L.A.?"

"I'm practicing law here in La Jolla." He pulled a silver card case out the pocket of his tweed coat and proffered a card.

"I've got the one you gave to my bartender." I fished the card out of my pocket. "Thanks."

"I have to tell you, Rick." The smile flattened out of his face. "If you don't already have an attorney, it might be time to consider one."

That didn't take long. I was a commodity now. Melody used me for an alibi, Heather used me for headlines, and now my old buddy Elk wanted to use me to pay child support.

"And here you are for my consideration." I let the sarcasm hang off the words. "What a coincidence. Good-old-times talk is over and now it's time to pimp for business."

The little boy lost look came back. Elk pursed his lips, and I thought for a second he might cry. Even if I needed a lawyer, I didn't want one this soft.

"No." He squinted and shook his head. "I don't even practice criminal law anymore. I specialize in estate planning."

"Oh." Another former supporter to win back.

"I just wanted to tell you that a couple defense lawyers at my old firm owe me favors. They're good and I could probably get you a discounted fee."

"I'm sorry, Elk. I'm a little defensive, myself, lately." I reached over to shake his hand. "That's very nice of you. If things get any worse, I may have to take you up on that. Please forgive me."

He gave my hand a dramatic one-shake.

"There's nothing to forgive, Rick. I still owe you."

"How do you figure that?"

"You saved me from a severe beating."

I racked my brain and finally pulled up what I thought he was talking about.

"You mean when we were kids at La Jolla Shores?"

"Ronald Jackson wasn't a kid and neither were his goons."

We were fifteen and Jackson was a high school dropout who liked to hang around teenage girls and act tough. The girls were from old money and thought it was cool to hang out with a loser ten years older than they were. One day Jackson and a couple of his toughs cornered Elk in the beach parking lot. I came along just as the pushing started.

They didn't know that I'd been boxing Golden Gloves for three years and hadn't lost a fight. Jackson made a move toward me and I dropped him with an overhand right. Then one of his toughs charged in, and I stopped him with a left hook under the ribs and a right uppercut. There was some huffing and puffing to try to save face, but that was the end of it. Jackson never bothered us again.

The next fall I blindsided Elk in practice and heard his collarbone crack through the ear hole in my helmet. The hit was legal, but one I could have held up on.

"I think we're even, Elk."

Muldoon's

CHAPTER TWENTY

Mount Soledad rose eight hundred feet above the ocean and had panoramic views of the Pacific, La Jolla, and San Diego. Even Mexico, way to the south. The famous cross stood forty-three feet high above the summit and had rested there for over ninety years. First wood, then cement. It was put there as a war memorial to honor all those who had fought for our country. Black granite plaques memorializing veterans had been added to the base of the monument over the years. My dad always saluted it when he took me up there as a kid. I would, too.

He stopped taking me there after the LJPD brass kicked him off the force. He stopped going anywhere after that. Except the liquor store. When I was old enough and had bought a car of my own, I'd sometimes drive up to the cross alone. I just didn't salute anymore.

I parked in one of the parking spaces that ringed the monument and got out of my car. Melody hadn't yet arrived, and no one else was there. Just me, the cross, and the view. By day, the view was spectacular. At night, it was magical. Scattered rainbows of lights from the restaurants, stores, and hotels of the Golden Triangle to the north gave way to the intermittent twinkles of house lights among the dark vacuum of hills rolling down to the black expanse of ocean rimmed by white splashes of broken waves.

I looked from the beauty below up at the cross, white and shadow above footlights, towering overhead. Thoughts of Colleen floated into my head. They always did when I climbed up the mountain and faced the cross. There was no distraction from the truth up there. No hiding the guilt. No running away from the fact that Colleen was dead because of me.

Car lights came off the main street onto the road that led up the hill to the monument. The car circled behind the cross and parked next to my Mustang. Melody got out and walked up the monument's steps to me. She wore jeans and a dark sweater, her hair in a ponytail, her face hidden in the shadow of the cross.

Two quick steps and she had her arms around me, her breath on my neck, cinnamon and lavender in the air. Just like the first night outside Muldoon's. She felt good in my arms, a longing satisfied. But I was still hungry for more. I'd missed her more than I'd realized.

But why? Was it just the sex? Or the need to be needed again? No, I'd already had that with Kim. Colleen had been the only woman I'd ever loved. Melody was so different from her, yet so alike. Strong, confident, yet vulnerable. Their voices were even similar. Still, there was something else with Melody. Something inexplicable, just out of reach.

Then Peter Stone's words echoed inside my head, "She could always make them fall in love with her." Had I been that easy? I took a step back and held Melody at arm's length. She tilted her head and her dark, almond eyes questioned me. I dropped my arms to my side and tried not to let those eyes pull me back in.

"I guess I should have called before I came down." A quiver of hurt in the gravelly voice.

"A lot's happened since you left."

"I know. I'm sorry." Her hand came out toward me, but I let it hang in the air until she brought it down empty. "It made the news in San Francisco because of Adam's connection to me. Other reporters even staked out our studio to try and interview me. I had to get away."

"Is that why you came back? To get away?"

"I came here to see you, Rick."

"Bullshit." I wanted to believe her, but wanting to wasn't enough anymore.

"It's true!" A trace of anger surrounded by hurt.

"Maybe it is. But there's always another reason. Something hidden beneath the truth." I put my hands on her shoulders and tried to penetrate her eyes. "First you tell me your source on the Albright story was the man who hit you, but you hide the fact that he was your ex-husband. Then you say Peter Stone is just some old boyfriend, but you don't tell me that you have something he wants. What's the other reason this time, Melody?"

"What did Peter say?" Her eyes flashed wide, then shrank back down.

"He thinks you have something the police didn't find." I squeezed her shoulders. "He told me that right after he had someone poison my dog."

"Oh, my God! Is Midnight all right?"

"Yes."

"Thank God. Rick, I'm so sorry I got you involved in all of this."

She sounded sincere. She always did.

"I'm sorry, too, Melody. I'm sorry I'm front-page news in the morning paper and that half of La Jolla thinks I had something to do with Windsor's death, including the police."

"What can I do, Rick?" Her voice caught in her throat. "What do you want me to do?"

"Tell me the truth or it ends here." I dropped my hands from her shoulders.

"What do you want to know?"

"Did you kill Windsor?"

"No." Her eyes held mine. She didn't blink. No deception that I could see. She looked exactly the way someone telling the truth would look. Exactly the way someone lying would try to look, too. It was one or the other. I just didn't know which.

"How did my Callaway Golf hat end up in your hotel room with Windsor's dead body?"

"I accidentally took it from your hall closet when I left early that first morning." She kept her eyes steady. "It was dark and I didn't want to turn on a light and possibly wake you. I thought it was my Giants hat. I didn't realize I grabbed the wrong one until I got back to the motel. By then, it was too late."

That's how I'd pictured it, but that didn't mean it wasn't a lie.

"Why did you leave it in the motel room?"

"Adam was still there when I got back." She shook her head and blew out a loud breath. "We had another argument, and I left in a hurry. I didn't have time to grab it."

Feasible.

"What was the argument about?"

"I wanted him out of my life. He tried to use the Albright campaign for governor story as a way to weasel his way back in."

Possible.

"What do you have that Stone wants?"

She took a halting breath and stared at my chest like she was debating whether or not to tell me. Finally, "Something that Adam had."

"What is it?"

Another pause. "Take me to your house and I'll show you."

"No more games, Melody." I grabbed her shoulders again.

"It's not a game, Rick, I promise. I can't show you here."

I searched her eyes. "Why did you come back?"

"Because I'm scared and you make me feel safe." She grabbed my coat at the chest and pulled herself into me. I let my arms accept her.

Colleen used to say she felt safe with me and that she knew I'd always protect her. And I had. Except for the one night that had really mattered.

"Let's go." I took Melody's hand and led her down the steps from the monument.

She stopped at the bottom and looked up at the cross and then at La Jolla sparkling below. "It's beautiful up here, but why did you choose here to meet?"

"This is where I come to face the truth."

•   •   •

Melody followed me down the mountain in her rental. A thin wisp of fog pushed in from the ocean. The road, steep and winding, traced through modest homes worth millions of dollars nowhere else but in La Jolla. The mansions above them, hanging off the mountain with views of the ocean, were where the real money in La Jolla lived.

I led Melody onto Highway 52, heading east. Back home. Where the people lived who worked for the owners of the hillside mansions.

I scanned the street in front of my house. No TV vans. Things were looking up. I pulled into the driveway, and Melody parked across the street behind me.

Bright lights exploded on the street and a cop car, light bar aflame, skidded to a stop behind me, blocking the driveway.

Running feet and then a gun at my window and a flashlight in my face. "Police! Out of the car, hands first!"

My adrenal glands vibrated my body, but I did as I was told. Someone slammed me against my car, kicked my legs apart, making me assume the position. Rough hands patted me down.

My mind rattled on overdrive. Were they going to arrest me for Windsor's murder? What new evidence could they have? Had Melody planted something on me at the cross and this was some sort of setup? Is that why she wanted to come to my house?

"Clean!" The cop who searched me yelled out to the street.

"Melody Malana." Detective Moretti's voice came out of the fog. "You're under arrest for the murder of Adam Windsor."

The cop behind me shouted to Moretti, "What about him?"

"Let him go. For now."

I turned and saw Moretti walking Melody, her hands behind her back, toward a slick-top Crown Vic.

Tears ran down her face.

"I didn't do it, Rick! You have to find the truth!"

Moretti guided her into the backseat of the car and slammed the door. He jumped in the front passenger side and the car drove off. The taillights left red smudges in the fog.

Muldoon's

CHAPTER TWENTY-ONE

Once inside my house, I called Elk Fenton and told him about Melody, Adam Windsor, and the cops. I didn't tell him everything, just about the arrest and Melody's connection to Windsor. He said he'd talk to his contact at the courthouse in the morning and find out when Melody was to be arraigned and if she had an attorney. I gave him my cell number, and he assured me he'd call as soon as he knew something.

I grabbed a beer from the fridge, sat down in my La-Z-Boy, and stared at the blank flat screen in the entertainment center. The picture in my head was much hazier. Could Melody have killed Windsor? The police obviously thought so, but I knew from experience they could be wrong. Most of the time, though, they were right. If they were right this time, maybe Melody was making up stories to implicate me. She'd already put my Callaway hat in the motel room with her dead ex. An accident as she claimed? Not if she'd murdered Windsor. The hat had me at the murder scene at a time when Melody knew I was asleep alone without an alibi. What else could she have planted to put me there?

My cell phone buzzed me out of my worst-case scenarios. It was too soon to be Melody. Besides, her one call would likely be to a lawyer. I pulled the phone out of my pocket to see whose call I'd probably ignore. It was Kim's phone number. I answered.

"Rick! Turn on *Channel Ten News*! Quick."

I grabbed the remote, flicked on the tube, and found channel ten. Just in time to see myself throwing Eddie Philby out the front door of Muldoon's. The picture was grainy and low-res, like a bad YouTube video, but clear enough to catch my Charlie Manson eyes as I turned toward the camera and stalked away down the entry hall.

In the era of Andy Warhol's fifteen minutes, I was already well into my second hour. Unfortunately, somebody had immortalized it on a cell phone cam. With the help of the news, I'd be viral in no time.

A blonde talking head summed it up for everyone, "Shocking video."

Then she went onto a story about a seventeen-year-old starlet's new haircut. I turned off the TV. My phone was still pressed to my ear.

"Rick, what happened?" Worry shrouded Kim's voice.

"How's Midnight?"

"He's fine." A pause and then a soft plea. "Rick, talk to me."

"Some punk was trying to sell drugs in my restaurant, so I threw him out. Maybe with a little too much emphasis."

"The news anchor mentioned that you'd been questioned in the Windsor murder and—" A deep exhale. "And she talked about Colleen. They tried to make out that you're a violent man."

"That's their job, Kim. To make it sensational and get it wrong. Then let someone else set the record straight after the fact."

"Ricky." Kim was the only person who'd ever used that name. Not family, not friends, not even Colleen. It was Kim's alone and I let her have it. "I'm worried about you."

"I'm fine." I tried to sound like I believed it. "You don't mind keeping Midnight for a few more days?"

"No, of course not. He's sitting next to me on the couch right now." She cooed something to Midnight. "Oh, before I forget. What kind of food should I buy tomorrow? I know you get him the good stuff."

"Damn. Sorry, Kim. I forgot all about his food. Don't buy anything. I've got a forty-pound bag sitting in the closet. I'll bring some over in the morning on my way to work."

"Ricky, take care of yourself."

I put the phone in my pocket and went outside to move my car around the corner to its new, permanent, parking spot. With my wild-eye cameo on the TV, there were sure to be more news crews or just Lookie-Loos hoping to find me home and see more of the same.

I got back inside and went into the kitchen to gather up some of Midnight's dog food to take to Kim's in the morning. I grabbed a saucepan from the pot rack and started shoveling brown pellets from the huge bag in the closet into a paper sack. On the third scoop I hit something that made a soft "clink" sound.

I reached inside the bag and pulled out a small two-inch by half-inch blue rectangle with a plastic loop on the end. A computer flash drive—a memory stick. The loop hooked around a key. The brand name Chateau was etched into the black plastic handle of the key. Just like the one I used to have to unlock the public storage unit where I'd kept my father's stuff after he died. Before I sold or gave most of it away.

Melody must have hid the drive in the dog food the morning the police told her about Windsor and took her downtown. She'd stayed behind in the kitchen a few minutes while I talked to the detectives. Was this why Melody had wanted to come back to my house tonight? Was she going to show me whatever was on that drive? Or was she going to try to take it back without me knowing?

Maybe there was evidence on it that would exonerate Melody and point the finger at someone else. Like Peter Stone. I went into the spare bedroom that served as my office and turned on the computer. After it booted up, I plugged in the flash drive and opened it. A menu appeared on my computer monitor.

There was only one folder on the menu, entitled with the letter A. I clicked the icon next to the title and the computer made a whirring sound and then a video image appeared, time stamped nine years ago.

A video image of a naked woman sat on the end of a bed with her head down. The camera shot was static, from the foot of the bed, and elevated. The bed was unmade and had only a fitted sheet on the mattress. There was a small leather case next to the woman and she held a hypodermic needle in her right hand. She crossed her left leg over her right knee at the ankle, spread her toes with her left hand, and plunged the needle into the V formed by her big toe and the one next to it.

Back on the beat in Santa Barbara, some of the hookers shot heroin between their toes to hide the track marks.

The woman dropped the needle and raised her head. She was young, early twenties, and pretty. But she was pale and more skinny than healthy, and her blue eyes were too old for her face.

A young Angela Albright stuck a finger into her mouth and fell back onto the bed in slow motion, like a leaf falling from a tree.

The video cut to another scene and it only got worse. Same room, same bed, same camera angle. Same Angela Albright. Only this time she was with a man. He put some money on the nightstand next to the bed and the two of them had sex. The clip didn't have any sound, but none was needed. The sex was rough, consensual, and demeaning.

More scenes of the same followed. Different men, multiple men, women. Always the same room and same camera angle. I got the sense that none of the participants knew they were being filmed, not even Angela. The camera was hidden, but someone had to have put it there. Adam Windsor?

Now Angela's drunken babbling in Muldoon's that night made sense. The manila envelope that had fallen out of her purse and she'd been so quick to grab back up; blackmail money. She'd been looking for the devil to pay him off, but I'd sent her home before he arrived. Adam Windsor showed up later. Video of the potential next First Lady of California shooting smack and turning tricks would be worth a lot of blackmail dollars. It was also a good enough motive for murder. Had Angela gone home, sobered up, and then tracked down Windsor in Melody's motel room and killed him?

It didn't seem possible. The drunk she'd been on would still be there when she woke up the next morning or afternoon. But the flash drive showed she knew her way around heroin. She might still know where to get it and someone else might have been holding the needle. Her husband? He had more to lose than anyone. Angela had said he'd been campaigning in L.A. that night, but Los Angeles was only a two-hour drive away. That left plenty of time to put down Windsor. But why kill him and not take the flash drive?

How did Melody end up with it and why weren't the police knocking down my door right now looking for it? Surely Melody knew that, at the worst, the flash drive would widen the field of suspects. Unless there was something on it that could hurt her.

I continued fast-forwarding through the images, looking for anything different from the debauchery I'd been scrolling through for the last half hour.

Something changed and I hit play to slow down the action. The room was different from the one in all the other scenes. Expensive furnishings, mood lighting. The angle of the camera was different, too. Much lower and off to the left. To the right, beyond a luxurious bed, the corner of a floor-to-ceiling window caught a high-up view of the Eiffel Tower at night. Next to it, below, the very top of a hot air balloon could be seen. Except this one was festooned with neon lights.

Paris. Casino. Las Vegas.

A couple seconds later, Angela jumped onto the bed. She looked healthier than in the other scenes. And happy. She beckoned to someone off screen and a man came toward the bed from the left. In profile, you could see one dead eye and a square chin.

Peter Stone.

He got on the bed and they started to make love. No money exchange. Nothing rough or demeaning. They looked like the sex meant more that just a physical release. I fast-forwarded and a minute later the screen went black. The Angela Albright show was over.

I sat back in my chair. Peter Stone, Angela Albright, Adam Windsor. Where did Melody fit in? Windsor and Melody had been married, but when? Before this? During? The time stamp was nine years old. Up until three weeks ago, Windsor had been in prison for the last eight years. Where had Melody been when the scenes on the flash drive went down? And why did she have the drive now? Were she and her ex-husband running a blackmail ring that picked up where it left off when he got out of prison? Or had she grabbed the drive so she could break a *National Enquirer*-style story that would catapult her onto journalism's big stage?

And what about Stone? Was a nine-year-old sex tape with a beautiful woman really something to fear? He may have tried to rebuild his image of a onetime casino owner, but everyone still knew he was from Vegas. Sex tapes were almost part of the Vegas résumé. It might be reason enough for murder to Steven or Angela Albright who had visions of the governor's mansion, but not Stone. Maybe he still loved Angela and was protecting her, but not from infidelity. The Albrights had only been married for six years, the tape was nine years old. There had to be more. Maybe it was behind the storage unit door that the key Melody left behind opened.

I drained three more beers and went to bed with more questions than answers.

CHAPTER TWENTY-TWO

In a moment between sleep and awake, something happened and my bedroom became very small. I opened my eyes and tried to listen with them. I didn't see or hear anything, but I felt something. I slowly pulled the sheets back and got out of bed. Then I heard a noise in the kitchen.

Someone was inside my house.

I suddenly wished the clerk at the gun shop had been willing to sell me something under the counter without a paper trail.

I crept out of my room in the dark. The cool night had hushed back down and closed silent around me. My cell phone sat on the table by the front door in the living room. Without Midnight, or a gun, the phone was my best defense. My eyes adjusted to the darkness, and I kept the lights off. I made it into the living room, ten feet from the phone, when a tiny beam of light shot out from the kitchen. A large, dark figure followed behind it.

I froze. My heart pounded in my ears. The light traced slowly across the room and then suddenly locked on my face. I jerked to the left and bolted for the door.

But he was too close.

I turned to face him before he reached me. He was dressed all in black, including a ski mask. Two inches of lightning crackled in his hand as he lunged at my chest. A stun gun.

Instinct took over.

I blocked his lunge with my left forearm, spun to my right, and caught his yarn-covered jaw with a right cross. It took him by surprise and the mask wasn't much protection. He staggered back a step. I bounced on the balls of my feet with my hands held high.

Ski Mask stabbed the stun gun at me again. This time I caught his arm and yanked it down on my rising knee. He yelped and the stun gun thumped onto the carpet. I kicked it away and went to work.

He tried to crowd me with his superior size. But I pistoned a left jab just as he stepped in with a looping right. The jab had a lot of shoulder behind it and snapped his head back as his blow bounced off my extended arm. I dug a right uppercut to his belly and followed with a left hook flush on his cheek. He stumbled against the wall. I grabbed at the back of his jacket to pull it over his head and finish him with a hockey punch, but caught his ski mask instead. It came off in my hand.

Even in the darkness he couldn't hide. The younger version of the hard boys who jumped me looking for Melody. He wasn't so tough without his big buddy backing him up. He lunged at me and I shot a straight right that caught him dead between the eyes. I heard the crack and the impact shot through my knuckles all the way up my arm. He slumped to his knees and threw both hands up to his nose.

My turn.

I bent over and grabbed his coat to yank him up. He was going to pay for poisoning Midnight. I noticed too late that one hand had slipped off his nose onto the floor. Lightning jolted me under my rib cage. My body clenched into a fist, and the world turned white. And then it went black.

"Where's the flash drive?" A voice echoed in the dark.

An alarm clock buzzed inside my head, and my body felt like a wrung-out dishrag. My mind was clogged with unformed thoughts bumping into each other. I blinked a few times and then held my eyes open. The living room was now lit. A spiderweb dangled down at me from the ceiling. Then the Gen Y tough guy's mug filled up my world. His nose now had a kink in it. A drop of blood hung from its tip, threatening to splash down onto me.

"Where the fuck is it!" His voice was thick, caught in his crooked nose.

I struggled to push myself off the floor, but my hands were bound together underneath me. I was naked, tied up, and about to be the M in an S&M scene. The kid kicked me in the side, and I stopped moving and started hurting. He held the black rectangular stun gun above my head and thumbed the trigger. An orange bolt of electricity danced in front of my face.

"Last chance, dude." The blood drop finally gave way and splatted onto my forehead. "Where's the flash drive?"

My mind started to clear. If he'd had a real gun, he would have shown it to me by now. Maybe he would stun me to death. Or just kick me in the side a few more times. I could yell for help, but more pain would be sure to follow. I could lie and try to buy some time. Or I could just tell him the truth and give up the only leverage I had in a game I wasn't sure I wanted to play anymore.

"What flash drive?" The game wasn't over yet.

"I warned you, dude. Now you gotta feel the heat."

"Hold on!" I braced for the shock that didn't come. "If I had this flash drive, why didn't you find it when you poisoned my dog and broke in here last night?"

He squinted and his blond eyebrows came together. "I didn't poison any dog. What kind of an asshole do you think I am?"

Irony was lost on him.

"Look, I don't have it. Whoever broke in last night must have it." I angled my head toward him. "If you leave now, I won't call the cops."

"You're not going to get the chance." He thrust the sparking gun at me.

"He says he doesn't have it. Says someone broke into his house last night and took it."

A surf-dude voice bounced around in my short-circuited brain. My eyes fluttered and then he came into view, standing in the entry to the kitchen holding a cell phone to his ear.

"I don't know." He looked over at me. "I think he's lying."

The plastic flex-cuffs around my wrists bit into my skin and numbed my hands. Hundreds of pinpricks stung my fingers. I scanned the living room and tried to envision a weapon that I could use with my hands tied behind my back before they went completely numb.

"Okay. I'll call you back."

I wondered who was on the other end of that cell phone. Stone? The Albrights? His mountain-sized partner? Whoever it was, they were directing the action. The kid was strictly muscle. And soft muscle, at that. He'd gotten lucky with me. If he was a pro, the tough-guy union had lowered its standards since my days as a street cop.

"Who you talking to? Stone?" I arched my neck to look at him. "You really want to risk jail for him?"

He walked over and looked down at me. His eyes got small and his smile got big. Pain was on the way. He kicked me in the ribs, and it felt like my chest caved in on my lungs. Bile pushed up my throat. I rolled onto my side and brought my knees up to protect my chest.

"No more bullshit." He gave me a squinty smile and raised his boot above my rib cage. "Tell me where the flash drive is, or I'll break every fuckin' bone in your body."

"Okay." I spit sour bile onto the carpet. "I'll tell you where it is."

CHAPTER TWENTY-THREE

"It's behind the bookcase." I nodded toward the large maple bookcase, that had once been my father's, against the wall directly across from me.

"Where behind the bookcase?"

"I taped it to the back." I raised my cuffed hands off my back. "Take these off and I'll show you."

"Nice try. Get up." He pointed to the corner of the room next to the bookcase. "Go stand over there unless you want the bookshelf to flatten your ass."

I rolled over onto my stomach, and a sharp stab in my side reminded me of the goon's last kick. I pushed my head into the carpet and inchwormed up to my knees. From there I stepped into a squat, one leg at a time, and then finally up. It had been a while since I'd been upright. I liked things better that way. I walked over and stood in the corner of room with my back to the bookshelf, my fingers brushing against its side.

"You try something stupid and you won't wake up the next time I put you to sleep."

I heard him move. When I thought he was on the opposite side of the bookcase and could no longer see my hands, I wedged my dying fingers between the case and the wall.

The bookcase was solid maple, heavy with hardcovers. He'd have to use both hands to pull the case away from the wall. It would take some force.

Maybe I could help.

With my fingers still jammed between the bookcase and the wall, I contorted my head around my shoulder and saw him slip

the stun gun into his back pocket and raise his hands up to the top
of the bookcase.

"I lied." I kept my eyes on him. "The drive isn't there."

"What the fuck?" He dropped his hands and came at me, stepping in front of the bookcase. "You're gonna pay—"

I gripped the back edge of the case and yanked as hard as I
could while I lunged off the wall with my right leg. The books, the
case, and I, all came tumbling down. On top of my attacker. He
groaned and squirmed, trying to free his legs pinned under the
bookcase. I did an inchworm-on-speed routine among the scattered
books, fighting to make it back to my feet before he could wriggle
free.

I won and stepped around Robert Crais's *Hostage* just as he
got one leg loose. I swung my right leg at his head like Charlie
Brown on the season's opening kickoff. Only Lucy wasn't around
to yank his head out of the way. He moved it himself. Just as I
started the downswing, he turned to look at me. His freshly broken
nose acted as a magnet, and the top of my foot smashed the target
with a crack.

"Shit!" I tumbled over the punk, books, and blood.

My foot throbbed. I wondered if the crack I'd heard had been
it or the remaining cartilage in the other guy's nose. His eyes were
slits that showed only white. I thought he might be dead. The only
thing moving was the blood trickling from his zigzagged nose.

I worked my way up to my feet and limped over for a closer
look. A bubble of blood percolated in his right nostril while a
stream of red meandered out of his left. He was alive and still had
a stun gun in his back pocket. I was still naked with my hands tied
behind my back. And my phone was still on the table next to the
door. I'd have a hard time dialing it. I thought about running to
my neighbor's and banging my head on the front door. The cops
would probably like that: onetime murder suspect caught in violent
homosexual bondage game. Heather Ortiz would have the byline
in the newspaper.

I squatted down with my back to the laid-out tough guy,

grabbed the edge of the fallen bookcase with my leaden hands, and strained to stand up. If he suddenly awoke, I would have been in a vulnerable position. Again. But he was as still as roadkill. I backpedaled over him and backed up the bookcase against the wall.

He lay on his back outlined by scattered books. Stringy blond hair splayed out around his head like a surf-angel halo. He was probably six four and weighed over two hundred. I had to turn him over to get at his back pocket. It would have been easy if my hands weren't numb and tied behind my back. I squatted with my back to him and grabbed his jacket. A couple of pinpricks in my fingers let me know they were still there. When I thought I felt the leather between my fingers, I tried to straighten up. I could feel his weight in my forearms and legs, but not in my hands. Before I lost the grip I dove backward and tumbled over books.

I scrambled up to my feet and saw that he was now on his stomach.

And moving.

His hands pawed the carpet in slow motion as if he were trying to dog paddle across the top of it. I was running out of time. I knelt down next to his waist and tried to find his back pocket with bloodless fingers.

"Heah—ma—funk—gun." The tough guy started to push himself up from the carpet.

He twisted away from me just as my right hand came out of his hip pocket. With something rectangular and heavy in it. I got both hands around it and my thumb found a metal bump. I lunged backward at him and thumbed the switch hoping I had the stun gun pointed in the right direction. I landed on top of him and kept my thumb pressed down on the switch. His legs kicked spastically and then stopped moving.

I rolled off him. He lay flat, like a bear rug, bleeding onto my carpet. I sectioned up to my feet and went into the kitchen and dropped the stun gun onto the table. When Hard Guy came to, it would be my turn to ask the questions and shock some answers out of him. But I couldn't do that with my hands cuffed behind me. I went over to the butcher-block island and fumbled with the wooden knife holder until I came out with a paring knife.

Hard Guy moaned and I heard him rustling on the carpet. I could barely feel the knife handle in my right hand and blindly tried to angle the blade at the plastic strap and my left wrist. I caught flesh. It hurt. Good. I still had some feeling left. I tried again. More flesh, more pain. Not so good.

I was still playing pincushion with my wrists when the dude rushed through the kitchen door at me. I ducked low under his arms, spun hard to my left, and the paring knife in my hand hit something hard and I lost the grip. Hard Guy yelped and tumbled past me into the kitchen table. He spun around to face me and we both looked at his right leg. The paring knife jutted out of his thigh.

"Motherfucker!" His eyes were wild like a maimed animal.

He pulled the knife out of his leg and screamed. Tears tumbled down his ruined face and he looked at the red blade. I braced for a charge, then glanced at the hole in his Levis. It was damp with blood.

He pointed the knife at my chest and took a step forward, then cried out in pain. His face went ghost and I thought he might pass out. He dropped the knife, clamped his hand on his leg, and staggered out the back door leaving behind a trail of whimpers.

I let him go.

I found the paring knife, slick with blood, on the floor and limboed it up with hands behind my back. I did more damage to my wrist than the flex-cuffs trying to cut them off. After five minutes, I gave up and fumbled the serrated knife out of the block. Better. It took me ten minutes to cut free of the flex-cuffs. By the time I was done, sweat poured off me and my left wrist looked like I'd played tic-tac-toe with a knife. The blood rushed back into my hands on the edges of razor blades. It took twenty minutes for the tingling to fade away.

I took a long, hot shower. The water stung my wrist, but felt good on the rest of my battered body. But not good enough to keep

Hitchcock's *Psycho* images out of my head. When I finally pushed them out, questions took their place.

I figured my attacker had to have been working for either the Albrights or Peter Stone. The Albrights would seem to be more desperate, but my money was on Stone. Hired toughs seemed like a better choice for an old casino boss than a campaigning politician. Although, sometimes it was hard to tell the difference.

But that didn't solve the mystery of who broke in last night. Tonight's intruder had broken a windowpane out of the back door to reach in and unlock it. Last night the lock had been picked. Why change the MO when the first one had been effective?

Maybe Stone and the Albrights had each sent their own goon on different nights. That would explain the different MOs, but it didn't feel quite right. I still didn't see the Albrights getting their hands this dirty, even by extension. Steven Albright had enough money to mostly bankroll his own campaign. If Windsor had blackmailed the Albrights, they would have paid him.

That left someone else. There were plenty of other people on the flash drive who'd paid to demean themselves and Angela. Nine years later, many of them had probably reached a station in life where they'd pay to keep evidence of their kinks locked in a closet. I just didn't recognize any of them.

Or, was I missing something? Was the real prize in a public storage unit waiting to be unlocked with the key Melody had hidden with the flash drive? I should probably take what I had to the police. Except they might use it as an excuse to lock me up. The new evidence didn't change the fact that my hat was found in Windsor's death room.

I got out of the shower and looked at myself in the mirror. Steam blotted out my reflection.

CHAPTER TWENTY-FOUR

My cell phone woke me at 6:50 a.m., robbing me of ten minutes of sleep. I grabbed it off the nightstand and checked the incoming number. Blocked. I punched on the cell and grunted a hello.

"Rick, it sounds as if I woke you." The voice was maple syrup over lemons. "You have my sincerest apologies."

"Stone." I sat up in my bed. He'd probably already moved on to plan B to get the drive after his goon failed last night.

"I'm calling to be of assistance."

"Like the guy you sent over here to break in last night?"

"More entanglements, Rick? You seem to be constantly at odds with your environment." A snicker. "As interesting as your reality TV wannabe life is, I'm calling about Melody. I need you to deliver a message to her."

"She's not here." I guessed Melody's arrest hadn't hit the news yet.

"Well, of course she isn't." Patronizing, like a politician at a town hall meeting. "She's in jail and it looks like she'll be there for a while. But you already knew that."

"If that's true, what makes you think I'll ever see her again?"

"She's Melody and you're a man."

"Last time I checked, you were one too. Deliver your own messages, Stone." A chuckle of my own. "Oh, I forgot. You like to send surrogates to do your dirty work."

"Ah, the blue-collar tough-guy routine again. Let's skip past the chest thumping." His voice lost a few degrees of its icy cool. "Tell Melody to contact Alan Fineman to represent her. She needn't worry about a fee."

I wasn't up on the San Diego legal community, but even I'd heard of Fineman. He regularly showed up on truTV as a talking head. It didn't surprise me that he and Stone knew each other. A big-shot attorney and a powerful semilegitimate businessman. The back end of what made America great.

"What's in it for you, Stone?" I already knew the answer, but I was good at playing dumb. Stone wanted a handpicked attorney so he could stay close to the investigation and bury any evidence the defense found that could embarrass or implicate him.

"I just want what's best for Melody." Somehow, he said it without laughing. "Whatever you may think of me, you know that Melody needs a good attorney and Mr. Fineman is the best. He's never lost a murder case. Convince Melody to do what's in her best interest. Goodbye, Rick."

The line went dead.

Stone was making bold moves, but they exposed him. He was playing from behind and wasn't used to it. His goon had failed to get him the flash drive, so now he hoped to bury it from the inside. He was desperate, but why? The images of him on the drive weren't incriminating and, at worst, were only mildly embarrassing. There had to be something more. I just hadn't found it yet.

I got up, got dressed, and felt the loss of my morning routine of letting Midnight outside. I scanned the morning paper over a bowl of Cheerios. No mention of Melody's arrest. That would come. I grabbed the bag of Midnight's dog food and headed for Kim's and then work.

Elk Fenton called me on my cell phone at 8:35 a.m. while I was in Muldoon's bar ordering from a liquor rep. Melody's arraignment was scheduled for ten thirty at the La Jolla Courthouse. She was being represented by Timothy Buckley. Elk had never heard of him and neither had I. Maybe Alan Fineman hadn't offered his services yet, or maybe Melody had turned him down. No matter Stone's agenda, it would be foolish not to retain Fineman as an attorney.

If I hustled, I could get my work done and get to the arraignment on time. And deliver Stone's message.

I finished cutting meat and fish by ten and went up onto the roof of Muldoon's with a canister of Freon. The compressor for the restaurant's air-conditioning system had to be replenished every month or so. The unit had leaked for years and Turk's short-term fix of refilling it with chlorofluorocarbons had turned into a long-term solution. There was probably a hole in the ozone over La Jolla that would make the Green Police shudder in their Birkenstocks.

I'd filled the compressor and was disconnecting the Freon canister when Turk came through the door onto the roof. His flip-flops crunched along the gravel and tar paper walkway that snaked around the vents and compressors. It sounded like an army marching to war. The look on his face made me the enemy.

"What the hell happened last night?" He stood in close, hovering over me. His face matched his fire-red hair.

There were many answers to that question. Just none that I wanted to talk about. "What do you mean?"

"The fucking video that's all over YouTube." His voice had a nasty edge that he'd never used with me before. "Don't tell me you don't remember going psycho on a customer last night."

"I caught him selling drugs in the bathroom." That suddenly didn't sound like such a strong defense.

"So you go all Rambo on him? You looked like you were out of your mind. We're probably going to get sued. I had to cut my trip short because of this shit."

"Sorry." I was.

"I don't even know you any more, Rick." His breath, hot on my face. "First the tough guys looking for some gal you hooked up with, then the Windsor thing in the paper, and now you go postal on some punk in front of the whole restaurant. Hell, the whole nation. And I gotta hear about it from Kris because you don't even do the stand-up thing and call me."

"Kris told you?" My corner was now empty.

"Yeah. She's worried about you, and so am I." He shook his head. "But I'm more worried about my restaurant. This kind of publicity isn't good for business. This is La Jolla, not L.A. That shit doesn't fly with old money. I got a call from Mrs. Fahey this morning. She says she doesn't feel safe eating dinner here anymore. We're gonna lose our regulars."

"So, you want me to take some time off?" Maybe hibernating for a few days wasn't such a bad idea.

"Rick." He blew out an exhale that sounded like a whale spouting and the anger washed out of his face. "It's going to have to be something more permanent."

My gut felt like Turk had stuck a knife in it and twisted. I had to fight not to lose my balance. Muldoon's and Midnight were the only two things *permanent* in my life. He couldn't really be taking one of them away.

"What do you mean?"

"Business has been down for a while, and we can't afford to lose any more customers. I've been away from the day-to-day operations for too long. It doesn't make sense to pay you when I can do the same job." His eyes left mine. "I'm sorry, Rick, but I'm going to have to let you go."

Go where? Muldoon's was all I had.

"You can't fire me, I'm your partner."

"My partner!" His eyes went big and his shoulders went back. "You've given me fifteen grand over the last two years. That doesn't even get you two percent. We're not partners. You're an employee."

Fifteen thousand dollars, seven years of sweat equity, twenty years of friendship, and I was just an employee. "You shook my hand. We had a deal."

"You haven't upheld your end. You needed to come up with a real business plan and get a loan. Buying the restaurant has been a fantasy, man. I should have put an end to it a long time ago." He sighed and put his hands in his pockets. "I wish I had so you could have gotten on with your life."

"Fifteen grand isn't a fantasy." My face splashed hot and I stepped in on Turk. "It's real money earned working here sixty, seventy hours a week while you're out chasing your childhood up a mountain or around a bar. Don't talk to me about fantasies."

"Don't make this personal, Rick." He flashed red again. "It's a business decision. You've gotten reckless and you've become a liability. Use this time to get your life back under control."

"Keep the self-help shit to yourself, Turk. Just give me my money and then you and I are done. It's not personal. Just business."

He looked down at me and sadness passed over his blue eyes, then flickered away. Back to business. He pulled a thick envelope out of his back pocket and handed it to me.

I ripped it open and saw a wad of hundred dollar bills.

"There's five grand in there," Turk said.

"Where's the rest?" I waved the envelope at him.

"That's severance." He folded his tree-trunk arms across his massive chest. "It's the best I can do right now. You'll get more when business starts to pick up. You know we've been losing money for the past few months. We don't have the extra cash right now."

"I don't give a shit! Go to the bank with a real business plan and get a loan. Just give me my money back."

"You can't expect to get your full investment back. While you were part owner the restaurant lost money. You'll have to take a hit."

"What investment? I'm an employee, not an owner. Remember?" I shoved the envelope in my pocket. "Consider the money a loan that just came due. I'll give you until the end of the month for the other ten."

"Then what?" He jabbed a finger the size of a roll of quarters into my chest. It felt like a jackhammer. "Are you threatening me?"

The whites of his eyes got big and he wasn't the Turk I knew anymore. He was a man mountain you didn't want to be on his wrong side. But he no longer had a right side. Something had changed in him. The whole morning was wrong. Everything about today was an overreaction. The Turk I used to know wouldn't have fired me. But this one had and his finger was still pounding my chest. I'd taken down bigger men before, and I welcomed the pain of a battle to go with the ache my life had become.

"Call it whatever you want." I knocked his hand away with my left forearm.

He exploded into me like I was the blocking dummy in a tackling drill. My straight arm glanced off his left shoulder, and we both spun sideways, but his momentum drove me down onto the rooftop gravel. I landed on the back of my left shoulder with the majority of Turk's two hundred fifty pounds on top of me. Gravel bit into me and the air exploded out of me, but I shot an elbow to his temple before he could leverage his superior position. The blow stunned him and I pushed off, rolled away, then spidered up to my feet. Turk was slower to rise. His ribs and head were exposed as he hand-and-kneed his way up. A kick to the head and I could finish him. I stepped back and dropped my hands to my sides.

We were already finished.

I pulled the restaurant keys out of my pocket and threw them down onto the gravel next to Turk. He picked them up and slowly rose to his feet. When he straightened up the rage was gone from his eyes.

I sat down hard on the air compressor and stared out at the ocean below. The office building behind Muldoon's blocked my view of the morning surf, but I could see the water out past the breakers. It lay still and gray and blended with the morning haze to smudge the horizon.

"Sorry it had to be this way, Rick." His eyes went soft like he wanted to say more. Like he was still my friend. But then he turned and walked back to the door that led off the roof. The crunch of gravel under his feet, an army marching away from ruin.

Muldoon's

CHAPTER TWENTY-FIVE

I left Muldoon's at 10:25 a.m.

Alfonso's, the Mexican restaurant across the street, opened in a half hour. A friendly bartender there was sure to serve me a liquid lunch of two-for-ones. A pathetic start to the rest of my life. There'd be plenty of time to wash down feeling sorry for myself and a less public place to do it. My car and a chance to further recede from life was three blocks up the hill. Melody's arraignment was three blocks in the opposite direction.

I started walking. The gray morning closed down around me and my pulse picked up. I felt eyes on me. There weren't many people on the sidewalk that time of day, but I sensed someone watching me. It could have been because of my starring role in the YouTube customer-abuse video or it could have been paranoia born from the residue of the last week. I scanned both sides of the street, but everyone seemed to be engulfed in their own little worlds.

I was trapped in mine.

The arraignment had started early, and I'd gotten there late. The gallery of the tiny courtroom was almost full. I sat in the back to keep out of view of the media types I saw scribbling on notepads. Thankfully, it looked like the judge had banned cameras from the courtroom.

Melody, in jailhouse orange scrubs, was already standing before the judge. Next to her was what looked to be a homeless man in a wilted business suit. Except he was her lawyer. He had a gray ponytail, a scraggly beard, and looked like he couldn't argue himself out of a drunk and disorderly.

I had to get to Melody and tell her about Stone's offer to

bankroll Alan Fineman for her defense. I didn't get the chance. The judge ruled Melody remanded for trial. Bail set at one million dollars. Back to jail. She turned and scanned the gallery as the bailiff cuffed her wrists. I didn't know if she'd killed Windsor or if she'd try to implicate me to cut a deal. Right then, I didn't care. I just wanted her to know that, in the worst moment of her life, she wasn't alone.

Not like I'd been in mine.

I stood and caught her eye just before she went through the door. She smiled for an instant and then her eyes clouded with pain and, maybe, shame. She dropped her head, and the bailiff led her out of the courtroom through a door near the jury box.

I turned to leave and saw Heather Ortiz standing near the front row of the gallery talking to a silver-haired man dressed in a three-piece banker's suit. Only thing missing was a pocket watch. He looked sad, yet resolute. Jules Windsor, father of Adam. Next to him stood Chief Parks in dress blues. His black mustache pulled his mouth down into a permanent snarl. He caught me looking and his coal eyes could have crushed diamond.

He broke from Heather and Windsor and headed right at me, his uniform snap-creased, polished brass gleaming. He was about my height, but heavier. The kind of weight that comes with age and fills up space, creating a presence. I held my ground at the door leading out of the courtroom. Parks looked like the kind of man you didn't want coming up behind you.

"Cahill." His voice sounded like a Mack truck radiator boiling over. "I'll lock you up if I find you're obstructing this murder investigation."

Something beyond hatred poured out of his eyes. I'd seen hatred before. Colleen's father, Santa Barbara cops, my own eyes in the mirror long ago. This was different, darker, malevolent. I felt it in my gut and on the back of my neck.

"How could I be obstructing your investigation?" Did he know about the flash drive? "I've got a right to be here, just like any citizen."

"If you have any information or evidence about the death of Adam Windsor, you need to hand it over to me right now." He leaned in on me, sending hate and cologne my way. The same strong cologne Detective Moretti wore. "This is your one chance. Next time it'll be jail."

Maybe Parks was right. This was my one chance to hand over the drive and the key and move on. Nothing I'd seen on the drive could hurt Melody. I could tell the cops the truth exactly as it happened. I found the evidence in the dog food. Melody must have put it there. Ask her why, not me.

I'd been in jail. I wasn't going back for anyone.

Parks pushed his face in closer, trying to read me. His cologne seeped under my skin.

Then it clicked like a nine millimeter chambering a round. The stink I'd smelled on my carpet the night someone broke into my house and poisoned Midnight. Cologne, mixed with sweat. The same cologne worn by Parks and Moretti.

One of them had broken into my house, poisoned my dog, and been willing to risk prison to find the evidence Melody had hidden. What else were they capable of?

I wondered if the man staring me down had been the one who poisoned Midnight. My hands closed into fists and my neck flexed tight. I held his hatred and gave it back to him. If he wasn't wearing the badge, I'd be the one asking the questions.

"If I find any of your evidence, you'll be the first to know, Chief." The last word came out like spit.

I spun away from Parks and out of the courtroom slamming the door behind me, sending an echo through the halls of justice.

I bolted out of the courthouse, the wooden steps creaking under my feet. A voice floated over my shoulder before I hit the sidewalk.

"Excuse me, Mr. Cahill? May I have a word with you?"

I turned and saw the homeless man who couldn't get Melody reasonable bail.

"Timothy Buckley." There was a trace of Texas hidden under

years of Southern California in his voice. He stuck out a leathery hand. "I'm Melody Malana's attorney."

I one-pumped his hand and waited.

"I understand you're a friend of Melody's. Is that true?" Buckley made it sound like it wasn't.

He squinted at me under the eaves of the wooden courthouse that was once a church. The steeple had been torn down to separate church from state, but Buckley sounded like he had me in the confessional.

I didn't have anything to confess. At least, not to him. "Why don't you ask her?"

Buckley smiled creamed-corn teeth at me. "You don't like lawyers much, do ya, pardna?"

"Compared to what?"

Buckley let out a hoot like he was calling the pigs back to the barn.

"You hungry, Rick? You like flapjacks?"

I didn't have a job anymore. Best to grab a free meal whenever I could. And the one thing I could do for Melody was convince this homeless cowboy to tell her that she needed a new lawyer.

"I could eat."

"Well then, follow me." Buckley slung an antique leather satchel over his shoulder. "There's a little ol' cafe around the corner that makes great pancakes."

I walked next to him along the sidewalk that led into downtown La Jolla. The morning haze still hung low, filtering pale sunlight.

Joe's Waffle Shop was a little hole-in-the-wall that stood as a civic treasure on Girard Ave. in Old La Jolla. Girard mostly maintained the small-town feeling that the whole village had once exuded. Family owned stores and restaurants populated nothing-special concrete buildings under palm trees that were as old as the town they towered above.

We sat on two bolted-down red and chrome stools at the counter. A glass pie case on the wall opposite us made me think of having a slice of pecan after the sock hop. And I didn't even like pie.

I'd always had waffles when I'd eaten at Joe's, but I followed Buckley's recommendation and the pancakes didn't disappoint. We small talked San Diego sports for a few minutes, but the whole time I felt Buckley measuring me. When I'd pause to eat, he'd narrow his eyes down on me like a scientist peering into a microscope.

Maybe there was more to this guy than a tired suit and whiskey eyes.

"Melody speaks very highly of you, Rick." Buckley wiped his mouth with a napkin. "Thinks you're a man of integrity."

I didn't like being schmoozed, but I didn't know where he was going. So, I stayed quiet and let him take me there. If he didn't know about the Angela Albright sex tape, I wasn't going to tell him. That would have to come from Melody.

"Is there anything you can tell me about the morning of Windsor's death that'll help Melody?" Buckley grabbed a pen and legal pad out of his satchel. "Now, you were actually at the motel that morning. Right?"

Buckley could play my "pardna" over flapjacks, but his job was to keep Melody out of prison. And he could do that by showing the jury that his client didn't commit murder because someone else did. Back on the force it was known as "SODDI." Some Other Dude Did It. Well, the cops had already looked at me once as that other dude. Buckley was sure to remind the jury of that fact.

"You obviously talked to the police, so you already know why I was there." I sopped up some syrup with the last bite of pancake on my fork. "However, I do have a message from a friend of Melody's that could be helpful to her."

"What might that be?" Buckley sat back in his stool and crossed his arms across his chest.

"I'm just the messenger, so don't take this personally. But a guy named Peter Stone has offered to bankroll Melody's defense if she hires Alan Fineman."

Buckley inventoried my face with sad eyes. "How well do you know Mr. Stone?"

"I wish I'd never met him."

Buckley slowly nodded his head. Time had worn down his face and I guessed that it had gotten help from alcohol. His brown eyes were pink and watery around the rims and a purple spiderweb ran down his nose.

"I reckon you're not the first person to feel that way." He put an elbow on the counter and rested his chin in his hand. "You think Stone's the kind of man to help someone out of the goodness of his heart?"

"I'm not sure he has a heart, but that's beside the point." This time I studied him. "I know you want what's best for Melody and Fineman is her best chance to get off. Besides, sitting second chair to Fineman would be a great opportunity."

"Son, I'm way past opportunities." His voice remained Texas iced tea smooth, but his eyes caught an edge. "But, you can tell your boss that I'll deliver his message to Melody."

"I don't have a boss, Buckley." Not as of a half hour ago. "I'd never heard of Peter Stone until a week ago, and I'd do anything to get that week back. But I can't."

Buckley pulled a toothpick out of his shirt pocket, nibbled on it, and then pointed at me.

"What happened to your wrist?"

I looked down at the bandages I'd put on my wrist to cover the slices I'd made trying to cut the flex-cuffs off last night. "I cut myself shaving."

"It seems you've had a run of bad luck lately." Buckley pinched his eyes down on me again. "You file a report with the police that you were assaulted, are interrogated by detectives for murder, get caught on video roughing up some citizen, and now this shaving accident. A lot of coincidences, eh, Mr. Cahill?"

Buckley was much better than he looked. Maybe Melody didn't need Fineman. Maybe I did.

"You trying to impress me with your homework, Buckley?" I

tried to swallow down the anger boiling up from the whole day. "Melody involved herself with some bad people and then brought them down on me. Maybe she didn't mean to, but they're still poking around in my life. Just like you are. I don't think she killed her ex-husband. But I'm not convinced enough to believe that you won't twist things around to try and make me trade places with her."

"So you're innocent. You got nothing to hide. Tell me what you know so we can both help Melody."

"I've been innocent before, Buckley. And that didn't seem to matter."

I stood up, pulled a ten dollar bill from my wallet, dropped it on the counter, and left. Outside, the sun had sliced through the marine layer and painted the day in light and shadow.

Muldoon's

CHAPTER TWENTY-SIX

The feeling of being watched followed me all the way home. I checked the rearview mirror a few times, but never spotted a tail. Back in Santa Barbara, I'd developed a sixth sense working the graveyard shift. Sometimes I felt something bad was about to go down before it happened. It was in the air. A tingle, an itch, a silence. Now I couldn't trust that extra sense. The last week had so frayed my nerve endings that a light breeze sent an alert up my spine.

When I got home, I grabbed a beer from the fridge and settled into the recliner. I had plenty of time to do nothing but think, no matter how hard I tried not to. Hopefully, I'd get drunk enough to slow my mind. I couldn't get away from the morning and the nagging feeling that Turk was right. Maybe I had been hiding from life in the fantasy that I'd someday own Muldoon's. It had given my life a purpose that had been missing since Colleen had died. But it wasn't real. I'd given Turk seven hundred and fifty a month to keep the fantasy thinly tethered to reality. A price I paid to believe the lie.

I buried the empty beer bottle in the trash and found another full one in the fridge. My house suddenly felt emptier than it ever had before. Almost as empty as my apartment in Santa Barbara after Colleen's murder. My last sanctuary now felt like a vacuum sucking out my insides. I'd come back to San Diego after Colleen because it had still been home. A place to heal and start life anew. But that life was over now. Turk had pulled back the hand he'd offered me seven years ago. My anchor had been cut loose. La Jolla and San Diego had nothing left for me.

I rented a duplex. I could give notice, grab Midnight, and walk anytime. Turk had put business before friendship, leaving me with neither. The only true friend I had left was Kim. The one person I'd trust to watch Midnight. And the best thing I could do for her was walk away, and let her finally move past me. She could start her new life while I started mine in another city. All I had left in this town were my father's shame and good memories gone bad.

My father hadn't walked away. He'd stayed and taken the looks, the whispers, and the accusations. He hadn't run, but after a while he'd crawled into a bottle and then an early grave. What had he proved? What did I need to prove now? That I could stay and take it? That I was as tough as my old man? I looked at the beer bottle in my hand and thought how routinely I'd pulled it from the refrigerator to fill up a little of the empty inside me. What would replace it when the empty kept growing?

Melody?

She might spend the rest of her life in prison, and if Detective Moretti and Chief Parks had their way, I'd have an adjoining cell. And what if she got out? She was beautiful, sexy, and made me feel that I could love again. But at what cost? I'd already lost my job, been hounded by the police, and had my name splashed in the headlines since I met Melody. And could I really love a woman I could never fully trust?

But if I left Melody and the town behind, the cops still wouldn't forget about me. If they thought I was dirty, they'd try to track me down. Even if I managed to evade them, I couldn't live my life running from something I hadn't done. Down deep, even as I grew to hate him for the man he'd become, a part of me wanted to believe that's why my dad stayed in San Diego. That he'd refused to run from something he hadn't done.

I remembered a ride-along he took me on when I was nine, about a year before it all went wrong. He was riding the squad car alone that night with me in the front seat. He pulled over a driver who'd been badly swerving between lanes on Torrey Pines Road. The man was obviously drunk. I didn't know what he blew on the field sobriety test, but I could smell the booze on him when my father put him in the backseat of the squad car. The sun hadn't gone down yet and it was a weeknight. Even as a kid, I thought it seemed like an odd time to be drunk. And unnerving to see a grown man cry. At that time of my life, my father only got drunk on weekends. Back when alcohol made him happy instead of mean.

My dad hadn't handcuffed the man, and I was surprised when we drove to the Pannikin coffee shop on Girard Street instead of the police station. We sat outside at a table under a pepper tree. Dad and the man drank coffee while I had hot chocolate under a burnt-orange sunset. The man sobbed for a while as my father put a hand on his back and spoke quietly to him. I didn't hear everything and knew better than to interrupt, but I heard Dad say that the man had responsibilities and his family needed him now more than ever. Finally, after three cups of coffee, the man had stopped crying and sobered up a bit. But his eyes still leaked pain, and it looked like his face might crack if you touched it.

We drove him up to a house at the top of Pearl Street instead of back to his car or the police station. Dad walked the man up to the front door and waited until he went inside. When he came back to the car, I asked him why he hadn't arrested the man for drunk driving. He told me that the man's son had just been killed in a car accident. I felt for him, but as a cop's kid I still saw things in black and white. Then my father told me the same thing he'd tell me a year later after he was kicked off the force and accused of being a bagman for the mob.

"Sometimes you have to do what's right even when the law says it's wrong."

He never said another word to me about his dismissal from the force. He and my mom fought about it behind the bedroom door almost every night. But if I never asked him about it, I could still hold out hope that somehow he'd done the right thing.

I wasn't a kid anymore and the only black and white in my life now was the squad car that pulled into my driveway when the police arrested Melody. But even after years of denial, hatred, and shame, I was still my father's son. He didn't run and neither would I. But I couldn't stand still and wait for the cops or Stone or the newspaper to write my story.

I'd write my own.

I went into my office and turned on the computer and Googled public storage businesses in San Diego. I found the website for the complex I'd used to store my father's property after he died. It was one of a chain of fourteen facilities around San Diego. The one I'd used was on Morena Boulevard, a couple miles from where I lived. Windsor's father, Jules, lived in La Jolla, but I didn't know about Adam. He'd only been out of prison for three weeks when he was killed. Hell, I didn't even know if the key Melody had hidden was his. Or the flash drive, for that matter. But I had to have a place to start.

I dialed the number given on the website on my cell phone. A young male voice answered, late teens or early twenties.

I thought about posing as a cop, but quickly changed my mind. It was an easy act for me, but one that wasn't worth the risk. Impersonating a police officer was jail time. Then I remembered Jules Windsor at Melody's arraignment that morning.

"I need your help, young man." I tried to sound old, important, and sad. "Can you tell me if my son was renting a storage unit at your facility?"

"Sorry, sir. We can't give out the names of our clients."

"I understand that, but I don't know what to do." I let go a long sigh. "My son, Adam, was murdered and I know he was renting a storage unit. But I don't know where. The things he stored there are all I have left of him now."

"I'm really sorry to hear that." A sigh of his own. "But I'm not allowed to give out names. I could get into trouble."

"Please, don't make this difficult, young man." Haughty old money replaced the sadness in my voice. "My name is Jules Windsor of Windsor Bank and Trust. My son, Adam, was murdered. I'm sure you've seen it on the news. If you'd like me to go over

your head, I will. I'm sure your employer and the local media
would be happy to know that you stood in the way of my claiming
my son's last possessions on earth."

I wasn't proud of impersonating a grieving father and bullying
a kid who was just doing his job. But this is what my life had become. I wouldn't play by the rules anymore. Peter Stone didn't believe in rules, and Detective Moretti broke them when convenient.
The rules had me teetering on the edge of a murder charge. I had
to play it my way now. But how many rules could I break before I
wasn't me anymore?

I buried that thought and let silence work on the kid.

He finally broke and looked up Adam Windsor on his computer. Nothing. I ran the ploy with the other thirteen facilities in
the chain and was only shut out by two of them. A manager and a
whiskey-throated woman who didn't care if I was "God looking
to clear out Jesus's stuff." She wouldn't budge.

None of the ones who'd checked their files came up with Windsor. Next up, I struck out with a California company that had
twelve San Diego locations and a national one that had twenty.
Two hours and forty-six calls and I had nothing to show except
that I was good liar. Not something I could put on the résumé
when I looked for the next job.

Seven calls and a half hour later, I tried the ploy on a facility in
Sorrento Valley, northeast of La Jolla. As soon as I gave the Windsor name the young woman on the phone was all sympathy.

"Oh, my gosh, I watched it on the news. I'm so sorry for your
loss. Let me look it up." I felt a twinge of guilt at suckering the
woman, but rode it out in silence. The clattering of fingers on a
keyboard echoed over the phone. "Hm. I didn't find one under
Adam's name, but I did find one under yours."

Coincidence? I figured if a man like Jules Windsor had extra
stuff lying around, he'd just buy another house to put it in.

"Really?" Playing for time. "I don't recall renting one."

"Well, you may have forgotten about it." More clattering of
keys. "You've had it for eight years, the payments are direct with-

drawals from your bank account, and your son was the first person to access the locker since I've worked here."

Eight years. The newspaper had said Adam Windsor got locked up eight years ago. Dean Slater, one of Muldoon's regular customers, said that Jules Windsor had kicked Adam out of his house for dealing drugs when he was a teenager. Maybe after the big drug bust, Jules had packed away any remnants of Adam to rid himself of his memory. Then Adam gets out of prison and the old man gives him the key to his old stuff.

What could be hidden away in there that was eight years old and had gotten Adam killed?

"Oh, yes." Back in character. "My wife must have made the arrangements. Could you tell me what unit number that is?"

"Three seventeen. It's the third building on the right after you go through the security gate, about half way down." She took a big gulp of breath. "Oh, that reminds me, you probably don't have the code to the gate, do you?"

"No." But I had a simple plan to get past that obstacle.

"Well, I can't give it out. But if you stop by the office when you come here, I'll open the gate for you."

"Oh, that's very kind." Not the sort of attention I needed. "But, I'm not sure if I'll be able to come by today. I'm making the funeral arrangements. I'll come tomorrow or the next day and I would appreciate your help then. Thank you very much, young lady."

After I got off the phone, I found the storage key where I'd stashed it in my office desk drawer and put it in my pants pocket. Then I went into my bedroom closet and rummaged around until I came out with a backpack. I grabbed a flashlight out of the junk drawer in the kitchen, stuck it in the backpack, put on my Padres cap, and went outside to my car.

My eyes were in the rearview mirror as much as on the road during the drive to Sorrento Valley. The hairs on the back of my neck were at half-mast. I still had the itch that I was being watched, but it had faded into the resignation that I was just paranoid.

Muldoon's

CHAPTER TWENTY-SEVEN

San Diego Self-Storage sat on Sorrento Valley Road across from the Coaster railroad tracks that connected North County with downtown. To the west, the scrub-brush-covered terrain pushed up from the Rose Canyon fault, above Interstate 5, until it peaked into Soledad Mountain. The cross was just visible on top.

I parked a half block south of the facility and got out of my car to surveil it on foot. It sat back from the street on a low rise and had a small parking lot next to the manager's office. The office had a large tinted window that faced the security gate across the lot. A sign on the gate read "Only One Vehicle Per Gate Code." A closed-circuit camera jutted out from a hedge and targeted the gate entrance.

I went back to my car and grabbed a screwdriver from the glove compartment, unscrewed my license plates, and tossed them in the trunk. I got in the car and watched traffic speed past on Sorrento Valley Road and waited. Then waited some more. Finally, after about an hour, a car slowed past me and turned up into the storage facility. I started my car and followed it up the driveway, then hit redial on my cell phone and put on my Bluetooth.

The lady in the car ahead of me stopped at the gate, stuck an arm out the window, and started punching numbers into the keypad on a metal stanchion. The same woman I'd talked to earlier answered the phone in the manager's office.

"I need your help." This time I went with my own voice. "My wife thinks she may have lost her necklace in your office the other day. Can you check your lost and found? It's got a little silver heart pendant on it."

I didn't know if they had a lost and found, but I figured, at least, there'd be a drawer where they kept lost items. Anything to keep her looking anywhere but out the window.

"I'll check."

Bingo.

I'd gotten pretty good at deceiving people. I convinced myself that the ends justified the means and added self-deception to my growing list.

The gate opened for the car ahead of me. I followed it though without having to enter a code. The bill of my hat was pulled down over my eyes, and I kept my head angled away from the surveillance camera. I'm sure passing through the security gate without entering an access code wasn't a capital offense, but it could be considered trespassing and I didn't need any heat.

The woman came back on the line. "I'm sorry, sir. I couldn't find a necklace."

"Damn. Well, thanks anyway."

I turned down the third row of buildings and followed it all the way down, passing unit 317. I parked around the corner at the far end, grabbed my backpack, and got out of the car. If anyone came snooping, I didn't want my car parked in front of Adam Windsor's unit. Surveillance cameras sprouted out of the side of the buildings about every fifty yards. I kept my head down and traversed the storage units on my way to 317. Most of the blue corrugated metal doors I passed had digital locks. I worried that Windsor's unit would too and that I'd sent myself on a fool's errand.

I was relieved to see that 317 had the old-style lock. I put the key in and held my breath while I turned it. A click and the lock opened. I felt relieved and nervous at the same time. Now I was committed. I rolled the door up, slipped inside, then rolled it back down, sealing myself in darkness. I fumbled in the backpack, found the flashlight, and turned it on. I scanned the room and saw a light switch on the side wall. I flicked on the overhead light and was surprised by the orderliness of the space.

Two dressers, a disassembled bed frame, and an immense head-board took up the back wall. A golf bag full of clubs, snow skis, a snowboard, and a bookshelf were the next row out from the wall. The rest were boxes, all shapes and sizes, taped, and stacked high, except for a wooden desk and office chair near the door. A black canvas laptop computer case sat on the middle of the desk and be-hind it was a hutch full of file folders and two old VHS videotapes. The name "Adam" had been scratched into the side of the desk long ago.

The computer inside the case was a newer model Sony VAIO, so someone must have put it in the storage unit recently. Adam after he got out of prison? I pushed the on button. It still had some battery life, but asked for a password once it booted up. I tried every variation of Adam and Jules Windsor, front and back, that I could think of. No luck.

I turned off the computer and pulled the two VHS tapes out of the hutch. The first was labeled "Angela."

The second one said "Melody."

Something told me the tape wouldn't be a video of Melody opening presents under the Christmas tree in happier times with Windsor. Melody had taken the key to the storage unit from Adam for a reason and it wasn't to gather up fond mementos. What was on Melody's tape? Scenes of her prostituting herself like Angela Albright? Had she taken the key before or after Windsor's death?

The police thought Melody was guilty and they didn't even know about the key and the video. Sooner or later they would. Beads of sweat suddenly popped along my hairline. If the tape had images Windsor used to blackmail Melody and the police found me with it, I was an accessory. Before or after the fact didn't matter. I'd do time.

I wiped down the first two tapes with my shirt to rid them of fingerprints and put them back in the hutch. If the police ever found this storage unit, they'd have to determine it was a crime scene to dust for fingerprints. It was a long shot, but I wasn't taking any chances. I started to wipe the Melody tape and then the words she shouted to me as she was being arrested floated through into mind. "I didn't do it, Rick! You have to find the truth!"

Would she really have wanted me to find the truth if she was guilty? Was the truth in my hands right now? If there was something on the tape that could help Melody, why hadn't she told the police? My father's words came out of my mouth, "Sometimes you have to do what's right even when the law says it's wrong."

The law and right and wrong could be sorted out later. My gut told me what to do now. I put the video in my backpack, then grabbed the other one and stuffed it in as well.

I pulled the file folders out of the hutch and perused them. They were filled with eight-year-old bank statements, electric bills, and other paper trails of a life frozen in time. The first two desk drawers held 1980s' baseball cards, a schoolkid's knickknacks, and some dated *Hustler* magazines. The bottom drawer contained an old Panasonic cassette camcorder. Probably the one used by Wind-sor to take the videos of Angela that he later transferred onto the flash drive. It was empty. I put it back in the drawer.

Then I put on my backpack and wiped down the files of potential prints and put them back in the hutch. Lastly, I wiped the desk and the hutch down. A bang on the metal door outside startled me and I jammed my knee up into the underside of the desk. Something brushed against the top of my leg and fell to the floor.

"Excuse me." The voice outside sounded like the woman I'd talked to on the phone.

My mind spun. If she opened the door, I didn't have a story to get me out of this one. But silence wasn't going to keep that door from opening. I put my hand over my mouth to neuter the chance of recognition.

"Yes?"

"We have to close in about a half hour, so please be finished by then."

"Okay." I checked my watch: 6:04 p.m.

I put my ear to the cool, corrugated metal door and listened for the sound of an exit. Nothing. I hadn't heard her arrive, so it would make sense that I wouldn't hear her leave. I stepped back to the desk and picked up the file folder that had fallen when I banged the desk with my knee.

"Mr. Windsor?" The woman hadn't left yet. "Is that you?"

"Yes." I tried to remember how I sounded on the phone. I muffled my voice with my hand again, just in case.

"Where's your car?"

This gal was too inquisitive to have an unlocked door between us. I might be able to age my voice, but my physical appearance would take magic.

"It's around the corner. I wasn't sure where the storage unit was."

"That's your car?"

My seven-year-old Mustang didn't fit the image of a La Jolla banker.

"If you must know, it's my son's." Haughty. "Now would you mind leaving me in peace while I sit with the memory of my boy?"

"Sure." Chastised. "Sorry."

I sat quietly in the desk chair and let silence convey an old man's sad irritation. When I thought she was gone, I opened the file that had fallen from its hiding place. Inside was a letter-sized envelope. I opened it and pulled out the single, folded piece of paper inside. It was an Elko, Nevada, birth certificate from 1979. The name on the certificate was Louise Abigail Delano. Mother, Elizabeth Nelson Delano. No father listed.

Who was Louise Abigail Delano? A girlfriend? A mark? I pulled my iPhone out of my pocket and Googled the name. There were thousands of hits for Louise Delano and plenty for Abigail Delano, but none for the three names put together. Louise Abigail Delano must have grown up to be someone important or had never grown up at all. I Googled the mother's name and got nothing either.

Windsor thought she was important enough to hide separately in a storage unit that held, undoubtedly, blackmail-worthy videotapes right out in the open. Maybe there was more about her that was hidden. I slid the chair out, bent down, and looked up under the desk. There was another file wedged in a seam between the underside of the desk and the side of the top drawer on the right. I pulled the file out and opened it. Inside was a black notebook-style ledger.

I checked my watch: 6:14 p.m. I still had time.

I opened the ledger. The columns on the left had dates, the ones in the middle had the names Stamp and Scarface, and the right had dollar amounts. Page after page. The entries started fifteen years ago and were listed every week or two. The dates were spread out over five years. Amounts ranged from one hundred to five hundred dollars. Stamp was the only name listed for the first year and the amounts were always one hundred dollars. Once the name Scarface starting showing up on the ledger, Stamp's amounts increased to two fifty. Scarface got five hundred every week.

Drug deals? Windsor had gone down for selling heroin, but the amounts were too small for a big-time dealer. The video of Angela proved he'd run at least one woman back in the day. One to five hundred could cover a variety of sexual acts. That made more sense, but Angela's video had shown a lot more johns and janes than just two.

The ledger must have meant something else. Like the notebook that I found in my dad's closet when I was eleven years old. It took years for me to understand what the dollar amounts that my father had written down meant. I wasn't a kid not wanting to believe the worst about my father anymore. The amounts in Windsor's ledger were payoffs to cops. Money paid to keep the police off Windsor's back so that he could run his women and deal "H" without the threat of being arrested.

It didn't take much of an imagination to come up with a couple of candidates for the nicknames. I thought of the stink of cologne left on my carpet the night of the first break-in of my house. The scent I'd smelled on both Detective Moretti and Chief Parks. It had been one of them. And whoever it was hadn't been looking for evidence to put me or Melody in jail. They'd been looking to destroy evidence to keep themselves out of jail. Suddenly, I remembered Moretti's tough guy in-my-face routine at the Brick House and the cleft lip scar under his mustache. Maybe he'd been clean shaven in his earlier days on the La Jolla Police Department.

Scarface.

I put Moretti in his early forties. The time frame worked. A little snooping and I could find out if he'd been working for LJPD fourteen years ago and who he'd partnered with back then. Maybe Stamp. Stamp could have been a real last name or a nickname. Either way, if he wasn't Moretti's partner, he could have been a cop from the San Diego Police Department. Windsor might have had women on more then one circuit. If Stamp was just a nickname penned by Windsor, he might be tougher to uncover. But I still had Moretti.

Then what? Take the information to Chief Parks? Not my biggest fan. And he was the kind of chief who'd thicken the thin blue line of protection around a fellow cop. Go to the state attorney general? What did I really have? A ledger with dates, dollar amounts, and nicknames that I'd stolen from a storage unit. I'd get laughed or chased out of Sacramento. That was a fate best left for politicians.

Maybe Heather Ortiz would be interested. A corruption scandal in LJPD tied in with a murder. In the days of dwindling subscriptions and shrinking newspapers, that was the kind of catnip any reporter would find hard to resist. Break the big story, turn it into a book, and then go on to be the next Ann Rule writing true crime.

But even for a newspaper reporter, I didn't have much. I needed more. There had to be something that could tie things together, point a more convincing finger. The laptop. I'd probably never figure out the password, but maybe I could find someone who could or find a way around it. I slipped the laptop case into my backpack.

As I did, I noticed the time on my watch: 6:28 p.m. That annoyingly efficient woman would be by to boot me out any second. I quickly used the bottom of my shirt to wipe down any surface I thought I'd touched. The desk, the drawers, the light switch.

Finally, I rolled the door up and peeked outside. No sign of the woman. I slid the door back down and closed the lock. I turned to leave and caught glimpse of a golf cart coming at me out of the corner of my eye. Dusk had squeezed the light out of the day, but I could still make out a female form behind the wheel. I brought my free hand to my face and turned away from the cart. I fought the urge to sprint to my car. Instead, I hunched over slightly and shuffled slowly toward it, letting out a breathy sob every few steps.

The car was fifty yards away. The golf cart thirty, and closing fast. I kept my hand to my face and kept up the fake crying. Even so with the backpack, the ball cap, jeans, a sweatshirt, and an athletic build, I doubted I pass for an elderly, wealthy La Jolla banker, even in the diminishing light.

"Can I give you a ride to your car, Mr. Windsor?" Same woman. The cart now crept a respectful twenty feet behind me on my unprotected side. The question in her voice sounded more for my identity than for the offer of a ride.

"I'm okay." I kept my head down and sobbed into my hand.

"Are you sure?"

I waved my hand above my head, kept sobbing, and kept walking. Finally, the golf cart slowly passed behind me and headed down the row of buildings. When it turned right, I sprinted to my car, got in, tossed the computer and backpack onto the passenger seat, and gunned it for the exit. I wanted to beat the woman to the front gate and leave before she could get a good look at me.

I made it to the gate in less than ten seconds and rolled over the pressure plate that opened it. The gate slowly opened inward and I waited for enough space to slide through. I kept my head angled away from the camera that sat on the right side of the gate. The golf cart turned around the last building and approached me from the left. It was twenty yards away and didn't have headlights. The woman could never get close enough to get a good look at me through the dark. The gate inched another foot open, and I stepped on the gas. I looked back at the cart and the woman pointed something at me with her hand.

A beam of light hit the side of my face just before my car broke free of the gate.

Exposed.

Muldoon's

CHAPTER TWENTY-EIGHT

I took a right out of the parking lot onto Sorrento Valley Road and whipped a U-turn at the first break in the divider and gunned it onto the 805 South. I had to fight the temptation to mash the gas pedal to the floor.

The woman had seen me.

If she'd recognized me from my picture in the *U-T* and called the cops, the least they could get me on was unlawful trespassing. The most, accomplice to murder, after the fact. Maybe even before the fact.

Headlights filled my rearview mirror as one would expect on the freeway. Still, the feeling of being followed crept back up my spine. Probably just the echo of the woman splashing the flashlight on me. I took my exit off the freeway and a few cars behind did the same, as would naturally happen any night. Still, I pulled into a gas station off Genesee and watched a couple SUVs and a dark sedan pass by.

Something didn't feel right.

I'd parked my car around the corner from my house and had just made it to my neighbor's driveway when I caught a glint of light and movement out of the corner of my eye.

Cars whizzed past on the road, but they were expected. Moving headlights were an intermittent constant any night of the week. This was something different, something out of place.

I lived on Clairemont Mesa Boulevard, but my section of the main drag through Clairemont was really a frontage road. A sprawling, disjointed mall sat across the street, separated by four lanes of traffic. It was really a series of strip malls shoved together at right angles. The out-of-place light and movement had come from the mall parking lot.

I glanced at the lot before I hit the walkway to my house. There were five or six cars parked next to the only two businesses still open after seven p.m., a wireless phone store and a pet shop. One car was parked alone down near the waist-high evergreen hedge that separated the parking lot from the lawn next to the sidewalk. It sat opposite my house, facing me. It could have been a store employee's, instructed not to park in front of the shop. But the spiked hair on my neck told me it wasn't. The make was a dark Chevy Impala, maybe purple or blue. Could it have been the sedan that passed by when I pulled into the gas station?

The parking lot's lone light pole stood forty yards to the left of the Impala and cast only enough light to put the car in shadow. Headlights from a passing car glinted off something behind the windshield, then the night refilled the vacuum. I couldn't see inside the car through the dark, but I sensed someone behind it watching me. An off-duty cop? A private investigator? One of Stone's toughs? All three were just different versions of the same bad news.

I considered not making the turn up the walk to my house and to just keep walking until I circled around to my car. I could stay in a motel tonight while I figured out how to fix my broken life. Or I could find out who was inside that Impala and decide what to do about it.

My life wasn't going to mend on its own. Too many people were still poking at it.

I took the turn and went up to my front door and into the house without a backward glance. Once inside, my cell phone buzzed in my pocket. I pulled it out and saw Muldoon's number on the screen. I let it go to voice mail. If it was Turk, I'd said all I needed to that morning. The call might have been from Pat or Kris or some other employee wishing me well. I wasn't ready yet for anyone's well-wishes. I was too busy trying to figure out how to deal with the people who wished me ill.

I went into my bedroom and changed into dark clothes. I left the light on and went down the hall. Hopefully, whoever was watching my house would think I was still in there. I grabbed the Bushnell binoculars I used at Charger games out of the hall closet and looked for my black Callaway golf hat. It took me a second to realize it was still in an evidence bag down at the Brick House. Instead, I pulled Melody's black Giants cap off the closet's shelf and put it on.

It fit perfectly.

I went into the kitchen and slung my backpack onto the table, then quickly went to a cabinet and grabbed a box of Ziploc freezer bags. I pulled the flash drive and the videotapes that I'd taken from Adam Windsor's storage unit out of the backpack, shoved them into plastic bags, and then buried them down deep into the forty-pound bag of dog food in the kitchen broom closet. My personal safe.

I grabbed my backpack and went out into the back yard. I crept along the grass on the side out my house, hunched over so as not to show above the wooden fence that guarded the backyard. There wasn't any dog crap to worry about stepping in. The thought of Midnight's poisoning spat adrenaline through my body, and I wondered what I'd do if I found Moretti in that car across the street.

I stopped my creep ten feet from the front gate, slowly brought my head up, and raised the binoculars to my eyes. It took a second to narrow down the focus and find my target. But the dark Impala was still there, pointed at my house.

The windshield was tinted, but I could make out a shape inside. The shape had its own pair of binoculars. Pointed at the front of my house. The old cop instincts were still good even if my last weeks on the force had been all bad. I kept the Bushnells pinned on the figure in the car, and it kept its binos pinned on my house. Minutes passed and my arms started to get tired, but I kept the field glasses pressed to my eyes waiting for the person in the car to drop his so I could ID him.

Finally, the binoculars came down, and I caught a glimpse of a face though the tinted windshield. More like an outline in shadow. The face looked down and all I could see was the dome of a head. The person was vaguely familiar, but I couldn't put my finger on why. I felt it more than saw it. I'd seen just enough to know the person wasn't Moretti, Stone, or the two toughs.

This was someone else who had a reason to follow me. I was running out of friends and replacing them with enemies.

The face came up and the binoculars back to its eyes. Then he brought a cell phone up to his mouth. A social call, or was he telling a superior I was down for the night and he was clocking out?

I needed to find out who was in that Impala and who he was working for, but I had to move quickly.

I slid back down below fence level, put the binoculars in my backpack and edged my way to the back corner of the yard. Zelda, my neighbor's miniature beagle, sniffed at me under the fence. She knew me well enough not to bark and probably missed her occasional playmate, Midnight. She wasn't alone.

I scaled the fence, out of view of the street, and dropped down into my neighbor's yard. Zelda shimmied up to me, her ass wiggling as much as her tail. I didn't have time to play. I went though the yard and over another fence into the backyard of a house that sat on the street behind mine. There was a light on over a patio in front of the lawn I now stood on. A dog started barking inside the house. Roared was more like it. I'd heard the roar before, but had never seen the dog connected to it.

A sliding glass door opened on the left side of the house, and a dog's head appeared at chest level. An American Mastiff. The head alone was the size of a pony keg. I didn't stick around to see its body. I shot around the opposite side of the house and heard the beast howling and thundering along the patio. Then a man's voice.

"Zeus, what is it?"

I launched myself onto the fence to the front yard and jack-knifed over it. I hit the ground and sprinted down an empty street with Zeus's Baskerville howl echoing through the night. He and his master had given up the chase in their backyard, but I didn't stop running until I got to my car.

I got in and backtracked the path I'd taken earlier that night, going an extra block on the street behind my house before I turned up onto Clairemont Mesa. I couldn't risk my car being spotted if the man in the Impala was sweeping my street though his binoculars.

Traffic was light and I pulled into the section of the mall that fingered off at a right angle from the one opposite my house. I drove up to the corner where the fingers met, paused at the stop sign, and looked over to where the Impala had been parked.

The space was empty.

I scanned the lot and caught brake lights at the far exit. Too far away to tell if it was the Impala, but I had no other options. I goosed it toward the car, which turned left out of the parking lot onto the main road out of the mall. Fifty yards away, my headlights hit the car broadside.

The Impala.

It turned right out of the mall onto Clairemont Mesa and veered into the left turn lane at the stoplight that fed onto Clairemont Drive. The light was red. I had time to catch up. I exited the parking lot, but had to wait for passing traffic before I could get behind the Impala. The light turned green and my target turned left. More traffic. The light went to yellow. I shot out through a narrow gap in traffic and made it through the intersection on the red.

The Impala was half a block ahead of me. I closed to within ten or twelve car lengths and kept it there. Just another pair of headlights in the rearview mirror. I followed it down Balboa Ave and across Mission Bay Drive.

I was in Pacific Beach now, Clairemont's big brother, and La Jolla's red-headed second cousin.

The Impala turned right on Lamont Street, and by the time I made the turn it was gone. I took a chance and turned right at the next cross street. I saw brake lights die up ahead in the tiny parking lot behind Lamont Street Grill. The door to the Impala opened and a face emerged as I passed behind it. A face I knew and had hoped never to see again. The mustache was gone and there was less hair on his head now.

But it was him.

Jim Grimes.

Detective Jim Grimes, Santa Barbara PD. The man who'd tried to put me behind bars for Colleen's murder.

Muldoon's

Chapter Twenty-Nine

Detective Grimes.

Why the hell was he in San Diego tailing me? Had something new come up with Colleen's murder? Even if it had, he wouldn't be running a solo operation in San Diego Police Department's jurisdiction. Grimes was by the book. He'd go through the proper channels. Staking me out alone in another PD's backyard wasn't proper in anyone's book.

No, there was some other reason he was here that had nothing to do with Colleen or the Santa Barbara Police Department. Whatever the reason, I was the target. And of all the men who now had me in their crosshairs, Grimes scared me the most.

He hadn't liked me from the start. Even before he thought I was a murderer. I was young and cocky and he was older and old school. Plus, he knew about my father, and I'd sensed he felt rotten apples fell from rotten trees. I'd bumped up against him at cop softball games way back when I was a rookie on the force. A lot of leg lifting and marking territory by both of us. He never mentioned my father, but I'd felt it in his attitude from the beginning. I was tainted and it was just a matter of time until my defective genes got the better of me.

I parked and followed the detective down the sidewalk. He'd turned the corner and must have been headed for the front door of Lamont Street Grill. I peeked around the corner and caught a glimpse of him just before he disappeared through the gate that opened into the restaurant's enclosed courtyard. He had a leather portfolio in his hand.

I knew Lamont Street well. It was the restaurateur's restaurant.

California comfort food prepared expertly. And the chef knew his way around a stockpot. His tomato garlic dill soup was a pool of crimson heaven. But dinner would have to wait. I had to find out if Grimes had come here for a quiet meal alone or to show someone the contents of his portfolio. No doubt, it had a file in it with my name on it.

I took a quick glance though the window in the gate before I opened it. A flash of outside diners, but no sight of Grimes. I entered the red brick courtyard that had seven or eight dinner tables. Half of them had diners. None of them were Detective Grimes. I scanned the windows that lined the main indoor dining room. Not there either.

I went up the steps under the wooden trellis and entered the restaurant. It opened onto a narrow foyer with a tiny hostess station just outside of the kitchen. A tan, blonde woman, probably just hours removed from the beach a few blocks down, welcomed me to the restaurant.

I quietly told the hostess I was waiting for someone and didn't want to be seated until she arrived. There were two dining areas I hadn't been able to see from the patio. One was down the steps from the foyer to the right and the other was in a separate room to the left of the hostess stand. Entering either would probably raise the heads of semiobservant diners. Especially if one of them was a cop.

I headed for the bathroom to the left of the kitchen and just past the entry into the small dining room next to the hostess station. I peered into the room over my shoulder and caught a glimpse of the back of Grimes's head. And the front of someone else's.

Timothy Buckley. Melody's lawyer.

The two of them were sharing a table and probably Grimes's report on me.

I went into the men's room and locked myself inside the lone stall, in case either of them needed to pee. The walls of the stall closed in on me like the bars of a jail cell.

Grimes and Buckley? What the hell was going on? Was Grimes

moonlighting for Melody's defense team in hopes of turning the case onto me and finishing the job he'd started back in Santa Barbara? It didn't make sense. If he was down here to put me behind bars, why wouldn't he have teamed up with the La Jolla Police Department? Maybe he'd retired and become a P.I., now free to pursue me on his own.

Whatever the reason, Grimes was sitting with Buckley right now relaying what he had on me. If Melody and Buckley had agreed to let Alan Fineman lead the defense, whatever Buckley had would make its way into Peter Stone's hands. If Grimes had followed me to the storage facility today, Stone would soon know it. I doubted anyone but me knew that Adam Windsor had a space there. But if I could get the woman in the office to talk, Stone's pros could too. They'd just be more direct about it, and when the woman was done talking they'd know that I'd been inside Windsor's unit.

My cell phone buzzed in my pocket. Muldoon's again. Somebody there really wanted to talk to me. Maybe Turk had my money or wanted to beg me to take my job back. Fat chance. I answered anyway.

"Rick!" Pat's voice was a hot sizzle. "You gotta come down here. There's some weird shit going on."

"I don't work there anymore." I tried to sound aloof, like the words didn't hurt coming out of my mouth. But they did. "Call Turk. It's all his now."

"What!"

"Turk fired me this morning. Didn't he tell you?"

"No! He said you were taking a few days off."

"Well, he fired me. So I can't help you." I spat the words out hard and jagged, trying to spread around my pain. But Pat didn't deserve to be the target. "Sorry. Hope it all works out. Thanks for the hard work you put in over the years. I'm sure I'll see you around."

"Rick, listen. Something's going on." Fear clung to his words. "Turk brought a couple of big dudes into the bar and told me we were lending them some liquor and beer. They took half our premiums. Ketel One, Black Label, JD, Courvoisier, everything. Two full boxes and four cases of beer. Then they went into the kitchen and came out with a couple cases of prime rib and filet mignon. When they left, they took one of the sofas in the hall. People were sitting on it, waiting to be seated for dinner and Turk asked them to wait in the bar. Then he just took off without a word. We've got a wait and Kris is in the weeds trying to work the hostess station and seat people all by herself."

I had Pat describe the men who came in with Turk. They didn't sound like my earlier attackers. Maybe this didn't have anything to do with me. Maybe Turk had either lost his mind or was selling the restaurant one piece at a time. That might have explained his behavior this morning. It didn't mean I had to care or could do anything about it. I had my own worries, starting with Grimes and Buckley in the other room.

"Rick, we need your help."

But I did care. I'd given the restaurant almost half my adult life. I'd hired every employee who worked there. They'd depended on me, not some absentee owner who'd decided to give the store away. I still had ten grand invested in Muldoon's. It might take a lawyer to sort out the legalities if Turk didn't come up with my money, but right now the restaurant needed me.

Finding out what Grimes and Buckley were up to would have to wait.

"Run a half-price special on all house liquor and draft beer." I left the stall and peeked out the bathroom door to make sure Grimes and Buckley weren't looking, then bolted though the front door and out of the restaurant.

I still had the cell phone up to my ear as I hustled along the sidewalk to my car. "Have the dishwasher and a busboy center the remaining couch so there's not a gaping hole there. Make sure Hector vacuums around where the old couch used to be. Give me a list of the premiums you think we'll run out of. I'll borrow them from Alfonso's and be there in fifteen minutes."

After he gave me the list, Pat asked, "Rick, what's going on?"

"Don't worry. It's under control," I lied.

Muldoon's

CHAPTER THIRTY

I got to Muldoon's by eight fifteen p.m. All three of the remaining sofas in the front hall were full of customers waiting to be seated for dinner. Busy, even for a Friday night. Some of the guests' eyes flashed wide, fingers hit smartphone keypads, and whispers hissed in the hallway when I strode into the restaurant. My life had turned into a giant fishbowl and everyone had now seen me crap in the water. But judging by the headcount, maybe my infamy was good for business.

I was famous just by virtue of being in the news and online. Good or bad, it didn't matter, you just had to be seen. Welcome to the United States of Celebrity. Maybe I should start selling my own line of cologne.

Kris and I quickly got the wait list under control, and Pat now had what he needed to make it through the night in the bar. I had to comp a few drinks and desserts to soothe some customers' jangled nerves, but, hey, the liquor and food costs were no longer my concern.

Kris did her job efficiently as always, but her smiles and conversation were saved for the customers. Me, she kept at a distance. My rough handling of Eddie Philby last night, coupled with the newspaper's finger-pointing, had shoved a wedge between us. The little sister-like affection I used to see in her eyes had been replaced with uncertainty and disappointment.

Celebrity is overrated.

Things had slowed down enough by ten to let Kris go home. She left with a rushed "Good-night" and without eye contact. I withstood the side-glances and the whispers of customers with practiced stoicism as I stood alone at the hostess stand. This wasn't my first swim in the fishbowl.

At ten thirty, my stoic facade sprung a hairline fracture when Peter Stone walked though the front door of Muldoon's. Overdressed in Italian silk, he showed me his dead-eyed smirk. Violence leaked from my eyes, but I quickly smoothed them into a flat stare. Best not to show your cards to the guy holding the rest of the deck.

"Stone." Murderer, possibly. Asshole, unquestionably.

"Rick. Delightful to see you." He looked at the bandage on my arm and the scab on the side of my face. "My, it looks as if the world has turned ugly on you. That must be discomforting."

"No goons to hide behind tonight, Stone?" I gave him a smirk of my own. "How courageous."

"Of course, you know all about courage. Don't you, Rick?" He stopped at the hostess stand and looked down at me. "A simple man's blunt instrument."

We stared at each other for a while to keep from peeing on the other's leg. Finally, Stone broke the silence.

"It's that everyman earnestness that's going to do you in, Rick." He showed me his teeth. "A conscience is a dangerous thing."

I had no idea what he was talking about, so I just kept up the stare.

"Have you spoken with our lovely Melody, now that she's a free woman?"

I didn't say anything, but he must have read surprise in my eyes.

"Oh dear." A hand over his heart. "You relay the message to Melody's lawyer about Alan Fineman taking her on like a good little errand boy, and she doesn't even call you to thank you when he gets her bail reduced? Yes, the world has certainly turned ugly for you, young man."

He could have been lying, but I doubted it. I had the feeling Stone used lies to get what he wanted and the truth to inflict pain. If Melody was out of jail, maybe she knew about Buckley hiring Grimes to tail me. Maybe she'd even given her approval.

Maybe my world had turned even uglier than Stone thought.

"You in for dinner, Stone? Drinks?" I was tired of being the stupidest guy in the room. "The band's on a break. You might be able to find some single women you can bully before they start up again."

"Rick, you never disappoint." He gave me the full Great White smile. "When I take over ownership of this dinosaur, I might just keep you on for your wit. Every kingdom needs its court jester."

The joke was on him. I didn't even work there anymore.

"I'm here to see Mr. Muldoon," he said. "The real owner."

His barbs had lost their sting, and I was tired of the game. I was tired of Stone, period. But because of Melody and Muldoon's, he'd wedged his way into my life. If I admitted I had what he wanted and would give it to him, would he go away or sink his hook deeper?

Or just erase me like someone had Adam Windsor?

"Turk's not here tonight. I'll tell him you dropped by the next time I see him."

"He'll be here." Stone swept around behind me and headed toward the bar. "Tell him I'm waiting."

Ten minutes later, Turk walked through the door and proved Stone correct. He didn't look happy to see me. I wasn't happy either. He was drunk. Not staggering, but his gait was wide and his eyes were red. Turk was mostly a happy drunk, but could turn mean quickly with the right impetus.

If I didn't light the fuse, Stone would.

"What are you doing here?" He leaned into the hostess stand and blew hundred-proof breath at me.

"Someone had to be here after you walked out." I nodded my head at a couple who came in behind Turk and headed for the bar.

"Don't tell me how to run my restaurant!" His voice boomed off the walls in the entryway. The band had started up again covering most of Turk's volume, but heads nearest the entrance of the bar turned.

This could get ugly.

I grabbed Turk's arm and tried to guide him to the front door. He shook my hand off, but followed me outside. A group of people stood in the courtyard smoking, so I went to the lookout spot behind the restaurant next to lawyers' offices. Turk trailed behind.

The ocean lay dark and infinite below, a cracked mirror to the night sky. Off to the right, the calm waters off La Jolla Shores lapped up onto the long, smooth swath of sandy beach. Dead ahead, the coastline turned jagged creating La Jolla Cove between saw tooth rocky cliffs. Waves crashed against the cliffs, patiently imposing their will.

I put my back to the lookout's metal railing and braced for Turk's arrival. When he got to me, he had a lit cigarette in his mouth. Further proof that he was drunk.

"I thought I fired you this morning." The cigarette bobbed in the corner of his mouth as he spoke out the other side.

"What the hell's going on, Turk?"

He pulled the cigarette from his mouth, let go a halo of smoke, and rested his barrel forearms on the railing.

"It's not your concern anymore." A hint of sadness took the place where I'd expected anger.

"Whether or not you fired me, I owe you for hiring me in the first place." A lump surprised me in my throat as I flashed back to the day Turk had offered me a job when no one else would even talk to me. "But you owe it to the people working in there to do things right."

He hit his cigarette and looked out at the water, but stayed silent.

"You've got that Vegas slimeball waiting in the bar to talk to you and two goons walking out of the restaurant with booze and a couch." I pointed back at Muldoon's. "Is Stone shaking you down? What's this all about?"

His head dropped and he stared at the ground.

"My old man started this place forty-two years ago." His voice, a rumbling groan. "My mom told me later that he didn't know a thing about the restaurant biz at the time. But he was an Old-

Country Irishman and wouldn't listen to anyone. By sheer hard-headedness, he figured out how to make it work."

He straightened up and clutched the railing with his hands, his eyes blank, starring inward. "I worked here every day as a kid and swore that when I was old enough, I'd leave here for good. When I got the scholarship to UCLA I thought, 'I'm done with this place.' Then I got out of college and went to see the world. Did you know I was running with the bulls in Pamplona when my old man died?"

I nodded. I'd heard the story before, but I let him go on. I didn't mind hearing it one last time.

"I was running for my life from cattle, and Pop died of a heart attack while carving them into steaks." A crooked smile contorted Turk's mouth. "At least God has a sense of humor. Anyway, my sister didn't have any interest in the place, and my mom couldn't run it by herself but refused to sell, so, fifteen years later, I'm still here."

"So now you can sell it to that asshole Stone and get back to running from the bulls and whatever else is chasing you." The words didn't come out bitter, just matter-of-factly.

"It's not that simple." Turk dropped his eyes. "Stone's going to tear Muldoon's down and put up a luxury hotel. He got the town council to approve zoning and he's already bought out these guys." He pointed to the lawyers' offices next to us. "Everybody would lose their jobs. Because of me."

"Then don't sell to Stone. Wait for a buyer who'll keep Muldoon's a restaurant." But I couldn't argue with Stone's acumen. This was prime La Jolla real estate, and he could charge an heiress's trust fund per night for a room.

"I can't." He flicked his cigarette over the railing onto the concrete staircase below and walked past me.

I grabbed his arm again, and he turned toward me. This morning didn't matter anymore. The words, the fight, the firing. Turk had been my best friend for twenty years. He'd been my family when I didn't think I had one anymore. He was hurting. He needed help. I couldn't let business, or anything else, get in the way of that.

"Tell me what's going on, Turk. We can figure this out together."

"It's too late." He tried a smile that never rose from a frown and his eyes went watery. Then he squeezed my shoulder and walked back into Muldoon's.

I trailed behind him wondering how he'd gotten himself into a hole that only Peter Stone could dig him out of. Turk's vices were varied: women, booze, and the risk of bodily harm when challenging the call of the wild. But he kept them all, except for the last, on a short leash. He'd had many girlfriends, but no children out of wedlock, and all his exes were still friends. He was a steady drinker, but rarely went on benders, and probably hadn't had to apologize the morning after to anyone since college.

The physical risk taking was another matter. I once watched him climb barefoot, without the protection of a rope, up an eighty-foot face while coming down from a mushroom buzz. That was back in college, but that part of him never grew up. I'd heard of more recent daring tales from his current climbing buddies.

But none of his weaknesses could put him in a situation where he had to sell Muldoon's in a hurry. Goons walking out of the restaurant with their arms full of product had the stink of a loan shark or bookie. Interest collected from an unpaid debt.

Gambling.

Del Mar was just ten miles up the road, but I'd never known him to bet the ponies at the track. I'd gone to Las Vegas with him once, and he'd spent more time trying to roll showgirls in the hay than dice at a craps table.

The only gambling I knew about was a few years back when we used to pool our resources and bet on college bowl games with a local bartender who acted as a small-time bookie. The most we were ever down was six hundred bucks and we halved that by winning a bet on the Rose Bowl. I quit two years ago when I finally realized the futility of betting on college kids with a month off between games. We never talked about gambling after I quit. I'd just assumed that Turk had done the same thing.

It looked like I'd been wrong.

A few minutes before eleven, Turk and Stone exited the bar single file. Turk, head down, walked by me and out of the restaurant without a word. Stone trailed him, head up, shark smile, king of the world.

"I look forward to talking with you again soon, Rick." He breezed by me, then glanced back over his shoulder. "Very soon."

The smile was gone. A flicker of malice gave life to the dead eyes.

Muldoon's

CHAPTER THIRTY-ONE

At eleven thirty, I went into the bar. The band was on a break, so I could lean over the bar and talk to Pat without shouting.

"You're going to have to close the restaurant down alone tonight." I had to make it to the Greyhound bus terminal before midnight. Besides, I'd given Turk my keys that morning. I couldn't lock or unlock anything anymore.

"No problem." He glanced around the bar like he was checking to make sure no one was listening to our conversation. Then he leaned closer to me and spoke in a low voice. "I thought you said Turk fired you."

"He did. I'm just not sure it stuck," I said.

"What's going on with him?"

"I'm still trying to figure that out."

"He came into the bar with some Wall Street dude and sat in the corner." Pat's eyes widened with concern. Stone did that to people. "Turk just stared down at the table the whole time. The other guy did all the talking."

"I think Turk got involved in something that got out of control." I kept my voice low and pushed closer to Pat over the bar. "When I figure out exactly what it all means, I'll let you know."

"Is the restaurant in trouble?"

"Possibly, but keep that to yourself for now. No need to get everyone nervous."

I turned to leave, but Pat's hand on my arm stopped me. "Believe it or not, I did just hear some good news."

I didn't think such a thing existed anymore. "I'm listening."

"A buddy of mine, Skip, bartends down at Manuel's." Pat

smiled for the first time all night. "He called me about an hour ago and said that LJPD set up a drug sting in the restaurant and just busted Eddie Philby for selling blow in the men's bathroom."

"Breaks my heart."

"Thought you'd appreciate that. Maybe your YouTube video bouncing Philby outta here last night woke the cops up."

The memory of my Manson-eyed glare on video took the luster off the only good news I'd received all week. I left the bar without another word.

I still had Adam Windsor's laptop in the trunk of my car. It wouldn't do me much good until I either figured out its password or how to override it. In the meantime, I needed a safe place to hide it in case someone came looking again. The pay lockers at the Greyhound bus station in downtown San Diego seemed far enough away and untraceable enough to suit my needs.

The bus terminal was on the bottom floor of an ancient mud-colored brick building on Broadway in downtown San Diego. Next to the modern glass-and-steel edifices that had sprung up around it, the building was an odd remnant from a passed-over era.

There were a surprising number of people in the terminal at eleven forty on a Friday night; young mothers shepherding flocks of kids, greasy haired Euro-students, and muttering homeless souls with vacant stares, smelling of whiskey, urine, and the tail end of life. Everyone was waiting. Waiting for loved ones. Waiting for a midnight bus ride to the next town with a cheap motel. Waiting to die.

I used to drop my dad off here when I was in high school and later home from college for the summer. My mom would get tired of his drinking and threaten divorce if he didn't stop. He'd take a bus up to Bakersfield and stay with his sister to dry out. I'd come back and pick him up a few weeks later after he'd sobered up. His eyes would be clear then, but there'd be a shame in them that I'd hated as much as the drunken anger they held before he'd left. The last time he got on the bus, he didn't come back for six months.

And that had been in a wooden box.

The terminal had changed a bit since I'd last been there fourteen years ago. 9/11 had changed a lot of things. The inner part now had a waist-high fence around it with a sign that advised that no one was allowed inside without a bus ticket. The pay lockers were inside the fence in the far left corner of the terminal. A single security guard patrolled the premises. Neither the fence nor the guard looked too formidable.

I went through the gate and was greeted by the guard. I told him I needed to use a locker, and he waved me through. That was post 9/11 security at the Greyhound bus terminal. Maybe I just didn't look enough like a terrorist. Or maybe a run-of-the-mill murder suspect didn't rate a pat down. No complaints.

The bus lockers were the kind that take cash or a credit card and spit out a paper receipt with a numerical code instead of a key or combination. They cost six bucks a day. I didn't know how long I'd stash the computer, but I didn't figure to go broke for at least a week or two. I put the computer with its case into the locker. The birth certificate and the ledger were also inside the computer case. I'd seen what I needed from them. Now it was just a matter of hiding the evidence for safekeeping while I figured out what to do with it.

My cell phone buzzed in my pocket just as I exited Highway 163 onto the 805.

Melody.

I debated not answering it. If I hadn't answered her call for help five nights ago, my life would be a whole lot different now. It would be normal. Routine, unexciting, safe. The life I'd needed and gotten used to after Santa Barbara and Colleen. The life I'd never be able to go back to now.

"Melody." The name felt like an anvil falling from my mouth.

"I hope I'm not calling too late." The warm gravel. It still tugged at me, even after everything that had happened. "I tried you at work, but you'd already left."

"I heard Fineman got you bail," I said.

"He's a godsend."

I didn't think even Stone would consider himself a god. Maybe a fallen angel. Like Lucifer.

She continued, "He got the judge to grant a hearing this afternoon and to reduce bail to two hundred fifty thousand dollars." I heard the slosh of liquid and then an exhale. Wine? Champagne in celebration of freedom? "I had to empty my savings and then go begging to come up with the twenty-five thousand dollars for the bail bondsman. I'll figure out how to pay everyone back after we win the trial."

"So with Fineman taking over, did you let your other lawyer go?" Maybe Grimes had tailed me and reported to Buckley for some reason other than Melody's defense.

"No, he's second chair to Mr. Fineman." Hesitant. "Why?"

"No reason." Except that it meant that the man who'd arrested me for murder eight years ago was reporting to an active member of her defense team. Was she aware of this? "Is Fineman using his own investigators or hiring freelance?"

"I leave the details to Mr. Fineman. Why, Rick? What's going on?"

"I just want to be sure that you've got good people working for you." I'd already said enough. I didn't want to tip off Grimes and Buckley that I was on to them. Not yet. "Doesn't it bother you that Fineman is working at the behest of Peter Stone?"

"It did at first. I almost didn't agree to have him take over. But after I met him, I felt much better." Another sip of whatever a beautiful woman out on bail drinks. "I know Peter must have his own agenda. But I trust Mr. Fineman and feel confident he's going to convince a jury that I'm innocent."

By casting the shadow of guilt over me?

I got on Highway 52. Four miles from home, my former sanctuary.

"Go with your gut." Mine was going in two different directions. Trust Melody and follow feelings that made me fall for her in the first place. Or run and don't look back.

"Rick. I want to see you." The gravel was rich and languid. "Tonight."

"I thought you'd be back in San Francisco by now." The feeling side of my gut was pulling hard, but I tried to ignore it.

"Mr. Fineman asserted our right to a speedy trial. It's in ten weeks. He thinks the DA has a weak case and doesn't want to give her time to make it stronger." A long slurp. "I'm staying at the Marriott. I could be at your house in ten minutes. We could— talk."

Back in Melody's arms. Even with all the background noise, it was the only place I'd felt like the man I once was in a long time.

"I don't think I can tonight, Melody." I wanted to. I wanted to wrap her in my arms and believe that the feelings of our first two nights together were true and everything else didn't matter. Or was this another ploy to get the flash drive and key she'd left behind? But I knew I was too weak right now to trust myself. "I'm awfully tired. It's been a long day. For both of us. Sorry."

"I understand." But I could tell by the hurt in her voice that she didn't. That she'd just needed someone who cared about her to hold her tonight. Someone she could trust. "Good night, Rick."

I couldn't trust either one of us.

Muldoon's

CHAPTER THIRTY-TWO

I still had a VCR hooked up to my TV. I had all the new gadgets, too. A flat screen, a DVD player, and a DVR. But I kept the ancient VCR for the one tape I only watched once a year.

Twenty-three minutes of Colleen. From the trip to Lake Tahoe when I proposed to her. It was already October and I hadn't watched it yet. Maybe this would be the year I finally stopped.

I popped the tape I'd taken from Windsor's storage unit entitled, "Melody" into the VCR, sat down in my recliner, and braced for the worst. I got it. The time stamp was two years earlier than Angela's, and the room and bed were different. But everything else was the same. Same camera angle. Same heroin needle between the toes. Same decayed life. Only this time the naked woman was Melody. Younger, pale, skinny, with faraway raccoon eyes.

And worse was still to come. Men, money exchange, rough, degrading sex.

When I'd first found the tape, I'd expected something like this. But it still gnawed a hole right through me. Had any of my time with Melody been real? Or had I just been another john, paying for sex with my protection, affection, and trust? Had I been that easy a mark? My face flashed fire. This was the first woman since Colleen I thought I might be able to love. A used-up heroin whore who still traded her body to get what she needed.

Or maybe she'd changed and the woman on the eleven-year-old tape wasn't Melody anymore.

Everyone's done something in their life that they wished they could change and try to forget. Some big, most small. All could be forgiven by God. All but one by man. But few sinners had their sins enshrined on videotape or shown on prime-time TV. Melody and I had that in common. Mine, what the media had convicted me of, was unforgivable. Melody's just hadn't been exposed yet.

Melody had to know about the tape. She had the flash drive of Angela Albright and the key to the storage locker. She'd probably already destroyed the drive that Windsor was surely blackmailing her with. Could she have gotten it away from Windsor without killing him? Didn't seem likely. But were the images really worth killing to keep out of the public domain?

Melody was on the cusp of an anchor position on the local news in San Francisco. After that, maybe network. She had the looks, the brains, and the pipes. A sex tape of her hooking and shooting heroin could derail all that. Or could it enhance it? In Celebrity America, it wasn't so much what you did, just that you were seen. She'd be seen. Virally. And even if it went bad at first, things could flip around.

The tape was eleven years old. After the initial shock, people would see Melody as a rags-to-riches story. The gutsy woman who pulled herself out of the gutter and went on to stardom. Even if she lost her job, there'd be a book deal, maybe a Lifetime movie, and a better job somewhere down the line. If she could handle the embarrassment, the tape might be a bigger break than she could have ever imagined.

Surely, Melody would have worked that all out in her mind instead of killing Windsor. But she still had the Albright tape and the locker key. Those were facts that couldn't be overlooked. She had to have gotten them somehow. When she did, Windsor had either been dead or alive.

I started fast-forwarding through the tape, only hitting play with the introduction of a new john. I didn't have to see the acts and couldn't stand to. Voyeurism loses its appeal when you're watching someone you know. And care about. Instead, I focused on the other men, trying to recognize any of them on the eleven-year-old videotape.

According to one of Muldoon's regular customers, Adam

Windsor had started his life as a blackmailer whilst a teenager when he tried to shake the man down on a construction site. By the time he started running women, he'd refined his trade. He hadn't taped Angela and Melody years ago in hopes that he'd be able to blackmail them in the future if they ever went straight. That had been sheer luck. His targets when he made the tapes had been the men and women, the johns and janes, who'd shared their bodies with, and inflicted their cruelties on, Angela and Melody. Maybe after he got out of prison, he'd put the finger back on some of his old victims, along with the new ones. The old ones were the wild cards in his murder.

I was forty-five minutes into the tape before I got a hit. The man on the screen was the only one shown who didn't pay. And the only one dressed as a cop before he wasn't dressed at all.

Boss Goon.

The block of granite who'd come looking for Melody in Muldoon's on Monday morning, who'd ambushed me, and who'd worked security during Mayor Albright's speech on stage with Chief Parks at the rec center. A cop. Former. I thought he'd been working for Stone, but he may have been solo. He had his own past that needed burying. He'd gotten a freebie from Melody on the tape. Could it have been in lieu of his normal payoff from Windsor? I'd already made Moretti for Scarface. Could the goon be Stamp, the other name in Windsor's payoff ledger?

Even if he was, why kill Windsor? The statute of limitations had surely run out on the crimes exposed on the tape and in the ledger. The hard boy didn't strike me as a guy who cared much about a bad reputation. He wasn't a cop anymore, he was muscle. He probably thrived on a bad reputation.

Good or bad rep, he was still a suspect. Right up there with the Albrights, Stone, and now Moretti.

And Melody.

I fast-forwarded, the sex acts a blur. The fast twitch movements had a numbing effect, but couldn't quite dull the pain caused by watching them. It was after one a.m. I didn't know how much more I could take, but forced myself to watch on. I slowed for a new john and sped up again. A minute later a spurt of red flashed on the screen. I paused the tape. The man, fetal, held his side, blood caught in mid-ooze between his fingers, Melody above him, her arm frozen in a downward arc, a knife in her hand.

Sweat boiled out of me, my breath went staccato. I fumbled the remote and found the rewind button and went back to the beginning of Melody's encounter with this new john. Shaved head, mid-thirties, fit. Not the kind of guy most people would picture with a prostitute. I was an ex-cop. I knew the world was full of all "kinds." The sex had started rough, but that wasn't unusual. Most of the men on tape with Melody had gotten off by abusing her.

A few minutes in, the man threw Melody onto her stomach and then yanked her head by her hair and she rose up on all fours. As on the other tape, this one didn't have sound but I could tell the man was shouting at Melody. He continued to wrench her hair and as her head whipsawed around the camera caught her face. Wide-eyed terror and her mouth contorting around the word, "No!"

The man pushed her face down onto the bed and thrust up inside her. Anally.

This wasn't role playing, or an agreed upon upsell for another hundred bucks. This was rape.

Melody's face grimaced, but her right hand shot forward and curved under the front end of the mattress and came out with the knife. She slashed it back behind her and plunged it into the man's side. I could almost hear his shocked shriek though the soundless tape. He rolled off Melody and balled up, blood running through fingers clutching his punctured side. Melody reared up and buried the knife in his chest, her face a demented mask. She pulled the knife out, the blade running red, and again cocked her arm for another stab. Her arm started to guillotine down and the static camera angle caught the flash of a door opening off to the left. Then everything went black.

I fast-forwarded and got nothing but the static of erased videotape and then rewound to the last image on the screen. The door had only opened a few inches before the tape cut out. I could only make out a blurred hand on the outer doorknob, not the person connected to it. But it had to have been Windsor. He must have been watching the live feed from another room and had rushed to intervene when things turned bloody. It looked like he'd been too late.

I dropped the remote, tilted back the chair, and stared at the static and saw nothing but the world turned upside-down.

Self-defense? With the first stab, yes, the second a stretch, after that, jail time. What had become of the bald man? Was it assault, manslaughter, or murder? Only Melody and Windsor knew for sure, and he wasn't talking anymore.

This changed everything. Melody now had motive that put her at the top of the suspect list. If she'd killed the bald man, Melody could still get her book deal, but it would be from behind bars. There was a statute of limitations on celebrity, not murder. When the spotlight dimmed, Melody'd still be in a cell. Where would I be?

I was sitting on evidence vital to a murder case. Evidence that I'd stolen and a case that the cops wanted to make me a codefendant in, not a witness. But a one-night sheet wrestle with a woman I'd never met before was a stretch for motive. If I walked into the Brick House tomorrow with the "Melody" tape, the cops might not care how I got it. They'd be happy to hammer in the final nail on Melody and keep the town council from closing them down.

I pulled out my phone and stared at Melody's number. One chance for her to plead her case and make me believe in her again? I thought of the woman I'd fallen for that first night, and then of the lies she'd told and the bloody knife in her hand.

I put the phone back in my pocket.

CHAPTER THIRTY-THREE

I woke up the next morning still seated in the recliner. The TV was on and James Cagney was standing on top of a high platform, the world aflame around him, shouting, "Made it, Ma! Top of the world!" Then everything blew up.

I knew how he felt, but from the other end. I had dynamite in my hands and I had to figure out how to get rid of it without blowing myself up. Not that easy, but it was time to quit playing hero and try to escape the whole Melody affair with as little damage as possible. Time to turn over what I'd taken from Adam Windsor's storage locker to the police.

Dropping stolen evidence from a murder case off at the police department didn't figure to be as easy as making a deposit at an ATM. I needed legal advice. I fished Elk Fenton's card out of my wallet and called his number. Seven o'clock on a Saturday morning must have been too early for him. I left a message on his voice mail to call me.

I had to be at Muldoon's in half an hour. Except I didn't. Not anymore. Turk hadn't offered to hire me back last night and after watching him leave Muldoon's with Stone, I didn't think there'd be a restaurant much longer anyway. I went into the bathroom to take a shower. Might as well start off my new life clean.

My house phone rang just as I stepped into the shower. I went naked into the living room to answer it, thinking I must have left Elk Fenton my home number instead of my cell. I picked up on the fourth ring.

"Rick. Heather Ortiz." She didn't wait for a hello. "Do you

care to comment on Detective Tony Moretti's comments in the *U-T* this morning?"

"I don't read the newspaper." But today, I'd have to. I hung up.

I went into the bathroom, wrapped a towel around my waist, then retrieved the morning paper from the front porch. The Windsor murder case carried Heather's byline and was still front page news. The article covered Melody's release on bond, the upcoming trial date, and a brief biography of the lead lawyer, Alan Fineman. The story continued on page A-7 and that's where my name showed up. Detective Moretti was asked if Melody's arrest had cleared me as a person of interest. He said, "We're still investigating the possibility that Miss Malana did not act alone."

Not exactly an exoneration. I scanned the rest of the article, looking for more bad news. I didn't find any except for LJPD. The mayor of La Jolla and the town council had decided to put to a public vote their desire to disband LJPD and the DA's office and farm out law enforcement to San Diego County's Sheriff Department. The expense of putting on a high-profile case forced the politicians' hand. Heather closed the article editorially, stating that anything less than a conviction might sway the public to the mayor and council's point of view.

The vote couldn't come soon enough for me.

I dropped the paper and sat down in the recliner. Suddenly, turning over what I had to the police wasn't such a good idea. If they thought I was dirty in Windsor's murder, I could be handing them my connection to it. I'd have a hard time explaining how I'd gotten possession of blackmail material that was motive in the case. It'd look like I was either Windsor's partner, murdered him with Melody, or was working a blackmail angle on my own. Admitting I'd stolen the evidence from Windsor's storage locker might be my best outcome.

With my history and LJPD's waning job security, I might be too big a prize not to pass up. I had to find a plan B.

I looked at the television. It must have been a marathon crime film weekend on AMC. I'd fallen asleep to *The Shawshank Redemption*, awoke to *White Heat*, and now *The Godfather* was on. Nice weekend to be unemployed, unless the police wanted to implicate you in a murder, you were being tailed by an ex-cop, and the woman you'd fallen for was probably a murderer. Twice.

I stood up to go take my interrupted shower and it hit me: *The Shawshank Redemption*. There'd been something about the movie that I'd told myself in a semiconscious state last night to remember. It hung just out of reach, but my mind told me it was important. The movie was about a man who goes to prison for murdering his wife. Obviously, close enough to home to spike a reaction, but that wasn't it. It had something to do with Adam Windsor and the clothes the inmates wore in the movie. Then I remembered. They'd had their Department of Corrections numbers on their shirts.

That was it. The DOC number. The only form of identification Adam Windsor had had for the last nine years before he was let out of prison three weeks ago. The number he saw every day on his shirt. Certainly, he'd known it by heart. Could he have used that as his password for the new computer he'd gotten when he got out of prison? I needed to see what was on that computer before I could figure out a plan B. Worst case, I'd destroy all the evidence and sever any further connection to the case.

I went into my office, booted up my computer, and pulled up the Nevada Department of Corrections website. It had an inmate search engine that required either the full name and date of birth of the inmate or his NDOC number. I punched in Windsor's name and date of birth, which I'd gotten from Heather Ortiz's first article about his death. The search came up empty. It must not have worked for released prisoners. I knew that a cop could get the DOC number, but I certainly didn't have any friends on the force. But I knew someone who did.

I found the business card in my wallet and called the number listed.

"Heather, Rick Cahill."

"I hope you're calling to apologize for hanging up on me." Not where I wanted to start.

"I'm sorry." I tried to sound sincere.

"Not believable." Still angry. "What do you want?"

"Off the record?"

"You're trying my patience." A pause. "Okay. OTR, for now."

"I need Adam Windsor's Nevada Department of Corrections inmate number."

"Why?"

"I can't tell you that, yet." Probably never.

"You don't seem to know how this game works, Rick." Pedantic, like a elementary school teacher. "You ask for quid and you offer me quo."

"I got better than quo." I paused to give her time to swallow the hook. "Police corruption."

"That's a little too general."

"Then I'll get specific, you find me a couple of cops from LJPD or San Diego with the nicknames Stamp and Scarface and I'll give you evidence that they were on the take for a known criminal."

"I need more than nicknames and a known criminal."

Heather was a reporter. Her only allegiance was to the story. Maybe after working the cop beat for a couple years, she'd grown somewhat sympathetic to the police, but I doubted she'd let that get in the way of a front-page story. She wasn't an ally, but with the police and Stone on my ass, and with Turk's back to me, she was the closest thing I had. Plus, she had access to information and information was my only weapon right now.

In the end, I might have to give her everything I'd taken from Windsor's locker and let her break it front page. I'd have to trust my freedom to her fidelity to the journalistic credo of protecting one's sources. For now, I'd investigate on my own, and give Heather just enough to keep her interested and willing to trade.

"I only know the nicknames, but they were on Adam Windsor's payroll ten years ago."

"Ten years ago?" I was losing her.

"It's in a ledger. I can show it to you."

"How did you come across this ledger?"

"I can't get into that right now."

"You know that withholding evidence in a murder investigation is a felony." A DA cross-examining a defendant.

Plan B could put me in the same cell as plan A if Heather decided to turn our little chat over to Detective Moretti. Another smart idea turned stupid.

"I'm not withholding anything. I have access to a ledger that proves police corruption." At least that was my take so far. "I'm certainly not going to turn over evidence to the cops until I figure out which of them are corrupt."

"I need more."

I had something else to give her. "See what you can find out about Louise Abigail Delano. Born November 19, 1979 in Elko, Nevada, to Elizabeth Nelson Delano. No father on the birth certificate."

"What's this have to do with police corruption?"

"I don't know. But it might have everything to do with who killed Adam Windsor. He had possession of the birth certificate and he would have been ten at the time the child was born. I doubt he was the father."

"Too cryptic, Rick." Back to stern teacher. "You've got to give me more than that."

"You'll get more when you give me Windsor's NDOC number." My phone beeped, but I let it go to voice mail. "I need to know I can trust you before I give you more. If the cops knock on my door with questions about what we talked about today, you'll never see the information I have that could keep you on the front page above the fold for weeks."

Silence again. Longer this time. "All right, Rick. I'll play it your way for now. But if I find out you're yanking my chain, your name will be in the paper every day until the trial is over. I'll play up your connection to Windsor's murder every chance I get and I'll tell the police what you've told me."

"Fair enough." I'd rolled the dice and now I had to make six, the hard way. Craps was not an option.

I hung up and checked my voice mail. Stone's voice pulsed in my ear. "Rick. I hope you're not still sleeping on such a fortuitous day. Meet me at Brockton Villa for breakfast at nine o'clock. You're not yet aware of it, but your life has changed. You have the opportunity to make it for the better." A pause. "Or worse."

The line went dead.

CHAPTER THIRTY-FOUR

I spent the next hour fast-forwarding through the Angela Albright tape I'd taken from Windsor's storage locker. It didn't contain any scenes that I hadn't already seen on the flash drive. Like the tape of Melody, it was obviously the master that the images on the drive had been transferred from.

I gathered the tapes and the flash drive and put them in my backpack. Then I went into the backyard and peeked over the fence. The morning marine layer pushed low and damp to the ground. The day hadn't yet awakened, but the purple Impala was parked in the lot across the street again, directly opposite my house.

Back inside, I called Yellow Cab and told the dispatcher to have a taxi pick me up in front of the UPS Store in Clairemont Town Square in ten minutes. I had two stops to make and one tail to lose.

I strapped on the backpack, exited my house, walked down to the corner, and took the crosswalk over to the mall. I scanned the Impala through the edges of my sunglasses, but only saw shadows behind the tinted windshield. Still, I felt eyes on me, watching. I passed by the lot where Grimes was parked and continued toward the Vons grocery store in the next section of the mall. Ten seconds later I heard a car door close behind me. I fought the urge to glance over my shoulder. The play was to let Grimes still think that I didn't know I had a tail.

I entered the Vons, cut down an aisle, and hurried to the back of the store. No Grimes, yet. I ducked through the employees only door into a storage room next to the meat section. It was dark and cold. Wooden pallets and plastic crates were stacked up in rows next to a large walk-in refrigerator, three times the size of the one in Muldoon's.

There was a loading dock somewhere that opened up to the outside at the back of the store. I just had to find it. I squinted through the darkness and kept moving north until I found the loading dock in the far corner. It had a big corrugated metal door that opened via a chain pulley system.

Except the door was padlocked to a loop at the base of the frame.

"Can I help you?" An irritated male voice spooked me.

I turned and saw a guy in a white butcher's coat with matching paper hat. He was more round than stout. The meat guy.

"You're not supposed to know I'm here." I tilted my head and gave him narrow bureaucratic eyes. "I'm with corporate and we're doing spot safety checks. Unfortunately, I've already found a violation." I pointed at the pallets and crates stacked next to the walk-in. "That is not proper storage of packing material."

I would have felt more authoritative with a clipboard in my hand and no backpack looped over my shoulders.

"Hey, I just cut meat." He waved his hands in front of him like a Broadway dancer. "You need to talk to the produce manager."

Apparently I didn't need a clipboard. "Get him."

Meat guy went out the door into the main store, and I scurried along the back wall looking for another exit. Fifty feet down from the walk-in, I found a couple square wooden doors waist high off the ground. Ten or so empty restaurant-size gray plastic garbage cans were lined up next to the doors. I pushed the doors and they opened outward and the gray morning seeped though the opening. I stuck my head out and saw an over-stuffed Dumpster eight feet below.

To the right, across the back parking lot, a Yellow Cab was parked in front of the UPS Store. I put one foot up on the ledge, then heard the door to the store open.

"Hey!"

I leapt through the opening and landed on a bag of something hard that twisted my ankle and bounced me onto the asphalt parking lot. I hit and rolled and came up gimpy.

"Hey! Stop!"

I shuffled toward the cab and glanced over my shoulder back at Vons. Two heads and one raised fist showed in the opening I'd just leapt from. The cabbie fired the ignition just as I opened the door. The car jerked forward and I dove in. The driver pounded the brakes, and I slammed against the back of the front seat.

"Get out!" Voice tight, Middle Eastern accent, frightened eyes in the rearview mirror. "I no want trouble!"

I didn't either. Sometimes you couldn't avoid it.

"No trouble." I took three twenties out of my wallet and dropped them into the front seat. "Let's go."

"I no want trouble." Less adamant, but foot still on the brake.

I casually checked the Dumpster doors at Vons. Shut. The manager either had a story to tell over lunch, had called the police, or was coming around back to investigate on his own. If the cops showed up and searched my backpack looking for stolen groceries, they'd find something more interesting. If they connected the dots with the homicide dicks, I'd be on my way to the Brick House, and the charge wouldn't be shoplifting.

I dropped two more twenties over the seat. No trouble didn't come cheaply. "Greyhound bus terminal, downtown."

The driver eyed me in the rearview mirror, and we still hadn't moved. Then the car eased forward out of the parking lot onto the street.

I spent most of the fifteen-minute drive downtown with my head cranked behind me looking for the purple Impala and cop cars. I spotted a few uninterested black-and-whites but no Impalas. The cabbie waited for me while I went inside the terminal. A handful of bleary-eyed travelers stared at nothing while I deposited my backpack in the locker that already held the birth certificate, Windsor's payoff ledger, and his computer.

The secrets locked away, I went to meet with the man who might have killed in an attempt to secure them.

The Brockton Villa had been a home at the turn of the century. Not the last turn, but the one before that. It sat across from the La Jolla Cove on Coast Boulevard, at the bottom of the hill below Muldoon's. The architecture was early-California bungalow and painted white. Twenty years ago, someone bought it, renovated it, and turned it into a restaurant.

I got there five minutes late and spotted Stone at a table on the patio, overlooking the ocean. No other customers were seated outside. The inside of the restaurant was full and there was a wait. Being Peter Stone had its perks.

"Rick, always a pleasure." His hard angled face sliced through the morning breeze. He gave me the smirk and waved his hand to the seat opposite him.

I sat down.

A waiter appeared instantly at my side and handed me a menu. "Coffee, sir? Juice?"

"Water's fine. Thanks."

"Right away. Let me tell you this morning's specials—"

"I won't be eating." I flat-eyed Stone. "Thanks."

The waiter walked away like I'd hurt his feelings. Stone looked at me like I'd made his day.

"Predictable as a politician with his hand out." This time his smile reached his eyes.

"Let's cut the repartee and the breakfast and just get on with it."

"Rick, enjoy the beauty of the morning." He swung his arm toward the ocean like a slow-motion matador without a cape.

The sun had slipped through the haze like fresh orange juice through cheesecloth. Small rollers crested out beyond the cove and curled leisurely toward the shore. Seagulls and pelicans glided inches above the water, stalking their own morning specials.

It was beautiful. It was La Jolla. It would have been soothing, seated across from anyone but Peter Stone.

"Get on with it, Stone." I leaned toward him to take up some of his limitless space. "I don't have all day."

"My boy." Another smile. "After this is all over, after you've made an intelligent decision, I think I might have you come work for me. I've grown tired of yes-men."

I squeezed my lips together and shook my head.

"Right. Down to business." The smile disappeared and he gave me the dead eyes. "Your friend, Turk Muldoon, has gotten himself into some trouble with acquaintances of mine."

I didn't think he meant fellow philanthropists. This was going to be worse than I feared.

"It seems Mr. Muldoon likes to put down money against the vagaries of sport." His mouth flatlined. "Sometimes, money he doesn't have."

Just then, the waiter showed up with Stone's breakfast, Coast Toast, Brockton Villa's decadent version of French toast. It fit.

"What does Turk owe?" I braced for the worst.

Stone pulled a crib sheet out of the inside pocket of his blue blazer. An echo from a bookie past. "One hundred two thousand, nine hundred dollars."

I sat back and brought my hand to my mouth. Turk had gambled his life and the restaurant away and now the bill had come due.

"Funny how little we know about those we know best." His dead eyes examined me.

"What do you want, Stone?"

"I think you know what I want." The eyes bored into me. "I'm well aware of your excursion into Adam Windsor's storage unit last night. The police might not know, but, of course, that could change. I want everything you took. Flash drives, documents, computer. Everything."

Documents. Did he know about the birth certificate? Was Elizabeth Louise Delano the key to the whole puzzle?

"Let's pretend I know what the hell you're talking about." I wouldn't concede this guy anything. Ever. "What's it have to do with Turk?"

"Mr. Muldoon and I are partners for the time being."

He waited for a reaction. This time I gave him nothing. I'd already written off Muldoon's, but I hadn't Turk. Not yet. He'd been the only person to reach down a hand when I'd been at my bottom. I couldn't abandon him when he was at his.

Stone continued, "I have considerable influence with Mr. Muldoon's, ah, bankers. I've paid the principal off with these fellows, but they are adamant about collecting the interest. This isn't the kind of bank Washington, D.C., bails out, and they are very meticulous about their reputation. It would be a bad example to leave a debt partially unpaid. They're concerned Mr. Muldoon might have an accident rock climbing." He paused, his eyes conveying the message before the words came out. "It would be a shame if he were to break a leg or something else and not be able to repay his debt in full."

"So, I give you what you think I have, and Turk is paid in full without having to worry about falling off a cliff or something else."

"I knew under that tough-guy exterior there was intelligence. And pragmatism." He took a bite of his Coast Toast. "In addition, you'll receive a commission for help in collecting the debt. Say, fifty percent?"

Fifty grand would be a nice life raft to float on while I figured out what to do with the rest of my life. Turk would be back at square one, but he'd be healthy. Stone would destroy the Angela evidence and do what he wanted with the rest. So what? The police had their killer in Melody. The images on the videotape had shown me they were probably right. Melody'd made her choices and now she had to pay the consequences. I had my own life to restart.

"What happens to the restaurant?"

"Its fate has already been sealed. Now you're determining Mr. Muldoon's." Dead eyes with a flicker of life. "And your own. You have until nine o'clock tonight to do the right thing."

He slid a business card across the table to me. An address was written on the back. "Don't make me wait."

I limped down the patio stairs to the street and looked out over the ocean. A seagull knifed into the water and reemerged back into the sky, his beak full with the morning's first kill.

Muldoon's

CHAPTER THIRTY-FIVE

I stiff legged along the sidewalk toward the long cement staircase that climbed up to Muldoon's. I checked the street for the dark blue Impala. Nowhere. Grimes hadn't found me yet. The day was still young.

The sun had peeled away the last layer of gray and glared down at me, forcing my route into the shrinking shadows. The morning air now had a wiggle in it. The breeze blew hot and out to the sea. A mounting Santa Ana. The Devil Wind that sucked the air dry of moisture, raked an all-day itch along your skin, and induced closeted pyros to light a match.

It was the kind of day where impulse and irritation guided one's decisions. Controlled men like Stone watched from above, content to rummage through the aftermath of ruin.

Turk must have been riding the Santa Ana winds for months, maybe years. One hundred grand. How the hell had he gotten so deep? And how had I not seen what was happening? I'd been cocooned in my own fantasy of someday owning the restaurant, unwilling to face reality. Hell, I'd stopped looking at the books over a year ago. What I didn't see wouldn't hurt me. We kept the doors opened, the bills eventually got paid. Everything was okay in my closed-off mind. I had had it all figured out without a real plan. In a couple years, I'd somehow come up with the money and Muldoon's would be mine.

Even if Turk had never laid a bet, I'd still be riding the same rudderless dream when I was fifty.

None of that mattered now. Stone had sifted through Turk's ruins and gotten what he wanted. Now he figured he could hold the threat of the cops over my head and throw some cash at me and I'd give him the rest of what he wanted. Maybe he was right. Maybe everything had a price tag. Stone thought mine was freedom from the cops with a fifty grand cherry on top. But how free could I really be if I accepted money from Stone? He didn't have a badge, but he didn't need one. He'd give me a suitcase full of green and I wouldn't see the string until he tugged on it when he needed something.

When a man like Stone buys you, there aren't any refunds.

But he wasn't the only one with leverage. I had what he wanted. He'd hidden the desperation under his cool-as-Absolut-Citron-fresh-out-of-the-freezer façade. But, it crept out with the fifty-grand enhancer. Sure, in his mind he'd own me when I took the money, but the amount was too large. An over bet. He was protecting a weak hand.

I struggled up the long cement staircase, hoisting my throbbing ankle one step at a time. The sun peeked over the office building above, branding the back of my neck. The Devil Wind funneled through gaps in buildings and spat broiled gusts down onto my face.

I finally made it to the top, all sweat sucked out of me by the wind, leaving a crackling itch behind. The front door to Muldoon's was unlocked and I went inside. The missing sofa was back in its spot along the wall. Stone had made everything right again, while he made everything wrong.

Turk was cutting filets at the meat table and Juan was peeling carrots at the veggie prep station.

"Juan." Both heads rose with round eyes at the sound of my voice. "Go get yourself a Coke and close the door behind you."

Juan did as instructed, and Turk returned to cutting steaks. He kept his head down, exaggerated interest in his work.

"I just had a conversation with your partner."

Turk continued to pretend I wasn't there.

"How long before Stone tears this place down and erects himself a Trump palace?"

"New Year's Eve is our last night." His head stayed down and the words came out as a confession. "You can stay on until then if you want. You're still on the payroll. Stone doesn't know that I fired you."

"But I know."

"Then why are you here?" He finally looked at me, the freckles of his youth faded with age, his blue eyes dulled with shame.

"I don't know. This is where I used to come when I had no place else to go." I scanned the kitchen that had once felt as home as my own and shook my head. "How did you let it come to this?"

"One win and four or five losses at a time." He put the knife down and let out a long sigh like a dead man's last breath. "After a while, the losses add up and you make riskier and riskier bets to try to catch even. I never did."

"You could have come to me for help. We could have figured something out."

"You were helping. Your seven fifty a month was covering the vig until it got too high." The big man I'd looked up to most of my life shrank before my eyes. "You never owned a piece of the restaurant. You owned a piece of my debt."

I wasn't a friend, I was a mark. Maybe that's why Melody had zeroed in on me. A scarlet M that everyone but me could see.

Turk walked down the hall to the office, returned with an envelope, and handed it to me.

"We're square."

The envelope was thick with bills. I looked inside and saw hundreds. Ten grand worth.

"Where did this come from?" Was he already skimming off Stone's investment? A dangerous practice.

"What does it matter? You're paid in full. You got out what you put in, Rick. That's the best deal anyone can get."

Maybe he was right. Take the money and run.

I left the kitchen without saying goodbye. One last spin around the dining room and lounge for memories. I turned to leave the lounge when a void over the bar caught my eye. The Irish bagpipes.

The Muldoon family heirloom meant for the son Turk hoped to have someday. The only thing of value, financially or emotionally, left in Turk's life. Gone. Sold to cover a debt. And I'd been holding the IOU.

The envelope stuffed with hundreds felt heavy in my hand.

I went back into the kitchen and over to the meat table where Turk still stood cutting meat.

I set the envelope down onto the table. "Buy the pipes back."

Muldoon's

CHAPTER THIRTY-SIX

I stood under the awning on the top step of the staircase that led up from Muldoon's to Prospect Street. The Santa Ana had wiped the sky clean of clouds, clearing the way for the unblinking stare of the sun.

I needed wheels. My car was still at home, probably under the watchful binoculars of Detective Grimes. Cab companies kept records of their fares. They might not have names, but they had locations, destinations, and times. And cabbies could give descriptions of their fares. I'd already given one cabbie something to remember me by. I didn't want a whole fleet of them to be able to give my travels to the police if the time came. I pulled my cell phone out of my pocket.

Kim answered on the second ring.

"I hope you're not calling to take Midnight home. He already feels like my best friend."

"No. But I am calling to ask another favor." As I said the words, it struck me that Kim was on the wrong end of our friendship. I took, she gave. Had it been that way when we were together? I didn't remember asking for much back then, but I didn't remember giving very much either.

"Name it."

Still ready to give without reservation. The guilt edged deeper, but it didn't stop me from asking once more.

"Can I borrow your car for a few hours?"

"Sure, I'm just relaxing around the house, talking to your dog. He's a good listener. Is your car in the shop?"

"Not exactly." I wouldn't lie to her, but I wouldn't tell her more than I had to, either.

"Ricky, are you in trouble?" Her voice pinched high. "Do the police still think you might have something to do with Adam Windsor's murder?"

"I don't know, but I need you to know that I had nothing to do with it."

"Of course you didn't." Quick, loud, allegiant. "I believe in you, Rick." Softer. "I've always believed in you."

It was nice to know I still had one person in my corner. Especially if the police found what I'd stashed in the locker at the bus station. I thanked her, and told her where she could pick me up.

Heather Ortiz called while I waited for Kim.

"Rick, meet me at the UCSD library in an hour." Her voice didn't have the command of her words. She sounded less confident than she had earlier that morning. "Bring the ledger you claim is Adam Windsor's and the birth certificate."

"Why the library?" It seemed like an odd choice for a clandestine exchange of information. The University of California at San Diego campus was in northern La Jolla. The library was an architectural focal point and sure to have plenty of students around, even on a Saturday.

"Well, it's convenient. Do you want to do this or not?" More edgy than angry.

"Make it an hour and a half." I hung up before Heather could object.

Heather wanted to meet in a public place. Maybe she was afraid to be alone with me behind closed doors without potential witnesses around. Or maybe she'd gone to the police after our conversation this morning, and they'd be there waiting to arrest me with the incriminating evidence. The extra half hour would give me time to surveil the library to make sure I wasn't walking into a blue ambush.

Heather's and my exchange of information had initially been based on trust. Right now there wasn't any on either side. I needed

Heather. She could use the power of the press to expose the truth hidden in the bus terminal locker. If the cops wanted me, that exposure might be the only thing that could keep me out of jail. But only if Heather didn't reveal me as the source. If she'd already gone to the cops, I'd never be able to explain Windsor's blackmail booty in my possession. I'd either have to get a lawyer or run. Maybe both. First, I had to find out where Heather stood.

A few minutes after I got off the phone, Kim pulled up in her green Rav4. I stepped out from under the awning and the sun seared down into me and sent in the razor-clawed Devil Wind.

I hopped into the car and was embraced by the cold blast of the air conditioner and Kim's smiling green eyes. They were bright emerald and their beauty always stunned me on the first glance after an absence. Her blonde hair was pulled back in a ponytail, full lips opened in a smile. She wore shorts and a tank top that showed off her tan, toned legs and arms. She looked like the tomboy next door who blossomed into a full-grown stunner.

Turk had called me an idiot when I broke up with Kim and told me I'd regret it. He'd been right on both counts. But when he asked why I'd done it, I couldn't come up with a decent answer. Still couldn't, not even to myself. Maybe it was because she wasn't Colleen. Or maybe it was because she was too perfect, too nice, too willing to accept me and not see the man I really was.

She was just too damn good, and I'd never measure up. It didn't seem to bother her, but it did me.

"Where to?" Kim asked as she pulled away from the curb.

"Back to your house so I can drop you off."

"Why don't you let me chauffeur you around?" Her hand dropped with measured casualness onto mine. "I've got nothing better to do today."

Her touch was warm under the cool of the air-conditioning. An inviting memory. The offer was tempting. It'd be nice to spend time with someone who was unconditionally on my side for a change. When I got past the guilt, Kim was easy to be around. She was smart and had always been a good listener, even when I didn't have much to say. I could have used her advice right about then. I could have used it the instant I met Melody. If I had, I probably wouldn't have had to borrow her car to go pick up blackmail material I'd stolen from a dead man's storage locker so I could trade it with a newspaper reporter for more information.

But the water had already crested that bridge. I didn't have a choice to go back to a normal life.

"That's a nice offer, Kimmy. But I'd better go solo on this one."

She waited for an explanation. I didn't give one.

"How's Midnight?" I needed to get us on a different track.

"He seems to be back to full strength." She patted my hand. "He spends most of the day staring out the front window, waiting for you to come back. Sometimes I sit there with him."

She squeezed my hand, then returned hers to the steering wheel. I didn't have an answer to her loneliness, only to his.

Muldoon's

CHAPTER THIRTY-SEVEN

I did a couple circles around the Greyhound bus station before I parked. No one appeared to have followed me. Inside, I opened the locker and took out the backpack with the ledger and birth certificate, leaving behind the tapes, flash drive, and Windsor's computer. I stashed the backpack in the rear compartment of the Rav4 and took off for my meeting with Heather Ortiz.

UCSD is located atop a mesa above the coastline, wedged between Interstate 5 and multimillion dollar homes. The Geisel Library was named after the man who gave us Dr. Seuss, a genius heard through a child's ear. The library sits in the middle of campus like a mother ship from a superior race, or a giant spider with a thousand rectangular eyes. I parked well back down the street, and hoped none of those eyes were looking at me.

I'd arrived twenty minutes early. Enough time to do a quick recon. Parked cars and eucalyptus trees gave some cover on the street, but the area around the inverted spider-legged base was flat concrete and grass with low shrubs in the back and a sunken patio in the front. I did a slow wide circle on my gimpy ankle and didn't see any cops. Of course, they might be waiting inside, but I'd left my backpack in the Rav4 that belonged to Kim. If they arrested me, it wouldn't be because they found evidence on me.

I held my breath and entered the library. Nobody jumped from behind a pillar and told me I was under arrest. I went up the elevator to the fourth floor where I could look out over the parking area through one of the spider eyes.

At five minutes to noon, Heather emerged from her Miata. She was alone. I watched her until I lost sight of her entering the library. I stayed at my perch for another couple minutes to make sure the cops hadn't thrown her out as long bait. Nobody followed her on foot and no black-and-whites or detective slick tops showed up. So far so good. I went downstairs and found Heather waiting in the lobby, facing the entrance.

"Heather."

She tensed at my voice and quickly turned.

"You scared me." Her brown eyes scanned me up and down. Not a come-on, a search.

"Why? Weren't you expecting me?" My antennae went full mast. I three-sixtied the lobby. Still no police bolting from the shadows.

"Of course." She tried to play calm, but she couldn't hold my eyes. "I just didn't expect you to already be inside."

"Your meeting. How do we play it?"

"You don't look like you came prepared." She put a hand on the strap of the leather bag hanging from her shoulder. "I thought you had something for me."

"I'm prepared."

"Okay." She let out an irritated sigh and shook her head. "Let's go up to the fifth floor. We should be able to find a private study room there."

"Wait for me outside the elevator on the fifth floor. I'll be there in five minutes."

I broke through the lobby and out the front door, hearing Heather's surprised, "What?" over my shoulder. I hustle-gimped up the stairs to the street where I'd parked Kim's SUV. Still no sign of cops or cop cars. It looked like Heather had played it neutral for now. The cops on one side, me on the other, her story in the middle. Fine, as long as she stayed there.

I grabbed my backpack out of the rear compartment and went back to the library. I took the elevator to the fourth floor and then the stairs up to the fifth. I circled around to the elevator. Heather was there with her back to me, facing the elevator doors. Alone. No cops. Still neutral.

"Heather."

"Shit!" She turned, her brown curls sailing, her face a snarl. "Why do you keep sneaking up on me?"

"I'm not sneaking up, Heather." I tried a smile. "We're just taking different paths to the same place."

"Don't get philosophical on me, Rick." Her face loosened. "It doesn't fit the profile."

"Yours or the police's?"

I expected a witty retort. Instead a frown tugged at Heather's mouth. "Let's go find someplace private."

There were small study rooms along the northwest wall of the fifth floor. We found an unoccupied one just back from the corner. Heather took a step inside it, but I went to the occupied room with a window next door and paid two students twenty bucks to switch with us.

I held the door open for Heather while she came in and sat at a small table against the wall. I sat opposite her, affording me a view through one of the windows to the parking area to the west. From there, I should be able to spy on the cops, Grimes, or someone worse if they tried to sneak up on me.

"What was that all about?" Heather asked.

"I like the view."

I pulled off my backpack and set it on the table. She did the same with her shoulder bag, then pulled out a pen, notepad, and handheld tape recorder.

I picked up the tape recorder, removed its batteries, and set it back down onto the table.

"Notes, yes. Tape recorder, no." I kept my voice friendly, as anger bubbled in Heather's eyes. "No need for my voice on tape or my name on notes. I'm anonymous or this ends right here."

Her eyes settled down and she studied me for a long time before she spoke. "If you're innocent, you're playing a dangerous game, Rick."

"I am innocent."

"Then why not turn over what you have to the police?"

"The police haven't always been fair with me." I looked toward the parking area. All clear. "I'm hoping for better treatment from you."

Heather studied me some more. She gave me a flat poker face, but I got the feeling she was hiding something. Something I needed to know. My antenna stayed up. That fence Heather was straddling might be leaning over to the police's side. If I pushed her on it, both feet might just fall into their camp. If I didn't push at all, she might end up there anyway. I needed to get all she was willing to give me now and move on. I'd figure out what to do with it later.

"Time to trade, Heather."

"Okay. Let's see this ledger you told me about."

I opened my backpack and pulled out Adam Windsor's payoff ledger and set it in front of me on the table, just out of Heather's reach.

"Windsor's Nevada Department of Corrections number first." I pulled a pen and notepad out of my backpack that I'd picked up at a Walgreens on my way over from the bus station.

Heather rolled her eyes and then opened her notepad and read the number off to me. I wrote it down, then slid Windsor's ledger over to her. She studied it quietly for a few minutes, scribbling down a few notes. Finally, she closed the ledger and looked at me.

"There's no mention of what the dollar amounts are for, and the nicknames could apply to anyone, not just police officers. In fact, there's no mention of the police anywhere." She pushed the ledger back at me. "This is hardly a smoking gun. If I took this to my editor, he'd put me back in the food section tomorrow."

"You can't tell me you don't know what this is." I slapped my hand down onto the ledger, thankful that I'd made Heather give me the NDOC number before I showed her the payoffs.

"Sure, this could be a record of payoffs made to police officers." Her hands went up in supplication. "I just can't prove it. Neither can you."

"You're an investigative reporter. Go investigate." I raised my eyebrows and my voice. "Did you even try to find information on cops nicknamed Stamp and Scarface?"

"Yes." An angry hiss. I'd struck a nerve. Good.

"And?"

"What about this birth certificate? Did you bring that?"

"Yes, but you haven't told me everything you know about Stamp and Scarface."

She measured me for a couple beats, let out a sigh, and then flipped back a couple pages of her notebook. "Okay. There was a cop who worked for LJPD who was nicknamed Stamp."

"Built like a brick shithouse with a blond crew cut?"

"Yes. Do you know him?"

"This is where you show me yours and I show you mine." I tapped the ledger and then leaned across the table. "If this thing breaks ugly, your byline will be page one above the fold for weeks. Probably get picked up by the wire services. 'Corruption in the Jewel by the Sea' or even better, 'Paradise Lost.' Some bullshit like that. Maybe even get you some talking head TV time. I can help get you there, but you gotta help me too."

"What do you get out of all this, Rick? What's your angle?"

I glanced out the window and saw a red-tailed hawk rise out of the canyon with something furry and limp in its talons.

"I stay out of jail."

"That's it?" She cocked her head and gave me raised eyebrows. "You wouldn't get even a little satisfaction bringing down LJPD on corruption charges after they retired your father for the same offense?"

"My father's epitaph was written long ago. Nothing's going to change that. Tell me about Stamp."

She gave me a poker face again. I gave it back.

Finally, she looked down at her notes. "Robert Heaton. Retired from LJPD years ago. Came from NYPD ten years before that. The rumor is that he used to wear a big gold ring with the initial 'H' on it. Supposedly, suspects he arrested sometimes had bruised 'H's

stamped on their bodies. Thus the nickname. He was quietly asked
to retire from both departments. He's a PI now. Discreet Investigations of La Jolla."

I'd been right. The head goon was the bad cop in Windsor's
ledger. Stamp Heaton. I thought of my own bruises and Heaton's
threats. He'd eighty-sixed the ring and the "discreet" part of his
investigations when he worked on me. "Who was his partner fifteen years ago?"

I waited for her to say Tony Moretti. The Pacino-size Scarface
with the cleft lip scar hidden by a mustache.

"Jerry Manley. Retired last year."

I tried to hide my disappointment.

"What does Manley look like? Any scars on his face?"

"No."

"Was Heaton ever partnered with Tony Moretti?" I wasn't
ready to give up on my theory yet. Maybe she had the chronology
screwed up.

"No. Why?" She seemed to be trying hard with the poker face
again, but her eyebrows wandered upward and her eyes followed
after. "Do you think Detective Moretti is somehow involved?"

I thought about telling her about the break-in, Midnight's poisoning, and the stink of Moretti's cologne on my carpet. But I held
it in. The mention of Moretti's name made her tense. I thought
back to the Windsor murder scene at the Shell Beach Motel and
Heather's demeanor while questioning the detective. The easy fa-
miliarity between the two. Possibly more than acquaintances?
Then back to the day Moretti and Coyote grilled me at the Brick
House. Heather had been the only reporter who knew I was there.
Her inside information had to have come from somewhere.

Moretti.

Sweat popped up on the back of my neck.

"How long have you been sleeping with Detective Moretti?"

Her face went crimson and her eyes hit the table. A denial now
would have been an insult. "This was supposed to be about police
corruption."

I had too much to risk to worry about the propriety of infidelity. I needed an edge. "Does his wife know?"

The red in her face turned to anger and her eyes went tight. "Are you going to blackmail me now, Rick? Is that what this is all about?"

"I need to know if you told him about our meeting today."

Her silence was my answer.

I grabbed the ledger, stuffed it into my backpack, and stood up.

"Rick, wait. It's not what you think—" Her cell phone donged in her bag. She pulled it out and looked at a text message. "Please, just wait. I have to make a quick call and I'll be right back."

She left the room and closed the door behind her. I slung the backpack over my shoulder, ready to leave, then noticed Heather had left her notepad on the table. I glanced at the door and reached for the notepad when my eye caught movement on the walkway from the parking area below. A man hurried toward the library with a cell phone to his ear.

Short. Porn mustache. An attitude I could feel five stories up.

Moretti.

Muldoon's

CHAPTER THIRTY-EIGHT

I grabbed Heather's notepad, tape recorder, and batteries, and shoved them into my backpack. Then I checked the window. Moretti was still visible, no longer talking on his phone. He'd make it to the entrance of the library in less than a minute and then up the elevator to the fifth floor. I bolted for the door, but it opened before my hand reached the handle. Heather stood in the doorway, phone in hand, a surprised look six inches from my face.

"I need to borrow your phone."

"Wha—"

"Your phone."

I grabbed it from her hand. "Thanks. Be right back."

She stood stunned, and I scrambled away from her and punched numbers into the phone while I held my other thumb on the end button. I put the phone to my ear, pantomiming waiting for a call to connect, and circled around the center column out of Heather's view. If she thought I was coming back, it would give me a bit of extra time before Moretti went on the hunt. Even if she didn't believe I was coming back, she wouldn't have a phone to warn Moretti that I was on the lam.

I put the phone in my pocket and pushed through the door into the stairwell and hyper-hobbled down the stairs. Each step, a jolt to my swollen ankle. By the time I reached the first floor, my shirt was damp with sweat from exertion, pain, and fear. I pushed through the door, eased around a corner, and waited. Ten seconds later Moretti entered the library and made for the elevator. He got in, the door closed, and I sped out of the building.

I shuffle-gimped up the stairs and across the concrete walkway to the parking area. Out from under the main body of the library I was exposed, hurrying to avoid human stares through spider eyes on the fifth floor.

I made it to the cover of the eucalyptus trees that separated the street from the overgrown canyon on the right. A rust-colored slick-top Crown Vic sat twenty yards in front of me. I froze, then ducked behind a tree trunk and peered into the unmarked cop car. Empty. Either Moretti had come alone or Detective Coyote was out there somewhere watching and waiting.

I hung behind the tree and scanned the street. If Coyote was stalking me, he was well hidden. I didn't have time to count every eucalyptus leaf or the sagebrush creeping up the rim of the canyon. Moretti would come bursting out of the library any second. Or call to alert his hidden partner.

Time to gamble. I broke from behind the tree and hustled along the street. Nobody jumped out from behind a car or out of a tree. Kim's Rav4 was still another fifty yards away. Ten feet before I came even with Moretti's Crown Vic, Streisand's "Don't Rain on my Parade" blared from my front jeans pocket. I pulled out Heather's phone and read the name of the incoming caller. "Tony." As in Moretti. Instinctively, I whipped around and checked the path to the library. Clear. He must have still been inside and realized that he and Heather had been duped.

I let Barbara keep singing and set the phone on the hood of the Crown Vic. The next time I talked to the cops would be through a lawyer.

I made it to Kim's Rav4 and exited the campus without Moretti catching up to me or being stopped by the campus police. Safe for now, but for how long? If I went home, would there be a black-and-white there waiting for me? Was there already a BOLO for my arrest cycling through LJPD patrol cars?

Nobody but Kim knew I was using her car. The cops probably hadn't ferreted out my friendship with her yet, but in time they would. Home and Muldoon's were out of the question. Kim's would be a risk.

There wasn't a safe play, so I made the only play I had. I headed south on I-5. I'd make the Greyhound bus terminal in fifteen minutes. Adam Windsor's computer was still in there in a locker. Heather had gotten me his NDOC number. It was time to see if my half-asleep epiphany of last night would work. The password to get inside Windsor's secrets.

My eyes were on the road, but my mind was somewhere else. Moretti.

Why had he come to the library alone? If it had been to arrest me, surely he would have brought Detective Coyote with him. Heather had said Moretti hadn't been Stamp Heaton's partner back when Heaton was taking bribes from Adam Windsor. But that didn't completely rule out Moretti as Scarface. He didn't have to be Heaton's partner, he just had to have been on the take. Or maybe Heather was covering for him and he had been Scarface to Heaton's Stamp.

My cell phone buzzed in my pocket. My breath caught in my chest. Moretti out for a second try? Did he even have my cell number? Easy enough for him to get it if he didn't. I pulled out the phone and checked the screen. I didn't recognize the number and let the call go to voice mail. Twenty seconds later, the voice mail tone beeped.

"Rick, it's Ellison. I got your call. Call me back right away."

Elk Fenton. He'd missed my morning call when I'd considered going to the police station with the evidence I'd stolen from Windsor's storage locker. Back when things just looked bad, but not horrible. From the urgency in his voice, things may have just gotten worse.

"Rick! Thank God you called!" Elk's voice was in my ear before the first ring ended. The normal effete goofiness replaced with red-lined gravitas.

Nothing good was going to come from this call. I fought the urge to push my foot to the floor and not let it up until I hit Rosarito Beach. Mexico. But ten-dollar lobster wouldn't taste as good if I didn't have a country to go back home to. And stealing Kim's car would be too big an imposition, even for me.

"Give me whatever it is."

I found a parking spot a couple blocks back from the bus terminal. Close enough. I figured whatever Elk was going to tell me, was better heard stopped than at full throttle while in control of two thousand pounds of steel and gas.

"I must confess, Rick. I've been following the Windsor murder investigation very closely since we talked the other night." A hint of the kid who wanted to be included slipped back into his voice. "I hope you don't mind, but I've put feelers out to some of my old contacts at LJPD and the courthouse."

"And what did you find out?"

"The DA is impaneling a grand jury Monday morning to try to get an indictment against you as an accessory in the Windsor murder."

CHAPTER THIRTY-NINE

The world went silent. Grand jury. Murder. Elk's words hung in the air. A gallows noose waiting to be tightened. I sat back in the driver's seat and stared, but saw nothing. The sun used the car's windshield as a magnifying glass. It felt like a laser cutting my heart out of my chest. The ghost of Santa Barbara had come out from the shadows. No more what ifs, no more hoping for the cops to see the truth. They had their own truth, circumstantial evidence knotted up with a wrong past.

It was Saturday. I still had two days until Monday.

Think. Work. Keep moving.

I turned the ignition on to run the air conditioner. Heat was pulsing inside me as well as out. I needed fresh air just to breathe.

"Why doesn't LJPD just get a warrant and arrest me now? Why go through the charade of a grand jury?"

"I'm sure you're aware of the precarious position the department and the DA are in with the upcoming vote on their very existence. They don't want to take any chances on a bad arrest. But," his voice grabbed the hint of a lilt, "it tells me they don't have a locked-down case either."

"They can't. I'm innocent." It wasn't a plea before a judge or a plea for help from Elk. It was statement of fact. Right now, it was all I had.

"When I worked criminal defense, I made it a practice never to ask my client about their guilt or innocence, but it always helped to have the facts on our side."

The more Elk talked, the more he sounded like a cocksure defense attorney and less like the goofy kid whom I wouldn't quite accept as a friend seventeen years ago. I think I wanted him as a friend now.

"I've got five grand in cash and no job, Elk. How much time will that buy me as a retainer?" I thought of the fifty Gs Stone had offered me, but wasn't yet sure how that was going to play out. I wasn't going to give evidence to a possible murder suspect and have him destroy it so I could pay my legal fees.

"I'll do my best to put you together with a top-notch criminal attorney. You'll have to work out your fee with whomever we get, but as I said the other night, there are a few who owe me favors. I'm sure they'll make accommodations."

"I want you, Elk."

"I'm not criminal anymore, Rick." He paused, maybe thinking it over. "I haven't tried a case in two years."

"I haven't been arrested for murder in eight. We both have some experience at this."

"I guess we do. Okay, Rick. If things don't go your way on Monday, I'm your man. We'll work out the money issue if the time comes."

"Thanks, Elk. Ah, I guess I should call you Ellison now."

"I've been using Ellison since I started practicing estate planning. I thought old-money La Jollans would think I was one of them." An amused exhale. "It is my given name, but I never realized how silly it sounded until I heard it coming from your mouth. Call me Elk."

"Okay, Elk." Niceties aside, I had to find out where I stood. "Why the grand jury now? I know the cops have my golf hat at the murder scene, but they've had that all along. Do they have something new?"

"In fact they do. A jailhouse snitch named Edward Ames Philby. He claims you contacted him the day before Windsor's death, trying to obtain heroin. The police are obviously cutting him a deal on his recent arrest for cocaine distribution."

Eddie Philby. I'd let my anger get to me and now it was pay-back time for the punk I bounced out of Muldoon's two nights ago.

Elk continued, "There's something rather odd about the deci-sion to impanel a grand jury, though. Rumor has it that Chief Parks is not on board. And that Detective Moretti went over his head, directly to the DA, because Parks wouldn't sign off on an arrest warrant."

Chief Parks on my side? Hard to believe. During my one face-to-face with him, Parks had looked at me like I was something he'd just blown into a handkerchief. Whatever his reluctance to lock me in a cage, it wasn't because he'd nominated me for citizen of the year. Something else was at play.

With his porn mustache and suffocating cologne, Moretti was a junior-size version of Parks. Going against his mentor would cre-ate a huge rift in a tiny station house. That could be career death. Was Moretti confident that Mayor Albright would be elected gov-ernor and take Parks with him, creating a void for the detective to fill? Was this an early sign to show the powers that be that Moretti wasn't afraid to make bold moves when justice was in the balance? Maybe the lone wolf routine at the library was an effort to bag new evidence that he could spring on the grand jury to further sep-arate himself from the chief.

"Philby's lie can't be taken seriously by a grand jury or any kind of jury." I squeezed the cell phone. "He's obviously dealing to get out of prison time and to get even with me for throwing him out of my restaurant. Anybody under the age of fifty has probably seen the YouTube video of me bouncing him the other night. Hell, they even showed it on the eleven o'clock news."

"In my experience with grand juries, the twenty-one to forty-nine-year-old demographic is not very well represented." He sounded lawyerly, like I was already on the clock. "It's more the fifty and above set. Successful and deferential to authority."

"Well." I was grasping for any edge now, no matter how rounded. "They probably watch the news."

"I don't want to be indelicate, Rick. But you seem like a man who takes things head-on. You did when we were younger." I heard a deep inhale and then a long exhale over the phone. "The video of you escorting Mr. Philby out of Muldoon's was not your finest moment. I wouldn't expect it to be presented to the grand jury, but it will be the invisible elephant in the room for those who saw it. We should probably hope that the jury members missed the news that night."

That edge I was looking for was as round as a cue ball.

CHAPTER FORTY

Backpack strapped over my shoulders, head on a swivel, I walked the couple blocks to the Greyhound bus terminal. The Devil Wind scraped its nails along my skin and the sun kept its piercing eye on the back of my neck the whole way. No one else seemed to take notice.

Inside the terminal, I paid my balance on the locker, opened it, and emptied all that remained inside into my backpack. Windsor's laptop, the Angela Albright tape and flash drive, and the Melody tape, joined the payoff ledger, birth certificate, and Heather Ortiz's notes and tape recorder. All the stolen booty from my recent life of crime. If the cops caught me with the Windsor evidence, the grand jury would be superfluous.

I was going to be arrested for murder. Again. The Santa Barbara police hadn't had quite enough evidence, but back then I'd already lost more than I could ever get back.

Colleen.

Now I was more innocent than I'd ever been in Santa Barbara. The police would have to fake a motive, but they had enough physical evidence to put me in Windsor's death room. They were coming for me. If not now, then two days from now. After that, I'd never make bail. I'd be in a cage until the trial.

I had two days, at most, to sift through Windsor's life and find somebody else to point the finger at and keep me from paying for my Santa Barbara sins with my freedom or my life in La Jolla.

I exited the bus terminal on foot, crossed over West Broadway, and entered Horton Plaza. The mall was five stories and six city blocks of bright colors and odd angles. It was a bit cheery and disjointing for my mood, but I waded through lazy shoppers and found the Starbucks on the first floor. The coffee shop had free Wi-Fi, and Windsor's laptop was new enough to be compatible.

I ignored the frou-frou coffees and ordered a ham sandwich and a two-dollar bottle of water. A small table in the back with a view of the front door served as an encampment. The first bite of the sandwich reminded me that I hadn't eaten all day, and I scarfed it down while I waited for Windsor's laptop to power up.

The Windows tone chimed and the password page appeared. This was it. Time to put my theory to the test. I found Windsor's inmate number in Heather's notebook and typed it into the password box. I hit enter. Dong. Invalid. I tried the numbers backward and got the dong. Next, I put the name Adam in front of the numbers. Dong.

With each new dong, I peered over the laptop toward the front door, half expecting a SWAT team to throw in a flashbang and crash through the smoke.

I tried variations of first and last name with DOC and NDOC, all over again backward and forward. Dong. Dong. Dong.

Dead end.

I slumped back into my chair and fought the urge to hurl the laptop at the wooden menu above the baristas. I'd risked prison time stupidly stealing the computer. An easy way for the cops to make a connection between me and Windsor that was never there. Now, probably the only way to keep me out of jail was to get into the damn thing and shift through Windsor's secrets.

Shut out.

The best thing to do now was wipe it clean of my prints and toss it in a Dumpster or the ocean. I stashed it in my backpack for the time being.

All I had left was Heather's notebook and tape recorder. I turned on the tape recorder and heard a low hiss like the recorder had been turned on but there'd been no sound to record. I let it run for a few seconds and got more of the same, then turned it off. Next, I flipped open Heather's notebook. It contained information on Windsor's murder and nothing else. Heather must have opened up a new notebook for each dead body she reported on. Kind of like a homicide detective and a three-ring binder murder book. One per customer.

The first page had Windsor's background and important dates. Birth, incarceration, probation, and death. Heather had written his full name down in her initial entry. Adam Nichols Windsor. She'd probably listed it in her article on his death, but I'd passed over it without remembering his middle name. I yanked the laptop out of my backpack and booted it up. When the password screen came on, I tried Windsor's full name backward and forwards with and without the NDOC number.

More nothing.

I stared at his name. Adam Nichols Windsor. ANW. I tried the initials alone and then with the NDOC number. All invalid.

Then I saw it. A&W. Root beer. A nickname he must have had to endure as a kid, and then in prison where the kids were just bigger, meaner, and the playground was fenced with concrete and barbwire. A hated nickname and prison. Two things he'd never forget. Two things that would always remind him of the people he had to get back at.

I typed in root beer and Windsor's inmate number.

Chime.

Desktop appeared.

I was in. Once it booted, I scanned his files. There were copies of the videos of Angela Albright and Melody, some violent porn, Excel spreadsheets of his payoffs, still with only the nicknames Stamp and Scarface listed, and a folder named "Empty Riches and Hard Time: The Life of Adam Windsor."

I clicked open the folder and found three separate files. One had e-mailed query letters Windsor had apparently sent to literary agents seeking representation for his memoir. James Frey with a real prison and no apologies. The query stated that he'd made mistakes, pimped women, sold drugs, and paid off corrupt cops, but had started to turn his life around when he was framed and sent to prison.

There were rejection letters in the file, but also a reply from an agent last week requesting the first fifty pages and an outline. The second file held an outline of Windsor's life and, thus, his memoir. All that was missing was the last chapter. Someone else had already written that for him. No chance for revisions. The last file was a draft of the memoir.

The outline was bare bones and chronological. Just a few lines per date. The word "father" played a prominent role, "Father Knows Best," "Wrath of the Father." "Father-Daughter Love" was way down the list right before "Framed." I wondered if Windsor blamed his life of crime on the fact that he wasn't his father's favorite. Wouldn't be the first time. Melody's name had a couple listings. "Cops on the Take" was another. The meat would be in the memoir. I shifted in my wooden chair and started to read it.

The writing was overwrought and sentimental with Windsor as victim. Rich only child who had everything but the love of his father. Every bad choice and bad deed played back to Dad's indifference or discipline. Adam owned none of it. He had the con excuse before he even became one; "It wasn't me."

I guessed that ruled out him not being the favorite. He was all his parents had. Lucky them. The Father-Daughter Love title to one of the chapters must have referred to someone else's family. Maybe a girlfriend.

I slogged through the first chapter, then scanned forward until I got to his pimping days. Windsor used to hang out on the San Diego State University campus and befriend pretty, but insecure coeds who were tight on cash. He'd get them gigs as arm candy for rich, awkward men and then introduce them to drugs. Pretty soon they were hooked and the gigs with the men went from awkward to rabid and were played out behind closed doors.

Windsor met Melody at SDSU. He set the hook so deep that she dropped out of school six months after meeting him and went to the sheets and the needle full time. He left out the important parts, like the hidden camera and the bleeding bald man. I guess some things were a little too real, even for a memoir.

He devoted a whole chapter to the cops he paid off, but he only used the nicknames Stamp and Scarface. He promised to name names in the final chapter of the book. So, Windsor was going for a double dip. First blackmail people and then out them in a memoir. Unfortunately for him, he never made it past chapter six. Hard to write when you're dead.

I already knew Stamp was Robert Heaton. He'd been the first to shake down Windsor after he busted Melody for prostitution. He'd sweated her in the back of his car until she gave up Windsor. She never went downtown, and Heaton put the squeeze on Windsor.

Scarface showed up in place of Heaton one night a year later and told Windsor that from now on he was to give Stamp two envelopes each week. One with two hundred fifty dollars, the other with five. Windsor wrote he didn't argue because Scarface scared him and because he felt an odd connection to the man. He explained it in his tortured prose:

"We both had been scarred in our youth. His scars were external, whereas mine were internal, but both left the same lasting painful impression. He took the high road as an adult and I took the low road, but we both ended up in a dirty back alley as grown men trading on the flesh of scarred women."

Scars of youth. Moretti's cleft lip, now hidden under a mustache, would leave a very visible scar, unshaven. Moretti was a bad cop then and a bad cop now. He'd gone rogue at the UCSD library, keeping his partner and his chief in the dark so he could ferret out what I had on him. He knew he could use Heather to freeze me out of the newspaper.

But the push to indict me through a grand jury didn't make sense. Was he trying to silence me? Had he silenced Windsor too and fudged up some evidence to frame Melody? He had to know whatever I had would come out in court if I was indicted and put on trial.

Unless he never intended to arrest me.

The grand jury indicts me, and I disappear to avoid arrest, never to be found.

Until someone dug up my bones.

Muldoon's

CHAPTER FORTY-ONE

Three o'clock. I had six hours until Stone expected me to hand over everything I'd stolen from Windsor's locker. None of it pointed the finger at me. Except that I had it in my possession. The only other link the cops had between Windsor and me was that he'd been in my restaurant the night before he died. Oh, and my ball cap was found in the room where he died. Three strikes. I could do the math.

I scanned the inside of the coffee shop. Still no one I recognized. The same with the tables outside. I was about to go back to Windsor's memoir when my brain hit replay.

Something was out of place.

I dropped my head so my eyes just peeked over the laptop screen and peered outside. There it was. The red light blinking danger. A man in a sweatshirt and ball cap pulled down low over sunglasses sat at a table outside. The cap was Dodger blue. Not a big deal, he could have been a tourist or one of the many L.A. transplants who lived in San Diego. The sweatshirt had been what triggered my mind's eye. It was eighty-five degrees outside with a wind chill of ninety-nine. Everyone else today was in shirtsleeves.

Flashing red light.

You might wear a sweatshirt if you were trying to change your appearance from earlier this morning. Something you did on a tail when you didn't want to be recognized.

Grimes.

The cap and sunglasses hid his face, but the military bearing I'd remembered from my time with him under the white lights in the square room was still there. I couldn't see his eyes, but I could feel them lasered on me though the mirrored lenses.

How the hell had he found me? Had he tailed me all day after I thought I'd lost him at Vons's this morning? No way. I'd have spotted the blue Impala. I had radar out for it all day. I couldn't have missed it.

But I could have missed another car while I was on the lookout for the Impala. Grimes had changed cars. Surveillance 101 and I'd missed it. He must have seen me leave the Vons's parking lot in the taxi and called the cab company to get the destination. The power of the badge.

Now I had to lose him all over again.

I pulled out my cell phone and dialed Yellow Cab. I told the dispatcher to have a taxi waiting for me in front of the Hard Rock Cafe in twenty minutes. I gave him my description and said there'd be an extra ten for the driver if he waited for me. I hung up and glanced at Grimes. He hadn't moved, but he would soon. He'd have to track me down after the fact again, but I wouldn't make it easy for him.

I went back to the decayed life of Adam Windsor. Chapter six, the last one he'd written, had him fleeing the corrupt cops of La Jolla and setting up shop in Las Vegas. Windsor worked out an arrangement with an unnamed casino boss. He'd fly out some of his college-aged girls from San Diego to play escort to whales the boss had comped in the casino. It was a win-win. The boss had access to fresh-faced call girls unknown to the local police, and Windsor could pimp women with mobbed-up protection without having to pay off Vegas versions of Stamp and Scarface.

Alas, it all went to hell when Mr. Casino stole Melody. So Stone cuckolds Windsor and his payback was blackmail over a video of him having sex with Angela before her last name was Albright?

It didn't add up, but I didn't have time to figure it out now. I powered down the computer and stuffed it, along with Heather's notebook, into my backpack. My cell phone buzzed in my pocket.

I took it out expecting to see Heather's number or, worse, Moretti's. Neither.

Melody.

"Rick." Sexy, raw gravel. The voice of a killer? Didn't matter. It still tugged at me, even after all I'd seen on videotape. "I need to see you. We need to talk."

"I'm in the middle of something."

"Tonight then. Your house."

I should have said no. Just as I should have that night she asked for my help. But I was all in now and I might be able to find out if her lawyers were going to point the finger at me. Even if my house hadn't been under surveillance, I wouldn't have met Melody there. The living room sofa, my bedroom. They were her turf now as much as mine. She'd already exploited my weakness more than once, I didn't want to give her another chance.

"Muldoon's. Courtyard. Eight o'clock." Back where it all began.

"I don't think out in the public is a good idea. Why not your house?"

"See you at Muldoon's." I hung up and left Starbucks.

Grimes stayed seated when I passed by him outside. Just a guy reading a magazine on a lazy afternoon. Ten steps past, I heard his chair push back. I walked around the mall for a while, window shopping, in and out of a couple shops, like a bored shopper, but always moving south from where I'd parked.

I checked my watch. Fifteen minutes since I called the cab company. Time to make my move. I turned a corner down one of the fingers of the mall. Grimes was at least ten yards back around the corner. If I ran now, I could lose him among the maze of shops and make my way over to Hard Rock and the cab. That was the smart play. The original plan. And the predictable one. I was tired of playing by everyone else's rules. Tired of being spied on, pursued, harassed.

I inched back to the edge of the corner I'd just rounded and waited. I bent my knees and rose up on the balls of my feet. A linebacker poised to deliver a hit. I sensed Grimes about to appear. I sprung into a fast walk and exploded my shoulder into his chest just as he turned the corner. A "whomph" blew out of him and his back hit the ground first, then his head. In football, they called that a decleater. In a mall, you could call it a cheap shot or even assault. Or, if no one knew your intentions, an accident.

"Whoa. Sorry." I reached a hand down to Grimes, a friendly citizen, sorry for the mishap. "I didn't even see you. You came out of nowhere."

A few shoppers had stopped in shock at the force of the impact, but they slowly moved along once they saw me lend a hand down to Grimes. He wouldn't take it. The jolt had knocked his sunglasses askew and one blue eye glared at me above the lens. Hatred, accusation, violence.

He reached around his back, and I suddenly feared he might come out with a gun or handcuffs. Back at SBPD, he'd worn a belt holster. He kept the glare on me and his arm movement hesitated, his hand hidden behind his back. Then he squeezed his lips together and his hand came out empty.

This time.

I kept my arm extended and let go the breath I hadn't noticed I'd been holding. Grimes rolled over onto all fours and slowly climbed to his feet. I grabbed him under his armpit to help him upright. He tried to shake my arm off, but almost lost his balance. Once he was steady again, I unhanded him.

"You should be more careful, Detective." I mocked concern. "You assumed no one was coming around the corner. Sometimes that first assumption can lead you down the wrong path."

He straightened to his full height, chest out, trying to convey the command he'd shown around the department and in the white, square room. But his cheeks and his ears burned red.

"I've been right about you from the start, Cahill." He whipped off his sunglasses to give me double barrels of hate. "One day, you'll stand before a judge for your wife's murder. That's a promise."

Anger and pain boiled up in me. That horrible night in Santa

Barbara flashed in front of me. Colleen gone forever. My life at a dead end. Justice blinded.

"Maybe if you'd done your job instead of pointing the finger at me, Colleen's killer would already be in prison." Rage, barely controlled.

"You can play that game if you want to, Cahill, but you and I know the truth." He'd regained his composure as I struggled to hold onto mine. "The polygraph, your neighbors, and Colleen's friend didn't lie. You did."

"Well, I guess the DA didn't have much faith in your case or he wouldn't have kicked me loose." I leaned toward him, invading his space. "Is that why you're here, Grimes? A chance to regain your tainted reputation? You were riding high until you pinned your star on my arrest. It's a little late for redemption, isn't it? Now that you're not even a cop anymore."

"You're on borrowed time, Cahill." He cut the space between us in half, so we were nose to nose. "You can feel it. The truth tightening down on you. That's why you're taking chances. You're nervous. You've got a backpack full of secrets that the police would love to see."

I fought my hands from going up to the backpack straps. A guilty man's move. He'd somehow caught up to me before I'd gone into the bus station. My game changer of confronting Grimes had blown up in my face. I had to get away.

Keep moving, stick the jab.

"The cops must not be interested in your theories. If they were, you'd be working with them instead of for the defense. Colleen's case gets colder and colder while you're down here playing Johnny Cochran."

"I quit the defense team an hour ago. Right after I saw you pull a computer out of that locker in the bus terminal. Strange place to keep one. Unless it doesn't belong to you." He gave me a smile that scared me more than anything that had happened in the last week. "John Kerrigan is my only client, and I've got one case. You. A whole file cabinet in my office has your name on it. John and I are going to take you down for his daughter's murder. Even if you're already in prison for Windsor's."

Grimes drop-stepped and swung his hand behind his back. I didn't wait to see whether he'd come out with handcuffs or a gun and try to make a citizen's arrest. I shot a hard right straight into his eye socket. He sat down like someone had whipped his chair out from under him. A woman's scream split the air. I blasted through wide-eyed shoppers and a maze of shops trying to find an exit from the mall. My ankle throbbed and grabbed at me. I ignored it and hit full sprint.

"Stop that man!" Grime's voice chased after me. "He's under arrest!"

A white security shirt flashed in front of me on the left. Small, young, and the fear in his eyes told me he wasn't fully invested. He reached for me and I pistoned a straight arm that caught him in the shoulder and knocked him into a kid in baggy jeans. They both went down.

His partner came around a corner up ahead on the right. The exact opposite of the kid rolling on the ground. Big, old enough to have been in some battles, and eager for more. Behind him, daylight. An exit from the mall. He knew where I was headed and cut off the angle. A straight arm wouldn't work this time and my ankle robbed me of all-out speed. I juked to my left so he'd think I'd try to evade him. The move got him on his heels just enough, and I shortened my neck, lowered my shoulder, and hit him in full stride.

Thunk. Head-to-head.

The impact knocked me dizzy and off balance, but I stayed up as he went down. I gathered myself and was back up to my limited full speed. A shuffle, huffs, and footsteps behind me. The guard was again in pursuit.

"Stop that man! He's under arrest!" Grimes's voice now echoed through the mall, losing volume.

Thirty yards away, the exit. Grimes kept shouting from farther and farther away. The huffs of the security guard were steady, thirty yards behind me. A couple of early-twenty dudes eyed me like they might make a play, but I buzzed by them before they got their hero up.

I hit the exit and broke hard to the left up 4th Avenue. Half a block to the Hard Rock Cafe. The cab was waiting and I jumped in and told the driver to roll just as the guard showed on the street. He gave up the chase, but Grimes came running out of the mall. He stopped and pulled a cell phone out of his pants pocket.

I watched through the cab's back window as he punched in a number and put the phone up to his face. I didn't have to hear the conversation to know that Monday's grand jury didn't matter anymore. There'd be BOLOs pointed at me circulating through squad cars from La Jolla to San Diego.

I had to either run for the rest of my life or stay and fight.

Muldoon's

Chapter Forty-Two

I switched cabs and the second one dropped me off two blocks from Kim's house. I didn't want the driver to have her address in case the police questioned him later. Kim looked surprised when she opened her front door. Midnight wedged past her and leapt his front paws up on my chest and lathered my chin with his tongue. His wagging tail percussioned against the open door. For a moment, I forgot that my life had turned to shit and enjoyed the homecoming.

Wind rattled the shutters on the windows and the moment passed. I checked over my shoulder for cops, PIs, or thugs, then slipped inside and closed the door behind me.

"Is everything okay?" Kim put her hand on my cheek. "You look worried."

"I need your help."

"Okay." She dropped her hand from my face and her eyes went wide with concern. "What can I do?"

"I need you to rent a car for me in your name. Your car's fine. I'll drop you by it when we get the rental."

"I'll do whatever you need, Rick." She walked over to the mahogany table in the dining room and sat down. "But first tell me what's going on."

There might already be a warrant out for my arrest. The more I told her, the more I'd put her in a position of aiding and abetting.

"If the police question you, I borrowed your car and then came back and forced you to rent me a car." Grimes had already made me in Kim's Rav4. He'd no doubt given the police the make, model, and license plate number when he called them after I escaped him at Horton Plaza.

"Rick, what's going on?" More fear than anger.

She had the right to know so that she'd at least have an option to walk away.

"The DA is convening a grand jury on Monday to indict me as an accessory to the Windsor murder. But there may already be a warrant out for my arrest."

Kim's shoulders slumped and she brought her hand to her mouth.

The words hit me as hard as they did Kim, but for a different reason. I was an albatross around her neck. First, by breaking up with her, and then staying just close enough by so she'd hold out hope and never move on. Now, I'd put her in real danger. I pulled her keys out of my pocket and dropped them on the table.

"Your car's parked on Second Street downtown, about two blocks north of the Greyhound bus terminal." I took thirty dollars out of my wallet and set it down next to the keys. "You'll have to take a cab to get it. Sorry."

I headed for the front door. Midnight fell in at my side. Head up, ears perked, he mirrored my movements, ready to go home and restart our once quiet life.

"Rick, wait." Kim got up from the chair.

I put my hand on the doorknob and Midnight growled, the hair on his back spiked, his eyes lasered on the front door.

Someone knocked from the other side. Midnight's growl grew louder. I snapped my fingers and he quieted, but his fur stayed at full alert. I let go of the doorknob, took a step back, and looked at Kim. Her eyes, green gemstones in white saucers. She walked over to me at the door.

Another knock, louder, urgent. Kim looked at me for instruction. I slid around the corner of the hallway, Midnight pinned to my side. Back pressed against the wall at a right angle to the front door, I nodded.

Kim took a deep breath and opened the door.

"Are you Kim Connelly?" The voice was familiar.

Midnight let out a low menacing growl. My hand to his face quieted him.

"Yes."

"Chief Parks, La Jolla PD."

I sucked in a deep breath. Only twenty-five minutes since I'd lost Grimes and the police had already found me.

"What can I do for you, Chief?" Kim kept her voice steady, formal. An upright citizen trying to help.

"Do you mind if I come in?" Park's voice had less of an edge than when I'd heard it at Melody's arraignment.

My hands went to the backpack straps around my shoulders. The evidence that would put me in a six-by-eight-foot cell in the Brick House hung like a target on my back.

"I'm afraid my dog doesn't like strangers. It's probably best that you stay outside." Cool, in control. A powerful side I'd never seen or maybe never noticed before. "How can I help you?"

"Maybe you could put him in the backyard while we talk." A cop pushing his badge around.

"I just watered out there. I don't want him to get muddy." She blocked the doorway, a blonde sentinel in tennis shorts. "What can I do for you?"

"Do you own a 2007 green Toyota Rav4?"

"Yes."

"Where is the vehicle now?"

"I'm not sure. I lent it to a friend." Concern lifted her voice. "Did something happen to it? Is there something wrong?"

"Who is this friend?" More a command than a question.

"Has there been an accident? Did someone get hurt?"

"Do you know Rick Cahill?'

"Yes." The knuckles of Kim's hand, still on the knob of the opened door, tightened to bone-white. "Is he all right?"

"That's up to him. Where is he?"

"I'd like to know what this is all about. You knock on my door and ask me cryptic questions and refuse to answer any of mine."

"You tell Cahill to contact me right away when you talk to

him." Kim's free hand moved forward like Parks was handing her something. "I'm the only thing that stands between him and a jail cell."

"What does that mean?" Real concern now. Her hand came back to her side with a business card in it. "Is Rick under arrest?"

"You just have him call me on my cell phone. It's written there on the card." He slowed his cadence and hit every word hard. "His time is running out. If he doesn't contact me tonight and give me what he has, I don't think I can stop this thing."

"What thing?"

"Tonight or it's out of my control." Fading away, like he'd turned and gone back to his car.

Kim closed the door, and I stepped into the foyer. The confident woman who'd held the chief of police to a draw had melted away. She looked dazed like she'd taken a shot to the chin, barely able to stay upright.

I put my arms around her and pulled her in. "Thanks."

"Rick." She pushed her hand holding Parks's business card at me, fear crowding her green eyes. "Maybe you should call him. He's the chief of police and it sounds like he might be on your side."

After our confrontation at Melody's arraignment, Parks would have had to have changed sides to be on mine now. But he'd come alone today, just like Moretti had at the library. And he'd tried to stop the grand jury that Moretti had spearheaded. There was definitely a rift between the two of them. I'd already made Moretti for Scarface, Windsor's corrupt cop. Maybe Parks had, too, and he'd figured out that I had evidence that could prove it. Could he really be my only shot of getting out of this? Or was it a trick to get me to show myself?

I took Parks's business card from Kim's hand. Maybe it was worth the gamble.

Muldoon's

CHAPTER FORTY-THREE

The gold '65 Cadillac DeVille drove like a whale in deep water. Mushy suspension and slow to turn. It had a black drop top, but I kept the lid on. My goal was *not* to be seen. Thankfully, the Caddy wasn't vintage, so I wouldn't attract any admiring eyes. Kim had borrowed it from a neighbor who was five years past driving, but who'd held onto it for chauffeured drives to the grocery store. It smelled of cat piss and baby powder, but the engine ran and it couldn't be traced back to me.

Parks already knew of my connection to Kim. The rest of the force was probably soon to follow. If they'd spread the net wide, they would have looked for car rentals in the names of my friends. The few I had left. Parks's card, unused for now, sat in my wallet. The backpack full of evidence was in the trunk.

Seven forty-five. Fifteen minutes before my meeting with Melody. Night clamped down and pushed the Santa Ana winds back where they came from. A fog had fallen into their void. I drove along Torrey Pines Road, the Caddy's jutting chin, like an icebreaker, cut through the mist. Headlights were smudged yellow orbs in the rearview mirror.

I parked down on Coast Boulevard above the ocean and across from the staircase that led up the backside of Muldoon's. Hidden in the fog, the staircase was empty and the rusted metal banisters were cool and slick in my hands. At the top, I stayed in the shadows and fog. Melody could have set me up, working with the cops and DA, to cut a plea deal. The courtyard in front of Muldoon's sat empty, too early in October for a dinner wait.

Ten minutes later, Melody emerged from the fog across the courtyard. Black pants, dark sweater, flowing midnight hair. Confident look of a television reporter instead of a frightened murder suspect. She took my breath away, and I silently cursed myself for allowing it. I receded back into the fog, a few steps down the staircase, and called her on my cell.

"Rick?"

"Take the staircase across the courtyard all the way down to the street."

"What's going on?"

I hung up and scuttled down the steps as fast as my gimpy ankle would allow. At the bottom, I hustled across the street and hid behind an SUV. I scanned both ends of the street for patrol cars or slick tops. Nothing. A few hand-in-hand couples strolled the sidewalk overlooking the ocean. No one gave off the scent of an undercover cop.

Melody emerged from the stairway. When I was sure she was alone, I stepped out into the street to show myself. She hurried over and surprised me with a long, tight hug. Cinnamon and lavender rose above the salty perfume of the ocean. Her touch took me back to the first night we met. Back to her naked body wrapped in mine. Back to the hope that I could love again.

I pulled myself back to now.

She unwound from me and her eyes held mine. Sad, yet inviting. Invitation or manipulation? Had that been the look she used with her johns? I ignored it and led her onto the sidewalk. We walked along the edge of Scripps Park, the crash of waves below us filling the night. Just another couple engulfed in the romance of ocean air.

"Rick." Melody stopped me with a hand on my arm. "I'm so sorry that I got you involved in all of this."

"Thanks, but you didn't come here just to apologize." I guided her off the sidewalk down onto the sandstone outcroppings that tiered down to the crashing waves. "What's the rest?"

"The DA is offering me a plea deal." Her voice was muffled

under the roar of the ocean. "Murder Two and I get twenty-five years. My lawyer thinks I'd be out in twelve."

"And?"

"The DA wants me to testify against you. They think you supplied the heroin that killed Adam."

Eddie Philby's jailhouse lie.

"And?"

"I'd never testify against you, Rick. Not even if I was guilty."

There were still a few weeks until the trial. The specter of life in a cell has been known to change people's minds.

I checked the sidewalk behind us. A couple paused to look out over the ocean. We walked down to the edge of the cliff, eight feet above the water. The mist off broken waves sprinkled our cheeks.

Melody was saying all the right things. Either the truth, or lies she'd rehearsed. I needed to knock her off script.

"What happened to the bald man?" The flash of red on the videotape and Melody thrusting the knife into the man's chest ripped through my mind. "Did you kill him?"

Melody's legs buckled. I grabbed just enough of her sweater to soften her landing. She sat with a thud, and I held on to make sure she didn't tumble off the cliff into the ocean. A wave smashed against the cliff and sprayed us in the face. I wiped the water from mine, but Melody let it drip off her chin.

"You saw everything?" Her voice was a raspy croak.

"Yes."

"Should I give you the sad hooker story? Or do you want to fill in the blanks on your own?"

"Whatever you like."

"You were a cop. I'm sure you've heard the sob story a hundred times." Self-contempt hung off each word. "Father molested then abandoned me as a kid. Years later, slick-talking Adam came along in place of Daddy, took advantage of my low self-esteem, and turned me out on the stroll. The tale is as old as time. Nothing unique."

"But you overcame it. That is unique." I couldn't help myself.

Melody could have remained a victim and lived a short, ugly life, but she fought, climbed out of the morass, and made something of herself.

"I had a whole new life. Then Adam got out of prison and tried to blackmail me. He showed me a flash drive he had with secret tapes he taken of me and my johns back a lifetime ago."

"So you killed him."

"No!" Raw.

"What about the bald man?"

"He haunts me in my dreams." She hugged herself like she was her own life jacket, adrift at sea. Her words came out shaky and wet with emotion. "I see that night over and over again. The knife I'd kept under the mattress for protection. The man forcing himself into me from behind. The one indignity I'd never allow. He took that from me. Then I stabbed him. Again and again. I couldn't stop. I wanted to kill him."

She collapsed into me, sobs convulsing her body. Pent-up emotion broken loose from years of control. I stroked her hair and gently rocked her. I knew what it was like to live with one horrible decision that had destroyed lives. Life moves forward, but the reverberations chase after you like yesterday's echo.

We sat huddled together. Waves crashing below us. Fog pulling the night down on top of us. Melody lifted her head up to me. Her eyes bloodshot, but unguarded.

"I never knew what happened to him, whether he lived or died."

"Why not?"

"Adam had a cop on his payroll who took care of it." She stared out into the burnt-charcoal night. "A month later, Adam and I moved to Las Vegas, and we never talked about it again."

"The cop, a big guy, blond hair, built like a truck?"

"Yes. I only knew him by the name Stamp."

So Heaton was in deeper than just as a bagman. Possible accessory after the fact. No statute of limitations for murder. Another name on Windsor's blackmail list? Another suspect with a reason to kill.

"Did you ever meet a cop Adam called Scarface?"

"No, but Adam mentioned his name a couple times. He was scared of him."

"Where did you go after you left my house that first night?" I asked. "The night Windsor died."

"I went back to my motel room, but Adam was still there." Her tan face, now pale even in the night, weary but still beautiful. "I crushed up some of my sleeping pills and slipped then into his drink. When he passed out, I took the flash drive and the storage locker key. Adam was alive when I left. I swear. Someone else must have gone in the motel room after I left and shot him full of heroin." Pain, fear, regret, in her eyes. "You believe me, don't you, Rick?"

I believed her eyes. "What were you going to do with the flash drive of Angela Albright?"

A big wave walloped the cliff and found a crack in the sandstone, shooting up a geyser of whitewater that slapped down ten feet from us.

"I started in the news business as an unpaid intern while I waitressed at night. It took me a while, but I've finally made a decent career of it." Her voice steadied. "Breaking the story about Angela Albright's past was going to catapult me onto the next level. Network. New York. D.C."

"You were going to destroy a woman who'd overcome her past just like you so you could grab the brass ring?" Maybe the only thing that had changed from the woman I'd seen on video was her career.

"That's my job, Rick. I get paid to expose the truth. No matter who gets hurt." She fixed her eyes on mine. Black marbles in a gray night. "And I was all set to do it. Then I watched the video and saw my wretched life played out all over again in Angela Albright's body. I'm not that person anymore and neither is Angela. Neither one of us deserved to have our pasts exposed."

"The nights we slept together, which Melody was that?" Did I want to hear the truth or a lie that would make me feel better?

"That first night, I was scared and you made me feel safe. I needed you on my side and I knew how to get you there." She held my eyes and touched my face. "But I came back the next night because I needed to see you. You made me feel again. Not just react and survive. I had to see if it was real. And it was. It is."

I knew what it was like to feel again. Melody had given me that. But had it been under false pretenses?

"But when you came back from San Francisco, it wasn't really to see me. You needed to get back inside my house and get the storage locker key you'd hid from the police. And tonight, you wanted to meet there for the same reason."

"Yes." She dropped her hand, but didn't let go of my eyes. "My feelings for you are real, Rick, but I have to survive. If the DA sees what's on Adam's computer, they'll have a motive and possibly another murder charge against me. I'd be lucky to get life."

"You could have asked me about the key instead of playing me. You could have trusted me."

"I've never trusted anyone." She dropped her head. "It was too big a risk to start now."

The fog pressed in closer and the ocean beyond the shore break disappeared into the haze.

"What are you going to do with the computer?" Melody's eyes had lost all their mystery. One emotion, fear.

Melody's fate and my freedom depended on what I did with that computer. If I turned it over to Chief Parks, along with what I had on Moretti, maybe he'd choose to believe me and convince the DA to drop the grand jury. Melody had put her survival first. Maybe I should do the same with mine.

But could I live with dooming Melody to life in a cell for a murder she may not have committed in order to clear myself? I knew what it was like to be judged guilty, but I hadn't yet lost my freedom because of it.

"What are you going to do, Rick?" Fragile, exposed.

"What I have to."

CHAPTER FORTY-FOUR

I sat alone in the Caddy and stared at two business cards belonging to men I wished I'd never met. Peter Stone and Chief Parks. Both demanded to see me tonight. One offering fifty grand, the other my freedom. All I had to do was show up and give them what they wanted.

Then trust them.

I pulled the items I'd taken from Adam Windsor's storage locker out of my backpack one at a time and studied them as if they possessed the answers to my problems. They didn't. They just reminded me of the mess I'd gotten myself into.

The last to come out was the tape recorder I'd stolen from Heather Ortiz at the UCSD library. I turned it on and heard the hiss I'd heard earlier that morning at Starbucks. I hit rewind and after a couple seconds Heather Ortiz's voice came on. She was talking to a Betty Brictson over a speakerphone, the recorder picking up both ends of the conversation. Heather introduced herself and explained that she was doing a story on Adam Windsor's murder.

"I don't know anything about any murder in California." Middle-aged, raspy voice full of cigarettes and hard living.

"But you do know Peter Stone, correct?" Heather sounded like she knew the answer to her own question. "He's living here in La Jolla now. Where Mr. Windsor was murdered."

"I don't see how this has anything to do with me. I don't want to be rude, but I have to—"

"But you worked as a cocktail waitress at the Starlighter Casino back when Mr. Stone was the casino manager, right?"

"Yes." Grudgingly.

"And then you left the casino when you became pregnant with Louise. That was right about the time Peter Stone married his boss's daughter and became a part owner, correct?"

The woman sucked in a harsh grab of air.

Heather'd been busy this morning after I gave her the name on the birth certificate. Betty Brictson was Elizabeth Nelson Delano. The name of the mother on the birth certificate of Louise Abigail Delano that I'd found in Adam Windsor's locker.

"I'm not suppo—I don't want to talk about that." Betty's voice was thick with emotion or a couple cocktails. Maybe both.

"It must have hurt when Peter chose his career over you and his daughter."

Stone was the child's father! The chapter title in Windsor's memoir, Father-Daughter Love. Stone and his bastard child. That's why he wanted everything from Windsor's locker. He wanted the birth certificate. But why?

Betty Brictson was silent for a moment. Then, "I miss her."

"Where is she? What happened to her? There's no record of her after her birth. Is she still alive?"

"She might as well be dead for how little contact I've had with her. I've seen her once in ten years and that was on television. She's too important now to talk to her mama." A sob followed by a line of hacking coughs.

"Who is she? What's her name now?"

"I have to go."

"Why did Adam Windsor have her birth certificate?"

Silence. No breaths. No coughs. Finally, "He was a vile human being and I'm glad he finally got what was coming to him."

The phone went dead and so did the tape.

Louise Abigail Delano. Illegitimate daughter to Peter Stone. Could she be the key to the whole puzzle? Too important to talk to her mother and only seen on TV once in ten years. She could have been any semicelebrity who flashed to the surface for her fifteen minutes and then disappeared back into the murk.

Who was Louise Abigail Delano?

Betty Brictson knew. But even if I could track her down, she wouldn't tell me. Stone knew, too, and he was waiting for me up in his mansion on a hill. But he'd take what I had and give nothing back. There was one more person who might know, but I doubted she'd talk to me either. If she did, she might have company listening in, but I didn't have any options left.

I looked out the Caddy window at the ocean below the cliffs. The fog had clamped down on the night. Water and sky wove together to form a gray shroud.

I started the car and drove though the sea of fog along Coast Boulevard. Headlights of oncoming cars smeared out into yellow halos sifted through a silk scarf. Stoplights were rainbow hallucinations. I cut back a few blocks through the soup until I hit Pearl Street and found the only gas station left in downtown La Jolla. An old phone booth sat next to the service garage.

I dropped in some coins and punched the big square numbers. Heather Ortiz answered on the third ring.

"Hello?" Low, almost a whisper.

"I guess you found your phone where I left it. Sorry about that. I didn't have time to stick around and talk to the detective." I tried to sound apologetic. Considering how she'd set me up for Moretti at the library, it wasn't easy. "I still have your notes and tape recorder if you want them back, too."

If Moretti and LJPD were triangulating cell towers, they'd be out of luck. A trace was possible, but I wouldn't be in the phone booth long enough for it to matter.

"I'll have to call you back."

I'd gotten the result I'd feared, but not the anger I'd expected.

"Wait. Before you do, did you find out who Louise Abigail Delano is?"

"No. But I found out Scarface lost his scars. Gotta go." Dial tone.

What the hell did that mean? Moretti's cleft lip scar was gone?

No, but it was now covered by his mustache. Maybe that's what she meant. She'd figured out that her bedmate was Scarface, but I hadn't found out anything I didn't already know.

I could either run, wait for the Grand Jury to indict me, or find some answers on my own. I still had Chief Parks's card, but his visit to Kim's house left me with more fear than trust. I was down to a Hail Mary. And the deity I had to entreat didn't answer prayers. He crushed them.

Stone.

CHAPTER FORTY-FIVE

Back in the Caddy, I pulled the envelope that held Louise Abigail Delano's birth certificate out of my backpack and wrote Turk's address on it. I ripped a blank page from Heather's notepad and wrote a note that the birth certificate belonged to Stone's daughter and instructed Turk to hold onto to it until he heard from me. He owed me that. If things didn't turn out as I'd hoped, if I got arrested, or worse, he'd know he had something valuable that pointed a finger at Stone. I stuffed the note into the envelope, then attached a stamp that I'd rummaged out of my wallet.

The La Jolla post office was just a block down from the police station on Wall Street. I dropped the letter into a curbside mailbox, making sure to stay out of view of the Brick House.

I'd need all the luck I could hold onto during my meeting with Stone.

Using my iPhone, I Mapquested the address he'd given me on his business card and set off. If I hurried, I could make his 9:00 p.m. ultimatum. He lived in one of the mansions populating the narrow streets that serpentined up the back of Soledad Mountain. Stunning views of La Jolla and the Pacific Ocean, out of reach of the common folk below. I recognized the house from my infrequent trips up to the cross at the top of the Mount Soledad. Unassuming from the front, its backside hung off a cliff, splayed out like a giant glass-and-copper crab ready to pounce.

A Mercedes SLK coupe sat in the half-moon driveway. I crept past through the shifting fog and parked on a side street above the house. Stone had told me to bring everything I'd gotten out of Windsor's locker, but he may not have known what everything was. I knew he wanted the flash drive of him and Angela Albright and the birth certificate. He'd get one but not the other.

I wouldn't give him Melody. Her secrets were my own for now, to be revealed later only if she took the DA's deal and flipped on me. Windsor's payoff ledger was my insurance policy against the police if they came after me without Melody's help. The birth certificate was my life insurance policy against Stone. That would stay behind, too.

I pulled the flash drive from my backpack and shoved it into my pants pocket. The backpack containing the rest of the Windsor booty went into the massive trunk of the Cadillac. The night fog was cool and heavy on my face. It seemed like days instead of hours since the Santa Ana winds had swept through town and left everything raw.

I made it to the house without being seen or ambushed. Maybe the ambush was waiting for me inside. The front door was a slab of hand-hammered bronze and loomed all the way up to the eaves. It looked like it could be lowered over a moat or open into a dungeon. My bet was on the latter.

I pounded the door a couple times, stepped back, and expected the worst. The door opened and I wasn't disappointed.

My stun-gun dance partner stood in front of me in full parade dress. Gold rings laddered up each ear, silver studs impaled through lip, and eyebrows. I had the sudden urge for a giant horseshoe magnet. The only metal missing was a stud through his nostril. That had been replaced by cotton packing to correct the nose I'd broken. I instinctively slid my right foot back a few inches and felt some flex in my knees. His mangled face lay flat, but his blackened eyes lasered violence.

The night was behind me, thick, gray, and black. One quick move and I'd be back into it. Even with my twisted ankle, I knew the kid wouldn't catch me on the injured leg I'd aerated with a paring knife two nights ago. But I stayed still and waited for round three to begin. If he made a move, I'd meet him in the middle. But he just stood there holding open the dungeon door. We stared at each other, waiting for the other to make the first move.

"Eight fifty-eight. Just under the wire." Peter Stone appeared over the kid's shoulder. Insincere smile stretched above the hard chin, shark eyes zeroed in on prey. "Luke, invite our guest in."

Seeing them together, I noticed the resemblance for the first time. Square jaws. Stabbing widow's peaks. Hard eyes. Luke's not quite yet dead, but on their way to Stone's shark stare. Take away the kid's broken nose and black eyes and the family bloodline was evident.

Father and son.

If I went inside, would I ever come out? How many holes had Stone dug back in the Nevada desert? Had he or Luke been the one who pushed the needle into Windsor's arm?

But if Stone had wanted me dead, he'd already had plenty of chances. No, he hadn't killed Windsor, not over a birth certificate. And if the certificate meant so much to him, I had leverage. It was time to trade.

Luke pulled the door open farther and stepped back. I entered, adrenaline at full pump, ready for the arm of Stamp Heaton to shoot out of the dark and lock around my neck.

It never did, but Luke stopped me with a hand on my chest. I tensed, ready to counter but Stone's voice stopped me.

"Simple precaution, Rick."

Luke patted me down, probably looking for weapons or a wire. I had only my wits. He came up empty, and motioned for me to follow his father. "Clean."

"Of course. Rick's a smart man," Stone said.

I didn't need his sarcasm to tell me that smart wasn't the proper adjective to use for someone who'd enter Stone's lair unarmed and alone. Desperate times.

Stone wore gray slacks and a blue La Jolla Country Club golf shirt. The normal waiting period to get accepted into the LJCC was about a lifetime. He'd been in town ten minutes and had somehow jumped to the front of a line where wealth was added up in generations instead of liquid assets.

I followed him across a grand marble foyer that swirled in black and white into a dark hardwood-floored living room. The entire back wall was glass and looked down on La Jolla. On most nights it must have been quite a view. Tonight it was a gray smudge.

Cold art and framed mirrors hung at sharp angles on the walls. I got the feeling Stone spent more time eyeing the mirrors than the art. Furniture: black, square, and uninviting. The room looked staged, rather than lived in. A realtor's imagination for the wealthy bachelor.

Stone stepped behind a polished mahogany bar. Luke stood sentinel at the edge of the foyer, guarding the exit. I caught his eyes, then moved mine down to his broken nose, then onto his wounded leg, and back up again. I finished the trek with a thin smile, reminding him that I'd beaten him with my hands tied behind my back. Evened up, he'd go down quicker this time.

"Yes, you and Luke have an unpleasant history." Stone's voice pulled me out of the challenge. "Young men and testosterone have a long journey to reason."

"I guess your son isn't, yet, as reasonable as you."

"Nothing gets past you, does it, Rick?" He shrugged his shoulders. "Well, I guess there's no hiding one's genes."

But I knew the last week had been all about Stone keeping the genes belonging to the birth certificate hidden. I'd use that knowledge when I had him on the ropes. Right now, we were circling and sticking jabs.

"Drink?" He held up a bottle of Macallan.

"Eighteen-year-old or twenty-five?" I asked.

"Eighteen." The same vintage I'd served him at Muldoon's that first night with Melody.

"Pass." I could use a drink, but scoring the minor point tasted better.

A genuine laugh escaped his mouth. "Really, after we conclude this small bit of business, you must come work for me." He swept a hand around the expensively decorated, unlived-in room with a view. "Even with all this, amusement is rare."

"I'll think about it." I glanced over at Luke and then back at his father. "Looks like you have good health coverage."

A low growl rumbled from Luke behind me.

"Cradle to grave." Stone poured himself a drink.

"Same go for your other employee, Stamp Heaton?" The tainted ex-cop with ties to Windsor, Melody, Scarface, and Stone. Linchpin to the whole sordid mess or bit player?

"Mr. Heaton is part time. We could work out something more permanent for you." He took a sip of his Scotch. "Come. We'll talk in my office."

Stone walked out of the living room to the entrance of a hall-way that shot off to the left of the foyer. He stopped and looked back at me when he realized I hadn't followed. Luke blocked the exit to the front door. If I broke now, I figured my football instincts could get me past an injured tough guy I'd already beaten once be-fore. I'd have room to maneuver in the open foyer. If I followed Stone into his office, the hallway walls narrowed retreat.

"Are you coming, Rick?" Stone gave me the teeth. "You didn't come all the way up here just for the view, did you?"

Stone was right. I still had a grand jury waiting to indict me on Monday. I'd come to get information that could keep me out of prison. If I ran now, I couldn't stop until I hit Mexico.

I walked out of the living room and followed Stone down the hall. Luke limped behind me. Photographs of Stone with major and minor celebrities covered the walls. Homage to his casino days in Las Vegas. There wasn't a single picture that didn't have an au-tograph on it. But there were no portraits of Stone with a wife or son.

The hallway led to an office at the far end of the house. A win-dow panoramaed around the entire left side of the room. The view matched the one in the living room. Luke stopped outside the office and closed the door behind me.

"You should feel privileged, Rick. No one is allowed in my office."

I didn't feel honored, only wary.

Stone sat down in a wingback leather chair behind a large mahogany desk. A picture frame sat directly in front of Stone, facing him. Maybe it was the one photo of someone close enough to him that a signature wasn't required. He motioned me to one of the two white-cushioned chairs that were on my side of the desk.

Stone opened a desk drawer and pulled out a thick letter envelope. He placed it next to a laptop computer in front of him and steepled his hands.

My muted phone vibrated my thigh in my pocket. It would have been rude to answer it when a man was about to offer me a wad of cash.

"I'm sure you're aware of the grand jury impanelling Monday. Fifty thousand dollars could go a long way toward securing an adequate attorney." He smiled. "Or give a jump start to someone who needed to leave town in a hurry."

I wasn't surprised that Stone knew about the grand jury. He had ears everywhere and fingers in every pocket. Maybe he'd been feeding the police information about me. That I'd broken into Adam Windsor's storage locker. Tightening the vise on me so I'd give him what he wanted and then hope to survive the courts or flee.

I pulled the tiny flash drive of Angela Albright's misdeeds out of my pocket and tossed it across the desk to Stone. He picked it up and plugged it into his laptop. The back of the laptop separated me from Stone and what he saw. I'd already seen it. A dark past best forgotten.

Life came into Stone's dead eyes. But the hard end of life. Pain. He moved his eyes over to the picture frame facing him then back to the computer screen. The pain pulled deeper. The only other emotions I'd ever seen in his eyes were malice and contempt.

I almost felt sorry for him. He looked up from the computer at me and I saw the eyes of a wounded predator. Then I felt sorry for myself.

"I take it you've seen this?" The smooth superiority was replaced by unhidden shame.

Stone ashamed of a tryst with a onetime hooker? It didn't add up. Were the eyes of the person in the photograph facing him adding to his shame?

"I didn't get any pleasure from it." The truth.

"Where's the rest?"

"What do you mean?"

"I want Windsor's computer, all other flash drives, and any original videotapes." Barely concealed anger pushed the shame out of his voice. "And the birth certificate."

Good. I'd gotten under his skin and knocked him off his cool control game. Time to push harder and see if any truth spilled out. "You mean Louise Abigail Delano's birth certificate?"

"Yes." Angry reptilian hiss. His eyes again shot toward the photograph in front of him and then back at me.

Stone might have once been a Vegas boss, but he'd make a crappy poker player. His eyes were a tell. The photo in the frame facing him was a picture of his daughter. I'd bet the fifty grand in the envelope in front of him on it.

"You mean your daughter?" I grabbed the picture frame and flipped it around.

Angela Albright smiled up at me.

Maybe I'd been wrong about the identity of his daughter. I heard a desk drawer close and looked up.

The gun in Stone's hand told me that I'd been right.

Muldoon's

CHAPTER FORTY-SIX

Adrenaline squeezed sweat out of my scalp and vacuumed a hole in my stomach.

"You overplayed your hand, Cahill." Hard stare. Rage on a strained leash. Light from the desk lamp glinted off the Kimber .45's stainless-steel slide as Stone pointed it at my chest. "You could have walked out of here with a pocket full of cash. Now—"

My flat face belied the fear raging through my body. Metalwork on the picture frame bit into my death-gripped hands. Sweat trickled from under my arms down my sides. I willed my muscles to relax and tried to slow my breathing.

"You pull that trigger and the tape of you and Angela in the sack goes viral, along with the proof that she's your daughter."

I was all in on a bluff. Time to see who was the better poker player. All I had riding on it was my life.

"I didn't take you for a blackmailer, Rick. Murderer maybe, but at least an honorable man." He squeezed his eyes down on me. "Fifty thousand dollars wasn't enough for you?"

"I don't want a dime from you. Whatever you and Angela did behind closed doors is your own business. I'm just trying to stay alive and out of prison. I leave here alive and you can have everything."

Stone studied me with predator eyes. A trace of humanity bubbled up in them. He set the gun down on the desk. I let out a breath.

"Adam Windsor was human detritus." His eyes drifted over my shoulder like he was looking at the past. "I let him run some women and drugs to my high rollers in the casino. Then I found out he was pimping his own wife, Melody. When I took her away from him and got her straight, he tried to get even."

Stone as hero. Saving women from prostitution. Even the ones he'd arranged to work in his own casino. I kept my eye on the gun six inches from his hand and listened to more of the legend.

"He must have come across Angela's mother while plying his trade. Betty had tried to blackmail me when she first had Angela. She spiraled from drugs to depravity and I never saw her or the child again for another twenty years. Then Adam Windsor came into my life."

His eyes rolled to my hands holding the picture of Angela. I set it back on the desk, facing him. The hurt was deeper now. He locked onto the photo and the pain that he'd inflicted upon others throughout his life leaked from his eyes.

"So, after you took Melody away from him, Windsor shows up with a new girl for you to try out and secretly tapes you with her." I shook my head. "Angela."

Stone had probably never talked to anyone about the darkest period of his life. Nine years with the guilt, humiliation, and anger boiling silently inside him. I knew how he felt. I tried to sympathize with the man who'd turned my world inside out and now held my life in his hands. I tried to stay alive.

"How did you find out?" I asked.

Stone measured me for a moment. His sharp gray widow's peak aimed at me in place of the gun. I didn't know if he read sincerity in me or just wanted to finally spill his guts after so many years of swallowing them. Maybe he knew he could unburden himself to me and I'd never live to tell about it. Whatever his reasons, he finally spoke.

"When Windsor brought Angela to me, I'd only intended to bed her once. My normal practice with a new girl." His usual rich baritone, tight in his throat. "But once I'd been with her, I didn't want anyone else to touch her. The next week a videotape of us in bed arrived in the mail. He'd somehow planted a camera in my bedroom. Then a copy of the birth certificate of Louise Abigail

Delano arrived. My daughter. I thought Louise's mother was up to something again. I wasn't smart enough to put the pieces together. A photocopy of Louise's driver's license came next. Angela's picture was on it. She'd changed her name since the license, but she was still my daughter. My biggest failing as a young man had been ignoring her existence and then this—"

Stone's shoulders sagged and his eyelids drooped. He'd aged a lifetime since he'd first sat down at his desk. I slid my eyes to the gun. His hand was six inches from it. The desk was at least four feet wide. I was a foot back from that and seated. Geometry wasn't in my favor. I needed to find another way out.

"Did Angela find out?"

"No. And she never will. I cleaned her up and got her out of Las Vegas, off to San Diego. And now she's made something of her life. I won't let it be ruined."

"So Windsor blackmailed you."

"Not until he got out of prison." The smug certainty returned to Stone's voice. "He never had the chance in Las Vegas. Somehow, a big drug deal he was involved in went wrong and friends of mine on Las Vegas PD arrested him. Some of his things miraculously disappeared. Then, by coincidence, he went before a judge I knew and ended up in prison."

Stone flexing his influence. But it didn't last forever.

"But he got out last month and picked up where he'd left off." I kept the ball in the air, afraid what would happen if it dropped. "And now the dirt he had on Angela could make him rich."

Windsor must have hidden the original tapes and birth certificate in the desk he kept at his father's house in La Jolla. Maybe his father never told Adam that he'd put all his stuff in storage until after he got out of prison.

"Show-and-tell is over, Rick." He rested his hand on top of the .45. "Time to give me what I want."

"You'll get what you want, Stone. I don't care if you killed Windsor. What you just told me was man-to-man. It won't go any further." I nodded at the gun. "Trust me or don't, but be careful with that Kimber because people know that I came up here to see you tonight."

"Nice speech, Rick. Are you warming up for your trial? Not very convincing. Especially since you know Melody killed Windsor, whether you helped her or not."

Stone had told me his deepest, darkest secrets. Why would he lie about killing Windsor now? Especially, when he still had the gun. Maybe he wasn't lying.

"Time's up, Rick." He picked up the gun and pointed it at my face. "Tell me where the rest of it is. Now."

"It's in a safe deposit box at Windsor Bank and Trust." I wished it were. "You're going to have to wait until Monday, nine a.m."

"How convenient. Let's see; dead wife. Dirty ex-cop father drank himself into an early grave. That leaves your sister in San Francisco and your mother in Arizona." He moved his finger from the slide onto the trigger. "I'm sure if one of them bothers to clean out the box years from now, when, and if, your disappearance is ever ruled a homicide, an accident can be arranged. And I'm betting your threat of the video going viral is a bluff. You're alone. You don't have any friends left."

His finger tensed on the trigger.

"It's in the car down the road from your house!" The words exploded from my mouth before a bullet could from Stone's gun.

Stone smiled shark teeth at me and kept the Kimber pointed at my face. He reached his left hand over and punched a button on his desk phone. I heard the door whoosh open behind me.

"Give Luke your car keys and tell him where the vehicle is," Stone said.

If Luke came back with the Caddy full of Windsor's blackmail booty, I'd disappear and end up buried in a hole. Luke shuffled his injured leg away from the door towards me.

I had one chance.

"Here." I pulled the keys from my pocket, turned in the chair, and tossed them to Luke. At his feet. I'd bet my life that he'd have a hard time bending his wounded leg down to pick up the keys. I gave him a Stone smile. "Oops."

I made it look spiteful, that I wanted to watch him struggle to pick the keys up. He glared at me, then looked at his father. I kept my eyes on him, not wanting to look at the gun I knew was still trained on me.

"Rick," Stone's voice had a trace of irritation. Good. "That chip on your shoulder has become annoying. Go pick up the keys and then slowly hand them to Luke."

I turned toward Stone, ignored the gun, and gave him some attitude, showing I was still a tough guy who wouldn't jump on command. His eyes narrowed and I got up from the chair.

Luke stood five feet from the open door, glaring at me. I could almost feel the barrel of Stone's gun pressing against the back of my head from across the room. I got to Luke and knelt down and grabbed the keys. Then I heard Stone's voice.

"Luke, shut the door." As usual, Stone was ahead of me. But maybe not far enough this time.

Luke started to step back as I slowly rose. I didn't know what kind of a shot Stone was or how much he valued his son. Time to find out.

I stabbed Luke with the keys in his bad leg as I dove behind him. He crumpled forward and a gunshot exploded in the room, putting a hole in the wall next to the door.

Too late! I made it through the door into the hallway trailing Luke's keening wail and the boom of another gunshot. A glass-framed photograph, shoulder high, shattered off the wall. Thirty feet to the foyer and the front door and escape. I juked to my right in the narrow hallway. My ankle gave out, and I bounced against the wall and tumbled down onto the cold marble floor while another picture frame exploded above my head.

I shot forward, a sprinter out of the blocks, and stayed low and fast. My ankle screamed. I stayed silent. Another painful juke. A gunshot and a burst of flaming air past my ear all at once. The foyer! I cleared the hall and made the front door in two strides. I yanked the giant brass handle, but the door held and its resistance slammed me into it. Footsteps pounded down the marble hallway behind me.

The deadbolt! I dislodged it, threw open the door, and fled into the night. The fog swallowed me, damp gray sheets fluttering against my face as I sprinted blindly for my car. I heard footsteps behind me, then a car door slam, and an engine rev. Tires squealed. I looked back over my shoulder and saw a smear of yellow against the gray curtain. Then it disappeared and small two red blurs took its place, then faded away with the receding car engine.

He'd gone the other way. I'd told him my car was down the street and he'd believed me. But he wouldn't go far before he figured it out, turned around, and came back at me. The road climbed, invisible, under my feet. My ankle robbed me of speed and balance, but adrenaline kept me upright.

I felt a void to my left and realized I'd made the connecting street where I'd parked the Caddy. It materialized through the fog, first a gold blob, then a sharp-edged rectangle. I jammed the key in the door and looked back at the intersection. No yellow smear, yet. I jumped in, keyed the ignition, and the car rumbled to life. I left the lights off and eased it through the dense night, not wanting the squeal of tires to give away my location.

Shapes emerged as parked cars and then I hit Via Capri, the winding downhill ski run of a road that led off Mount Soledad. I risked the lights. The visibility was only marginally better than running blind. I checked the rearview mirror. The night stayed burnt charcoal behind me.

I'd eluded Stone for now, but he wouldn't stop until he found me. I knew his secret. His pride couldn't let me live. I could go to the police with what I had, but their minds where already made up. They'd fit me for a cell and make the evidence fit right next to me.

Via Capri flattened out after a long steep fall and T-boned a street that back roaded to Interstate 5. I could be in Mexico in half an hour or L.A. in two. I'd spend the rest of my life with my eyes in the rearview mirror and my back to every wall.

There was one other option. A long shot. I pulled out my cell phone and saw the last incoming call was from the same person I wanted to dial.

Heather Ortiz.

Muldoon's

CHAPTER FORTY-SEVEN

I checked my voice mail. Heather had left a message. Cryptic, as it was.

"Rick. Heather. I found information that can help you. Meet me at my house in fifteen minutes." A pause, then quickly in a hushed voice. "Be careful."

I pulled the Caddy to the curb and killed the lights. The call had come twenty-five minutes ago. I punched Heather's number. After five rings, her voice mail came on and I hung up. Could this be a setup Moretti had arranged? Maybe he figured he now had enough on me and didn't need to wait for Monday's grand jury. Heather lures me in from the cold, Moretti gets the arrest, and she gets the exclusive story. The hushed "be careful" at the end of the message a nice touch to make it seem we were in this together.

But she hadn't left her address. Had she expected me to remember it from our two-year-old one-night stand? Or had there really been a reason she had ended the call quickly? Maybe her message had been real and she'd found something that could help me. Heather was my last hope to avoid a life on the run. But she might be a false hope that took away my last chance to make that run.

I had to take the risk.

I started the car and turned around. When we'd hooked up a couple years ago, Heather had rented a house on a side street off La Jolla Boulevard behind a Chinese restaurant.

I took Hidden Valley Road until it dumped onto Torrey Pines Road. The fog had started to thin at the bottom of the hill. Headlights, no longer flickering candles behind stained glass, were now visible at a hundred yards. I did the long *L* from Torrey Pines to

Pearl to the boulevard, through the center of town and finally saw the restaurant appear through the gloom.

I cruised past Heather's cottage, scanning the street for police cruisers or detective slick tops. Nothing. I did a two-block circle, finally parking a couple hundred yards away, around the corner from the cottage.

The lifting fog still kept a low ceiling on the night. I dialed Heather one last time, hoping she'd pick up and I could get a better read from a live voice. Voice mail. I exited the car and slowly walked toward her house, my eyes alert to movements and shapes. A streetlamp cast down a bright halo of light on the corner of Heather's street. I avoided it, stayed on the far sidewalk, and went down half a block before approaching the house from the opposite side.

A raised wooden deck above a small yard fronted the house. Muted light pressed the edges of vertical blinds across a rectangular window. A porch light stood dark above the front door. Heather's red Miata sat in the carport to the right of the house. I touched the hood. Warm. Heather or someone else had parked her car there recently. Why didn't she answer her phone?

My gut told me to run, that Moretti and a SWAT team were waiting for me inside. But a voice deeper inside told me that I had to make sure, that I'd hidden from life too long to have to spend the rest of it on the run.

Heather was still my one hope. My last hope.

I traced low along the Miata to a window on the side of the house. I peeked in at an angle, afraid I might see a SWAT helmet shield staring back at me. Safe. Just a white curtain with shadowed light behind it. The carport swung around behind the house leaving a little oval patio off a back door. The door had a white-curtained window that, again, gave the hint of light within, but nothing else.

I slunk down and tried the knob. It turned. I stayed low and slowly opened the door, my ears as alert as my eyes. The only sound was the low hum of a refrigerator. The kitchen was a straight shot through an archway into the living room. A light out of view lit a bookshelf and desk against the far wall, and the arm of a burgundy couch in the foreground. No SWAT team.

Moretti could have been hiding around the corner of the living room, but I doubted it. The house had a lifeless feel. Still, like an empty stage. I crept through the kitchen into the living room and saw the full length of the burgundy couch. Heather lay across it, one arm dangling to the floor.

Dead.

Eyes open, staring at eternity. Her mouth, stretched open for a last gulp of air that never came. Finger-shaped bruises ringed her neck. Death's grasp.

My knees gave way and I almost went down. If I'd never given Heather the information about Windsor's payoff ledger or the birth certificate, she'd still be alive. Moretti or Stamp Heaton on Stone's orders had killed her, but I'd been responsible, too. Just like with Colleen.

When she'd needed me, I hadn't been there.

Bile surged up my throat, and I scrambled down the short hall-way to the bathroom and purged my body into the toilet. On my knees, gripping the commode. Again. Finally, I flushed, sat back against the wall, pulled a towel down from a rack, and wiped sweat from my face and residue from my mouth. Then I folded the towel inside out and wiped down the commode and the handle.

I took the towel back out to the living room and wiped any-thing I thought I might have touched. Heather lay frozen in death, as Colleen had in the Santa Barbara morgue years ago. Heather deserved to be found while the beauty she had in life could be pre-served, not eviscerated by the twin horrors of death and time. But I couldn't call the police, not even anonymously. They could trace the call and identify my voice.

Something about the room was off. A void. An emptiness I couldn't finger. I looked around and caught the desk in front of the window. A printer. But no computer. No purse with a reporter's notepad either. I went down the hall to check her bedroom to be sure.

No computer, no purse. Whoever had killed Heather took the information that could have put them in prison and kept me out of it.

I went to the back door, wiped it down and used the towel to open it. I closed the door the same way and stepped onto the patio. Cigarette smoke hit me immediately. I froze and saw a round man next door pulling a butt from his mouth. His patio paralleled Heather's back door. An outdoor light spilled just enough glow to illuminate my face. I turned my head down and away and walked along the carport as calmly has I could fake. A waist-high brick wall separated us.

The sidewalk was just a few strides away, then I could break off to the right and circle back to my car.

"You a friend of Heather's?" It was more an accusation then a conversation starter.

"Yeah." I kept moving, but felt his presence mirror me across the fence.

I bolted across the street.

"Hey! Stop!"

I could tell from the fading sound of his voice that he hadn't pursued me past his driveway. But it wouldn't be long before he checked on Heather and the sirens came. I pushed hard on my throbbing ankle and made the far corner. No one chased me, so I doubled back on the next block down and headed for the car. I ditched the towel I'd taken from Heather's house down a sewer a block from my car. A minute later, I cranked the Caddy's ignition and pulled out from the curb.

No cops, no sirens, no screams of discovered death. Yet.

My choice had been made for me. A life on the run. No life at all. I headed for I-5 South.

Mexico.

CHAPTER FORTY-EIGHT

I didn't have a passport, but I'd only need one if I was coming back. I wasn't. I had about a hundred bucks in my wallet. That wouldn't last very long. Not even in Mexico. I pulled into a mini-mall in National City and withdrew my daily max of $400 from an ATM.

My phone vibrated in my pocket as I took the on-ramp back onto the freeway. Kim. Maybe Heather's murder had already made the news and she was calling to warn me that the cops had put up roadblocks. Too soon. Maybe she just wanted to tell me that Midnight missed me and, by implication, she did too.

What could I say to her? Midnight was hers now? Sorry I wasn't the man you thought I was? This way our break would be final. She'd be forced to finally move on with her life without me hanging around the fringes. At least Midnight would have a good home. I let the call go to voice mail.

Chula Vista passed by into my rearview mirror. San Ysidro, next. A few more exits and I'd be at the border. If the cops had a roadblock there, I'd ditch the car and my life on the run would begin on foot.

The phone buzzed again. Kim. I suddenly wanted to hear the only friendly voice I had left one last time.

"Rick." Urgent. "I need your help."

Finally payback for all the times she'd helped me without need for explanation. Unfortunately, my debt would remain unpaid.

"What's wrong?" I stalled for time while I figured out how to tell her that I'd never be able to help her or see her again.

"I'm up at the cross and my car broke down." The words came

out quickly like fear had run them together. Kim wasn't one to panic over a broken-down car. "They must not have known I was up here when they locked the gate. I can't get my car towed until tomorrow, and I don't have any money for a cab."

"What are you doing up there?" The clock on the dashboard read 10:25 p.m. LJPD closed the cross down at ten every night.

A road sign rolled past. The border was a mile away.

"I came up to look at the view." Her words, breathy with emotion. "Like when you used to bring me up here."

Another sign. Half a mile to the border.

"I'm sorry, Kim." My heart folded in on itself. "I won't be able to see you for a while. Goodbye."

I put the phone in my pocket and slunk down in the seat. Ashamed. I'd failed the second woman in my life who'd ever loved me. Just like the first. Only, Kim would survive.

A sign appeared out of the thinning fog: LAST U.S.A. EXIT BEFORE MEXICO.

The fog. The cross. The view.

You couldn't see twenty feet past your nose in the fog on Soledad Mountain tonight. There was no view.

Kim was in danger.

I punched her number on my phone and whipped across three lanes of traffic and blaring horns to just make the last U.S. exit. Voice mail. I left her a message that I'd be there in twenty minutes, circled under the overpass, and rocketed the Caddy north, back onto the freeway.

Moretti, Heaton, or maybe even Stone, had gotten to her, hoping to get to me. If they didn't think I was coming, they wouldn't need her anymore and kill her. I prayed she was still alive and had gotten the voice mail.

I rummaged Chief Parks's card out of my wallet and dialed his number while I punched the Caddy up to eighty-five. I didn't trust Parks with my own freedom, but I had to with Kim's life. His voice mail came on and I left a message that Kim was being held at gunpoint at the cross. I put my phone in my pocket, then pulled it out again. I couldn't depend on Parks checking his messages or me making it to the cross in time to save Kim. I dialed 911.

My freedom for Kim's life.

My phone beeped before 911 could pick up. Chief Parks's number on hold. I hung up with 911 and took the call.

"Cahill, I've got an officer down and an ongoing SWAT operation at La Jolla Shores." The cell reception was scratchy, but I could make out excitement in his voice. "All squad cars are employed, but I'll try to get at least one unit up to the cross. I'm on my way there now. You'd better not be pulling my chain on this."

"I'm not." I couldn't risk being wrong.

"Don't do anything stupid. I just hope we can get some men there in time." He hung up.

The fog thickened on my drive north. I exited the freeway and wound my way up Via Capri. My radar went up for Stone's Mercedes as I traversed his home terrain. Not a single headlight, but maybe he was already waiting up at the cross.

The fog closed in tighter. Instinct took me up the mountain as I drove faster than the gray wall beyond my headlights would let me see. I sensed I was approaching the summit and turned off the lights. I slowed and craned my neck looking for the entrance to the cross.

My phone vibrated. Turk. I ignored it. Then I saw a horizontal silver smudge through the gray. The gate to the road that led up to the monument. Closed. Either I'd beaten Parks up here or he'd locked the gate behind himself. That didn't make sense if he was expecting reinforcements. No, I'd gotten here first. I couldn't wait for Parks or a patrol car. Kim might still be alive and the fog would give me cover.

I parked on the tiny shoulder opposite the gate, turned off the switch to the Caddy's inside light, and quietly got out of the car. My phone vibrated. Turk again. We didn't have anything left to talk about and never would, but he'd called me twice in fifteen seconds. Maybe he knew something I should. I whispered hello and kept my eyes on the shifting fog behind the gate.

"Rick!" More emotion in one word than I'd heard out of Turk in a lifetime. "A couple of detectives were just here looking for you. That reporter who's been on your ass was murdered and they think you did it. What the hell's going on?"

Maybe Parks's get-out-of-jail-free card didn't extend to Heather's murder. But I didn't have time to deal with it now.

"I gotta go."

"Wait! These guys have a hard on for you. I got the feeling it's shoot on sight and read you your rights later. Go to the police station and turn yourself in before they get to you. Where are you?"

Maybe the cops had put him up to the call. Maybe he was really concerned. It didn't matter. Right now cops with guns might be the only thing that could save Kim's life.

"I'm at the cross." I hung up and ducked under the single-bar gate.

I peered into the fog. It muffled the sounds of the night down to a loud silence. I shuffled forward and found the sidewalk that meandered around the parking lot and up the hill to the cross.

At the top of the hill, a breeze pushed the heavy air and a car appeared twenty-five feet in front of me. A Crown Vic slick top. A detective car. It was parked just below the steps that led up to the cross. I froze. The fog swallowed the car again and I strained to hear voices, footsteps, anything.

Nothing.

I took a step forward and sensed movement behind me. Too late.

"Don't move." Something small and hard poked into my back. The barrel of a gun.

Muldoon's

CHAPTER FORTY-NINE

A bear paw of a hand patted me down while the other one pressed the gun to my back.

"Kneel down and give me your car keys and your cell phone." Stamp Heaton stepped around in front of me and leveled a Smith & Wesson .44 Magnum at my chest.

I did as I was told. He stuffed the keys and phone into his coat pocket. Then he kicked me in the nose. Heaven's light exploded and my head hit the sidewalk.

"Go down and find his car and bring it up here. Lock the gate behind you." A voice out of the night.

The same one that had been behind the police spotlight the night Melody and I were pulled over. I'd heard it since, but hadn't been able to connect it with that disembodied voice until tonight when it came blind out of the dark again.

La Jolla Police Chief, Raymond Parks.

Scarface.

The cologne on my carpet, his not Moretti's. Windsor's words in his memoir about the crooked cops' scars of his youth. Acne, not Moretti's cleft palate. Heather telling me that Scarface had lost his scars. Plastic surgery. The man with the shiny buffed cheeks. Prettying up to follow Mayor Albright up to Sacramento and start his own political career.

My head throbbed and my nose felt like it had been shoved into my brain. I lay still, pretending to be unconscious, blood pooling against my lips. I didn't have a weapon and didn't even know where Parks was. Right now, playing possum was all I had.

Then I heard the executioner's metallic aria; a slide racked to chamber a round in a semiautomatic pistol. Adrenaline buzzed through me. I had to move. Now. Somewhere to my left, maybe twenty-five feet, scrub brush edged up to the parking lot from the north side of the mountain. If I could just get up without being shot, the fog might give me cover and then it was a downhill tumble to Interstate 5.

My muscles tensed. One, two—

"Heather Ortiz is on you, Cahill." The calm voice of a moment ago, now a hard rasp. "Windsor sealed his own fate as soon as he starting writing a book. His death should have gone down as an OD, but that pissant Moretti had to get ambitious and your girl Melody filled the bill. Then you had to be a fucking hero and bring Heather into it. Hell, I liked her. All you had to do was sit on the sidelines and keep your mouth shut. You stupid fuck."

Footsteps. Close.

I pushed up off the ground, but a kick to my ribs sent me back down. Pain vibrated along my right side. I sucked in air in short gasps through my mouth, my broken nose useless. I stayed down and hoped the cops had been with Turk when I told him where I was. Time was my only weapon, if I had one at all.

I eased up to a sitting position. Parks stood over me, a Glock nine millimeter hung loosely in his hand like a surgeon at ease with a scalpel. Coal eyes burned down at me through the fog, his mustache pulled his face into a permanent frown.

"You're all alone, Cahill. No officer down. No help on the way."

"Where's Kim?" The iron taste of blood tangled in my words.

"She's on you, too."

"Where is she?" I shouted, but the fog swallowed the echo.

"Shut up!"

Yellow smudges rolled up the hill. As soon as Heaton searched the car and found Windsor's payoff ledger, Parks would kill me and Kim. If he hadn't killed her already. The Caddy stopped behind Parks and Heaton stepped out.

"Search it." Parks said.

Heaton fingered the car keys, walked around to the trunk, and opened it.

"Does Parks know you're working for Peter Stone, Heaton?" Maybe a rift would buy me time. I wiped blood from my lips, but my shattered nose kept pumping out more.

"Nice try, Cahill." Parks said. "But Stamp has always been on my team. Stone just didn't know it."

"Where's Kim?" I pictured Kim lying still, eyes open like Heather Ortiz. Then she was Colleen on the steel coroner's table in Santa Barbara. "Please. Let her go. She doesn't know anything."

"What's he talking about?" Heaton stepped back from the open trunk, my backpack in his left hand. "Who's Kim?"

Heaton didn't know. He'd helped Parks to cover his own ass, but didn't know all that Parks had done.

"It doesn't matter." The chief barked commands like Heaton was still on the force. "What's in the backpack?"

"Does he know that you killed Heather Ortiz, Chief?" I said.

"Shut up!" Parks backhanded me with the Glock. The barrel's sight sliced open a gash above my right eye. Blood streamed down into my eye and joined the flow from my nose.

"What's going on, Ray?" Heaton's normal gruff baritone leapt up an octave. His right hand down at his side holding his gun. "I don't mind roughing up this asshole, but I didn't sign on for murder. Tell me he's wrong."

Parks spun toward Heaton and an explosion shook the night. A dark dot bloomed on Heaton's forehead and he collapsed straight down like a puppet on broken strings. His gun clattered to the ground.

I sprang to my feet and bolted for the edge of the parking lot when I heard Parks's voice.

"Stop or you're dead!"

Personal defense experts preach to keep running in a situation like this, that it's hard to hit a moving target. Peter Stone had proved that tonight, but I'd just seen Parks spin and put a bullet in a man's forehead at twenty feet. My back would be an easier target, even while running.

I froze and prayed for the cavalry to arrive.

"Turn around and walk toward me slowly." He had the Glock trained on my chest.

I did as told and he backed up when I got within ten feet of him. He halted after a couple steps.

"Okay. Stop right there."

Parks looked back and forth between Heaton's still body and me as if he were measuring the angles. He might as well have been measuring my casket. I was a prop in Parks's play. Heaton and I get into a gun battle at the cross and kill each other. The trail back to Parks is erased and he goes off with Albright to Sacramento. But that still left Kim.

"Sit down and don't move." I sat down and Parks walked over to Heaton's fallen body.

"What did you do with Kim?" Time was my ally. If I could get him talking, I might have a chance of surviving. And if I didn't, maybe the extra few seconds would save Kim.

Parks opened the backpack with his free hand and looked inside, then back at me. "You killed her."

Tears welled in my eyes and washed the trickle of blood. "You motherfucker!" I rose up to start a suicide charge when Parks stopped me.

"Whoa! You haven't killed her yet. She's in the trunk." He nodded over to the Crown Vic parked ten yards away. "You set yourself up nicely, Cahill. Some of your hair, extra from the hat you left in Windsor's hotel room, will be found in Heather Ortiz's house. I wouldn't have gone to the trouble if I'd known you were going to walk all over the crime scene on your own. I just heard it on the scanner. Some citizen saw you fleeing Heather's house. You are one stupid son of a bitch, Cahill. Just like your old man. You have to be stupid to get caught."

"You don't think you'll get caught?"

"You just brought me the evidence I needed." He pulled Windsor's ledger out of my backpack and waved it at me. "Goodbye, Cahill."

"What about Windsor's book?" I braced for impact. "I copied it on a flash drive and mailed it to a friend. If I don't show up at his house on Monday, he'll send it to the police and the newspaper. Windsor named names. Like Scarface."

"You don't have any friends, Cahill." He pointed the Glock at me.

"Hey!" Turk burst through the fog.

Parks spun and fired at Turk just as I dove at him. The Glock went off again and pain ripped through my left shoulder and my left ear went deaf. Turk, Parks, and I all hit the ground at once. Only Turk had stopped moving.

I lunged across Park's body and grabbed for the gun with my live hand. But it wasn't there. It was on the ground ten feet away. Parks clamped his hands around my neck and squeezed, digging his thumbs into my Adam's apple. Rage burned in his black eyes. I choked out a cough and fought for air. None. I shot a right to his nose and his hands released, but one found the hole in my shoulder and tore at it.

Pain blast furnaced through me. Parks pushed me off, scrambled to his feet, and lurched to his gun. I sprang backward toward Heaton's body and spotted his Smith & Wesson. I grabbed it, spun around on my back, and fired five rounds at the dark shape my one good eye could see just as the Glock went off and punched a hole in the Caddy next to my left ear. Parks was still upright and I pulled the trigger again, but the cylinder was empty. I dove over Heaton, expecting the last gunshot I'd ever hear.

Silence.

I looked up to where Parks had been standing. He wasn't there anymore. I lowered my eyes and found him. Laid out on the asphalt parking lot, black eyes staring at nothing, the gun off to the side. I walked over to him, bent over and picked up the weapon. The ground started to roll as I rose. My ears felt clogged with cotton and the night closed around me in a narrowing pipe. I wouldn't be conscious much longer.

Turk lay still, face down twenty feet away. Parks's car with Kim in the trunk a few strides in the other direction. I started to turn toward Turk when I noticed the holes. Two bullet holes in the trunk of the Crown Vic. Right in my line of fire when I emptied the gun at Parks.

I bent down and got the keys out of Parks's pocket and staggered over to the car. The night kept rolling in on me as I fumbled the keys into the lock and threw open the trunk. Kim lay still inside, blood pooled below her head.

I fell to my knees, saw a floating rainbow above two fuzzy orbs of light rolling toward me, then slid down onto my back. The last thing I saw was the forty-three-foot cross looming over me like a giant dagger.

Muldoon's

CHAPTER FIFTY

I opened my eyes to bars of shadow across a wall. I figured I was in a jail cell until a nurse's face appeared in front of mine. She said something about window blinds and I closed my eyes.

The next time I opened them, I saw Detective Moretti frowning down at me. Maybe I was in jail. Or hell. I checked the off-white walls, mounted television, and IV needle in my arm. No, still the hospital.

"Is Kim alive?" The words were sharp in my throat and came out raspy.

The image of Kim wedged in the trunk of Parks's car, lying in a pool of blood, hurt worse than the hole in my shoulder. I held my breath and waited for Moretti's answer, as if the verdict of Kim's life was at his command.

"Yes." Moretti's frown flattened into a straight line. "She's going to be fine. She sustained a blow to the head from her captor and was knocked unconscious. She has a few stitches, but no lasting injuries."

"She wasn't shot?"

"No. She's very lucky."

"Thank God." Tears welled in my eyes. The first tears caused by joy since before Colleen was murdered. Then I remembered Turk lying still, facedown, on the asphalt parking lot below the cross.

"What about Turk Muldoon?" Again, I waited for Moretti's verdict.

"He's alive. In ICU. The bullet fired by the assailant lodged next to his spine. The doctor says he'll survive, but may never walk again."

The tears of joy dried up and a dark hole opened up inside me. Turk had set aside our war to help me when I was in trouble. He'd saved my life and paid for it with his freedom. He'd no longer be able to view life from eight thousand feet up, dangling off a granite face.

"You want to tell me what happened up there, Cahill?"

I figured Moretti hadn't shown up in my hospital room to hold my hand. I told him about the whole night, but left out the evidence I'd taken from Windsor's locker. And Stone. I'd deal with him on my own.

"That's quite a story, Cahill."

"It's the truth." But not the whole truth. "Kim can verify it."

"I talked to Miss Connelly." Dark eyes bore into me. "When Mr. Muldoon's conscious, I'll talk to him, too."

"Okay." I waited for what he hadn't told me yet.

"People died because of you, Cahill." The rage built in his eyes. "You withheld evidence in a murder investigation. If you would have turned that evidence over to me, Heather would still be alive. Now the fucking media is going to make you out to be a hero."

"You don't have to worry about the media, Moretti. I don't want anything to do with them."

"Shut up." He closed the door to the hospital room, then moved a chair next to my bed and sat in it. "You're a grade A asshole, Cahill. You stick your nose where it doesn't belong and leave dead bodies and broken lives in your wake."

I couldn't argue with him.

He continued. "Well, there are sixty-seven lives hanging in the balance because of you now. The people employed by LJPD and the District Attorney's Office."

Now I understood why he'd used "captor" and "assailant" when referring to Kim's and Turk's injuries. This wasn't about justice. This was about survival. LJPD's survival. If La Jollans knew the police chief had died a three-time murderer and not a hero, they'd surely vote to disband the department when the proposition went on the ballot.

"Let me tell you the official story." He leaned in on me, his cologne reminding me of the man I'd killed at the cross. "Stamp Heaton and Adam Windsor used to be partners when Stamp was on the force. Heaton protected Windsor from arrest when he was running women in La Jolla. Then Windsor got out of prison and decided to blackmail his old partner. Heaton killed him, then killed Heather when he learned she was on to him. Then he kidnapped your old girlfriend to lure you to your death because you knew too much."

"That's quite a tale, Detective, but it doesn't explain Chief Parks's showing up at the cross."

"Parks had Heaton under surveillance and got to the cross in time to save you and Miss Connelly, but unfortunately died in a shootout with Heaton."

"What if I don't play along with your bullshit story?"

"Right now, Heather's case is open and you're still a suspect. We have a witness who is convinced he saw you fleeing the scene." He gave me a smirk. "Of course, he could be mistaken and some compelling evidence that Mr. Heaton committed the crime could come to light."

Moretti had built a house of cards that could be brought down by the slightest bit of investigative journalism or me opening my mouth. But when those cards came down, I'd be at the bottom of the pile again, a suspect in another murder. I'd need a lawyer, and I'd be under the spotlight again.

I'd lived with a lie for eight years, I could live with another one as long as innocent people didn't get hurt. Heaton wasn't a murderer, but he wasn't innocent either. But I wouldn't ask Kim to lie for me. My self-preservation had its limits.

"You're going to have a hard time convincing Kim that it wasn't Parks who kidnapped her. That's the one loose end that unravels your little yarn, Moretti."

"Like I told you, Cahill." He leaned closer. I could make out

the cleft lip scar under his mustache. "I've talked with Miss Connelly. She understands the seriousness of your situation, as I'm sure
Mr. Muldoon will when he regains consciousness."

Kim, still looking out for me even after all I'd put her through.

"Detective Coyote going along with all this, or haven't you told
him yet?"

"Detective Coyote is taking an early retirement." He dropped
his eyes.

"There's one man with a conscience. What happened to yours?
Is it tough to sleep at night, Moretti?"

"I sleep fine. It's not like Stamp Heaton was a saint, Cahill."

"Neither was Parks, but now you've made him one."

"Where he's going, it won't matter." He grabbed the guardrail
of my hospital bed. "Do we have an understanding, Rick?"

I nodded my head, but I didn't think I'd get much sleep tonight
or anytime soon. Moretti stood up to leave, but I stopped him.
"And the evidence you found in the backpack of Melody and Angela Albright."

"Doesn't exist." He walked to the door and opened it.

"One last thing, Moretti." He turned hard eyes back on me.
"When you questioned Melody about how my Callaway hat ended
up at the Windsor crime scene, what did she say?"

He told me and left.

An hour later, Kim came into my room. Her head was wrapped
in a bandage, but her green eyes were clear and beautiful. Joy and
guilt hit me hard in the gut all at once.

"I'm sorry," I said.

Tears welled in her eyes, emeralds in pools of rain. She came
to me and delicately hugged me, avoiding my bandaged shoulder,
stitched brow, and cotton-packed nose. Hot tears dripped on my
neck.

"How can you say you're sorry?" She unwound from me and
pulled back. "You saved my life and almost died because of it."

"I put your life in danger. If I had just taken what I had to the police instead of playing hero, none of this would have happened. Heather Ortiz would still be alive."

"You didn't have a choice, Rick. You did what you thought was right. You always do. You're a good man."

Kim had always believed in me. She'd only brought up Colleen once, early in our relationship, just to let me know she'd listen if I ever wanted to talk. I never did. I let her believe that I was an innocent victim who'd been unjustly hounded by the police and the press.

"I was supposed to pick up Colleen from the library the night she died." I looked up at the blank television screen in the corner of the room, not wanting to see the change in Kim's eyes that was sure to come. "It was a ritual we had. We never broke it. No matter what. She'd study at the library until closing, and I'd come by in my radio car to pick her up and take her home. It was against Santa Barbara PD procedure; just one of the rules I broke back then.

"We'd had a fight before my shift started that night. We had a lot of fights back then, but this one was bad. Furniture thrown, broken plates. She didn't like that I spent so much time with my ex training officer, Krista. She told me that I'd changed from the guy she'd fallen in love with after I became a cop. That I'd become short tempered, callous, and full of myself. I could have blamed it on working the streets, seeing what depraved people did to each other. But she was right. I was just too puffed up behind the badge on my chest to see it then. When I finally did, it was too late."

I dropped my head, and Kim put a hand on my arm. I shook it off. I didn't deserve her sympathy.

"I was still pissed when I went on patrol that night and knew where I could find a sympathetic ear. Krista and I did spend a lot of time together. We'd bitch about the job and our spouses over lunch or a beer. The things only another cop could understand. Not a civilian, like Colleen. Strictly everyday bullshit. But there'd been a different, unspoken, undercurrent at our last couple of meetings. I knew her detective husband was out of town on a case and convinced myself I'd only go over to her house to talk. We did talk. For a little while.

"When I got out of her bed, I caught my reflection in a mirror and saw for the first time that Colleen had been right. I didn't like the person staring back at me."

I looked at Kim, but she wouldn't look at me. I didn't blame her. She must have now wondered if I'd betrayed her while we'd been together. I didn't. Only Colleen. The one time. On the last night of her life. It had cost me my only love. It had cost Colleen everything.

That night in Santa Barbara came back at me and filled me with the same dread. Back in Krista's bedroom, a huge hole opened up in me for something I'd once had and now had ruined. I wanted it back. I wanted to be the man Colleen had fallen in love with again and realized I never could. But I had to try. I'd go to counseling, quit the force. Whatever it took.

I needed to see her, to hear her voice. To confess.

Kim still couldn't look at me, but I had to get it all out. Finally. "Colleen had called my cell phone twice while I was in bed with another cop's wife. My calls back to her went to voice mail. Panic gripped me. A graveyard shift's sixth sense. I knew something worse than my sin had happened. I raced to the library, but got there an hour late. Colleen was already gone. Forever. Her body was discovered on the beach the next morning."

Kim didn't say anything for a long time. When she finally spoke, the hint of affection in her voice that I'd always taken for granted was gone.

"Why didn't you give the police your alibi when they arrested you?"

"I should have. Then the police might have looked for the real killer instead of focusing on me." I looked out the window, but saw only the sun's glare. "I told myself I was protecting Krista, but I knew deep down that I didn't want my fellow cops to know that

I'd committed the unpardonable sin of sleeping with another cop's wife."

"You were willing to go to prison for that?"

"No. If it had gone to trial, I would have shown the world who I really was. But the DA dropped the charges because they found unknown hair on Colleen's body that wasn't mine. Detective Grimes was still convinced I'd killed her, but the DA didn't think he could get a conviction. But none of that changes what I did that night."

I finally looked at Kim, but she wouldn't meet my eyes.

"That isn't who you are now, Rick. And it doesn't change the fact that you risked your life to save mine."

But I knew from the sound of her voice that something had changed in her. I missed it already.

Melody came by the next evening. Freedom, or maybe a tanning booth, had brought back the caramel color to her skin. Her dark eyes, as smoky and sexy as the first night I saw her.

"Oh my God, Rick, are you okay?"

She kissed my forehead. Either because it was the most likely area that wouldn't hurt, or because I wasn't worthy of deeper affection.

"I'll live."

"I can't thank you enough for what you did. Without you, I'd still be in jail."

That was probably true, but I didn't feel like a hero.

Melody sat with me for a half hour. She told me she had to fly back to San Francisco for work, but would be down next weekend, as she had a job offer in L.A. to host a daytime talk show. The benefits of celebrity victimhood.

"If I take the job in Los Angeles, I'd only be two hours away." She stroked my hair. "We could see what life's like without the police trying to put me in jail and without you getting shot."

She kissed my lips this time, and the memory of our first night together rushed back at me. She said goodbye and stood up to leave.

"When the Detective Moretti questioned you about how my Callaway hat got in your motel room the morning Windsor died, what did you tell him?"

If the question surprised her, she didn't show it.

"That I'd grabbed it by mistake out of your closet."

"So you didn't tell them you didn't know how it got there?"

"No." The lie wouldn't let her eyes meet mine. "Why?"

"I just wanted to be sure." And I was. Melody had let me dangle on the edge of the Windsor murder as a potential suspect. Another option in her feral instinct for survival.

"I really do care about you, Rick." She turned and left.

In her broken way, I believed she did.

She didn't come down to see me the next weekend, or ever again.

Muldoon's

EPILOGUE

Three days after I got out of the hospital, against doctor's orders, I drove my car over to Elk Fenton's office. I got what I needed and then went to Turk's house. He was still in the hospital, but out of ICU and on his way to recovery. Not recovery of his former life, but of some kind of life. I sifted through his mailbox, found what I was looking for, then headed over to San Diego Gun.

Ten days had passed and my life had changed more than once, but I still had need for a gun. I picked up the Ruger .357 Magnum and bought a box of Magtech ammo.

At six o'clock the next morning, I drove over to Stone's house and parked where I'd left the Caddy a week ago. My left arm in a sling, I hammered on the drawbridge front door and returned my right hand to the heavy pocket of my bomber jacket.

Stone opened the door in a blue terrycloth robe. His eyes were alert, but he hadn't been awake long enough to tame his gray mane. I pulled my hand from my coat and held the Ruger loosely at my side. Stone's eyes tracked the gun, then came back to mine.

This was going to end today. How it did, would be Stone's choice.

"Well, Rick," he opened the door wide, "I see we have some unfinished business. Come in."

I stepped inside and off to the right so I could see him as he shut the door. "Your office."

He led me down the hallway. All photographs were hanging back in place. I checked the wall inside his office that had been punctured by the first shot he fired at me. Not even a mark.

Stone saw me examining the wall. "Some mistakes are easily erased."

"Sit, Stone, but keep your hands on the desk."

He did as told and I took the same seat opposite him I'd chosen a week ago. The morning sun hadn't yet climbed up the back of Mount Soledad and the panoramic windows behind Stone only hinted at the ocean below in gray relief. I set the gun down on the desk and pulled an envelope out of my back pocket and placed it next to the gun.

"You're now legally part owner of Muldoon's Steak House. There's nothing I can do about that." I rested my hand on the desk between the gun and the envelope. "But I can stop you from forcing Turk out and tearing the restaurant down to put up a hotel."

"You think the threat of a gun is going to stop me?" He gave me sharp teeth and dead eyes.

"No, but what's in the envelope will."

"You have my attention."

"Louise Abigail Delano's birth certificate." I took the certificate out of the envelope and held it up so he could see it. Then I pushed the envelope across the desk to him.

Stone opened it and pulled out the document Elk Fenton had written up for me the day before. "What's this?"

"An agreement not to sell Muldoon's or close it without Turk's consent. Sign it."

He looked at me and smiled, then signed the contract and slid it back to me. I checked his signature and put it back in the envelope and placed the birth certificate on the desk. I stood up, put the gun in my pocket, and reached across the table with an open hand.

Stone tilted his head and his smile grew larger. He hesitated, then finally shook my hand. I turned and headed for the door, leaving the birth certificate on the desk.

"You don't think my lawyers can break this contract, Rick?" The confident, languid baritone from the first night we met.

"Maybe." I stopped and looked at him. "That's why I shook

your hand. I know you won't break that oath because you believe in honor. And if you do, I'll come after you."

I left without looking back.

Late that night, I sat with Midnight in the dark and watched the video of Colleen and me in Lake Tahoe the weekend I proposed to her. The video cut to the part where we camped at nearby Fallen Leaf Lake. Colleen was cooking over a Coleman stove and didn't know I was filming. Her blonde hair in a ponytail, sparkling azure eyes pulled up at the corners in a smile, she sang softly to herself as she flipped bacon on the stove. She looked up, embarrassed when she saw me, then her face melted into the smile that told me she wouldn't want to be anywhere else but there with me. It was the look I held onto after all those years and summoned when I could get past the guilt.

I turned off the tape and cried.

A week later, I went back to work at Muldoon's. Stone stayed away. I worked one hundred and forty-nine straight days until Turk finally rolled through the front door in a wheelchair. I quit the next day.

I've since found a new job. Private investigator.

Now strangers come to me with their problems and I try to solve them. I do it for money, not for love. It's easier that way. Fewer people get hurt.